ADVANCE UNCORRECTED GALLEYS
256pp   ISBN 1-57962-076-0

Pub Date: November, 2002   Cloth: $26

Toucan Whisper, Toucan Sing

a novel by Robert Wintner

The Permanent Press Sag Harbor, NY 11963

Library of Congress Cataloging-in-Publication Data

Wintner, Robert
    Toucan whisper, Toucan sing / Robert Wintner
        p. cm.
    ISBN 1-57962-076-0
    1.   Hotels—Employees—Fiction. 2. Mexico—Fiction 3.
        Hotels—Fiction. I.Title.

PS3573.I63 T68 2002
813'.54 – dc21

                                                            2001036620

Printed in The United States of America

THE PERMANENT PRESS
4170 Noyac Road
Sag Harbor, NY 11963

*For Marty Shepard, who is at home on the reef,
with garish color and profound innocence.*

Other Books by Robert Wintner

Whirlaway

The Ice King

Horndog Blue

Hagan's Trial & Other Stories

The Prophet Pasqual

Homunculus

The Modern Outlaws

Lonely Hearts, Changing Worlds

I

Modern Times

Crystal teardrops tinkle in the chandelier hanging from the ceiling of the eighteenth floor to the Grand Foyer. They shimmer and shape the light and set a tone for the prices in the Gift Shop just ahead. You can't help looking up and knowing in advance that they're only fair, the prices, considering this kind of elegance and good taste.

Pinched snug from the rear so the high-quality cotton conforms to the muscular plastic torso, T-shirts of superb design and imagery offer the exotic flair of the place and can continue to do so long after *Hotel Oaxtapec* guests go home. These Ts cost more than a normal T, but while you might save a few pesos elsewhere you would hardly accrue the exotic identity these Ts can provide for years to come.

They capture the essence in the air with their colorful illustrations, so you can feel the tropical tingle in winter in your chilblain loft in northern Minnesota, even under a sweater. You may even recall the hot breeze whispering love and anarchy in nature, just as you feel it here.

You want to buy one of these mementos to have and to hold, to wear and feel again from far away. You want others to see it too by simply looking your way, so they'll know where you've been and will see the full range of your experience.

So, surrounded by such comfort and potential for exotic character, what are a few extra pesos?

On the front of each T is a wild animal silk-screened in garish pastels, lifelike as the species recently roaming, screeching, and preying here. They don't anymore, those wild others, nor can their screech and scratch be heard beyond the hill or down the road.

The only habitat over the hill is employee housing. Hardly marbled and mostly lit by naked bulbs, these modest bungalows are a blessed billet for the likes of Antonio Garza, who rises yet again from flat on his back to sitting up. As if taking a tally of his power to make more money in tips on a single morning than his father made in a week on the road crew, he counts, "Eighty-two."

Down and up again, he represses the grunt, "Eighty-three…"

Antonio knows the value of sit-ups. They're very close to money in the bank. Beyond intrinsic value he knows that doing them first thing in the morning is worth plenty. Just look at today, waiting until after eating, before siesta, with the day half-done and the day's energy half spent. He will reach a hundred twenty before deciding if a hundred twenty-five will do, or if today feels good for a hundred fifty. He knows the hundred fifty standard must stick once established, so he mustn't press prematurely. But he also knows that today *is* the day the bar will rise. A washboard stomach doesn't last forever, nor can the ripples deepen without strenuous effort. Then again he is late, a condition common to a man on the rise but never acceptable to a punctual man. For the sin of tardiness he will give penance. "Eighty-eight. Eighty-nine."

He remembers, like it was only this morning, the day long ago when Milo the Beach Manager told him with no warning to take off his starched white jacket and go. It was a moment of startling chagrin. Who could not foresee the ax, given Milo's apparent envy? Yet close on the heel of this apparent ax was certain joy on the tip of Milo's finger shooting seaward with Milo's pronouncement, "Go to the jet skis."

¡Ay!

The jet skis could not be called a promotion by anyone but Antonio, who proved his prowess by drawing more guests to the jet skis than his predecessors and delivering a happier ride than ever before, thereby generating more revenue and additional goodwill. It was a simple progression from the jet skis to the towboat that pulls the big banana, and from there to pulling the parasail. Antonio made them laugh no matter what their fantasy, as he does to this day. Fast or slow, *no problema*; he eases them into spending as if that's why they came, as if spending is to fun and sun what tequila is to margaritas.

From the jet skis and the parasail he sent them back to their chaise lounges by the pool talking about "the wonderfully entertaining fellow working the beach. You really must experience him." Thus came the rewards. "Ninety-four. Ninety-five."

It was only a matter of time, never mind Milo who can't see the value of rippling muscles and a glittering smile—and a nonstop monologue to make that smile contagious.

Now he, Antonio Garza, is maestro of pool activities. Soon he will have more money than a coffee can will hold. He won't get another can but will next fill an entire plastic bucket, one of those five-gallon buckets that begins full of *jalapeños* but then is promoted to holding the Garza fortune.

Five gallons of money?

¡Chihuahua!

It seems too much to imagine.

Then again, it depends on the currency. You could have a million-*peso* bill and need only a little envelope. Or a check. It could be made out for...anything!

Hey, what else can you think about in a strain like this, upping the bar in one jump by twenty percent? You think twenty percent is a gain to sneeze at? No. It is a gain to measure and feel, each huff to the next.

Antonio's best T-shirt hangs neatly in his closet, facing front so the sleek panther is ready to spring, even between washings. Shiny dark and graceful as any beast, he and panther are ready for one more wearing before washing, because washing every day will wear him out. Besides, Antonio detects playful curiosity in the women by the pool when he and panther ripen a bit. Mrs. Mayfair likes it. Then again, he must use caution in all things, given the risk of misperception on a rise so rapid. Far from predatory, Antonio Garza is only playful and willing.

Mrs. Mayfair would buy him another expensive T at the mere hint of desire, so he might drop a tacit word or two. She'd surely take his hint to heart quick as a white-eyed tit on an early worm. She would buy three Ts and get so lovey, clingy and tonguey that frankly he'd rather ripen.

"A hundred eleven. A hundred twelve," each syllable of each number receiving clear enunciation. "A hundred thirteen. A hundred fourteen."

This keeps the pace slow and even, allowing for proper form on each sit-up, so that each can make its rightful contribution.

She's smart like that, Mrs. Mayfair, so rarely does she miss a beat between herself and Antonio. He smiles in pleasant recollection of Mrs. Mayfair's warble. He hears her whispering her hot, coarse need. What else should a young man recall while doing sit-ups? Does she not contribute to his overall campaign? Besides, he hears her because her need is endless, with no regard for a man's limits or private moments.

Still, she's more alive than most, and who could tire of her body with the matching red hair? His smile is sustained on her refrain that he please "Make me feel wanted. Please, Antonio. Make me feel…"

Wanted? Okay.

So instead of one hand behind her head he put two, accelerating the roughness she seemed to long for. Well, he hopes she longed for it. She seemed eager at the time for the two-handed head grab and the vigorous pumping action.

"One hundred twenty-two. One hundred twenty-three."

No, he should do the right thing. He will buy a second T-shirt on his own. "One hundred twenty-four."

His father condones this decision based on manhood and independence. His photo hangs on the wall by the table beneath the tiny Jesus.

Gustavo Garza died a man of no means, except of course for the immortality made available to a man through his sons.

Antonio and Baldo often stare at what remains of their father with the same glazed gaze they shared over the simple grave and wooden box holding he who kept them fed and for the most part clothed. Nobody cried, so most surmised that their dazed wonder was not for their father but rather for the uncertainty of tonight and tomorrow. Antonio was too old for crying anyway, a man already in the technical sense. Besides that, he was overwhelmed and stupefied at his father's passing.

Baldo was young enough but neither cried nor whimpered. Some doubt his grasp on the meaning of loss. Some doubt his grasp on any meaning. Some doubt that he's ever uttered a sound, but Antonio knows better. Baldo knows right from wrong and wants to fit in, as long as it fits with what he knows. He speaks with a nod or a gaze, a skewed glance or a sudden turn. He looked up to Antonio at their father's funeral, and emitted a tiny, fearful croak like that of a fledgling bird teetering on the edge of the nest. Looking down at life's reward, Antonio put an arm around his little orphan brother for assurance; they would make do. So they have, thanks to Antonio, who sees things for both of them and translates as necessary for his younger brother, who often needs help in seeing the fit.

Baldo makes another sound as well. It was first heard years ago on the night their father brought home a gift of a tiny bird on the cusp of fledging. Floppy and downy as any nestling, it suffered further disadvantage from too much beak. How could such a bird ever fly if it could hardly lift its head?

Gustavo Garza picked it up from the ground, where it had lolled and squawked beside the fallen tree where its nest had been. The tree and thousands more had to go so development could proceed with a roadway. With a roadway, the world can arrive.

The roadway should have been built sooner, with so much beauty for tourists here at hand, including the weather, the water, and the languorous sandy beaches. Progress is not free but requires a few minor casualties, like a dead bird here and there. But you can't stop progress for those who would perish anyway, given their limited ability to move out of the way.

Gustavo knew these things as he knew the indiscretion of a D-9 Cat with a front-end loader, so he stepped in front of the grumbling earth mover to reach the fledgling bird. At times a man of sentiment, Gustavo Garza that time reached for a token to bring home, for his sons to see and play with it before it died.

Gustavo picked it up again a few hours later to set it out back for a quiet death under the stars. That's when Baldo barked, which is the second sound we know he can make. From deep within came the startled complaint, until the little bird was brought back in. Back inside Baldo held it. He stared at it, cooed in its face, and finally jammed a bean down its throat.

It was cooked and mushy, the bean, and required some follow-through to work it down the tiny gullet, but it filled the bill and was followed by another. Then they sat and stared at each other, Baldo straight ahead while Toucan, as the little bird was called, looked at his mentor sideways, one eye at a time. They helped each other along, one stuffing, the other gobbling, then cocking his head with curiosity and longing.

Antonio remembers those days of strange noises from under the table where Toucan lived. He laughed along with his father; neither knowing which fledgling made this noise or that. Baldo was a child then and Antonio was hardly more, yet their father spoke to the elder as the repository of a father's teaching and a father's responsibility. Hardly loquacious as his elder son, Gustavo crooked a weary finger at Antonio and nodded sanguinely. "Your brother is different," he said, which of course any boy of twelve could plainly see.

Of course, a father is partial, so the mute boy was spared the quirky profile but was rather viewed as both more and less. As a workingman on intimate terms with the daily vicissitudes of food and shelter, Gustavo surrendered now and then to sentiment but not to gloss. He leaned in and said, "He knows things. I cannot tell you what he knows. I see things myself and don't know what they are. I…sense things but don't know what to make of them. Baldo, your brother, knows things that you and I cannot know. He knows."

Knows what?

Well, Gustavo said he didn't know what, and maybe Antonio isn't too sure either. In the next few weeks Toucan dropped his baby down and sprouted feathers and was moved to the old cage outside the little *casa*, because a chicken belongs outside, no matter what its shape or size or color. Baldo moved the cage from the ground to a rickety stack of bricks, because Toucan was no chicken and should not have suffered ground hazards after surviving so much already.

Gustavo died a few months later. He gazed up glassy eyed and feeble, saying he made many mistakes but always did his best. On a sigh he was gone.

Things changed when Gustavo died.

For starters, in the week following the burial, Baldo smashed the cage with an old board, then beat it to a mangled mess. There it sits, once a birdcage, its perches and swings now broken and mangled in a heap.

Toucan watched the thrashing from a nearby limb, presumably enjoying the demolition of his confinement.

Baldo didn't exactly speak that day, but he mimicked Toucan's guttural surge. Their harsh duet entertained and relieved both of them.

"A hundred forty-eight. A hundred forty-nine. A hundred fifty."

There, it is done. A hundred fifty per day will be the new standard and will be done in the morning. Antonio does not stop but goes directly to a hundred stomach crunches and a hundred twenty-five push-ups. Make that a hundred fifty each, for balance and symmetry and penance in advance. A little credit on hand can't hurt.

Antonio remembers his poor dead father, gone now these past five years but seeming absent for much longer. Well, maybe it's six or seven years. Time changes its pace for a boy with no father in the formative years, at once an orphan yet a father to his younger brother.

Dead already at an age younger than Mrs. Mayfair is now, Gustavo Garza showed twice the wear and tear and asked for *nada*, except maybe some warm *tortillas* for *los niños*. Maybe it's best that he died.

Antonio ponders death, because such thoughts also occur during blind, dumb effort. He huffs and knows that his father's early demise was not best. How could death be best? It cannot be. Antonio wonders if his father could have taught him what he's learned on his own. We can never know how Gustavo Garza might have influenced his exceptional son, the elder one.

Perched stoically below the tiny Jesus, Gustavo peers at his sons with just the right thing to say for all occasions. Mute as his younger son, Gustavo seems wiser now, knowing those things that eluded him in life. Yet his surviving image still shines with a patina of dried sweat, as if toil bespeaks his afterlife as well. A photograph can't sweat, unless it's a miracle, like the famous Madonna that cries, and not from a leak in the roof. So, perhaps such a miracle is here before us. Heaven knows he sweated more in a single day than Mrs. Mayfair in a month of poolside tanning sessions.

Mrs. Mayfair suffers her own travail in her own way, feeling unwanted like she does, giving with such generosity as if compensating for gross inadequacy elsewhere. Antonio wants to tell her that any more adequacy might blow a fuse, and that would be something in such a healthy young man. It's not that he wouldn't want to keep up, but he can't, because her appetite is relentless and her needs not nearly as complex as his own.

I mean, she only has to lie there, which she hardly ever does, but maybe life would be easier for all parties if she would. Perhaps she could be more adequate in the realm of silence, which is not to say she should shut her yapping mouth, but she should silence herself every now and then.

Mrs. Mayfair may never feel the bliss of silence, except for the blessed moments when he, Antonio, shuts her up. But that's hardly serene, with her gurgling noises between ecstasy and choking. And what if she does choke? Then what? She always wants more and more, even insisting that he hold her by the ears and stuff the leak in her chatterbox.

At least she knows what a good sweat feels like. And he has to admit that she does grow eerily calm when he does the thing with his mouth. It isn't risky, because it's only his tongue and not his *pinga*. Moreover, he doesn't hesitate, nor would any modern man hold back if he understands a woman's sensitivity or the potential of a morning's tips. Tongue diving like no tomorrow, he makes her happy. Is not helping others with their issues of self-esteem among life's greatest pursuits? He feels good about himself in the act of giving. Moreover, he feels three entire mornings of tips flowing from mere minutes of an easy flick just so, between the lips. Is this not the return promised by the New Economy, in which working smart can richly balance working hard? Is this not win-win for everyone all the way around?

Well, of course it is.

He asks Mrs. Mayfair for nothing. She sets the rates; a hundred fifty pesos for the thing with his mouth was her idea. It seemed spontaneous at first, until the three fifty-peso bills seemed always ready, folded on the dresser. More are on hand in neatly folded threes under the mattress. She makes no secret. The money is not hidden there but is there for convenience. Antonio vows to one day seek the mother lode.

Lyria calls him disgusting and says he knows very little of risk. But what does she know, cleaning rooms with no exposure to affluence and personal charm beyond what is flung to the floor or left on the toilet rim? What can she know of the subtle transformation from a pocket full of money to a tin can filling up? Can she tell the difference between a pile of *pesos* and the upper level of money called capital? No, she cannot. Nothing is what she knows. Nor can he teach her what he has learned from years of exposure and through sheer, raw instinct. Antonio is qualified. He will rise rapidly in this world of new development. He tells Lyria it's not so bad because she, Mrs. Mayfair, is clean smelling and only forty-one. Lyria says that she, Mrs. Mayfair, is fifty-one or fifty-six, and it doesn't even matter what she smells like, as if anyone cares or wants to hear about such filth.

"She's dirty. You think you're the only one, Antonio?"

Antonio thinks he could have gone to one hundred fifty push-ups a long time ago. But it's okay that he waited, because if you push the reps too quickly you get these huge biceps bulging like papayas, and they're simply out of balance with your forearms, your delts, and your abs. And I suppose your pecs and even your traps if you think about it. So waiting was the right thing to do.

"Seventy-three. Seventy-four."

Am I the only one? Maybe I am. Maybe I'm not. Mrs. Mayfair came only once a year until last year. Now it's twice. So why would she double up if she were getting it elsewhere?

Lyria laughs scornfully. Where is her husband getting it? Does he wear the cover? You are teasing evil, Lyria says.

But Antonio doesn't need negativity and tells her so. Furthermore, he will not confide in her if she abuses the privilege. Besides, he wears the cover. And Mrs. Mayfair is very hygienic, which you can plainly see. And besides all that, she, Lyria, sounds like a jealous woman, which is foolish.

The privilege? You call it a privilege to hear about you and that *puta*, which makes me want to puke?

Lyria was never delicate but now seems farther from the soft touch than ever. Still, her accusation and yelling are playful in nature and no different than all those years ago, since she first caught him peeing on her leg in the bath they shared as children. She yelled then, too, but can you blame her?

Any little girl will yell when she discovers you peeing on her leg. Lyria's been steady through the years, a sister to the one and perhaps a surrogate mother to the other. Why can't she see these things as they really are? At least Baldo retains the mystique and secret wisdom of a person of silence. Lyria is a shrill young woman whose every thought is volubly shared with everyone. What can she know? Why must she yell and accuse? Why do I confide in her? Well, because she is the only one. And no matter what she says or how loud she says it, a different mystique surrounds her. Perhaps it resides in her shape, which is so different from what it was. And her innocence, biblically speaking. She ripens rapidly. Soon she will be ready for plucking. This will be a time of joy.

Do you wear the cover on your tongue? Lyria wants to know.

But he will never answer such harsh questions that serve no purpose other than to make a man feel wrong. "One hundred thirty-seven. One hundred thirty-eight."

It has been known for years that Antonio and Lyria will marry. And happy day it will be, perhaps with minimal yelling. She will be his love forever, which she surely must know as well as she's ever known anything. Still, who in his right mind would respond to such caustic interrogation so devoid of civility, much less compassion or understanding?

Hardly a little girl anymore, her raven hair falls profusely down her back, and her dark eyes glare with conviction. Racing to finish her womanly growth, already she blazes inside and out. You can see it if you look, but it's too bright to stare directly into and too hot to eat. One day Antonio Garza will see and taste the fire.

Is he not the hot tamale for her corn shuck? Of course he is. So why must she make him so unhappy with such noise between now and then?

¡Ay Caramba! Who can take it? Nobody is who. She knows this, falling silent only when he takes his leave. He turns back as if for more abuse, but she's done. He really only wants another look, however brief. She fills out with specific succulence in the gentle curve separating the girl from the woman. She seems to taunt that curve just as she taunts all things, until she appears ready to split from too much ripening, too much juice and sweet pulp inside. He wants to lay her naked and run his palm through the slalom course from her ribs to her thighs, over hill and dale and back and maybe then some. He will not yet divulge this desire. She would take him entirely wrong, most likely assuming his attraction is merely the lust of a teenage boy, which he is not, though the lust feels the same, and he wants to roam those hills and spelunk the caves too. But the hot depths of womanhood must fully ripen in the spirit and heart to catch up with the body so that all can be savored at once, as a wife should be. Such is the moral standard of people who would marry forever, not to mention the standard of good taste in those on the path of goodness.

He compensates self-denial by facing her scorn, knowing the cold drenching will be like gasoline on coals. They will fuel the passion when the match is made and the lust blazes, and Antonio and Lyria will laugh at her former derision.

Meanwhile, her derision proves her desire for him and her concern for his welfare. Will not Antonio and Lyria consummate their union soon in a bonfire of delirious joy with flames soaring skyward? Will not a love sweetly anticipated be sweeter still, once it emerges from the clouds of abuse and denial?

After all, for whom did she adopt the habit of shaving the hair from her armpits, if not for him? She sees the women of affluence by the pool, women whose armpits are smooth as ceramic. Antonio wishes she would catch on and shave the coarse hair from her calves and outside her high thighs while she's at it. He knows many men would find her hairy legs repugnant, but he does not. For one thing, he grew up among women with hairy legs. For another thing, you can't see the hair in the dark. But Lyria will one day sit poolside as the maestro's wife and should have creamy thighs for the occasion.

Like Mrs. Mayfair, who likes to keep the lights on during services, and who lathers cream in dollops on her thighs while lounging by the pool. Antonio suspects great effort and some discomfort in achieving such a lustrous hue up her thighs to the narrow patch of radiant red above the sliver that matches the hair on her head. Not that she creams the sliver, not by the pool anyway, but she does push the cream up under the elastic in her strange, provocative way. Who knows? Maybe leaving the lights on is sweet reward for a woman's effort toward beauty. Maybe one day Lyria will work as hard.

At any rate, the hair outside of Lyria's high thighs could stay as far as Antonio the man is concerned. He only thinks it should go for practical reasons. He considers leaving the lights on with Lyria, though he doubts she would allow it, even in deference to beauty and love.

Besides, Lyria's beauty is unique, not so self-conscious or staged. Lyria will be well explored in the dark, and he knows what softness will lie in the fur of her thighs.

So what does it matter? Long run; short run; who cares? He loves her as he has since the hair on her legs was downy fuzz. He could never condone removal of the hairs from the edge of her Fertile Crescent as the women by the pool do and as Mrs. Mayfair does, as if a woman and a racing car both need a stripe up the center. Antonio knows the two are different; both can be fast and expensive, but a woman should have a proper bush, and if it sticks out the sides of her bikini, who's to mind? Who is required to look, except for one who enjoys such a view?

Then again, a woman seems so much closer to social evolution if she works as a waitress rather than a maid. The maids have hairy legs. The waitresses are smooth, svelte, and shapely, with a slow swagger. "This way, please." Lyria can't be a waitress; she won't shave her legs, because cleaning is one thing and servitude is yet another. But still, maybe she will soften.

"Yes, my father," Antonio tells his late father. "I have learned many things I would like to share with you to see what you would say. I sweat like you. I work very hard for my money like you did." He rises, pulls the chair out, and sits to count his morning tips. "But it's different now. I wish you could see. It's more money. Much more money."

He savors the count to forty-eight pesos. In only two days he can have another T-shirt, the toucan, the most beautiful of all in his opinion and perhaps the nostalgic favorite as well, symbolizing that which Baldo knows or might know some day. Still, he wanted the panther first; it's so lean and muscular, with electric eyes and a willingness suggesting high voltage.

¡Ay!

He feels the impracticality of another hundred-peso T-shirt but also senses a level of opportunity unknown in former times. Can you weigh potential on the same scale that you weigh *tortillas*? Is not a hundred pesos meager capitalization for viability? Flamboyance may tip the balance in the long haul.

Such is the complexity of his world. Antonio sees how the affluent tourists feel at home in the company of a man like himself if his exotic side is properly presented. By deferring to such sensitivity, a toucan T could bring additional barriers down.

Antonio is not so much concerned with garnering the favors of another Mrs. Mayfair. But a firmer toehold among the men might ease them into asking his opinion from time to time. He knows it's only a matter of time before such men come with their money for more development and realize that local knowledge is a premium.

Antonio waits for his late father to chime in with his fatherly *dos centavos*. Gustavo wore T-shirts, but not like these. Never new, they simply appeared as their predecessors tattered to failure and could no longer stop a breeze or soak a sweat or even admonish motorists through their stained shreds to *Drink Coca-Cola*, or to remember *Avis. We try harder.*

Remnants of *Avis* and *Coca-Cola* now line the shelf over the table. Antonio reaches to touch the cotton cloth; rotten and coarse as a laborious life, it crumbles.

Sitting and staring, Gustavo would hang his head for absolution from the little deity, to whom all praise, gratitude, and requests are due. If a few pesos could be spared for a small round bottle of mescal, his indeterminate woe would be shared with his sons as well. One played under the table while the other looked askance and asked his father what was so wrong.

"I don't know what to do," Gustavo said.

Do? What can you do? Antonio bows his head again all these years later in abeyance to his father's uncertain guilt. What did he do wrong? Nothing, is the answer; it was only the mescal that clouded his vision. Was he wrong to work behind the heavy equipment, clearing a swath through the jungle? No again, he was only out of synch with modern times. The men of development would have built the road no matter what, because roads must be built. Tree clearing is back-wrenching work, which was a commodity to be thankful for.

"Father," he says to his late father, "toucan and panther and weasel and the little birds must move out of the way. They must adapt like us. You cannot stop progress."

Well, Gustavo has little use for such assessment at this point, yet he is urged to see the light and shed the ignorance from the Garza legacy. Such suggestion may not be within a son's proper place, but Antonio senses comprehension in the spirit of his late father. Gustavo must have sensed something in life, because he wasn't entirely ignorant, even when the mescal slurred his speech. Nodding sanguinely and shaking a finger he instructed, "Each is a life, my son. A life like yours or mine. Or maybe better."

Better? He asks himself and implores aloud, "How can it be better, Father? Those cats and birds are wild animals. They spend their days looking for a little seed or a mouse to terrorize, or hiding from whatever terrorizes them. But look at us. We have all of this now, a place to eat and sleep with four walls around us to keep us safe and away from the bugs and to take care of our business in private. I don't understand how the animals have anything better than we have here. Progress is good, my father."

Gustavo smiles wearily when Antonio flows with youthful vigor. He smiles just as he smiled until the night near the end of his life when he said, "It is a matter of pride." Antonio waited, but his father was done.

"Are you not proud, Father?"

I am proud of you, Antonio, he so much as says. Please keep me that way. Antonio hears him and answers, "Yes, father."

Antonio has no doubt that family pride will be sustained. Yet he also knows that neither his father nor the little deity can change the ultimate law of humanity, requiring us to lead, follow, or get out of the way.

Just look: the Garza brothers adapt and move daily past the baseline called survival, inching surely to prosperity. Antonio knows his father's smile will be justified for years to come, for him and for his unlikely younger brother too.

Baldo crawled out from under the table and gazed at his father's mournful mumble over something or other about wild animals sent screeching in the face of progress. Soon after, he gazed at the simple wooden box, and years later he gazes still with his simple wooden knowing. In Baldo something ferments like yeast and sugar, blowing off when you least expect it. He's sweet if the balance is right but can explode if it's not.

Well, maybe it's a phase he's going through.

Antonio inventories his father's legacy and knows it might be seen as paltry. Gustavo Garza left enough money to spend in one minute in a *tienda*, but he left something else that may germinate to greatness, and from greatness can come the money to buy the *tienda* itself. His father left Antonio the tenacious spirit. As for Baldo, inheritance seems a different egg altogether, for Baldo got *nada*. Well, maybe he got more than that. Maybe he got sweetness too, for two beings sweeter than Baldo Garza and his poor dead father have yet to breathe the sultry air of *Oaxtapec*.

Well, enough of wonder and legacy, sweetness and madness. Antonio flashes his warmest smile, which is soft and happy but is not a grin. With humility, not pride, he reveals his perfect teeth to tiny Jesus. The teeth he got from his *madre*.

The coffee can brims with eight thousand pesos at two point nine one to the dollar. Antonio wishes his father could just once hold the tin can and feel its heft and then shake the small fortune so they could laugh together. He wishes to reach in just once for an idle handful and shower his father with money. Just once he would like to treat his late father to a meal of too many *tamales* with both *mole verde y mole rojo,* and enough *frijoles, arroz y tortillas* to make his belly ache, and a few *cervezas.* They would scorn the mere thought of *mescal,* Antonio and his *padre.* They would crown their comfort with some of the new tequila that costs more than man's wage used to be and tastes like thin air but warms your fingertips and your heart before popping a sweat on top of your head.

Gustavo often said the best was yet to come, and maybe this is it, this fantasy of prosperity and the very best of eating and drinking between father and son.

Antonio savors the moment and vows to live as best he can, with no regrets and with love for what comes his way. Look how much has come so quickly. Twenty-two already and well on the rise. Well, twenty-one and eight months, which is practically the same as twenty-two. Bowing his head again with respect and deference to his late father and tiny Jesus, he genuflects quickly and turns to see his brother watching from the doorway.

Baldo is sixteen now, still thin as a weed but taller than most and gaining the swagger common to adolescent boys. He stands in silhouette before the blaring siesta sun; his sinewy muscles stretch along the bones now, his limbs at last looking heftier than straight lines between the joints. The machete hangs like an extension of his left arm, not grasped and not separate. A huge green coconut is snug under his right arm, and he waits, perhaps observing or seeking approval. "What?" Antonio asks. "No thirsts today?"

Baldo nods; yes, we had some thirsts today. He stoops and sets the coconut at an angle on the stone threshold and with an easy slash from overhead, cuts the husk to the nut close to one end. Spinning the coconut to the opposite angle, he cuts again, twists, pries and pops the top to reveal a hole for drinking.

He offers the nut to Antonio, who takes it for a short drink and returns it.

Baldo tilts it up and drinks long and hard, until Antonio asks if he's trying to swim to the bottom. Baldo comes up for air and stares off. Coconut juice blends with the sweat on his neck and runs down his chest.

He walks over to the table and empties his pockets of twelve pesos. These are his own tips from a morning on the beach where he opens coconuts and serves them with two straws and ice cubes—purified of course—to hotel guests who sign a chit and add a tip and who sometimes throw in a peso or two.

Antonio nods and counts and adds both piles to the coffee can.

Baldo removes his shorts in preparation for siesta and goes outside again, where he cleaves the coconut with another slash. The blade whispers, rendering two halves with a good core of sweet, tender meat. Baldo knew this would be the case, because Baldo knows coconuts and saved this one for home.

They eat.

Baldo may be innocent, but a boy who stands nearly two meters tall in his bare feet and swings a machete of another meter while dangling a ten-inch *pinga* should know the difference between innocence and carelessness. It is one thing to cool off and another to waltz around the *casa* with a semi-swell.

What if Lyria walked in?

Antonio wonders if Baldo knows the facts about men and women. Besides needing guidance on innocence and nakedness and the wise thing to do, Baldo needs instruction on the difference between a tool and a weapon. The machete should rest on a shelf most of the time, just as the *pinga* should be inside the trousers most of the time. Perhaps a boy is more comfortable sleeping naked, but no boy needs to sleep with a machete.

Well, this too may be a phase he's going through. But how many phases can an elder brother be expected to process all at once?

Antonio will speak with him one day soon, man to man, because it is time. Perhaps it will be today, after siesta. For now the heat prevails and the brothers surrender, stretching into the curve of their hammocks.

Outside, the cicadas pick up their pace for the apex of the afternoon. The weak breeze goes flat; the fronds hang limp, the hammocks sag and soon the brothers snooze. Antonio dreams of myriad bugs rubbing thighs in celebration of the heat. Sweat rolls from his face and chest. Baldo sweats less but dreams more, twitching and flopping like a dog still running and jumping through his dream. He hears cicadas too but dreams of a different rasp and resonance, which is simply Toucan's song outside, though Toucan has flown the coop, as it were. Perhaps he, Toucan, dreams as well this afternoon, twitching like a bird who watches his dog run and jump.

Toucan went to live in another cage at Jimi Changa's, the wild tourist restaurant and discotheque across from the hotels. Jimi Changa specializes in Mexican cuisine, and both diners and revelers keep Toucan awake long after his bedtime. Such is the nature of progress, which has served to enrich Toucan's life as well, providing him with many new friends and admirers who squawk in passing. Some even offer fingers for a nibble.

Baldo wants the lights out and silence so a bird can get some rest, because a bird as glorious as Toucan needs neither disco dancing nor sour drinks with cheap whiskey. This is not the life that was promised when Baldo was told that sooner or later a man and a bird must work. This is not the life for a man or a bird.

But Jaime Ruíz came with an offer.

Jaime's friends once knew him as Jaime the Weasel but only because of his long, skinny nose and long, sparse mustache and not because of any bad characteristics. Now he actually calls himself Jimi Changa and is fairly famous in the region. The Weasel promised that such a bird and such a place were a natural match. Moreover, Jaime poured two hundred pesos into the can and promised more if Toucan survived the year, thus proving the progressive nature of beneficence.

Baldo dreams of revelers and wild diners and wonders in his dream: why is Toucan caged, when I already smashed it for him?

II

Let Him Sleep

Baldo rolls over without falling out because he's rolled over in his hammock since time began. Now that he's bigger the mesh presses more, leaving its woven pattern along his flank, his arm and leg. He sleeps like the dead, not a care in the world, heavy as bricks with no concern for the mortar. Let him sleep. Nobody cares if Baldo is late. For all we know they won't care if Baldo doesn't show up at all. Of course they would make timid reference to the missing drinkboy. He makes them nervous, and they would rather have drinks served in glasses with napkins on trays, as drinks should be served. Perhaps he is colorful; but would the tips not accrue to them if he didn't show?

That's okay. Antonio cares about Baldo's punctuality and performance, because he's bringing Baldo along on the way up. He first introduced Baldo as his assistant, his *compadre*, and his *vaquero*, necessary to herd the tourists into line. The managers relent, knowing the value of Baldo and that of his brother, Antonio, the rippling one, the golden boy, as it were. Antonio brings them back in droves for his brand of laughter and carrying on, so Baldo is okay until the cows come home. Just never you mind whom Baldo makes nervous.

At the little table under the family shrine at *Casa Garza* Antonio empties his pockets of two hundred per day to Baldo's twenty or sometimes twenty-five, and this too is okay for brothers taking care of each other as best they can. They care for Lyria too, as their girl and their woman, whom they love like a sister and whom Antonio will soon take as a wife.

This sibling love going to romantic love is not what you could call incestuous, because Antonio is waiting as men have waited through the ages, if the prize is worth waiting for and embodies the ultimate purity of womanhood. A weak man doesn't wait; he takes, insisting that his beloved stoop to the ficky fick before wedlock.

What pure woman ever wanted that kind of thing without the commitment? What can the act of love become if it's rushed to occur outside the eyes of God?

Of course Antonio is not her brother by blood, and her father died long before Gustavo, so the brother-lover concept merely describes a love that will roll over in time to reveal its brightest side. She merely needs time to allow the roll to occur naturally, to wed as a fully developed woman.

Then comes the ficky fick.

Antonio spreads his T-shirt across the table and irons it with his hands, careful not to crease his panther. He can wear it two more days without washing if he wants to, because today is Saturday. Tomorrow turns over with mostly new tourists who won't play along anyway their first day, and even so, his shirt comes off in the first five minutes to get things warmed up, to get the women going, which invariably brings the men along. Well, sometimes it brings them along, unless they're self-conscious of their own poverty of ripples. Or maybe it's their wealth of dimpled rolls that makes them scowl at him. He pulls the T-shirt on and decides to wear it to the last minute before buying another one, which may be today and may not be today.

Besides, if Mrs. Mayfair stays another week, as she threatens, she might buy him a new T in spite of his resistance. These and other potentials accompany thoughts for the afternoon and evening shifts, beginning with pool aerobics, pool volleyball, and then bingo again. Bingo tensions will be relieved with a round of float walking, in which a string of small floats is stretched over the pool, and we see who can walk to the end without falling off. Some of us already know whom, and it's not because he's had so much practice. Antonio Garza is an extreme physical specimen with extraordinary skills in many, many areas.

Okay, we'll wrap up the daylight hours with beach volleyball. That should sustain the lively spirit of float walking and will include everyone, even those with much less skill, for they are only here to have fun. Twilight will begin with good cheer all around, with good mingling and recalling the highlights and hijinks of both the winners and losers, blending to general schmooz and quick inventory of the blessings we share.

Beach bar revenues are rarely discussed between Antonio and the managers, because he works the guests into a thirst, then massages them toward the perfect quench. Oh, let a day pass with no drinks; then they'd let him know the score. He knows instinctively that a good lead from the beach to the bar means forty patrons ordering forty drinks. At twenty *pesos* each, it's a pretty *peso* from one sundown to the next. Nobody says boo, but such economic stimulation does not go unnoticed. A career path in most cases depends on cohesion such as this exercise in clockwork timing and maximum resource utilization. Antonio has the knack. The afternoon shift waits for the rising curtain no less than a play on a stage. *Overture, dim the lights. This is it, the night of nights.* Maybe it's only Bugs Bunny who sings that one, but it fits so well.

Prepping for the show, Antonio poses and flexes, checks his teeth and his nose for strays and goes in close for quick scrutiny of his face. With a little pluck here, a little pinch there, a scrape and a squeeze, but not so hard as to make a red spot, soon all is well. He stands back for the big picture.

Ay, perfecto.

For the afternoon shift he rolls his T-shirt sleeves to the notch between his biceps and deltoids. He rolls a cigarette pack in one side as seen on TV. He poses again in the mirror and takes the cigarette pack out. He doesn't smoke, for one thing. He only brought this empty pack home to see if he should. It crushes too easily for another thing, so maybe the new crush-proof box would be better.

But it seems foolish to interrupt the beautiful curvature from bulging biceps to definition deltoids with a lumpy box.

These things are simply known by what the mirror says, though an outside admirer might think him already perfect.

Antonio practices a few moods in the mirror, moving between a great big smile and a grin. Between the two is a vast difference. One is warm and fuzzy and the other is greedy and perverse.

He practices stern authority, anger, and, of course, amusement. He feels the cliff edge of his high, angular cheekbones. He puckers up, not with vanity but to better apply the sunscreen to his lush Latin lips. He wonders with amusement how much his lips weigh, and how much insurance they warrant from Lloyds of London at a hundred fifty pesos per tender kiss with so many years ahead. He sweeps his frizzled hair back. It springs forward again, so he bulges his eyes and gapes his mouth to match the voltage in his hair. He smears a double dab of hold'em into his stubborn frizz, gives it a half-minute to set up and brushes it back to its proper wave. Each wavelet crests with a shimmer of light as he slowly turns to profile to see how big his beak really looks.

It's big, but who cares? It balances his face. That's character. Of this, we can be assured because it is often said in a whine and a whimper. *Oh, Antonio, you are the most handsome man in the world. Oh, oh, oh.*

Antonio smiles at the man in the mirror, seeing what they see. He thinks he is surely not the most handsome man in the world. But who can know for sure?

He relaxes, daubing scent on either side of his neck and under each arm, and along his inner thighs in case Mrs. Mayfair wants to see him after cocktails, before dinner. He feels that she will stay another week, which should be good for another six hundred *pesos* plus gifts. If she weren't planning on staying, then why would she go these last two days with no needs?

No, she would not. She is most demanding on her last two days. She calls it her storing-up time. But when does she expect her stud stallion to store anything up? This would be good to know. Never mind, a rich *gringa* gets what she wants if she's willing to pay for a private show with a performance like no tomorrow.

In a minute he's quaffed, scented, unruffled, and ready to go. He turns to Lyria in the door. She has only just wakened and shuffled over from next-door, looking sleepy as a child in her rumpled dress. She is staring at Baldo's floppy *pinga* but hardly sees through her glassy eyes. Antonio plucks Baldo's baggy pants from the hook on the post and chucks them across what should be covered.

He steps deftly between Baldo and the open door and closes the distance to Lyria. He stands before her, not so much hovering or honing in but merely sensing her. In this intimate but safe proximity he senses as well the exquisite agony of romance and hopes she feels it too. He wants to tease her on his own terms, wants to flirt with what he knows is waiting under the soft, cotton rumples. But he is careful here too, lest he rumple the prospects nurtured for so long. Lyria will be his in a year or two, when he has the money, and his own sons will view the world in dollars instead of pesos.

So instead of playfully squeezing her breast like it's a bicycle horn that may not beep but will surely wake her up, he merely watches her gentle breathing, and he waits. In a rare moment she responds like she does sense the sweet agony. Would he like to meet later for dinner, if he's not working? This last is reference to his side job, but he notes with pleasure that her reference is civil, deferring politely to his efforts toward extra income, as she should. After all, he fully intends to share.

"Yes, I would," he says. "Saturday night." Baldo stirs with a guttural groan, proof of vocal chords. "Baldo will come too. Okay?"

"Okay. I will make…"

"No! No make. Tonight we celebrate. Baldo will take us out. For dinner and dancing!"

Baldo drags his legs over the side, swinging the hammock perilously to the vertical. He sits as if in pain, holding his head, groaning lowly. Lyria goes to the sink, where she moistens a towel and spreads it over his shoulders. She rubs his head and tells him to wake up. With playful petulance she demands to know why a boy so young can't wake up. Antonio watches, wishing the playful petulance could be applied to him from time to time rather than the stern criticism she most often gives him.

Then again he is the elder, and Baldo is only a boy.

Now she rubs Baldo's head vigorously, admonishing him to rise, to go and serve the thirsts, to split enough coconuts with great flourish to pay for dinner and dancing. He no longer groans but takes to the stimulation on his scalp like a pup who can't get enough.

She turns away so Baldo can wiggle into his pants. She asks Antonio, "Celebrate what?"

Antonio shrugs, secretly relieved that she does not suspect his motive for dining out, which is to have dinner apart from Rosa, mother of Lyria and matron as well to Antonio and Baldo. Antonio loves Rosa, but she is too fat and worried for him to relax. "We celebrate what not. Celebration is important, you know. Baldo. Come." Baldo adjusts himself, ties the draw string, and rises to follow, not yet fully awake but shuffling his feet, dragging his ragged camp shirt in one hand, holding his machete loosely in the other. Passing Lyria, he glances up sideways with a shy smile like the same pup who suffers beatings for peeing inside, yet who can't tell what he did so wrong. Perhaps this shy apprehension is also Gustavo Garza's legacy to his second son. With a wistful sigh Antonio smiles too.

Lyria tussles Baldo's hair.

Antonio waits, then steps near her for a hug. They touch cheeks but not groins, because this is the *abrazo* that conveys warmth among family members with a commingling of spirits. He lingers in her scent to convey his intention, which is forever. She stands for it briefly but then enforces punctuality. It is time for the second shift.

What? Do you want to be late?

She watches them go, her boys; no, her men.

She has not forgotten Antonio's cruel request of only a week ago, to know if Lyria had a photograph of Rosa as a girl. "But why would you want to see such a thing?" Lyria asked, but feared that she knew what Antonio wanted to see. Rosa's beauty is in her heart, not her body. Lyria sees it and knows that Baldo sees it too and Antonio would if he had a brain in his head, which she sometimes doubts. Rosa is, in a cruel word, *gorda*. But she is only as fat as her heart is big and her arms are open and her table is set for giving.

"That's an easy question," Antonio said. "I want to see if she looks like you."

"You mean to see if I will look like her!"

"No, Lyria. You accuse me wrongly yet again. I did not think of that." But he let it go and will not ask again to see Rosa's picture. Of course he was guilty of such fear, which may be the shape of Lyria to come, because twenty years roll around before you know it. She easily gains two pounds per year, which become six or eight pounds in a few years, because such things gain momentum. And forty or sixty pounds will make her very fat if the wondrous process of filling out has no end. He fears her failure in beauty, and she knows it, because Antonio thinks of everything, and everyone knows it. He lets it go but ponders the mysteries of love and fat.

Lyria wonders why he presses relentlessly what has no importance except to convenience or impressions on others or money, money, money. Why does he treat her condescendingly but then respect perfect strangers? Why must he distance himself like a father to a child? She is not Baldo. Maybe Baldo needs restraint and discipline, but she does not. What keeps him from the tenderness every woman craves? Why must he feel her intimate parts so brusquely with a grab and a forced laugh instead of a caress? The *gringa* bitches by the pool believe him to be the real man of Mexico. So why must his *machismo* melt down like yesterday's *queso* in her presence?

Is she not a woman?

Yes, she is a woman, with a woman's needs and a woman's awareness of the modern world and its changing ways. Well, *en casa del herrero, cuchillo de palo*. The blacksmith's mare and the shoemaker's children are the worst shod. How can he remain so blind to that which would trigger any blacksmith to fan the flames and bang the anvil?

He treats her like a novitiate even though they're practically betrothed and have been since before they stopped sharing a bathtub, and everyone knows that too. And if those who comprise their community were to be surprised, it would not be that she had lain with Antonio or even that she swelled with his child but rather that they had never lain together at all, that he had not even attempted to share her inner warmth.

Oh, that would surprise them.

She watches Antonio stride boldly for the hilltop at the same hurried pace in which he strides for the future. Baldo never exactly wakes up, but he catches up at the crest. He straightens with a rhythm in his lanky gait, not a swagger, really, but a lope. Hardly the showman his older brother is, Baldo is merely graceful and silent with a certain unknowable quirk bespeaking happiness on his very own terms.

As Baldo approaches, stretching another inch here and there to maximum lank, his feet and hands swinging to the ends of their natural arcs, Antonio advises that a man should take care with his machete. A man doesn't let his *pinga* dangle for all to see. And a man absolutely doesn't swing a machete near his dangling *pinga*.

Baldo laughs short, perhaps at the imagery of *pingas* harvested by machete. At the main road he looks not left or right but strides boldly across such as an uprooted tree in a swollen stream might enter a greater flow. Antonio shakes his head, wishing his brother a greater arrogance and a lesser stupidity, for one can be cured and the other is a tale of a different telling. As it is, Baldo emotes the happiness of a tree, pure and dumb.

Across the road they wait for the bus, which is full. Once squeezed in they give in to its hypnotic effect that lulls them to sleep on their feet for the ten-minute ride down the road to the world of progress, development, and hot and cold running dollars.

Milo, the pool and beach manager, waits for the Garza brothers with anticipation. Antonio has seen it too often to respond. Some returning woman has asked for the maestro, or maybe two guests have sat for thirty minutes with no coconut juice. He nods steadily to indicate resolve, so Milo can calm down and the show can go on, once these critical problems are remedied.

Antonio scans the pool deck for familiar faces but sees only Mrs. Mayfair, who stares back intently as if to lock his gaze with her own. This afternoon she wears her grasping-hands bikini, the one with nothing between her breasts, so her sternum is exposed between the lift and spread of her sizable *melones*. The cups of this bikini are scalloped on the edges and remind Antonio of hands grasping the breasts from behind as he sometimes does. He smiles dismissively; he is not behind her, he is working. So please.

This morning she wore her red bikini that allows her breasts to hang close together with dramatic cleavage and dramatically heightens the reds in her dramatically red hair. The red is fetching and suggestive, but the grasping hands hold the breasts higher and spread them apart, so they're more spherical and not so oblong. He has examined the grasping hands she now wears to see what magic is in this simple black fabric that elicits such buoyancy in her *tetas*. The cups look soft and natural but, alas, are stiff with fiberglass beneath the fabric.

She watches and plays along with his preference for lift and spread by sitting up with a deep inhale, until the bottom part of her *chichis* cannot be contained by mere fiberglass and won't go back in the cup, until she exhales and tucks them back in. She well knows that the bottom part sticking out drives him wild.

But this is not the time or place. He's working. He shakes his head and looks away, so she relaxes and tucks back in, because he's right, public displays with hungry eyes can disrupt the reverie around the pool, which can threaten a livelihood.

With new intuition he thinks now that she is leaving. She *must* be, with this flagrant display of receptiveness. He can do without the display but is willing to fill her need as long as she understands that it must be quick, because he has plans with the family. Well, not that quick, but not more than an hour, or two on the outside.

Baldo gathers six coconuts for a group slash for the happy hour rush. But Milo intervenes again, after taking a call and making small talk to a guest. Today is very important, he tells Antonio. He waits for the meaning of 'importance' to sink in. Baldo grasps the importance before him, hacking coconuts. Milo moves to stop him and make him pay attention but then moves back. Baldo swings effortlessly with an impressive resolve that no man could absorb and tell about, especially Milo, who flinches in the line of fire. Only a fool would step farther in to such a swing.

Anyway, it is very important, today. By the power vested in him, Milo, under the auspices of *El Secretario Pesco* and the Mexican Navy, Baldo is hereby promoted.

Stepping forward, Antonio asks, "Promoted?"

Baldo replaces the hacked cap of his second coconut and seeks its proper fit. Once all six are cut and the caps are set neatly in place, he will prepare the straws; two straws in each with the paper wrappers bunched up at the top. This presentation appears fresh and sterile, which purity is very important to a hotel guest who wants a refreshing drink and no more. The ice cubes will be added prior to serving by the bartender, whose hands are on a higher level of purity. Otherwise, they would melt too soon, allowing the drink to water down and warm up, which is not acceptable to anyone and would generate no tips. The liquor too is dispensed at the bar if the guest wants liquor. Baldo is not allowed to handle the liquor. Liquor is valuable.

"Yes, a promotion. As of today—make that tomorrow. No, today. As of today, Baldo will be..." Milo steps up as Baldo fiddles with the caps. He sets a stubby hand on Baldo's shoulder and announces in a harsh whisper, "*El Capitán de las Tortugas!*"

"Captain of the Turtles? Do the turtles need a captain?"

"*¡Ay, sí!* Not just any *tortugas. ¡Las chicas!*" With a spurious grin and the marginal flourish of a chubby man, Milo turns to the six plastic tubs now lining the low wall beside the steps leading down to the beach, or up to the pool deck if you're going the other way. A parasol has been installed overhead, and, peering into the shade over the rims, Antonio squints to adjust his vision. In the tubs are baby sea turtles, just hatched, maybe twenty to a tub. He comes back out to the bright light and asks what is expected here of Baldo.

Milo explains that all of Mexico is now changing.

Antonio nods in compliance.

Milo goes on to say that *El Secretario Pesco* of the Federal Government of all of Mexico has decreed, and the Navy will enforce the law, that anyone taking or tampering with turtle eggs will face fines and imprisonment. The Navy has taken what eggs it can find and secured them for safe incubation. These babies are part of the seasonal hatch, distributed to hotels on appropriate coastlines for safekeeping for ninety days. In only ninety days these small turtles will grow big enough so that ninety percent of them may survive instead of merely two percent. The time has come to restore the turtles: no more turtle steaks or turtle soup or turtle oil or turtle shells.

No more.

Just look: a swimming pool lined with guests who are willing to pay four dollars—four dollars!—for a simple drink by the pool. Willing to pay *six* dollars for something fancy. Willing? Nay, they are happy to pay and looking forward to paying again and again. With tips! Does Antonio realize what this means?

Hey, to whom does Mister Milo think he speaks? Who knows better or stimulates more paying for more drinking? Who profits more from the happiness of *Hotel Oaxtapec* guests than Antonio himself does?

But Milo is a bump on the proverbial log, so Antonio merely nods once more as if to confirm comprehension, as if to say, Oh, so that's how it is.

Baldo hacks his sixth and final coconut. He glances up briefly at the dialogue and determines that he will not be missed for a brief run to fetch the straws, two each, which makes twelve straws in all.

"What can Baldo do? He is very busy serving coconuts. He is very conscientious with his work. He makes them happy. They love him."

Milo nods condescendingly. "He is the man for the job. He will now be part of Hotel Security. He will wear a uniform. There." Milo points to the khaki pants and matching shirt with official sleeve patches. It hangs on a wire hanger from a low limb of a nearby tree. "He will be proud to serve the turtles and the hotel, and we will be proud of him." Milo shifts quickly here from pride to confidence. "Antonio, I have seen your brother walk the beach. No other man I have known—and I will call him a man now that he is grown; no other man takes such effort to return the boxfish to the waves whether they are alive or dead. He gathers rubbish with no regard for hotel boundaries. He throws dinner scraps to *los pelicanos* when they have nothing else to eat because the small fish have not appeared. He swims alongside *los cocodrillos!* Who but a crazy man would do such a thing? I will tell you who. A man who walks with God is who. A man who is touched by St. Francis himself. Antonio, do not doubt the wisdom of this promotion. Today we are blessed. You are blessed. Baldo is blessed. We are all blessed. And so. It is late. You must prepare for bingo. No?"

"But what of tips? He makes tips with coconuts. The turtles will be happy, but will they pay tips?" He pokes his head into the shade again for a display of the antics that make him invaluable poolside. "Hey, *chicas!* You got some money? Hey! What you got in there?"

"Antonio, I am told from on high that it is no longer acceptable to have Baldo near the pool, near the guests. Do you now see how much we are blessed?"

Antonio feels the sting of this uppercut but shrugs it off as a true champion must and presses his case. "You want to affect the livelihood of my family here."

Milo nods and opens his mouth to speak but cannot, for first he must calculate the amount of money required to make Antonio happy without straining the budget. After all, how much can anyone be expected to pay for a babysitter of turtles? It wasn't Milo's idea. Nor does *El Secretario* provide a budget but rather advises the hotel that it will be good for business, just you wait and see, and don't forget the fines and imprisonment.

Baldo finishes prepping the last of his twelve straws so that anyone desiring their thirst quenched with a cool, refreshing drink can now be served by adding ice cubes, garnish and liquor if necessary. A simple slice of lime will do for garnish, this late in the day, because the evening hour is less playful and more serene and calls for less garnish than the midday drinks. Midday drinks get two slices for eyes and a pineapple wedge for a nose and a little paper parasol for a hat. Oh, they do like the midday garnish. He scans his inventory and nods, set to go, recalling the days not so long ago when he would need fifteen or eighteen straws to get it right. Not anymore; twelve up with no mistakes, and though this isn't exactly the same as Antonio's unique skill at float walking, it is a proficiency resulting from diligent practice and establishes his rightful place as one of the two Garza brothers.

He stands straight and turns to where Antonio waits and Milo stutters over this and that. He looks up at the new parasol over the wall beside the beach steps as if it didn't exist before his preparation was done. He too steps into the shade with a squint and then leans into it.

Milo and Antonio turn together at the sound of Baldo's gasp and the high-pitched, eerie squeal of a mute in undeniable ecstasy. Baldo reaches into the shadow and backs out grinning, his brow wrinkled as if in anguish, holding a baby turtle gently near his face with both hands. The little turtle flaps all four legs briefly, then stretches its little neck up to Baldo, practically touching him nose to nose.

Milo nods and grins. "So. You see?"

"Milo. You are right. No man is better than Baldo at many things. *Las chicas* among them. How much does it pay? He makes thirty, sometimes thirty-five pesos a shift now."

"That's too much."

"Too much for what?" Antonio waits while Milo ponders what. "Milo, I know what we can do. Baldo can watch the turtles while serving coconuts."

Milo shakes his head. "No. It is decreed. Twenty-four-hour security for the turtles. The other is decreed as well. No more Baldo by the pool or the guests."

"Twenty-four hours? How can he work with no sleep?"

Milo nods. "He will take time off to sleep. And to eat. And to take care of the rest. You will see that he is clean and groomed."

"Milo, has he yet to be unclean or failed to groom?"

"He will be paid... Two pesos per hour. No. Twenty pesos per day."

"You said two per hour."

"But he needs time off. Antonio, this is best. Besides, nobody really knows what the hotel guests are willing to leave tips for. Or how much. Eh? Do you not think they will love the man who loves the turtles? Do you not know how our guests most often express their love?"

Antonio knows what makes the world go round. He cannot refute Milo's logic, but he also knows that a bird in hand is often worth more than the murky whim of hotel guests. They tip to ensure continuing comfort. But to tip simply for the love of turtles? This is highly conjectural. He sighs audibly, factoring twenty pesos times six days times four weeks. Well, times seven days, really, if this is only a ninety-day promotion. Baldo will be here and so will be paid. And make it times four point three weeks, really, because Mrs. Mayfair's husband is in business and always insists, she says, on factoring four point three weeks to the month. Otherwise you take it in the shorts, she says he says, which is okay if the shorts is where you want to take it, but not okay if you're out to make some money.

Antonio further understands the importance of initial agreements. Now is the time to bump twenty pesos a day to twenty-five, or at least to twenty-three, but no sooner does he turn to speak than Milo's waddling rump is all that's left to see as it bounds for the lobby. Milo beat him to the punch with urgent distraction. Well, it's true; Baldo is the best, already counting, inspecting, observing, checking for life and viable turtle spirit; in a word, nurturing.

A new guest approaches. Petite in a classy one-piece with a gold chain and a suitably expensive watch and long, blonde hair, she lets her eyes drop to Antonio's abs. He watches and waits and lets the electricity ripple its magic arc to her lovely orbs. He fixes her gaze, then stops, subtly facilitating a lifting of the eyes with a gentle flex of a perfect pectoralis major. His shirt is still on, but she sees and blushes and asks in delightful confusion if today will be bingo.

"Ah, yes! Bingo!"

He bounds for the head of the pool, leaving the new blondie flushed in his wake. They love the rejection; she'll be along for more. Plugging in his little amplifier and testing for sound with a spicy salsa disco number that challenges all stillness, he gyrates shamelessly side to side, in and out. He smiles warmly as the Latin lover of your dreams, and soon poolside attention is all his. At least the attention of the women is his; this is a given. He holds the microphone provocatively and says, "Testing, *uno, dos, tres...* Hey! Wake up! No more *siesta*! Time for bingo! Wake up! Er! Er-Er! Er-Errrrrr! Wake up! Bingo! We play for twelve beers today. Not all at once, because it's too early to be drunk. Maybe later. Okay*, amigos y amigas. Doce cervezas hoy dia*! Wake up! No more *siesta*!"

He stacks his bingo cards behind his jar of dried beans. He preps his music and glances up to see that Milo is back and yakking at Baldo, who towers over the short, fat manager with a simmering glower. Each grasps the handle of Baldo's machete, causing Antonio to grab the mike again and hurriedly announce once more to get ready and hold the fort, "Er! Er-Er! Er-Errrrr! Wake up! Bingo! Come up for your cards and your beans!" And he bounds back around the pool to see what's up.

"You don't need a machete to guard the turtles," Milo insists.

Baldo grumbles and reddens and easily tightens his grasp beyond the limited strength of Milo.

"Why not, Milo? Let him have the machete. Who ever heard of a security guard with no weapon? What? You want to give him a carbine? That would not look very nice."

Milo scowls. "He needs no weapon! It scares the guests."

"No, they think this is colorful. They think we all carry these things around, just like our fathers did. Just as they think the coconuts are colorful." Now Milo reddens at the mention of his unskilled father and lets go of the machete with a scowl. Turning squarely to face Antonio and stepping forward, he huffs and puffs but doesn't say that enough time has been wasted already on this half-wit brother who has passed for too long as an "assistant" and makes far more money than he should. But such is understood; Antonio reads the prevailing sentiment as though it was written and says, "Milo. Make it twenty-five."

"What? Make what twenty-five?"

"Twenty-five pesos a day. Here. Here is the machete." Antonio takes the machete from Baldo easily, as only he can do.

Milo turns and walks, shaking his head. "I better not hear," he says but doesn't say what he better not hear.

Antonio hands the machete back to Baldo, who sets it down on the top ledge of the wall because he needs two hands to properly care for the small turtles. Milo has left a fish fillet, which Baldo now tears to small bits. Antonio watches briefly and taps Baldo on the arm. He tells Baldo to wash his hands, miming the act of washing with emphasis on rinsing all the soap and never allowing suntan lotion into the turtle water. Baldo stares with a grimace and a nod, first imagining the awful potential of poisoning by suntan lotion, then comprehending the remedy. "Where will we be with buckets of dead babies?" Antonio asks with brutal practicality. The idea is drawn in pain across Baldo's face as he's off to clean his hands.

Antonio bounds back, scans the pool, and asks the microphone, "Is everybody ready?"

"*Síííí,*" they reply.

"Okay." He spins the basket with his biggest, warmest smile, which is not a grin, and pulls out a ball. "B twenty-three. *Bay vente tres.*" The game is on. "For two beers we play this game. *Dos cervezas.* Up, down, diagonal. Any which way, one line. Okay. G-seventeen. *Hey, diez y siete.*"

III

A Mostly Uneventful Evening

Bingo passes uneventfully, except for the third game requiring two diagonals plus both a vertical and a horizontal for four *cervezas*. Four guests playing poolside all call at once, "Bingo!" and demand the full payout. But four beers each times four winners makes sixteen.

¡Diez y seis cervezas!

What do they think, that I have an endless supply of beers to hand out like candy? Let them demand. The game paid four. Period. No more discussion.

¡Terminado! ¡Hola, cabron! ¡The nerve of some people!

As if that isn't enough, the new blondie lying on the first chaise lounge facing the head of the pool plays with her bingo card between her legs, which are spread in such a way that no man seeing her can think of his mother. It is no accident that she spreads them, the legs, with her most provocative display for the most alluring eyes before her. They sparkle in Antonio's head, hinting playful thoughts. She plays along, demonstrating her flexibility by bending studiously forward for a most titillating buffet, which is hot, not cold.

Smorgasbord is cold, even in Mexico at your finer hotels, and a man rising with the tide and times knows the differences in such things, down to nuance and flourish. She seems alone, available, wealthy, interested in the maestro, and between one and two decades younger than Mrs. Mayfair.

Not one to take defeat lying down, Mrs. Mayfair holds the attention of four men convening here to discuss annuities and to fish. Their foam cooler full of beer and ice represents the height of rudeness to those whose ancestors made the ultimate sacrifice so that their modern descendants could earn a decent wage by shagging beers for tips by the pool. Some people will never learn, no matter how much affluence and influence they wield. These four businessmen from *El Norte* look like brothers, with the same ruddy hue and beer bellies that sag like *boda* bags filled for a long journey. Antonio thinks another pair of hands must hold such bellies up so the first pair can wipe them free of the sweat and smegma assuredly growing in the dark crevasses beneath them. These modern moguls look eleven months pregnant as they strain against the *gordo* guts hanging over their droopy shorts. They wear gold chains and are very burned on their chests and shoulders. They laugh and drink until the beer trickles down their necks and onto their chests and tickles them into great, good cheer. They taunt each other over who will win tomorrow, who will lose, and why. Matching boisterous wagers, they yell that one city or another will defeat the rest.

Ain't no way in hell 'ey won't.

They savor prospects for Sunday and six hours on the beds in their rooms watching American football.

Interspersed in their joviality are gamy glances at Mrs. Mayfair and lewd suggestions, but none stare longer than mortal men can look at the sun for fear of melting their eyes. They look away with playful smirks for each other when she looks majestically off.

Antonio smiles, wondering what each would pay for what he is paid for. Ah, Mrs. Mayfair. She can work a poolside as deftly as he, and Antonio hopes she feels gratitude for what he has shown her. He hopes as well that one of these fat red men will strike a chord, because the maestro is frankly too tired to squeeze her in tonight. Well, maybe not too tired but certainly not predisposed. He would honestly rather introduce the new blondie to his twilight cocktail program, and he doesn't want to keep Lyria waiting too long. And Mrs. Mayfair gets so emotional. Well, he shall see what he can do.

Things are mostly uneventful beyond the pool as well, except for three tourists in the chaise lounges down on the beach, who call shamelessly for *joven* to bring some cool, refreshing drinks, right now if you please. Baldo is playing with pieces of fish fillet, then changing the water in each tub after dinner because it's fouled by the mess the baby turtles make, as babies will. He asks Antonio to please keep an eye on *las chicas* while he requisitions another tub, because anyone can see that a spare tub for changing will greatly facilitate the task at hand. Baldo nods fore and aft. He spreads his arms and chops his choppers, and the message is conveyed. And that would be that, except for the three helpless *gringas* down on the beach who need cool refreshment and *pronto*.

But what? You want what? You want the maestro to fetch you a drink? This is not in my contract and seems unnatural, Antonio thinks, scratching his *huevos*. Then he smiles; after all, it is nothing but show biz, where a headliner sometimes helps with the props. He moves casually into service, shagging ice cubes and garnish with his bare hands at no extra charge. Then he serves the three coconuts. He waits for the tip but there is none, perhaps in deference to what is obvious to all involved, which is simply that a maestro does not serve coconuts on the beach.

Never mind, happy hour is here.

Response to the floating squares is marginal and worse; it's embarrassing when two little boys want to try it, which isn't the same thing at all when you think about it, because they only weigh fifty pounds and can walk easily to the end.

So? What does that mean? *Nada* is what. What can Antonio do, outshine mere boys? Give them a beer? I don't think so. Pool volleyball generates an equally weak response, but some weeks are like that, where the crowd is devoid of life. Let them sleep.

Antonio cranks the Latin love ballads to deepen their slumbers, and in another little while he whispers into the microphone, "Wake up. Beach volleyball. No more *siesta*. Er! Er-Er! Er-Errrrrr!" Let them sleep. Meanwhile, Antonio is well served by shagging coconut drinks if he is covering for his errant brother. Baldo will handle both jobs better tomorrow once the babies are nestled in and a routine is set. As for Baldo serving drinks, he has not yet been instructed otherwise. Tomorrow he will resume. Just wait and see.

Antonio is amazed at the traffic in coconuts, which is more than usual. He calls on Baldo to prep another six. Antonio doesn't mind covering now, because the tips are adding up, and though Baldo looks like a child at play in the sand, tomorrow will be like yesterday with yet another revenue source. The coconuts will continue adding pesos to the tally, and along with them the little turtles may yield the greatest tips of all, which are those paid in tribute, which is certainly nobler than convenience and should not be overlooked as a viable revenue center.

Baldo has moved the plastic tubs off the wall by the beach steps because the setting sun comes under the parasol and hits the babies directly. He restores them to the shade by setting the tubs inside the wall. At sunset they will go back on the wall, and tomorrow morning they will go outside the wall. A rhythm in nature emerges, and Baldo moves more gracefully with each passing hour as if ordained and risen, guardian of the turtles.

As the sun sets, the new blondie orders a double strawberry margarita, tips thirty pesos for personal delivery from Antonio and hands him the lotion for her shoulders. She removes one strap, carelessly revealing a breast that is much smaller than either of Mrs. Mayfair's but is nonetheless plump and pert and inviting to the touch. Mrs. Mayfair is of course watching, but she can't very well follow suit without a Sawzall to cut through the fiberglass.

"You know," Blondie says. "You're very good looking."

"Yes, thank you." Antonio says. "I wear contact lenses. I don't take them out for swimming. Do you find that amazing? I can show you my trick in one hour. Here. You don't need this. The sun is down now. Excuse me." He hurries off to nowhere because he's too tired for such complexity, even with such a blushing young blondie. But don't worry; he'll know what to tell her before the hour is up. And if he doesn't know, so what? She'll be here a week.

To his unfathomable gratitude Mrs. Mayfair is accepting the lead of a fat red man. She casts a furtive eye back for revenge or regret; Antonio can't tell which. He only hopes the fat, red man will dress well and will neither sweat nor smell like a pig, that he will treat her gently or roughly as her taste predicates. Who knows? Maybe he, the fat red one, will even give her a hundred pesos for her trouble.

Ha. That's a good one, and he, Antonio, laughs at his own joke, turning to yet greater relief. Just there under the poi sienna, leaning languorously against the trunk, Lyria waits and watches. She has seen his indifference and strength in the face of shameful temptation. This bodes very well as proof of his long-standing love, for Mrs. Mayfair obviously represents no threat but in fact serves the family objective with wonderful practicality, providing money and relieving pressure. The young blondie, however, could mean trouble on the home front.

Antonio warms to the surge of victory in circumstances that could have gone either way as he warms to the sight of Lyria. Pointedly curved, smooth, and sharp in every detail as a brand new Chevrolet, she waits only for the one who will turn the key and drive her home. Like an elixir, she fills him with energy and light, because he is the one.

"Would you like to meet at eight?" she asks.

"Yes, I said I would meet you at eight." Antonio doesn't slow down but sends his affection in passing, employing a technique tried and true with the poolside women, because all women are the same in certain areas. She reminds him as he passes that they had yet to set a time, and for all she knows, *algo sucedió*; that is, something came up, or maybe it will come up between now and this evening.

Slowing only to train his grievous hurt on her, he assures her that nothing came up nor will it. "*Ocho. Perfecto.*"

She watches, granting him the smile he needs, knowing he's showing off. She wishes him free of his constraint and considers an act of daring. If she doesn't take the initiative, who will? She eases out and down the road to prepare for a night out.

In thirty more minutes, it's over. Day is done for the Garza brothers, who have assured poolside happiness since coffee time this morning. Happy hour turns to dusk and then twilight as the infantry digs in for one more. A few troops turn to dinner, a few to more deliberate intake, and a few take one for the road on their way to somewhere else.

Antonio ducks behind some shrubs to pull a handful of tips from one pocket and put them in the other. He doesn't need a count to know he topped a hundred twenty. At least! Maybe more. He only needs to balance the weight. Now he looks like his balls are swollen, but who cares? It's getting dark. Time to go. And maybe they are!

He fetches Baldo, but Baldo looks up like a man entrenched, a man for whom departure is as likely as that of a lioness leaving her cubs. Palms up, he shakes his head vigorously and very nearly whispers, "*¡Las chicas!*"

Antonio has neither scolded Baldo nor disciplined him for a long time, not since Baldo was two heads shorter. Antonio tells him that he must come, that these babies are already hatched so nobody needs to sit on them anymore, that twenty-four-hour security is a figure of speech, and nobody expects anybody to guard round the clock. He must come home and clean himself and eat, and besides, he is scheduled to take Lyria and him to dinner. And dancing!

Baldo shows his palms again and with his machete points at the crimson sky over the breaking waves, where *las tijerillas* make their way with suspect stealth. These scissortail cormorants love the nestlings of others, and once their feeding begins, it's only a matter of minutes before *las gabiotas* arrive, seagulls screeching and diving on the hapless plastic tubs.

Antonio explains that no man can sit ninety days without coming home to bathe, sleep, eat, and take care of the rest. Baldo shakes his head and stamps his foot. He mimes that Antonio will bring him things to eat and Lyria as well. As for sleeping, he will bring his hammock and pillow and a light cover to this place. He'll have all he needs, and so will *las tortugas chicas*, because it is time for Mexico to change its ways.

This last is a loose translation, Antonio knows. But he gets the gist and feels the tenor of his little brother's insistence. Size is power, he thinks, and though he doesn't doubt Baldo's need for discipline, he, Antonio, will not be the disciplinarian.

With neither threat nor ultimatum, Antonio urges Baldo to come along ten minutes, only ten, just up the beach, from where they can watch the turtles and hurry back if necessary. Baldo ignores him then shakes his head. "Baldo!" Antonio yells as if at a bad dog. He further explains that they will keep watch from up the beach. They must, in order to see and know if in fact Baldo should stay, or if he can come home for just a while.

Baldo declines.

Antonio insists.

Baldo won't move.

Antonio turns away and turns back. "All right. Nine minutes. You must grant me this, Baldo. As you are my ward for all I've given you. Come with me."

Baldo rises, looks into each tub and out at the *tijerillas* who now dive beyond the surf and pluck little fish easily as from a bucket. He looks at Antonio and holds up nine fingers. They walk in silence. Antonio carries his T-shirt on his shoulder now because it stinks. He may stop in the gift shop on the way out for his new toucan shirt, but maybe he'll give Mrs. Mayfair another day or two. A hundred *pesos* are nothing to sneeze at. Baldo carries his machete loosely, as is his custom, in case he needs to run back in a hurry for the slaughter. He looks back at the plastic tubs every few steps. He scans the birds working the surf.

Silence is normal for Baldo but rare for Antonio, who tells himself it's not so bad that his brother is obsessed with one thing if not another. What we have here is opportunity. What will happen if the hotel guests catch on to the man who guards the babies night and day? Appreciation will happen, which can lead to tips of significant magnitude with proper management.

Antonio knows of the tips given on cruise ships at the end of the week in lump sums and ponders such a program for turtle appreciation. It is important to keep an eye open for dynamic application, especially with a brother like Baldo. A brother like Baldo could hamper those of the unseeing eyes. But Antonio has turned his unusual brother into an asset, not a liability.

Has not Baldo capitalized on his disadvantage so far? Does he not carry his weight? Will he not evolve with proper guidance toward a tangible contribution, for which society will express its gratitude in tips?

Antonio can easily ask these questions and know their answers by simply opening his eyes and seeing, which is exactly what he's doing.

IV

Algo Sucedió
(¡Something Came Up!)

Life can change when you least expect it. Antonio has always known this, but then knowing that life makes sudden turns does not make the road ahead less surprising. Antonio will remember these moments in the days and years to come, just as a man who puts his weight on a first slick step and slides irretrievably down the stairs will remember his failure to anticipate total loss of traction. He will as well remember that first giddy freefall, in which the world of order suddenly loses its binding.

Antonio will remember the man fishing, walking into the surf with complete disregard for getting his clothing wet. He will remember the trousers with their houndstooth check that tell you this man works in the kitchen of an expensive hotel or else he did at one time before he was fired, or else he stole the pants. Or maybe he bought them or they were handed down. Never mind, the trousers disappear as the man wades to waist deep, wetting his red-and-yellow plaid shirt as well and hurling his baited hand line over the breakers before they break over his head. The water recedes to expose the fisherman still standing like a rock. The fisherman shakes the water from his head and pays the line out rapidly so the undertow can carry his bait deep to where the big fish swim. He backs up to the dry sand and keeps things taut so he can feel the bump and run. The brothers watch. The fisherman glances back. Antonio returns the man's look with a wave and a greeting. "*Buenos noches, Señor.*"

The man nods and the Garza brothers walk on—except that Antonio is walking alone. He looks back to see that Baldo has stopped and now stoops slowly as if struck by the kind of internal affliction felling men far older who are usually infirm. Baldo picks up a fish that flops in his hand. Antonio walks back and says, "He's alive, Baldo. You can carry him to the surf and release him."

Baldo is gasping again, more gently now than a few hours ago when joy overflowed with baby turtles. Now he is stricken with grief, for the fish in his hands is a trumpet fish, first cousin to the sea horse but much bigger. This one is two feet long and thin by nature, maybe three inches in diameter. Its head isn't exactly shaped like that of a horse, but it and its cousin both have elongated jaws prominently rounded, big oval eyes, and a snout also like a horse's but again, much thinner. But this one is maimed, its jaw broken halfway back from the nose to the eyes. Baldo lays it on the wet sand and kneels before it. He places his palms over it like a shaman who knows some magic, but Baldo only sobs through labored breathing before raising his machete and removing the balance of the head with a casual but decisive stroke. His own head hangs limp as if broken at the neck, as if the scope of his loss is complete.

Baldo looks up to his brother with anguished eyes, imploring him to right this wrong situation.

Antonio shrugs and softly explains. "Baldo. There is nothing we can do here. The fish is dead. You have ended his misery, and now he is dead. We can do no more." Baldo looks down at the fish again. His mouth opens and closes as the fish's recently did, but Baldo is not gasping for air; he is, rather, mouthing the words, *mi amigo*. This fish is known. This fish is a friend of his; he would recognize this fish anywhere. This is the fish he saw only a few days ago, hovering weightlessly over the reef. His small pectoral, dorsal, and caudal fins flapped fast as the wings of a hummingbird and his big eyes rotated to stay full of Baldo, who blew bubbles overhead.

Look at this fish and say it isn't so, that this is not the friend who looked up with the same greeting and recognition these last two years since Antonio pulled enough pesos from the coffee can for a mask and a snorkel. This is Trumpet fish, who swims backwards when he wants to and hovers nearby and changes color at the sight of a friend.

Baldo weeps, holding his machete gently to his chest, coddling the cold, stained steel. He weeps pitifully, as if for a death in the family, though the deaths in the family never caused so much weeping.

The fisherman pulls in another trumpet, unhooks it roughly, and holds it like a stick for breaking. "Wait, my friend," Antonio calls. The fisherman waits but will not look back at Antonio. Rather, he remains poised for the kill, anticipating the plea.

"It is a life, my friend. A life," Antonio says. Now the fisherman looks back, but he doesn't speak. He waits to see if that is all Antonio has to offer. Antonio presses his point, which isn't his point at all but that of his late father, who speaks through him as if bearing witness and giving voice to the *alma*, the inner spirit a father might pass to his sons. "It is a life like yours, or mine, or maybe better."

"No, my friend," the fisherman says. "It is not. It is dead." He breaks this second trumpet fish as well along its jaw and tosses the still flopping fish up higher on the sand, where it can perhaps reflect on the error of its bait-stealing ways while it waits to die.

Antonio says, "Come. Come, Baldo." He moves quickly from this cruel scene as the man untangles his line and puts another piece of fish on his hook. But Baldo won't budge, and the fisherman too is in apparent need for further resolution.

"Three hundred *pesos*," the fisherman grumbles. "Three hundred *pesos* is what the hotel for *gringos* is willing to spend on one pelican with a broken wing. Three hundred pesos to mend a bird. A bird, so that it can try again to steal my bait. As God is my witness, *Señor*, I will break any fish or bird that takes the food from the mouths of my children. Only a man with children to feed can understand this. You cannot. You cannot, unless you have children to feed like I do, and a wife who is already big again with..." He hurls his line again over the incoming waves. "Ah..."

"Come, Baldo. Come." But Baldo will not come. "Look, Baldo. He is using fish for bait, just as you feed fish to your turtles. Well, maybe he uses blue fish as you do and not a friend from the reef, but still, it is..."

"A friend from the reef?" The fisherman gingerly feels his line and may have interest on the other end. "What is a friend from the reef?" He relaxes with this novel concept and is prepared to discourse further with these boys who cannot yet know the world as it must be known.

These are nearly the fisherman's last words as he backs out of the water, just before he turns to the startling sound of Antonio's shrill outburst, "*¡No-o-o-o! Baldo! ¡Para nos Madre¡*" Antonio knows that his plea is of no use. Something rises from a deep recess within the heart of his little brother. With a head wag slow as a verdict, Baldo will not be denied. His shoulders slump as his eyes squint into focus, and he draws from below the waist with both hands on the machete. He swings from the earth to the firmament, meeting the neck and clearing the crown with a thump and a squish on a casual, decisive stroke, a stroke the trumpet fish of *Oaxtapec* would call a happy stroke.

The fisherman's last complaint is "*¡Jesu Cristo!*" before his face is cleaved, and he learns the dance of the fouled trumpet fish—if not with the same flop, then at least with similar surge and twitch. Baldo stands before the headless man, grasping his machete more firmly than is his custom, but that's only because of this rare occasion calling for two hands, and because he is risen as well to a state of extreme agitation. The man faces him, as it were, until following the suggestion of Baldo's gentle shove. He falls back in the lapping waves.

The half head washes up and back and up and back. A single *gabiota* senses tidbits and lands nearby to get a feel for temperaments in case nobody will mind him taking a piece of cheek or sampling an eye.

Antonio chases him away, not for decency but to prevent a frenzy of seagulls. That would surely give them away.

Baldo kneels by the second dying trumpet and ends its misery with dispatch. Stunned in their daze, the younger brother whimpers and weeps while the elder gazes at the surreal yet inevitable scene. Thoughts swarm: *How could this be? At least it has been.* Baldo kneels in supplication to the departed soul, the one with fins and scales, until he looks up and runs back as the *tijerillas* make their move on the baby turtles.

Then Antonio stands alone, wondering what next to do, knowing mistakes must be few.

Jesu Cristo is right; what has happened here? Antonio asks this of himself, knowing full well what has happened. He knows from the depths of his past and everything he has seen and heard that big events come along in every life, and then you choose to take action, or you let nature take its course. Ah, but there, my father, he thinks, is the difference between a life of circumstance and a life of sentient control. *Jesu Cristo*, the fisherman said, yet already Antonio wonders if the fisherman said these words.

How did *Jesu* let it come to this? Was this fisherman a bad man? Well, he was bad tonight, not to mention more foolish than Baldo could ever be. Who could not look at a six-foot boy skinny as a chili pepper carrying a machete and carrying on over a dead fish and not look again?

Crying and grieving, his eyes dark as the demon's who stole his voice, does not Baldo tell you point blank who he is? Baldo is insane, a condition known only by two men in the world, one of whom sleeps in the dirt. Make that three men, another of whom sleeps with the fishes and will dream the liquid dream tonight and all nights forever more. "Thou shalt not kill," Antonio tells the half head as it flops in the wave wash, reminding the fisherman of rule *numero uno*. True, Baldo killed as well, but Baldo is his brother and more. Baldo is a man who is not quite a man but rather a soft and foolish boy and perhaps an avenging angel besides and, maybe, the dominant factor in tonight's discord.

Antonio is proud of his analytical power in the face of certain danger and drags himself through these thoughts by sheer will. He likewise drags the body up by the heels to where the waves won't catch it. He tucks the half head under a floppy arm and wraps the fingers around the brow.

He scans north and south for walkers.

With a frightful commotion to the north, Baldo makes it a night of carnage, saving his baby turtles. But Antonio sees no human traffic. So he rinses his hands, checks himself for unsightly stains, and strolls casually north like a man out for a twilight constitutional.

He can use the towrope from the big banana but should not use the towboat because the boat is moored beyond the break and would require swimming with the headless body in tow. Unless of course he had a rope long enough to secure the ankles and reach beyond the breakers. He could swim out to the boat with the other end. But he has no such rope, and besides, it would be too heavy to pull through the breakers. Well, he could, but still. What would he do with the half head? He could get a pillowcase from Lyria, but that would take too much time. Make no mistake; he could do any and all of these things if he had to, but he knows the one thing he must do above all, which is the best possible thing to do in this given situation.

He will use a jet ski. He can lash the ankles and leave the body in the shallows, then maneuver the Jet Ski from the shallows through the break with Baldo's help. Then, very slowly, to keep the noise down, he will drag the body halfway to the *Rock of Oaxtapec*, maybe three miles out, give or take, where the bottom sinks to five hundred meters. The half-head will fit in his T-shirt as if swallowed by the panther itself.

He moves deftly and quickly with no time for hesitation, knowing as he measures progress that he must quell whatever agitation remains in his unbalanced brother. What he knows amounts to everything necessary to solve this grizzly dilemma, including the laws of buoyancy resulting from gaseous decomposition. A corpse will pop to the surface in no time, if it's not properly weighted. Antonio breathes deeply and slowly to better facilitate the separation between what he knows and what he feels. Time will come soon enough for reflection and assessment. He must sink the fisherman with certainty.

Scanning the items of every day he thinks of poundage but discounts them one by one. The chaise lounges are too big and bulky and besides, they're plastic. The anchor from the boat would be perfect but its absence would establish a weak link of its own. And what about the half-head? He could tether the shirt to the body, but then the shirt as well would give him away if the head popped to the top, which he doubts it will. But either the head or the body could rise with the gasses that build in a few days, so the T-shirt is also untenable. He sets these and other potentials aside for a stroll farther north, to see what Baldo is up to.

At least the scene is quiet if not tidy. A dead cormorant with a broken neck lies in the sand. Another one, badly injured, whimpers nearby. Also whimpering and strewn with feathers and blood, Baldo is beside himself with grief. With his head bowed in mourning he laments the lifeless infant in his hands, willing its return but failing. Antonio sits beside him and leans close for emphasis. He grasps Baldo's arm with gentle but great pressure for further emphasis, and he tells Baldo that the baby turtles will be safe for now, now that the marauders have been successfully chased away.

Baldo holds up the five fingers of one hand. Five babies are lost, all taken except for this one left behind.

Antonio reiterates his joy over Baldo's successful defense of the remaining hundred and eighteen babies. He says he is proud and confident that these babies will reach maturity with very little additional mortality. He pulls Baldo's arm and whispers with urgency that they must turn their attention elsewhere, however, or their lives will be lost, spent forever in prison cells.

Baldo is inconsolable; he doesn't care about the rest of his life but, rather, moons over the dead baby in his hands, until Antonio reminds him that going to prison tomorrow, or maybe later tonight, will leave these babies unguarded, leave them to certain death. Baldo rises and steps forward, responsive at last to the reality at hand. He strolls south. Good. Antonio will gather the towrope and—"Wait, Baldo. Help me. We need the jet ski."

Okay, Baldo is waiting, but what can be used to hold the body down, and where can the head reside?

Antonio scans north and south again. All is calm. Only the night drinkers stir like another set of gentle waves at the pool bar where they commiserate on the meaning of life. Always nearing the crux, they agree further and have another round. "Baldo, wait! Wait for me! I will be right back! You wait!"

Okay, nothing for it but to duck inside for a pillowcase. Ah, ha! And a mop bucket, to clean up this mess. A mop bucket? For what, to mop up the sand? Hey, the turtle nursery is bloody with feathers. The guests don't want to see this or know this. They want these babies unharmed. We will make it so, maestro Antonio and Baldo, my assistant.

This story will fly, Antonio thinks, running across the vacant deck on his way in to the laundry room, which is happily open and empty. He shags a pillowcase and then another, just in case, and around the corner, as if luck is favoring his receptive mind, is a mop bucket. Bending his knees, not his back, and looking up, he stoops to lift, grunting for the sixty pounds of it, which shouldn't be enough to draw a grunt but the bucket is so cumbersome, so far from his body.

Finding a bucket this easily is very good, until he jumps, startled by Inez of the night shift in the laundry room, who stares in disbelief that Antonio doesn't even know how to wheel a mop bucket. "It has wheels," she says, pointing them out. "It rolls. You can roll it. You don't need to carry it."

"Ah!" Antonio says. "I am so foolish. Ha ha." He rolls it out to the foyer, heat flashing from within and without under the glare of Inez, who must wonder. He stands straight and tells her, "I must clean the... by the pool, you know. We have a mess." Inez lightly nods, so Antonio nods too, confirming the consensus between them. Then he shrugs and stoops to push the bucket on his way.

"How can you clean with no mop?" Inez calls. Antonio laughs and shakes his head. He cannot, of course. She hands him the mop while he continues wagging and laughing, and he pushes the bucket much easier now with the mop to steer it by.

He must lift the bucket again for the steps down from the lobby and the steps up to the pool, but that's okay. Even a cumbersome sixty pounds is nothing next to a hundred fifty each of sit-ups, crunches, and push-ups. He wonders if his grand total should not be an even five hundred, but then he would have a hundred sixty-six for sit-ups and push-ups and a hundred sixty-seven for crunches. Wait, two times six is twelve plus seven is nineteen; it should be a hundred sixty-seven each for sit-ups and push-ups, and a hundred sixty-six for crunches. But who can remember so many odd counts?

And why must I consider push-ups and crunches at a time like this, when my faculties must remain clear and focused on the job at hand?

Antonio fills the bucket slightly in the pool for the benefit of anyone watching. Then he pushes it to the wall by the steps to the beach and mops a bit here and there. In a minute he casually scans east for random *romanticos* idling under the stars at the far end of the pool, innocent bystanders who may be called upon to say what they saw. But luck is holding. The pool deck is free of guests. So he quietly sets the mop down, empties the bucket into the sand, and carries it southward.

Darkness prevails now but thins under the half-moon rising, swollen yellow and beaming across the beach. Choreographing as he trudges over the sand, Antonio cheers himself onward with proper attitude in this time of strenuous effort. He will complete this task only with correct mentality, even as the mop bucket goes to a hundred pounds and a hundred twenty, and he surges on sheer will, confident his faith in mindset is well placed.

He stops mere paces from his goal and sets the bucket down. Breathing hard, he fixes his hearing on the madness ahead, then squints against the blinding truth of what he sees. He buckles under a breaking wave, disbelieving, and stands awash in the faint rasp of Baldo's gurgling gibberish and coconut hacking. Another sound nearby is the frenzy of *las tijerillas*. They circle and swoop in a rare evening feed.

Antonio will remember these soft hues that shade this eternal impression of his brother. Neither rage nor grief but rather a misty, serene calmness surrounds this small industry. Mincemeat remains of the fisherman, and though *las tijerillas* and *las gabiotas* and all their cousins could finish the feast laid out for them under the stars, the waves can catch the rest and wash it away. Like a fresco preserved for the years remaining to Antonio Garza, the scene burns its imprint of Baldo's simple solution to life's relentless challenge.

Baldo is not like other people. Baldo feels something unique to himself and the wild animals, something unfelt by other people. Moreover, Baldo feels nothing, like here on the beach, mincing a man to bits with all the emotion of taking out the trash. This too is unlike other people who would call Baldo dangerous. But isn't efficiency among predators a blessed part of nature? Baldo is efficient and practical, besides deliberate, reflecting his superior place among survivors.

It's important to ascertain the positive and establish credit where it's due, lest people think him daft. He's not. Just look at his logic in resolving this mess, first removing the sandals, then sliding the trousers off, and finally removing the shirt, button by button, then folding this clothing neatly for future use among the living. What's more, disrobing the fisherman facilitates the dicing, because a blade loses efficacy on fabric and in fact grows dull.

For now, Antonio leaves the mop bucket behind with the towrope partly inside and partly hanging out. He notices that the half head would fit neatly inside if wedged by the roller and lashed down. But such synchronous fit must be set aside for all the difference it makes now, which is *nada*, thanks to the insanity pumping from the heart and coursing through the veins of his flesh-and-blood brother.

Baldo could as easily be prepping coconuts for a shift, though his current pursuit seems less precise relative to placement of straws with the paper pushed up just so for proper presentation. No need here for lime slices and a pineapple wedge for eyes and a mouth. No more eyes, no more mouth, this fisher is down to *ceviche* in a ghastly marinade beyond lemon and salt. But the birds screech delight and stuff their gullets with bountiful repast in a way Antonio can only hope his late father cannot see. Baldo raises the blade and slashes, so the big, bony chunks will be rendered to bite-size bits, lest the poor birds struggle and choke.

The last thing a careful man wants is to leave a grizzly mess. Antonio fears the attention a flashlight might draw, but how else can he see that the big chunks are accounted for? So he shines it to see and reviews. He paces and ponders and finally deems the scene clueless.

Baldo washes his hands and blade in the surf, cleaning his fingernails, plucking bits and squishes from his eyebrows before heading back north to where he is most needed. Antonio watches him with growing disbelief, Baldo's so mechanical, so matter-of-fact, folding the trousers and shirt over the *huaraches* and strolling up the beach like a regular Joe.

All right, it is okay. It is good. Well, maybe not so good. But maybe it is somewhat good that he recovers so quickly from such a challenge.

Antonio submits to his own insistence, backing slowly from the scene. Smudges in the sand melt further with each set as the waves wash the beach and erase what has been. Nothing will remain by sunrise. Yet, backing up, he stumbles over embers in a shallow pit left by the fisherman. Beside it is a basket with three corn tortillas, an avocado, a tomato, two limes, a half-empty bottle of *mescal,* and one *cerveza*, perhaps to cleanse the palate. Plus a bent, rusty knife.

Antonio will scatter the hot coals to the sea and so too with the foodstuff, except for the beer, which he should drink for his nerves and besides, the fisherman's palate is ultimately cleansed.

But no, a whole avo and two limes drifting in would clearly indicate traces of what has been, and the basket washed up on the surf would point as well to foul play. No, best to leave this little scene intact. Did not the fisherman say he has children? Will they not seek their father? They must know where he fishes, and by leaving these things as they are, the solution presents itself. The fisherman is gone; like a fish taking the wrong bait, so too did he take the errant step into the surf, where an undertow took him deep, or maybe a shark, or maybe both. Yes, maybe the undertow took him deep and then the shark ate him, or the shark dragged him in and chewed him up and then the undertow took him way out. Who knows? But look: all his things are here just so, so he must have run into trouble in the surf, which is of course exactly what he did.

Antonio now sees the two maimed trumpet fish, no longer flopping or gasping. With a headshake he picks up the beer and opens it, and with a long pull that feels like morning dew on a desert floor, he drains it. He feels calmer still with the belch that follows. He scans north and south at the glistening beach, awash in the half-light of the half-moon. Misty phantoms swirl above the surf.

"It was a life, my friend. A life."

Drifting between hard efficiency and contemplation of a soul passing, however evil it might have been, he stoops to the mescal and wraps it carefully in his shirt. He uncorks it awkwardly with another section of shirt and tips it up to cleanse his own palate, hesitating on the notion of lip prints. Then he guzzles liberally and waits for the revolting liquor to do its job of changing a man's outlook.

Dropping it in the sand, he strolls slowly north a hundred yards with the beer bottle. He fills it with seawater, wipes it down, and, holding it with a grab of shirt, hurls it beyond the breakers. He watches the splash point but sees nothing resurface, so he returns to the dead fire for the bottle cap. Rubbing it as well, he carries it in a fold to knee-deep water and drops it.

Then he hurries back north, seven-thirty already, and he can't be late, not now. "I was having dinner, Your Honor, with my fiancée. We are engaged to be married."

V

Dinner at Eight

At least Baldo has the sense to shag the mop bucket back to his outpost and then use it, however senselessly, to mop the feathers and blood from the sea-wall steps. He could just as easily fill the bucket and pour it over the mess, but he mops, dragging the damp head through the sand and pebbles like a fool, but a wise fool who knows the value of an explanation, even if it makes no sense.

The dead bird is gone. Antonio sees this as Baldo sees him shuffling near in a rare display of fatigue and perhaps early senility, talking to himself. Baldo nods up to the surf, indicating burial at sea for the late bird. The wounded bird rests quietly in a makeshift nest with his feathers carefully straightened over the makeshift dressing that binds the distorted wing. Baldo has torn strips from his own T-shirt. Beside the bird is an oyster shell filled with water, in case of thirst, and a small piece of fish, in case of hunger. The turtle nursery is buffed and organized like a well-oiled machine. Antonio reels briefly on the logistics of matching stories, on the need for parallel details that will cohere precisely to cover the last thirty or sixty minutes. It would be one thing if he and Baldo could engage in rational dialogue to compose a narrative with no holes, to troubleshoot, modify, and polish the finished version as necessary. But this is quite another thing. At least the situation lends some value to a mentally disturbed brother who is mute. Perhaps what has transpired tonight can be buried in obfuscation, just as the corpse was buried at sea.

He sits beside Baldo and sighs. Baldo nods and parrots his sigh. Baldo smiles and shrugs, relieved, it seems, with justice dispensed. Or maybe relief derives from cleaning up the beach. Or maybe Baldo is happy because his babies are resting peaceably again. Antonio shakes his head, leans close, and says, "We sat here since happy hour. We did not walk on the beach. No, no. Forget I just said that. We walked on the beach. The other way. We saw nothing. Nothing." Baldo sits up straight, curls his lips back, sets his tongue behind his teeth, and mouths *Nada.*

Well, for all Antonio or anyone knows, Baldo is as mentally undisturbed as a man or boy could hope to be. He beheaded another man as casually as hacking a coconut; this is true, but this other man was engaged in multiple commission of the same crime.

¿Que? ¡Ay, cabrone! Imaginary voices from the upper level heckle and jeer. *You compare a man's life to that of a fish?*

Antonio's eyebrows rise like flotsam as he weaves through the breakers with a smooth response: *Yes, well, it was two fish, actually, Your Honor. And who knows how many fish before we got there?* He grimaces at this glib flirtation with the firing squad and follows a falling star with a wish: *How I wish I had another beer.* He muses over what is worse, one beer or no beer at all. And as if the evening were made for dreams come true, good dreams and bad dreams, Baldo reaches into the shadow at the base of the wall by the steps between the beach and the pool and pulls out a beer. He hands it over to Antonio, who cannot accept without first knowing where this beer came from and how it was purchased. Baldo smiles and shrugs and flops his arms in a silly reenactment of prepping his pants for washing, which begins, of course, with emptying the pockets. That is, the fisherman had enough for three beers with a peso left over.

"Where is the clothing?"

Easy, it's in a pillowcase just here, ready for delivery anywhere you might like.

Antonio nods and wonders. He drinks when Baldo urges him to drink. Baldo waits with another beer, because one is enough for him, and besides, he got the third one for Antonio. The third beer slows things down and smoothes them out, and Antonio eases into the easy sense a few beers can make.

I will be late for dinner because I was on the beach, Your Honor, having a few beers with my brother Baldo. Baldo is unusual, Your Honor, a boy of rare skill and potential who applies himself with diligence. We spend this time together to enhance his further development.

Antonio nods, sustaining himself, and stands, telling Baldo he will return later with something to eat. Baldo shrugs and rises as well, to step forward and lean over and look in on his *chicas*. He makes sure they are resting well and that none are having bad dreams after the evening's rude intrusion. Antonio takes the pillowcase full of the fisherman's clothing and steps up to the pool deck. He looks back to see Baldo adjusting the injured bird.

He stops in the lobby *tienda* for three more beers. No, make it two, which will make five altogether. No, make it three, in case Lyria wants one, or two; no, make it four. Four beers, please.

He knows that any man must be crazy to pay three times the price here in the lobby, but he feels crazy. He has the money. He is on the rise, and the beer is here. And this pounding chaos in his head could absorb all the beer in the cooler.

He is surprised and gratified when Juanita the clerk rings in a fifty percent discount and dourly informs him that he is an employee and therefore entitled. Antonio loves entitlement but is none too certain that employee classification fully recognizes, much less captures, his essence.

Think of it: an employee might need to restock a cooler, but he is responsible for the basic happiness of the hotel's most precious commodity, its guests. Two hundred people look this way every day for fun. You call that an *employee*?

Never mind. He pops a beer for the walk out front to the bus stop and laughs when his arrival at the curb is timed perfectly with the bus. He doesn't break his stride but steps right on board and smiles like a happy man. He welcomes the view of a full bus, because these people saw me Your Honor, heading home after a few beers.

Besides, it's good to stand up on the ride home on a night like this, because too much luck must average out sooner or later. Besides that, a beer is easier to drink while standing up.

Across the road and up and down the hill feels like a long way from a few hours ago, but it's not. Carrying the extra beer is a good thing too, because it distracts anyone's attention from the pillowcase. Still, he would like to burn the pillowcase if he can find a fire. Maybe he'll build one.

In the meantime, he tosses the bundle into a corner and plops onto his hammock, suddenly feeling age catching up and surging ahead. *Dios mio*, the mesh never felt so good. Ohhhh, he moans, helping the tension ooze from his muscles and bones. Mmmm, he shifts for another angle of release. Ahhhh, he reaches for one more beer, but it's just beyond his reach, but that's okay. Lyria will be here soon to hand it over and sit beside him carefully so as not to tip him from his hammock.

¡Caray! Can you believe the nerve? He will soon share his disbelief with her. Four beers each for four winners in a single game? Is their good fortune supposed to spell doom for my own? No, let them drink one and buy three more if it's three more they want to drink.

Or maybe she will swing her legs up and they will lie together. What can it hurt and who can it scare with clothing on in a hammock, least of all Lyria, who could lie back and spread her legs if she wanted to, but what can he do in a hammock, arch his back like a *pelicano* and dive for his dinner? A man can do nothing on a hammock, except perhaps for a gentle feel here and there, which can only enforce the bond between himself and the woman of his dreams.

True, his gluepot is full, but such is the way of true romance in the beginning, and besides, Mrs. Mayfair won't leave without a formal goodbye. Then he can coast with indifference to the blondie for two days, after which she too will be served.

Sexual desire is an old familiar for him but only now emerges in Lyria. And a girl needs time.

Proper timing underscores Mrs. Mayfair's contribution. She should be invited to the wedding, which perhaps should be soon. He ponders the night of nights, or perhaps a lazy afternoon. He will deny himself the pleasure of others before immersion with his beloved. Not that it matters with such a renewable head of steam. Two hours should be adequate. Besides, Mrs. M will doubtless have a special wedding gift for the groom.

Feeling his *pinga* rise to the kindness and generosity of his friend from the north, he deflates directly in deference to a day that began a long time ago. Er er-er er-errrr, he thinks, drifting, drifting. *Jesu Cristo*, what a mess.

He half mumbles, half snores, falling quickly and soundly asleep. Time enough, he dreams, for a short, revitalizing nap. Then he will rise and clean himself, and they will go for dinner and stay out late and maybe dance. Maybe he will touch her breasts and breathe fast as he tells her of his intentions. Maybe she will want to touch his *pinga*, which could lead to trouble but may help her overcome her fear of such a ruthless beast who can be a most agreeable fellow, once you get to know him. Er! Er-er! Er-errrr!

But maybe this is not a good plan, he is still such a young man, and no woman, not even Lyria, would allow customer relations with Mrs. Mayfair if he and Lyria were married. As the saying goes, *Antes que te cases, mira lo que haces*; before you marry, look what you do.

You multiply a hundred fifty pesos times four for an average week but sometimes six, depending on her need to be needed, and once it was eight. Already you're talking terrific loss, and then you multiply that by two, because she now talks of one week not being enough, and then multiply by two again because she comes twice a year now.

"What, are you *loco*?" he asks, suddenly waking to her vigorous insistence. One scent of her tells him he has let a rare opportunity pass by, for she smells of sweet gardenia, and he sweats like a fat man from too much beer. She shakes her head and appears to be disgusted, as if this is not the evening she had in mind. Moaning again like a much older man, he swings his legs over. He breathes laboriously, hurrying himself into coherence and then calming himself. He offers her a beer. She declines, standing pertly back as if to see what he has to say for himself.

He smiles and says, "Well, then. I'll have one for both of us." Rubbing his face and head as if to clear the fog, he reaches another beer, drinks half of it and says, "Please, sit down."

"No, thank you."

"Lyria, please. We have trouble tonight. Very much trouble." She waits, and so he tells her of Baldo's promotion to *El Capitán de las Tortugas*, which makes her laugh, but more with amusement for Baldo's antics than with tolerance for Antonio's shenanigans. He moves directly to Baldo's obsessive concern for the baby turtles and his, Antonio's, attempt to bring Baldo home. From there they went for a walk on the beach and, as luck would have it, encountered the fisherman who lopped off the trumpets of Baldo's friends, the trumpet fish. Or at least he, Baldo, thought they were his friends, and they likely were. At least they could have been. But anyway, Baldo cut the man's head off.

She waits for more. He shrugs, *terminado*.

"He cut the man's head off?" She thinks Antonio is onstage again, exaggerating as if Lyria, who has known both him and his *schtick* ever since when, is supposed to laugh on cue like a good audience. But he's late and dirty and smells like a butcher, which could be the lingering scent of the aging *puta* for all she knows.

Lyria simmers with disappointment verging on rage with a dash of disgust. Tonight was not meant to be a casual rendezvous but a Saturday night of anything goes with a possible inching toward who-knows-what and a certain probability of you-know-what. "So what? You think this is funny?"

But Antonio is not reaching for humor. He reaches low instead with both hands and slowly rises to neck level with his best air machete. "*Sí*. He cut the fisherman's head off." Antonio drags a finger across his neck, then nods to the corner. "There. His clothing is in the pillowcase. The fisherman's clothing."

"But what of the man? Where is he? And why is he without his clothing?"

Antonio shakes his head. "Please, don't ask. The poor fisherman is without much more than his clothing. He is without his head, and worse yet, without his life. Satisfy yourself to know that he was put to good use." He stops shaking his own head and goes to a nod. "Recycled."

She turns and walks to the doorway for fresh air and fresh perspective. She moves seductively as a beautiful woman in a dress and high heels, though these are not high heels but only sandals, because she has no high heels. Where would she wear such shoes? Cleaning rooms? Having dinner with Rosa? No, she needs no high heels, but even with sandals a man can imagine how gracefully her dress would fall past the curvature of her lower spine and over the luscious ripeness of her hindquarters if only she were propped just so. Just look at how much grace flows forth this very moment. And for what? For a crazy story from a man who remains blind to everything?

Antonio, however, isn't blind to some things. He sees the grace. He wants to step up, hike her dress, and feel her high thighs but determines quickly that discretion here will pay off in a few short hours. She will be smooth as rayon. Tonight, his gluepot will bind the woman of his future. High thighs will be his. He will kiss the space between them. Then we'll see who calls him disgusting, when she trills like Toucan over fresh berries. Too much waiting is no good. Abstinence beyond a point feels *mas larga que la cuaresma*, longer than lent.

She comes back and sits beside him. "This is terrible," she says.

He shrugs. "It could be much worse. Everything is taken care of."

"How can you say such a thing; everything is taken care of? The man's clothing is there in a pillowcase."

He shrugs. "I will burn them in the morning."

She can't believe his casual response to a heinous crime. "And where is Baldo?"

"Where else? Baldo is exactly where he wants to be, where he should be, babysitting the babies." He smiles at his own grace, offering the soft opening to a few hours here together, alone at last on a Saturday night with the whole world waiting between now and sunrise.

She stands again, requiring him to check his balance. "We must take him something to eat. He must be starving. He eats nothing all day, you know."

"He eats nothing all day by choice. And he sleeps with the turtles by choice." Antonio rises. "I will only be a minute. Then we can go as we planned. We can take him something to eat. Okay? Okay."

From behind the curtain he tells her they will dine at Jimi Changa's, because he feels good in spite of a very demanding day. She won't respond when he talks like *Rico Suave* on Money Street, so he ignores her silence. He says he has decided on lobster for himself and one as well for her. She hasn't eaten lobster since seeing them walk in a line a mile long across the ocean floor on The Discovery Channel in the hotel laundry room. Baldo watched too, seeing the face of God.

Antonio watched too but still craves lobster, even as she refuses a reply. He finishes washing his armpits, butt crack, and scrotum, reaching deep under his nuts with a daub of scent just in case. "Hey, Jaime the Weasel owes me something, so maybe tonight we let him pay. *Con langosta.*" He sorely wishes his new T-shirt was in hand for such a night but resigns himself to a camp shirt with a pattern of tiny *gabiotas* winging across the front and back and around the sleeves, too. It's not a bad shirt. It's just so regular for such a night.

He emerges and steps up behind her where she stands facing the night sky in the doorway. He bends to kiss her neck softly, to set the mood and to eliminate the distance he feels has grown between them. It's only a minor misunderstanding that will soon be repaired. She moves away in irritation, but that's only her way of telling him that his gesture is not enough. She wants more, which is what she will get, the whole *enchilada*, before or after dinner, at her leisure.

They watch the night sky for a minute more, perhaps thinking of stars twinkling or the moon waxing or love or youth or passion.

He bends near again until his lips barely touch her neck and whispers that she is a beautiful woman.

It is just this expression and this sensual contact that she has imagined for so long, but it falls shorter on the second try in the gruesome context of events. Her skin tightens under his lips as if to repel him, but he perseveres here as in all things. Resistance will melt and move with warmth. Just you wait and see; like a dam bursting it will soon flow forth.

Perhaps it would flow if Lyria could ease the nagging questions. How can he be so casual after disposing of a body on the beach? How well can you know a man, if you've only known the boy? She stands motionless with no resistance, and Antonio senses discretion may still be the better part of breast-tweaking.

He takes her hand for the lovely stroll to Jimi Changa's, where some disco dancing will follow an extravagantly touristic dinner with cocktails. Then we will see what's up and who's ready. Glancing back in the shadows, he sees her beauty enhanced in the half-light. Unbuttoning another button on his shirt, he sighs and squeezes her hand.

It isn't so bad, not talking but simply walking, holding hands, in a way cementing the bond between them. They haven't held hands since they last peed in their pants together, and the years have changed the feeling in their fingertips. Now they're electric, wired for transmission and reception. When she twitches as any woman might, holding hands with Antonio and sensing the eruptive potential of any given evening, he gives her a rest and leads the way like a lead dancer. Up the sidewalk and onto the patio of Jimi Changa's they arrive. He is as handsome as any young man; she is as beautiful as a starry night.

They pass the cage bought cheap by Jaime Ruíz because of so much rust covering its ornate Victorian grillwork. Now the old cage is painted white but shows up electric blue under the black light overhead. Toucan perches inside, solitary as a single bird in a very large cage. It's past his bedtime, so he's in his sleeping position with his bill pointed back and tucked under his wing. But he's given up on sleep, and his eyes move with the movement around him as the wild diners come and go. Antonio belches in passing, and Toucan jumps with a squawk.

"I belched," Antonio explains, but Lyria pushes him onward as if she knows better. At least Baldo isn't here, and they're spared that embarrassing scene, with the hyena squeals, the gyration and genuflection, the preening and cooing between birds of a feather.

Antonio knows this place, where judgment is instantaneous and measures a man by the woman on his arm and the respect shown by the maitre d'. It's hard to say why a weasel like Jaime Ruíz is so admired and famous. Yet he has everyone performing according to the social standard here. Some of these men are fat and red. Some have gray temples. All appear to be flush.

Antonio announces softly, with confidence, "Two, please." He palms twenty *p* into the hand of the host, who is no older than himself and just as eager to fill a role.

The host quickly inventories Lyria up and down and what's in his hand. He looks surprised, then he takes the lead with authority. "This way, please. I have a beautiful table for you." So the gavel falls, and judgment is secure. Lyria avoids looking back at those who ogle by keeping her eyes straight ahead. Something makes her wince. Never mind. She most likely shaved with a dull blade, and a little black nub stuck to her dress stings when it's pulled.

Antonio smiles with serene confidence, carrying himself with the poise of a man out on the town. They wend their way through the maze of lesser echelons, on their way to the top.

The diners obsequiously observe as they remain obsequiously oblivious, until Antonio notes the presence of the hot salsa dance combo, *Autoridad*, musical misfits who will charge the evening with a throbbing pulse after an exquisite dinner.

The scrutiny gauntlet is the first course at Jimi Changa's. It's why they come, to ignore it and then sit and burn whoever comes next with merciless assessment. And it's fun, or it could be fun and would be fun if not for the nemesis of the common man, which is circumstance, that, in the end, must occasionally be faced. But Antonio has not been among the common ranks for quite some time now. So, *qué pasa aqui?*

Alas, the sting in Lyria's panties is Mrs. Mayfair, having dinner with a fat red man with gray temples, who appears unqualified for Mrs. M's favorite forced march. He's so red he matches her hair.

Mrs. Mayfair watches Antonio far past the dictate of good taste and in fact gazes shamelessly. And she's grinning! And now nodding as she rises repeatedly in her seat as if responding to a little portable *pinga* on the upthrust, which no man or woman would put past her after one look at that dress! It leaves nothing to the imagination, including what a man might do with such a woman. Or better yet, what such a woman might do to a man. Oh, she is her own magnetic field.

Tonight Mrs. Mayfair dines with a man of commerce, like her husband, Mister Mayfair, though this is not Mister Mayfair, because Mrs. Mayfair purred only yesterday, or maybe the day before, that Mister was freezing his lilywhite buns on the frozen tundra of Texas, just as he deserves.

Besides, this man is more attentive than a husband would be. What husband would look so fervently down a dress? He appears mannerly, moneyed, and patient, and perhaps he will have a bit of luck *a esta noche*, unless of course he suffers coronary complexity in the stretch. She's ready to romp, as anyone can see. But who can blame her for having fun?

Mrs. Mayfair helps this man along, out of his stodgy shell. He nods at her husband's fabulous success with one development after another. They share a wonderful understanding, she says, she and the Mister.

She gazes off, igniting her date's curiosity, because it's a game you play, or you watch until the fire burns to ashes and you wish you'd played. Still, a man who lives in a shell is wary of social blunder. It makes such a mess, and nobody wants to live in a messy shell. Easy as a move can be, it can also be elusive.

He smiles, assessing a back flip with a gainer and a full twist on the one hand and belly flopping on the other.

She shares her quest for fulfillment. She lives to the fullest, she says, with everything she wants most of the time, because nobody gets it all the time. Most integral to her happiness is creature comfort. "I make no apologies. I love to be warm and soft. I'm not a bad person, and I love it. So there." Another key component is sex; make that good sex. "I love good sex, and my one wish in life would be for great sex once every day in the morning and once again every day in the evening. Is that too much to ask?"

Mrs. Mayfair's escort is so heavyset with worldly experience relative to restaurant dining, that an observer might think she only taunts him. The jowls flap, the gout hurts, and the skin flashes crimson. Apparently cognizant of the fleshy treasure before him, he remains tentative. Perhaps she's merely jerking his chain. But why would she do that? He ponders the parameters of good taste and says, "Yes, well, no." He frowns and smiles again. "I suppose it's not. Too much, I mean. To ask. I...haven't given it much thought."

Like hell, she thinks, plucking the paper parasol from her *piña colada* and twirling it before her eyes as *señoritas* used to do. Well, they did it in the movies, anyway.

Frederick Wendell leans forward as if to clarify his position on the subject, rising slightly to facilitate movement or relieve pressure. Then he eases back again like a man of global import. "You know," he begins timorously, looking up with a crooked grin, so much as saying, *This is the best I can do. Is it adequate?* "You're a very beautiful woman."

She touches him lightly, looks down, and admonishes, "Oh, aren't you sweet?" He knows that tonight he will get none, until the touch goes to a grasp, giving Frederick Wendell hope that his concession to beauty is suddenly adequate and that he will shine till midnight or fatigue, whichever comes first. He may rise again in the morning, before he simply must return to Dallas.

But she's looking past him, and he shudders, sensing the husband, unannounced. He follows her gaze but can't find her focus. All he sees is a Mexican boy and girl dressed in department store clothing, endearing them on one level but causing regret on another. End of an era, Frederick Wendell thinks, when the help eats at the same restaurants.

Antonio wonders if a man was ever tested so frequently as he has been these last few hours. Siesta seems like a hundred hours ago. He knows the odds of random encounter remain constant at *medio a medio*. So who can be surprised? It's a small town.

Lyria sees Mrs. Mayfair, who isn't exactly making a scene but is ogling long distance, stretching her neck and waving like it's grand reunion time.

¡Hola! Sí? But Antonio calling across Jimi Changa's in response to her wanton leer and patently seductive greeting would surely throw fuel on the fire. Maybe just a nod and a fond smile will suffice in light of her generosity and understanding. But no—

"Antonio! Darling!" She turns to Frederick Wendell, who Antonio recognizes from the fat and red contingency poolside but can't be certain with so much tailoring. Who can fathom hundred-dollar trousers, a hundred-dollar shirt—dollars!—and a five-hundred-dollar suit on a man who brings his own Styrofoam cooler to the pool? The *gordito* who has no pride smiles like a pooch caught sniffing the *flan*, a cheap pooch unworthy of instant pudding much less this smooth and creamy company.

Mrs. Mayfair stands and embraces Antonio like she hasn't seen him in years, and he fears she will whimper like she did on Tuesday with his tongue thrust between her legs with such proficiency she nearly triggered the smoke alarms. No, wait; it was Wednesday. Where does the time go?

In his pocket he comforts his sleepy *pinga* that, like a troublesome child, seems so sweet when it's napping. The other hand grasps the three crisp fifties that will pay for his romantic dinner with Lyria, in case Jaime the Weasel is not here tonight and another scene must be avoided. He grasps those three fifties plus two more or maybe three, in case they find the magic rhythm leading to true romance after many sour drinks, a long, exquisite dinner, and hours of disco dancing.

Mrs. Mayfair is still embracing Antonio, practically writhing, rubbing her *melones* against him so he can feel the dark *jalapeños* protruding from the ends, as if such grotesque presentation of her mutant nipples through sheer translucence isn't enough.

Who can see such a woman with such *tetas* rubbing against Antonio and not imagine him suckling like a piglet? Nobody is the answer, because the translucence is enough to stir mild nausea in any decent woman, especially with those wiry hairs growing horribly around the ends.

Mrs. Mayfair gushes in matching translucence and flourish, telling Frederick Wendell, "You must meet this man. Antonio. He's fabulous! Really, he can do anything. And I'll tell you something else; if you want a good point man for your project, Antonio is the man. Antonio! It's *so* good to see you out. Who *is* your young lady?"

Shy and tentative as the teenage boy he was only last year, or the year before anyway, he bows like a cleric and says, "This is my friend, Lyria."

Lyria looks at him with startled confusion. My friend? Is it not more than that? Especially in the face of this *puta*? She wonders briefly what she would best be called, for they are not betrothed, nor has the subject been broached. So what could he say, that she is his future wife? Would she actually want that introduction to the woman who sucks his *pinga* while he holds her ears? Of course Lyria cannot be certain that he holds her ears; he often exaggerates shamelessly. Even so, such an introduction may not be desirable, but still, *my friend*?

"Isn't she lovely? Where *did* you get that dress, dear? I adore it. Oh, you must forgive me. I just never know when to shut up."

Yes, you do, think Antonio and Lyria, in synch at last, or at least in concurrence. Lyria imagines the worst, with the gagging and gulping and the obscene mess running down her chin and, for all we know, gumming up those fake red curls. Antonio warmly recalls a kinder, gentler largesse.

"This is Wendell Frederick."

The fat red man who travels with a Styrofoam cooler rises and offers a puffy hand, as rich *gringos* are compelled to do. He leans forward and mumbles, "*Buenos noches*. Frederick Wendell."

"Oh! My! I *meant* Frederick Wendell!"

Frederick Wendell blushes, his sunburned apoplexy purpling around his half smile. He wears a khaki suit and a tie, as if this were a sixty-year-old movie. He won't look at Mrs. Mayfair now, much less down her dress, lest anyone in view suspect him of the worst. He is focused on keeping his shell clean.

Mrs. Mayfair beams in the light of her own making, her splendid bronze bosom presented on a satiny platform rather than grasped by fiberglass hands. The deep and endless cleavage pre-empts the lift and spread, but any reasonable man, including Antonio, thinks this display only fitting and proper. Evening calls for formal presentation, unless you're dancing after dinner, in which case lift and spread might be more appropriate and less floppy. Which is the main problem with huge breasts and cleavage longer than the Line of Demarcation between what is owned by the church and all else. Oh, Antonio knows his history; he took a correspondence course, for the background and the polish.

"Antonio!"

"Yes."

"I asked you what your young lady does!" Mrs. Mayfair moves like initial tremors, rumbling plates below the surface, sliding boulders over plains like mere toys.

"She works."

"I'm a maid at the hotel. I clean your room. Under the bed. In the bathroom. A maid."

"Oh, and what a lovely job you do! You know…" She leans forward in a display of spherical grandeur. "Wendell plans to build a hotel. A very nice one. I'm telling him he ought to look into you kids, you know, for some real ground-floor connections."

"I don't clean rooms on the ground floor," Lyria says.

Antonio blushes. "Oh, my," Mrs. Mayfair giggles, covering her mouth and the *faux pas* as well.

Since no one else has anything to say, Frederick Wendell takes the lead with a twenty-four carat phrase plucked directly from the handbook of the worldly wise. "It's been pleasant meeting you."

Antonio, missing nary a beat, replies with a bow, "Yes. The honor is all mine."

Now Mrs. Mayfair is blushing. Frederick Wendell looks puzzled. Which leaves only Lyria to unabashedly lead her friend like the boat with the engine towing the big banana.

Antonio doesn't mind, but feels none of the romance and sensitivity appropriate to such an evening. He orders wine. Lyria can't believe that anyone in his right mind would pay as much for a glass of wine as two bottles would cost back in the neighborhood. He wants to tell her that certain events in life have nothing to do with money and in fact transcend expense. Besides, it will likely be free! Because of the bird! But why start? He would sooner savor the buttery complexity of an exotic vintage while living in the *esprit* of *esprit de corps*. But he sips and feels tired, which is only natural. And guilty, which is not a good sign.

She takes his hand in both of hers and scrunches forward like Mrs. Mayfair with less firepower. He is amazed again at her fresh scent and flawless skin. Still, he regrets the apparent motive of her body language, which is to gain advantage, to ask for and to receive. "Please, Antonio. I cannot be happy here tonight. I want to come here again with you, I think perhaps sometime soon. But not tonight. Tonight..."

She pauses, and into the interlude he lopes, "She only..."

"Not her. I worry for Baldo and what you said. Please, let us get something hot in a bag and go to him. You can drink all you want."

Well, he has to admit: he should cut his losses. All is well with Lyria. They simply picked the wrong night to express their love over romantic dinner and wild discotheque. He is very tired anyway, and it's not easy, reading the left side of this menu without factoring the shifts required to pay for the right. And where is the Weasel when you need him? No, a smart man saves his load for opportunity.

So, okay for now, we go, maybe stopping at Manny's Tamales on the way for some tamales and pickled chilies. We'll get out of there for thirty pesos for three of us, instead of two hundred forty pesos here for only two—and that's *before* the wild dancing and the drinks.

Oh, and the tips!

VI

A Time for Reason and Rest

Not only does Baldo appear to be mentally secure on this night or, for that matter, on most nights, he seems more sanguine than most. He is more reposed than most men picking up a check at Jimi Changa's. Stargazing in glittering communion as blithely as some people might watch TV, he knows the difference between nature and discotheque.

Here he has the cool sand to soothe his feet as he lies back astride these seductively comfortable chaise lounges. He has the moon in its risen glory and the stellar bodies twinkling overhead. Here is unbound fantasy in the untold populations inhabiting some of these twinkles, and glistening solitude with no populations on the rest. Peace and gentle slumber cover the turtle babies like a soft blanket, imbuing their tiny hearts with security and perhaps a small knowing of the love of a boy who would give his all for them and then some. These things are here for the taking, for free.

At the discotheque, on the other hand, are noise, sweat, and lust arcing short circuits for a pretty peso. Does not a wealth of natural riches mark a man as wise?

Antonio can't remain oblivious to violent events. But who can tell what worry lurks below Baldo's placid surface? Antonio suspects Baldo's natural redemption to be so complete, that his violent slaughter of another human is already settled on the still bottom, fuzzy with first growth and blending with the rest. Unless of course Baldo's worry is merely masked by serenity, just as the tall grass can hide gooey *pollo* squat among the cool green blades. Surely Baldo must understand what has happened here.

Yet Brother Baldo relaxes with his tamale and lemonade as if worries are for poor people, for those less secure in their calling. Who can tell if remorse for the fisherman is among his concerns? He shows little but guilt for the death of a cormorant and the condition of the cormorant's cousin. These birds committed no crime beyond feeding, as nature requires them to do. They did not kill wantonly or for sport. So why should they suffer?

When Antonio and Lyria returned to the beach with the oily, aromatic bags of dinner and a few more beers, Baldo was gone. Not to worry; he was only down in the water, waist-deep in a pounding surf, conducting his special mass for the blessed slain. He emerged naked, which was only practical, since a man in wet shorts is far more vulnerable to eruptions of the skin.

Still, Lyria didn't need to stare with such scientific intensity. Has she never seen a *pinga*? Well, come to think of it, she most likely has not. Which was a good reason to laugh; just wait until she sees the magnitude of her destiny.

Baldo stared in disbelief that his wise brother could find anything humorous on such a night. Antonio shook his head. Never mind. So Baldo pulled on his pants—the new pants that are the lower half of his security uniform. He took them from the hanger on the tree where they'd hung all day. No need to soil them with so much work to be done. Donning the official shirt of the security guard's uniform as well, he cut a different figure. Still remotely and perhaps idiotically serene he seemed more sanctioned and, yes, more employed by society in general. Antonio smiled proudly and patted Baldo on the back for doing so well. He wanted to say, Good boy. Good boy, Baldo, but he held back to avoid further confusion.

Baldo was either too tired or too distracted to celebrate. He adjusted the bedding and water dish of his convalescent bird and stroked its head feathers with a finger. He stared at the bird, whose head grew heavy as it lolled off to sleep. Baldo smiled in confirmation of a night on the mend; things were progressing as well as could be expected under the circumstances.

Easing back onto his chaise lounge he eats quickly, guzzles his lemonade, wipes his mouth, and gazes up at nothing, or proof, or perhaps meaning and guidance in the firmament.

Lyria watches him as if to see the wheels turning or some inkling of movement between the ears. Her curiosity seems scientific, as if he is a rare creature indeed, a wild one with an unpredictable nature, available here for personal observation.

Antonio eats a *tamale con pollo y poblano* in a cornhusk. Its warmth and simple flavor dull the edge of the razor-sharp evening, so he reaches for another, this one in a banana leaf, which takes longer to unfold and requires more room to prepare for eating. This one is so messy and drippy you could never eat it in a fine restaurant like Jimi Changa's where you would pay eighty-five pesos for it instead of eight pesos, which is what it should cost in the first place. It isn't even so big, but... *¡Ay!* This is how a *tamale* should taste.

He swills another beer and belches, realizing the importance of dullness from time to time for a man on the fast track. He farts out loud, looking up to see who will laugh, ready to quip about the barking tree frogs or the mice on motor scooters that are out tonight. But Baldo remains moony, and Lyria keeps her vigil. Oh, well, a man who can fart out loud in peace and comfort is a lucky man too. No doubt about it, dull is good, and from time to time, fat has its merits. Thinking of which, he wonders if Wendell Frederick is now mounting his matron. He thinks not.

Still, you never know; *Señor* Wendell is one of her kind, and with the lights turned low, fat blends with shadows and really is no bother until morning. Who knows? Maybe he, Wendell, was once adept at the thing with his mouth, which skill a man never loses. If lost he can find it again. Mrs. M can make a man want to find it, especially if she's having a good night and especially again if he, *Señor* W or whomever, is drunk or hungry. He looked hungry. But then surely Mrs. Mayfair would be more selective, unless her hunger ate her discretion, or maybe she needs to be needed in compensation for Antonio's preoccupation with another.

Antonio farts again and finishes his beer.

Who knows how many hours pass between the last of gazing and eating and drinking and farting and the first of gentle slumbers? Somewhere in the night Lyria retires from her chaise lounge to the sand, where she eases back on two cushions propped against a palm tree. Baldo is beside her, curled like an infant mammal not yet weaned from the nurturing warmth of motherhood, not yet exposed to the cruel requirements of this world. Her hand lies fondly on his head, which lies gently in her lap. They breathe deep in this position when sleep finds them. This is not a lascivious scene but rather one of familiarity and brotherly, sisterly love. So Antonio laughs at the irony of the scene were Lyria to observe it and the roles were changed to other, familiar players, namely himself and the M.

Oh, Lyria would insist that his tongue was all but between her legs if the head was his and the lap was Mrs. Mayfair's. Never mind; this scene is not only pure and loving, but of practical value as well. Bringing dinner late to Baldo and then innocently falling asleep will help assuage the lament in the morning from *gorda* Rosa over her virgin daughter staying out all night. *No problema ahora*, not while babysitting little Baldo and his baby *tortugas*.

Hours pass between Antonio's practical strategy in the middle of the night and his sudden waking at sunrise. His eyes open before his slumbers have properly ended. He looks north and south, up and down, and sniffs for the trouble that feels tangible in the air. He lies still and breathes easily, instinct telling him that sudden movement could bring on the bite or sting if in fact the snake or scorpion he senses is also awake and alert. He reaches for alertness and feeling and in a blink knows that he will never make it home to change and prepare in time for another day of fun. But so what? This is Mexico, the land of *mañana*, of laughable delay and balmy blue skies to fill the time of waiting. Can he not compensate with the verve and example of a true maestro on any given morning or afternoon? Of course he can.

Though a man tangibly rising in social status is intuitively
attuned to get up and get going, Antonio drifts back, suffering
fatigue from a most demanding evening. In sweet surrender he
sleeps again briefly and sorts the images. Color and movement rise
and fall like the tides and break like the breakers; swoop like a
machete in a harsh harvest. Images flash and darken with the pulse
of a blinding new day that throbs with horizontal sunlight on his
closed eyes.

Everything is garishly red and smells like dog breath, until he
turns away from the blinding light and presses his cheek into a
cold nose. Eyes open on Lyria sitting and staring beyond the black
dog who sniffs his face. Above her are three men in uniform.

One is Baldo.

One holds a leash; he and the third man have machine guns
slung over their shoulders and nightsticks on their belts.

Antonio swings his legs over and sits up with a long and
mighty stretch and a yawn to match, opening his mouth wide
enough to swallow the beautiful crisp morning. So wide does he
yawn in deference to the greatness of another day in Paradise that
his eyes squeeze shut again. He holds this pose briefly to set the
scene and himself. Closing his mouth, smacking his lips and
easing his arms to the same angle as He who died for our sins, he
opens his eyes, looks up with cheerful optimism and says,
"Buenos dias."

"Buenos dias, Señor. Have you slept here all night?"

Antonio looks troubled briefly, and then nods. "Well, yes, I am
sleeping here since falling asleep here after dinner."

"And what time was that?"

"Well, it's hard to say, since dinner was takeout tamales from
Manny's, which really are superb and only eight pesos, which is
incredible if you happen to have read the menu from Jimi
Changa's lately. We went there first, to Jimi Changa's, that is, and
would have stayed for more than a single glass of wine that cost
half as much as six tamales… Hey, we got one left."

Antonio smiles to himself in the paltry shadow cast by his
down-turned face. Will the young men in uniform expect a glass
of wine? He picks up the bag and looks inside. *"Sí."* But he

doesn't offer it, because a fine line is tricky enough without a foolhardy lean to one side. So why did he lead with a straight chronology in reverse? Where can that go but back to happy hour, which establishes a presence here?

Well, that's okay, because a presence somewhere is a fundamental requirement of reality and/or existence. Is it not, Your Honor? And right here is where existence occurred for me, no, for us, no, make it only me. Why not only me? Am I my brother's keeper? Or my sister's? But let's not rush the details or mire scenarios in strict chronology. A circuitous route might be best for now.

Antonio considers, "Eighty-five pesos for a tamale? It's ridiculous." Okay, let it drop, lest undue attention be drawn to the circles. "Why do you ask? What is wrong?"

"Were you here yesterday afternoon?"

"Yes. I work here. I must work here this morning, and I must go home and prepare. I am the director of poolside activities here at the hotel."

"How late were you here?"

Antonio shrugs. "What? Five-thirty. Six. I don't know. I can tell you it was no longer light, but not quite dark. What time was that?"

The two with guns confer. Antonio looks at Baldo and nods halfway and then at Lyria with the other half. Back to the men with guns and sticks, he says, "I must go now." He turns away with a singular quickness up a step. He tells the police, "I must go now. It's time for work. Everyone must work or things will turn back to how they were. If you need more information, everyone who was here yesterday will be back in only one hour, when we can talk as long as you like."

But unlike the longest walk that begins with a single step, this single step comprises the entire walk. One of the policemen intervenes with his nightstick and insists, "Please. You will you come with us?"

Antonio doesn't follow but displays a look of honest curiosity. "Can you tell me what is wrong?"

"A man is dead."

Antonio waits. When nothing more is said, he shrugs, "So?"

"Murdered, *Señor*. Here, on this beach."

Twisting his honest curiosity to socially conscious concern, he allows for brief, personal agony before repeating the assertion. "Murdered? On this beach? When?"

"Last night, *Señor*. Please, you may have very valuable information for us. You may not even know it. We will have a word with your manager. You will be excused. When we're done, we will bring you back."

A word with the manager will not be necessary, for the time to begin work is now, and Milo watches from the top step leading to the pool deck. He nods slowly with a wry smile, assenting to Antonio's absence and affirming a wry truth. He, Milo, has known all along that it would come to this, and though he's too much a gentleman to say so, his smirk reflects his further understanding that Antonio's absence may span the entire morning, perhaps the afternoon, and maybe thirty years to life.

Antonio forfeits a moment's composure in registering the verdict in Milo's eyes. Milo is master of nothing but what the New World of tourism has taught him, which is a practical envy to match his practical greed. Who knew he would turn so quickly against a loyal colleague? But then who thought he wouldn't, given the chance?

The policeman now asks how long Lyria and Baldo have been here. He already asked Baldo but got *nada* in reply and then learned from Milo that the boy doesn't speak but was yesterday appointed to guard the little turtles in accordance with the decree of *El Secretario Pesco* and the Navy. The cop's posture corrects slightly in audible range of such monumental authority.

Milo further explains with churlish annoyance that the job of guarding the baby turtles is described as round-the-clock. "But who can be expected to babysit turtles around the clock?" Milo turns his palms up and turns his head with fey indignation. He waits for an answer with growing exasperation over this scene on the pool deck. Affluent guests arriving only yesterday don't need a disturbance, much less news of violence on the beach.

The cop is not *simpático*, shifting his machine gun to his other shoulder with a grunt and curling his lip to reveal teeth at once terrible and perfect. Hardly his own but perhaps better suited to his calling, they flash like polished steel in the morning sun. Stainless steel uppers and lowers serve to clarify the source of real power in this emergent world of wealth and comfort. He turns to better question the mute boy's girlfriend, the one whose lap he slept in, because a cop needs answers, even from a woman who may be loosely connected to The Secretary of Fishing himself. He glares with keen intensity to be sure.

She hangs her head. Well, she is female. What can she know? And what could she have done? Commit such a crime of violence? Every policeman knows the fury of a woman scorned, but she is not such a woman. She is submissive, possibly partially mute herself. She was with the mute boy. What does that tell you? "Tell me," the policeman says to Antonio. "How long have your friends been here?"

Antonio won't look at Baldo or Lyria. Baldo can swing either way here but will likely play along. Glancing north and south, east and west, like a man seeking the big picture, Antonio sees no machete, so he glances up and steps out on a limb. "They must have come back later," he says. "I came here to spell my brother, so he could have time to clean himself and eat. And be alone."

Let Milo stare. What does he know?

"I fell asleep. Now they are here."

"So you had wine by yourself? Then you went for tamales by yourself, and you brought them back here?"

"No. And yes. I brought the tamales back here by myself but then I was not by myself, because my brother was here with the girl." But no sooner is Antonio pleased with his sophistry, referring to Lyria blithely as *the girl* and leaving her name out of it, than the cop looks troubled.

"But you said you spelled him so he could eat. Are you saying he left to eat, or he ate here and then left and then came back?"

Antonio realizes he has stepped unwittingly into logistical stalemate, for which nothing will do but *finesse de force*. "And so?

You are talking now in circles. I don't know what you're driving at, Your Honor."

Now the cop laughs sardonically with an appalling display of dazzling steel, indicating the last of free dialogue until the lawyers are retained. "I am driving at nothing but the police station, *Señor*. Please. Shall we go?"

Antonio shakes his head and prays with dire urgency to his late father that both his younger brother and his nearly betrothed are granted the common sense to continue standing still as bumps on a log while he trods off to Babylon. Or is it Gomorra? This may be the last chance for communication until a private space can be secured, which may be never. Luck must be given room to breathe for any chance to stay alive.

Looking up only at Milo, Antonio says, "I'll be back as soon as I can. I wish these fellows were less presumptive."

Milo arches his eyebrows but only in mockery of a fool, of a wannabe highbrow on his way to the *jusgao*. Presumptive? Ha! Oh, Milo has known the inevitability of this embarrassment, and though the arrogance doesn't surprise him, the sheer, raw bravado is a sight to behold, here before God and the law. Milo smiles ruefully at his presumptive maestro. Guilt was inevitable and now is presumed, unless innocence can be proven beyond a reasonable doubt, which it obviously cannot be. Where does he think he is, *en los Estados Unidos*? Too bad, my friend, that we are only *un poquito* to the south.

Antonio Garza is familiar with intense gazing from svelte, blonde *gringas* honing on his mid-section. But this intense gaze seethes with the envy of burrito-built Milo, whose sweat flows like runoff in the shade. Perhaps the justice system appears dark for now, as it too hones on Antonio's midsection. But what can the *gordo* manager Milo gain from such unbridled contempt? Does not Antonio fulfill the responsibilities of his position? Are the guests not happy and in some cases thrilled?

Well, if you're not too fat and green with envy you could see the happy faces around the pool or get up off your fat, hairy ass and read the happiness on the comment cards. Oh, Antonio keeps them coming on. Er. Er-er. Er-errrr! That's Milo's rub. He will not rise. Such is the way of a five-star resort spotlighting Antonio and his muscles and giving him the sweet reward while the fat manager must change his shirt twice a day.

It's a sad dawn indeed when the cock won't crow, but neither will he hang his head in shame or remorse. Back by late brunch is what he'll be; just you wait and see. This Antonio conveys to his roly-poly manager as he continues up the steps and passes so closely he can smell the *frijoles y huevos* on the *gordo's* breath, already sour as putrefaction. Antonio winces in disgust and shakes his head. *"Comida frijoles y eructar jamón,"* he says in passing. You eat beans and belch ham, meaning that Milo will never rise from the basics, even as the maestro demonstrates how easily the job is done.

Let Milo fire me. Let him try. Let him explain poolside that he, the fat bastard of a whore for a mother, is now maestro for the guests, of whom thirty percent on any given week are repeat guests. Repeat! At these prices! And for what? A puff pastry of a manager with *flàn* where his spine should be? *No lo sé, pero no lo creo. Ha!*

Antonio crosses the arched bridge over the pool. He walks as resolutely as an innocent man, which the morning forces him to be. He moves with dignity, impervious to the slings and arrows of relentless circumstance.

Still, he wishes his feet didn't shuffle so much from too much beer and too much tamale and way too much yesterday. Heavy legs must clear the steps from the pool deck to the brunch terrace.

Difficulty compounds when the cops behind him grip Antonio's biceps on approach to the lobby. Here is the perfect place to make a run for it, which they must not allow. Antonio pauses with a scornful laugh and an easy flex that throws off the grubby mitts of the little cops as easily as flies flicked by a stallion's tail. Stainless steel teeth? Ha. Ask your dentist for muscles of steel.

But his small triumph is brief. The cop who doesn't talk responds to resistance with a sneer, showing he has not yet marshaled resources for new bridgework in steel, and the ivories remaining are more rotten than not, mere stumps in a once-youthful sneer. Perhaps he has seen Antonio at work and now cowers in his inner self, knowing he will never ascend to such levels. At any rate, upon losing his grasp, he unslings his automatic rifle and lowers the barrel to nudge Antonio's kidney, which pushes back by sheer reflex. But this is a machine gun, wood and steel, not a horsefly or a grubby mitt. A gun feels no muscle flexing and kills a man's pride here in the lobby. The stump-mouthed cop achieves his own small triumph over circumstance and briefly feels his dominion.

This is humiliation, which can foul the balance of an entire life. Antonio stops short and turns to lock eyes with the cop pointing the gun. This is wrong, he wants to convey, and with sheer confidence of expression further conveys to the punk cop that bullets are nothing.

He stands taller and breathes casually, expanding his chest like a bull frog so much as croaking, *Go ahead my little cop, shoot me many times*. The cop will not meet this gaze but prods again, into the ribs this time. Antonio wants to take the gun away from him but sees Baldo watching just down the steps. Baldo pleads with silent eyes.

Antonio checks his anger, because rectitude in men is less forgiving than in nature, and survival is now of critical importance. So he nods slowly, turns and walks as directed through the lobby at gunpoint for the guests to see and murmur recognition of the one known as Antonio, or Tono by the end of the week. He is what? Chief suspect in a murder on the beach?

Lyria comes to the fore, surprised and confused at this maddening presumption. Baldo straightens his uniform to begin another day of work, oblivious to the world of men and their guns, focusing on the needs of nature and its salvation. He moves to the morning task of feeding the baby turtles. Then he'll change the water and arrange the tubs for maximum shade.

Lyria can only stare, striving to know whether Baldo is actually so callous to his brother's arrest, or if Baldo performs for the manager as well. But with guests in full migration to the dining room and the pool, industry calls. She seeks the younger brother's

eyes for understanding, for something to go on, if not a plan then
at least a tacit collusion, a time and a place to meet and talk. Well,
not talk, actually. But Lyria can approximate dialogue with Baldo
as well as anyone, except of course for Antonio.

But Baldo is mute and moreover numb to her silent call.

So she gathers her things and strides resolutely back to the
chaise lounges where Baldo preps breakfast for his baby turtles.
She rifles the sand as if searching for her sandals, waiting to gain
his attention. She doesn't look at him but says lowly, "*Nueve
horas.* Baldo! *Nueve.*"

Baldo won't look her way but nods and continues ministering
the needs of his new ward, the injured bird, who is amazingly alive
and awake, accepting care from this unlikely mentor by
swallowing gobs of fish stuffed down his gullet.

She can only hope for the best, that Baldo's emotions and
instincts are not as mute as his speech and will apply to his own
flesh and blood as they do to a lice-infested, half-dead bird. She
can only accept his oblique affirmation with faith. Her faith fails,
however, on remembering what she now misses, which is not her
sandals but the machete, without which Baldo looks like an
amputee. He so often holds the machete either as an extension of
his arm or else cuddled to his chest like a loved one. And now it is
missing. Anyone who ever watched TV knows that without a
murder weapon the prosecution has nothing.

She shuffles the sand to find it. If she can find it, she can go up
for a towel, come back and wrap it and then dispose of it. She
looks up to Baldo's grasp, his half-smile and half-nod seaward.
So, he does know. At least he seems to know.

Milo steps forward. Baldo returns to the motion of only a
moment ago as if nothing intervened. Lyria puts on a show of
exasperation for Milo, who turns away to tell a guest it was
nothing, nothing. A minor matter that will be cleared up in no
time. Lyria drops a shoe and kicks sand over it, and as Milo turns
back she brightens. "Ah! Here it is!" She smiles gratuitously and
hurries to begin the new day of delivering happiness by way of
cleanliness to the guests of our deliverance. "I will change my

dress," she says in deference to Milo's countenance. He scoffs. What does he care what a maid wears?

At the top of the other steps leading to the brunch terrace above the pool, she looks back and sees a woman and five children to the south, the family of the fisherman, she thinks. She further fears the circumstance emerging, which is the need that will fervently remove her from the ranks of those destined to succeed. She needs money and power, great money and great power, which might as well be a need to fly, or to make *caga* that smells like gardenias.

Lyria feels a mortal difference between last night and today. She has met the source of her anxiety, and the source met her. More importantly, at a level we can safely call critical, that source is now the source of salvation. Lyria must speak with Mrs. Mayfair, who springs to mind just as water flows freely in a weary traveler's fancy.

Need is the overwhelming sensation of the hour, and it is upon her and her men. Just as any man or woman from any class in Mexico knows, so Lyria learns of the fundamental need of a radically different practicality. Antonio is gone forever, unless this basic need can be met.

Stocking her cart in the laundry room, filling the modular holders with soaps, shampoos, lotions, cream rinses, shower caps, shoe cloths, tissues, toilet papers, bath towels, and face towels, she cannot imagine how to make contact again with the Mayfair woman without looking entirely suspicious.

For one thing, Lyria is dark-skinned. For another, she has nothing to wear but this foolish dress that won't do by the pool, and even if it would, she shaved her legs, and how in the world would *that* be construed? A maid by the pool in a party dress with shaved legs? She's mixing in, attempting to climb; that's how. Next thing you know she'll be attempting to climb out, ordering fancy drinks with fruit slices for facial features. No, that won't do and will only result in her losing her job, which is all that separates her from the fundamental abyss, on the edge of which she can barely live the lovely life through next week. Unemployment would starve her and her poor mother.

The only alternative is her maid uniform. She thinks this in the act of changing into her uniform, the spare she keeps for mid-week, and here she is changing on Sunday. No; it's a bad idea. Maids at the pool are in violation of hotel policy and again she would risk immediate termination.

Yet properly attired and with her cart stocked, she sees another way. The clock says seven-thirty, so she isn't so late, maybe fifteen minutes, or thirty, depending on early checkouts for early flights.

Watching the clock, she moves with faith and beyond with the most fervent prayer; that a lowly maid can rise *como el burro que toco la flauta*, with the best of luck, like the burro who played the flute. She knows she has only to knock on the door—Mrs. Mayfair's door—as knock she must. The shortest route is often best and is always a straight line, or so Antonio would say. The straight line in this application will require information from the room monitor. Asking is easy as punching in the letters to spell the filthy name, and she experiments with spellings for Mayfair, beginning with Mefer on floor two but going directly to Mayfair, because the red-haired whore with the *pechas grande* is not Mexican, nor does she stay on the twelfth floor. This we know for certain. If the *puta* were on the twelfth floor, Lyria would have changed floors for practical reasons.

If Lyria can only find the room number, she can simply go and knock, which will entail the risk of running into the maid for that floor, but that risk is certainly better than the pending avalanche at poolside. She can most likely see where the other maid's cart sits and then duck down to Mrs. Mayfair's room at the right time. Alone. Without her own cart, which she will park on the twelfth floor as if working there.

Good. But where is the whore dog daughter of a whore? Only up to floor nine in her search of the listings, Lyria fears an assumed name, or perhaps the name of a man. Or of several men. She scans, losing the composure so recently gained, fearing too much time lost in this hopeless search. She jumps when Theresa comes in. Running her gamut of silly facial reactions to this guest leaving, that guest staying, those guests checking out sooner or later, Lyria wonders how anyone can be as stupid and slow as Theresa. Taking another lesson from Antonio, she casually goes back to the listing by names of the guests and finds Mrs. Mayfair, finally, in 1801, the nasty bitch. She, Lyria, should have known that such a shameless one would need the best room in the hotel for her pornographic games. Never mind, because the past is no more than imagery that may well be gone forever, imagery of a hard-working young woman who loves and the chance to raise a family in moderate comfort. Imagery compounds with *pinga*-thrusting and ear-holding, because circumstance can make for strange bedfellows. But if all is lost, what difference will it make?

Meanwhile, at the bottom of the lower steps between the pool deck and beach, Baldo tends to the turtle babies with one eye southward. The woman and children rifle the dead coals and tortillas. So what is Baldo to do, tell them to stop? No, he only watches with one eye and wonders what kind of man could go through the motions of finding a woman and having babies of his own while living with so little regard for the lives of others. Did he think his hunger a justification for murder? Baldo stops and stands straight and considers himself as a murderer but then shakes his head. This is a very difficult reality to accept. Condemning a man to death may seem justified in a moment of passion, but here he stands with little pieces of innocent fish. Is he not guilty?

No, he is not. For one thing, these little pieces were game fish, creatures of high speed and predatory habit who understand the nature of killing or being killed. Trumpet fish are reef fish merely seeking contact and dialogue. They hurt nothing and eat only the tiniest specks, and a tiny speck doesn't know if it's swimming in the dark depths of an ocean or on its way to becoming a fish turd anyway, so no harm is done. No, he, Baldo only enforced the greater law of God and nature, which stipulates compassion and quickness in all killing, or at least in most killing. This law often differs from the law of men. And women—like the one now shrieking lament, hurling faggots and avocados.

What is she mourning, the loss of love, or the loss of her provider? She looks unlovely, but Baldo suspects that most women do, sooner or later, once the marriage and children are done with. He suspects the same of men, but men are different, as long as they can make the *pinga* stand up straight. When a man grows very old and cannot perform, then he too is of little use. Baldo cannot reason how or why it is that the men stay with the women when the women turn too ugly for what the men want. The men may turn ugly too, but the women always want what the men have, as long as the men can pay. But none of these things matter. Nor does Baldo care who turns what or when, for he thinks he'll grow old in the company of thriving and abundant nature, in which beauty fades and comes again every day. He won't worry for any woman or man, especially if they are old and ugly.

He suspects that some men and women do stay in the bond and care for each other and that the reason is love, which comes from familiarity and convenience. Maybe what is intimately known becomes part of oneself, which must make a thing easier to love, because we love our self. If we didn't, we would change. You might think nobody would want to fuck a trumpet fish, but then another with just such scales and funny fins and long snout would want to.

Or, take the tone-deaf bird, who most people assume to live without romance with such a discordant serenade. *Rrrik. Rik Uk. Urik Rik. Rrrrrik.* Yet those from whose heartstrings a chord is plucked, also know that a call of love, however ghastly, is tuneful to she of the similar feather, beak, and persuasion. Only once did Toucan warble his throaty song, sounding more like Gustavo Garza after a night of drowned sorrows than a troubadour. Toucan's effort for vibration and tone comes no closer to melody than a big fat bill stuck through the bars can come to flight. Toucan mostly only whispers, yet some comprehend his forlorn rasping and what he wants to say. He does say it. He wants something different. Who in the world could not see this or hear this or know this? This comprehension is as well the stuff of love. Yet how loveless the world remains for him.

Baldo speculates that love comes from memory too, which has a way of shaping things for the good, lovably. His love for his mother is perhaps greater than it would be in person, had she not died and taken her nasty habit with her. At least his father called it a nasty habit and called it good riddance when she left with the last of it. Baldo was only a baby then and knew her so briefly that she remains unsullied in memory as the lovely woman who introduced him to touching and whetted his appetite for the suckle.

His few memories of her have played a million times but still they play with fervor, recalling her just as she was, which was perfect and silent, like him. *De tal madre, tal hijo*, he laughs; from such a mother, such a son, which is a joke of course, because everyone knows a son should reflect his father. His father appears frequently in his thoughts as well, yet the years of struggle soil the memory of his poor father with fatigue, poverty, hunger, and a paltry longing that seems his prevailing legacy.

Still, the perfect love he holds for his long-dead mother can't be the same as romance. Romance makes a *pinga* grow tall and requires candles and flowers and perhaps some chocolate. He wonders if he would have wanted to fuck his mother and glances down. No, he knows such a thing cannot be good, or else the boys on the street wouldn't glare with such hatred when making reference to it.

What he knows with greater certainty is that the fisherman was guilty of murder, cruel and senseless murder, which must be the very worst kind. He, Baldo, feels neither guilt nor regret but rather relief that such a man no longer exists. He did not choose to enforce the law of nature or wield the hand of God any more than he could have chosen to refuse. He simply yielded to the ineluctable source within, which he feels with certainty was God and is God, so soundly was the need for action revealed to him. The action was easy insofar as it came natural as sunrise, without thought or predilection, merely swinging decisively at that which is wrong, which is different than right. As for two wrongs failing to make things right, well, life is a messy business. Justice is approximate, equations hardly ever balanced.

Such assessment could be damned in church, but Baldo is content to conduct his own services, they're so much easier to follow. *Jesu Cristo*, the fisherman said, as if *Chuco* Himself would condone such sinful behavior there at the scene of the crime in God's own surf.

What? A wanton casual murderer can relax with Chuco, Who picks his teeth and reads a newspaper while standing by with Divine Intervention for the evil fisherman who idly murders trumpet fish while waiting for a decent bluefish to swim along? No, *Señor, Jesu* doesn't fish. He has greater consequence to process, like cruel and senseless murder.

Like his brother before him, Baldo wonders how The Maestro let it come to this, and why a skinny, mute brother like himself was chosen to swing the blade of justice. He returns to his work with vigor as the woman and her children slog laboriously up the beach under the burden of what the fisherman left behind and their grief over his loss, whatever that loss represents.

Lyria knocks on the door and listens, perhaps for the fat red man in Mrs. Mayfair's room. Hearing nothing, she knocks again and could then enter, in compliance with hotel policy that allows entry and a good-morning call after two knocks. Knocking a third time to be sure, she doubts she'd find the fortitude to knock at all if Antonio wasn't on his way to jail.

With no response to her three knocks, she fears a lost chance. She unlocks the door, opens and calls, "*¡Buenos dias!*"

She hears the eighteenth-floor maid only four rooms down and ducks back to avoid further botching, but as slim chance narrows to nothing, Mrs. Mayfair speaks, "Nnnnn. Oohhhhh!" Lyria laughs, though the night and day are further from humor than any in her life. She wonders if this is what Antonio wakes up to as she steps quickly inside to see the truth many women fear, which is first thing in the morning.

Lyria stands triumphantly before a badly hungover woman in her mid-fifties whose ridiculously orange hair with platinum highlights is mashed and ratted like yesterday's mop. Mrs. Mayfair rises rickety as *los muertos* in October, her face sagging with smeared foundation, her huge breasts hanging like overripe *casabas*, one of them plopping out the stretched sleeve hole of her nightie. Mrs. Mayfair oozes like a lump of melting wax. She tucks her stray *pecha* back through the sleeve hole, squints, and says, "Go away, please. I'm not even up yet."

"I am Lyria," Lyria says. Mrs. Mayfair falls back on her four pillows and moans. "Antonio is in jail. They say he is guilty of murder." That works; like time-lapse spore growth Mrs. Mayfair is up, pushing the covers aside and hauling her legs over.

She repeats the news as sleepy people do to gain time and awaken. "Murder? In jail? What?" Her consciousness rises slowly like little bubbles here and there from the depths of her slumber. She reaches for something to grab onto but only flounders among the surface flotsam of her age and the abuse she's endured. Wiping away the detritus first with a knuckle, then with the back of her hand, she looks out the window and regulates her breathing. "Where's my bra?" She sees it on a far chair and shakes her head.

"Come in. Sit down," she says.

VII

Women United for Justice

Down on the beach Baldo will not stop working, even as the sorry, haggard woman stands before him with her children and tells him the bandits killed her husband.

So? What does she want him to do?

She zeroes in on the only uniformed guard on the beach, as if restitution was ever so available. "They killed him," she says. "Killed him." Baldo looks up and smiles halfway and finds himself stuck, staring at a five by three mound of flesh so loathsome it inspires pity. She is so fat you can't see her pregnancy until you wonder how fat can protrude from fat, and why it would jut from just under the sternum. Then you see it and wonder why she wants one more. Maybe she doesn't but doesn't want damnation from the Pope either. Or maybe she drinks like her poor dead husband once did, and her liver is big and round as the world and just as crowded, like that of Joaquin the old bartender. "And now he is gone."

Baldo returns to his work and leans into it with renewed focus so the sorry woman will see he is busy rearranging his tubs for a new angle in which to count his babies again.

"Do you know them? Were you here?"

Baldo works, because a mute man is often deaf as well. Yet he stops again to face this woman, to ease her burden with sympathy. She is not guilty like her unfortunate husband, and this should be a time of forgiveness and truth, within reason. Because anything less than truthful will be found out. So he raises a forefinger to his mouth and shakes his head, meaning he doesn't speak, which she understands after a few renditions.

"Did you see them?"

He shakes again, opens his arms toward his little babies then brings his fingertips back to his heart with a shrug. This she cannot decipher any more than he intends her to. So she waddles back and forth until Baldo must finally turn away, and she turns too, her bulk moving ponderously as a ship on loose moorings.

She whimpers and asks, "Who will feed my children?"

He looks up as she sees the injured cormorant in the shade and steps near it. He steps near it too, to intercede if necessary. She asks if he is going to eat it. He wants to shake his head and explain to her that neither he nor this bird will feed her children. He wants to tell her that he will try to heal it so it can fly again, but he finds himself nodding. She says it would be a blessing on both him and the bird if she takes it to feed her children. Three children wait with dull eyes and snotty noses. Another child is twenty paces off and higher up in the softer sand of a shallow dune, squatting over its growing pile of runny turds.

Baldo takes a moment to see if he might be missing something. He shakes his head and explains the situation by opening his arms to the injured bird then bringing his fingertips to his chest again. He wants her to see what she's been missing, which is the difference between this bird's behavior and her husband's crime. One merited personal sacrifice in deference to the law of God and nature while the other does not. But he only watches as she raises a howl in further lament, and he knows nothing that either of them could convey would make a difference to the other.

So the whimpering woman and her children trudge north up the beach. Baldo watches with certain relief in knowing that a love was not ended last night. He rearranges but cannot count the babies, because he's too preoccupied wondering what the fisherman got out of life. He stops and stands straight and watches the shrinking waddle, trying to put himself in the fisherman's shoes late one night after catching or not catching fish. Walking home to darkness and hunger, snoring, foul smells, and too many children, what can a man think? *Caramba*, now I will lie with my fat wife and relieve myself in that rank opening between her legs?

Baldo shudders and returns to work, thanking himself as the fish and the birds should thank him and, if truth be told, as the fisherman should thank him too.

Lyria can't get the story quite right to the point of satisfaction. She cannot answer the endless stream of questions spewing from the old lady with the notable *chichonas* on the other bed, because she only got the story in bits and pieces herself. Mrs. Mayfair will learn the parts that fill the empty spaces soon enough. But the story makes no difference in the telling anyway, and besides, an accurate chronology at this point would be rare as Toucan's song and just as jumbled.

With exasperation and impatience rising more quickly than she herself can rise, Mrs. Mayfair waves her hands to bring on the reason, the logic and fundamentally sane behavior she *knows* humans are capable of, so she can understand, please. What has happened in the few short hours since last seeing Antonio and his "friend"? Her animated urgency has the effect of jiggling her grand *melones*, so that even Lyria stares.

Lyria catches herself and wonders if she fits the profile she's heard, of women who desire women and don't even know it. She would like to feel these *chichis* for firmness and heft, but she's only curious to see if the doctor put something inside to keep them from sagging too much, and she would like to compare them to the feel of her own breasts. Her own aren't nearly as big but seem much nicer with high-pointing nipples. These are long and droopy, perhaps from years of suckling many men, and big, dark chilies dangle from the ends. Who could be aroused?

Nor is she curious in the least to see these ominous nipples shrink and point. They're so big; each would take a willing mouthful to gather it in for proper suction. Lyria can't see what Antonio sees but she has no doubt his mouth is willing. She suspects him pleased with this liaison in spite of his tired refrain on practicality. Moreover, the certitude of this hefty set may be fading. They're big but must be sagging more this year than last, unless of course Mrs. Mayfair always sagged.

Who cares anyway? Lyria does not, especially in light of these cheap, dazzling goods. Who would avoid her but a fool?

What normal male within a thousand miles would not like to feel *my chichis* or do the thing with his tongue? I am young and fresh and like *ice crema* over *caga* next to this mountain of whore fat. But does he even suggest, or try, or insist? No; I get a goose and quick feel. It's disgusting.

Mrs. Mayfair, hardly an insensitive woman, snugs her nightie with two hands. She doesn't mind Lyria staring; the human body is natural, and so are the wonderful gyrations within its reach. Furthermore, you don't compile Mrs. Mayfair's resume in the ways of the world by precluding potential, especially if the one man who makes her come is involved—or his girlfriend. But this is hardly the place or time for idle fantasy. The one man is in a far more tawdry fix and must be processed on a higher plane, or a different plane, at any rate. Mrs. Mayfair surrenders her need for logic but cannot grasp the simple truth. Repeatedly she asks, "He cut a man's head off?"

"Baldo. Not Antonio. But the police have taken Antonio."

Mrs. Mayfair can neither calm down nor stop her head from shaking. "And then you went out for dinner?" She shifts on the edge of the bed and smoothes her hair to no avail. "I need a minute to think." So she thinks. Lyria watches, avoiding the chest. Mrs. Mayfair's idea rises on a moan and a half nod and emerges with a sudden reach for the phone. She jumps when Lyria cries, "*¡Ay!*"

"What?" Clutching her heart with both hands, she looks up in startled anticipation.

"*¡Ay!*"

"What?"

"*¡Ay! ¡Ay! ¡Ay!*"

"Child, you must tell me what's wrong with you."

Lyria grabs that which has caught her stare, which is not the dribble on the pillow but the entire pillow itself, which she shakes, and attests, "*¡Ay!*"

"What?"

"The pillowcase! Antonio left the pillowcase! It is full of the fisherman's clothing!"

"Left it where?"

"At his place!"

Mrs. Mayfair then accomplishes three behaviors at odds with each other. She slumps into eerie calmness for one, as she blushes like a maiden for two, and makes the call she began making moments ago for three. She tells the man who answers—Lyria knows it is a man, because women like Mrs. Mayfair know men, only men—she will need counsel within the hour on a matter of dire urgency. Lyria wonders if dire is a sexual term but thinks it unlikely. Not now. That would be too much. How could she?

Mrs. Mayfair says she will be in touch directly but now must hurry to gather information. In the meantime, "Mr. Balsom *must* be found. I hope I make myself clear!" She hangs up and holds her face in her hands briefly before insisting, "We must hurry. Wait here."

She rushes to the bathroom for a pee, a tooth brushing and a ten-minute shower that fogs the mirror over the dresser. She calls out that she won't be a minute, and in twelve more minutes is very close to achieving dry hair. Lyria approaches the door to check room-cleaning progress on the eighteenth floor. Who can worry about cleaning rooms on the twelfth floor at a time like this?

Slowly opening the door for a peak out, she faces Maria, the eighteenth-floor maid. Lyria smiles and frowns. It's her turn to blush, which she presents as a hot flash with a semi-swoon, indicating severely urgent symptoms including nausea, headaches, dizziness and fainting spells. She mumbles that it's because of her time and perhaps a touch of the flu; please, don't come near.

"Who are you talking to?" Mrs. Mayfair calls.

"Please. I may be contagious."

Maria leans aside for a look inside, so Lyria tells her she only stopped here to return this guest's shoes from the lost and found but now she may need to go home for fear of falling deathly ill or worse, making a guest sick.

"Who are you talking to?" Mrs. Mayfair steps out of the bathroom, speaking loudly over the hair dryer. "Ah. Good. What is your name?"

"Her name is Maria."

"Maria. Can you clean...um...um..." She waives her hands and says, "Please forgive me, dear. What is your name?"

"My name is Lyria."

"Can you clean Lyria's rooms today? She's not feeling well and neither am I, so we're going together to get well. *Comprendez*? Here's some money for your trouble." Mrs. Mayfair doesn't count the bills she pulls from her purse, but Maria and Lyria do. Twenties. Three of them. Dollars.

Denial disgorges from the ages and Lyria's gut, but she swallows it back down as Maria brightens with understanding, faith, trust, dedication, application, concentration, and the rest. "Yes. I clean. Very clean. Very, very clean. You will see."

"Thank you. Thank you. You go clean. We're very busy." And out the door Maria goes, until Lyria opens it again and calls to Maria that her cart is stocked and ready on twelve. Maria returns and hands a twenty to Lyria, who reaches to take it but stops; she feels the pain but refuses with insistence that the money is for Maria, to be sure.

Back in the room Mrs. Mayfair's hair is extremely close to dry and should need no more than another minute or two to hold the spray net. Her face is mostly corrected and improving with great gobs of ghastly red lipstick, a liberal troweling of foundation, a tuck-pointing of eyeliner, a smear of rouge to simulate facial circulation, and a trace of shadow for the coy suggestion. She turns around modestly to face the closet and drop her nightie so she can dress. Lyria assesses the back end, which doesn't sag nearly as much as one might expect.

Mrs. Mayfair turns back and says, "It's not true that one size fits all, but here. You can wrap this snug and it should look fine." Lyria stares. "You can't very well walk out of here in your maid's uniform, can you?"

"I have my dress downstairs."

"Tsk. Tsk."

Lyria is certain this tsk tsk will not translate, so she asks instead, "They will not see me in this?"

Mrs. Mayfair says, "Put it on," as she rummages for extra sunglasses, a sun hat, and a scarf. Lyria complies, soon looking like a starlet incognito. "Well, it's still you, but if we go together, and I keep talking, and you keep your face on me, we can be through the lobby in no time. Okay?"

"Sí."

In two minutes that spans ages they're in a taxi. Mrs. Mayfair lays a hand on Lyria's thigh and leans forward to ask the driver, "Do you speak English?"

"Oh, no," the driver laughs. "*Hablo poquito. Hablo poquito Español tambien.*" He laughs again.

She removes her hand and speaks lowly to Lyria. "We're compromised by leaving together. Maria compromises us. But I don't know how else to do this without some compromise."

"What is compromise?" Lyria asks.

Mrs. Mayfair whispers, "It's what every day comes down to. We've been seen. Others can say we're together. I want you to tell him to drop us off at a commercial establishment that's walking distance to the place. You know, where what's-his-name lives."

Just like a floozy, Lyria thinks; she is in his grasp one day but can't remember his name the next. Still, she does seem concerned. So Lyria sits up and asks the driver to let them off at the dry goods shop on Juarez Avenue. In a few minutes they arrive.

Two steps onto the curb Lyria removes the sun hat and glasses, leaving Mrs. Mayfair as the single object of all the staring eyes, or at least the object of most of the staring eyes; some widen on the unlikely, dark-skinned figure who for some reason carries a broad-brimmed hat and Hollywood sunglasses in the blaring sun. Down a hill and into an alley and down that they walk, until Lyria points out the place. Mrs. Mayfair checks fore and aft like a mother prepared to stay back if anyone is looking. But the coast is clear, so they enter the humble *casa* together, and there it is, lying on the floor where it was casually tossed.

"What do we do with it?" Lyria asks. "Antonio was going to burn it this morning, but they took him away."

"Burn it where?"

Lyria shrugs and points to the dusty ground outside. Mrs. Mayfair shakes her head and sinks again into deep thought. She paces the small abode in puzzlement and wonder. The puzzle is how best to dispose of the evidence. Awe derives from seeing the private side of her private stud. Stepping to a hammock, she feels the mesh and pushes as one might press a mattress for firmness. The hammock won't resist, so she turns and sits, whooping when the hammock lets her fall a foot before catching her. "This one is for Baldo. That one is for Antonio," Lyria explains, thinking Mrs. Mayfair might like to test the hammock of her lover. Oddly enough, she does, rising with difficulty, going to Antonio's hammock, easing onto it and lying back. Lyria sits in Baldo's hammock with waning tolerance.

"I don't know how you people do it," Mrs. Mayfair says.

Lyria feels the sting of condescending distinction. She wishes for a *pinga* to plug the old whore's head right now; but then what satisfaction would that bring, and to whom? "Ah!" Mrs. Mayfair announces when a heel snags in the mesh that nearly flops her to the floor. Righting herself and standing in the vertical world of superior judgment, she says, "We need a bag or something." Lyria finds two plastic grocery bags, and Mrs. Mayfair says, "We really shouldn't stay here."

They leave. Sure enough, as they head back the way they came, Mrs. Mayfair holds back, pulling Lyria's arm and urgently whispering, "This way!" So they turn and hurry the other way.

"We can't get out this way," Lyria says as they round the corner at the bottom end of the alley. But they have no choice; the voices of men at the top end approach as the women did only minutes ago. Down on their knees on uncommonly common ground covered by fine dust that smells of cat piss, they struggle through a hole in the chain link fence. The dust actually softens the friction. The smell thickens on passage through the decrepit shrubbery that squeezes and snags their dresses. Mrs. Mayfair wiggles and whimpers but won't complain, which conjures disgusting imagery but compensates for her prior superiority as well. Lyria wishes the whore cow would hush.

As if crawling through the black hole of social parity, they stand and adjust their visible selves. Shooing the dust and twigs, Lyria is ready to proceed. Mrs. Mayfair brushes her knees as if to brush away the holes in her nylons. Lyria smiles and nearly explains that some things cannot be brushed away, but she contains herself, because superiority is a two-way street. Instead of speaking from the high ground, she simply replaces her sun hat and glasses.

Still adjusting within and without, they hurry on, winging up the street like birds of a feather. Mrs. Mayfair carries the pillowcase in the plastic shopping bags. Where to? Mrs. Mayfair knows the world; Lyria knows the neighborhood. Together they lead and follow on their way to salvation for their common love.

At the corner, Mrs. Mayfair says, "We need a telephone."

Lyria looks neither left nor right but leads the way across, explaining that such luxuries are not common to the neighborhood, that a *larga distancia* place is only three blocks up and two blocks over, but it's very expensive and not a good connection and conversations are easily overheard. In fact, no place would be better than the hotel for efficiency, privacy, and clarity.

Mrs. Mayfair looks back like a woman pursued, then takes the lead into another alley, a shady dead-end offering respite from the sun but little else for a modern woman. She sweats profusely but her foundation, shadow, and liner remain firmly in place. Lyria sees and wonders how she does that.

"I don't know if this works here," Mrs. Mayfair says, digging in her purse for her miniature telephone, the kind that cost ten times a normal telephone but gives you only a tenth of the size and weight. Turning it on, she urges, "Come on. Come on. Come on." They must wait for a connection, she explains, showing Lyria the little window with its little pictures of ears and telephones, megaphones and phone books and many odd, squiggly lines. At least a pause and a bit of shade allow the elder to catch her breath.

She holds it when Lyria steps intimately near, so close that their noses must turn aside to avoid collision.

Their eyes meet in the blur of shameful proximity. The elder's are confused, the younger's resolved. The younger proceeds into the elder, who is pressed against the wall more awkwardly than on that first press of the first boy ever attempting intimacy with the amazingly young, flamboyant, and beautiful Lena McSwain all those years ago. Now, in a shadowy alley in Mexico, the still flamboyant and beautiful Mrs. Mayfair gasps, "My dear..."

"Sh..." Lyria closes her eyes and raises a hand to cover Mrs. Mayfair's eyes, yet they sense the men who moments ago entered the alley from the top and could only pass this way by squirming through the hedge at the bottom, just as the women have done.

"Oh, God," Mrs. Mayfair whispers, dropping the prima facie bags among the trash littering the alleyway. "Oh, God."

"Sh." They breathe and wait.

"Why not just leave it here?" Mrs. Mayfair asks.

"Because we cannot," Lyria advises, which is, of course, the reasonable response. Pressure eases as the manly footsteps fade, and a moment of awkward friction seeks graceful transition.

"Ah! We have a connection!" Mrs. Mayfair says, helping them along and punching many more little buttons than a normal telephone would require. While waiting, she explains to Lyria that Rudolph might be game as a red-nosed reindeer, but he's also the best lawyer money can buy. "I don't care if you're in Texas or Timbuktu, Rudolph knows who to call."

Lyria tries to see the relevance of Texas or reindeer, both of which she has seen in books. Christmas is approaching, but how does Texas or Timbuktu relate to Antonio's fix, unless, of course...

"Rudolph Balsom, please. This is Lena Mayfair calling again, urgently, if you don't mind. Yes. Yes. Thank you." Covering the tiny talk hole with her garishly red-nailed finger, Mrs. Mayfair nods sanguinely, as if the fix is on; the lawyer is in. "Rudolph! Oh, darling, how *are* you?" So Mrs. Mayfair proceeds to gush sweet nothings and "remember whens" and "Oh, those were the days, I mean, *really*! Oh, don't. No. No. Yes. Yes, I do. I do... Listen, Rudolph, I'm in a bit of a situation here..."

So Mrs. Mayfair begins anew, relating the details of the bit of the situation we find ourselves in.

Lyria listens as patiently as possible, which isn't too patiently. A young person intimate with the neighborhood and its practical standards may see the benefit of lawyers and international phone calls at a time like this and may also understand the need for womanly wiles, but tawdry whimpering at such a time feels wrong. Antonio needs help now.

Mrs. Mayfair talks and talks and still has made no mention of liberty *or* money. Lyria is aggravated to hear such frivolous carrying on preempting what is so important. She shakes her head vigorously; Mrs. Mayfair should stop.

Mrs. Mayfair responds with concern to such a display; "Hold on, please." She puts her finger over the tiny talk hole again and asks, "What, dear? What is it?"

But Lyria can't say what it is, cannot simply blurt a demand for freedom or ask what the terrible cost will be. She laughs instead; if life was that easy she wouldn't be a maid in a hotel, wiping black, curly hairs from toilet rims. Antonio this minute sits in a steel cage in a concrete jail surrounded by men with guns. His confinement is impervious and complete, save the wily ways of an aging *puta gringa*. So resistance fades. Lyria shakes off her wrong instinct to stop this last hope for salvation. Mrs. Mayfair proceeds, listening now to what will be done on the one end and what should be done on the other. Instructions are simple and concise.

Mrs. Mayfair then sinks again into the sweet and gooey like a hapless monkey in swamp mud, signaling the ultimate promise that awaits between her legs for the powerful man on the other end, who is undoubtedly aided by recollection of unseemly past encounters. "Bye, love," Mrs. M coos, pressing the tiny button victoriously.

Lyria picks up the plastic bags, and it's done.

Putting her little phone away, Mrs. Mayfair straightens herself again as if another hedge has just been cleared. "We need to wait two hours. He needs two hours. He says he may only need a few minutes, but he wants two hours. He says we should find a place to wait. I suppose he could call me, but I don't want to confuse things now. I mean, these things don't work all the time and you never know. I mean, I do know it often doesn't work. Don't ask me how I know, but I do. I don't want to think he's going to call, and then have it not work. You understand, don't you?"

Lyria nods sideways, indicating conditional understanding.

"Tell me, dear. Have you... have you had lunch?"

No, Lyria has not had lunch or breakfast or a glass of water, the mention of which recalls the weakness in her knees. Why does Mrs. Mayfair ask this question? When could she have had lunch? In the taxi when no one was looking? "No, I have not had lunch."

Mrs. Mayfair nods; they must eat, and after a suitably poignant pause, she reminds Lyria of the special needs of a woman like herself, who is only here on a visit—this with a gentle touch to the forearm, woman to woman. A *gringa* is most susceptible to the perils of microorganism, making this particular situation one of trust and confidence. Even from ice cubes. So she will be most happy to treat, if Lyria can lead the way to a safe place, safe meaning one with a safe bill of fare, meaning *sans* the little squirmies, because Mrs. Mayfair feels they're on the right track to a bail-out.

Ice cubes too, now. Don't forget the ice cubes.

"*Sí. Hielo purificado.*" Lyria is not a fool. She knows what a fat whore with the shits looks like.

Lyria does not know what a bail-out is but senses that some things can and should move forward without her comprehension. She knows the place to go, six blocks over and three blocks up, and so they head out again, still in step but at a slower pace with two hours to kill. They breathe easier, as if progress is theirs and the Sword of Damocles is stayed for now. Lyria leads but follows the tenor of the situation. It changes with Mrs. M waxing lyrically over the lovely town, its prolific flora, and sensational views.

Lyria imagines the concrete miasma comprising the land of wealth and power.

Mrs. Mayfair chortles over the quaint houses and charming landscapes. "To think, you can have all this with no, you know, gated communities. It would never work at home."

Lyria neither nods nor shakes but stares obliquely at the harsh opposite of all things quaint and charming, which is jail in Mexico. She sees moreover what Mrs. Mayfair does not see. She wants to broach the subject of jail in its innate difference from one country to the next, not so much in the violence and homosexuality common to all jails, but in the foregone torture common to Mexican jails.

"Do you know," she begins, only to be interrupted.

"This is so nice. I like getting to know you. I have so few friends. You wouldn't think that. I mean, I would think you wouldn't think that. Tell me, dear, what kind of menu does this restaurant have?"

"What kind of menu? It has things to eat. What other kind of menu does a restaurant have?"

"No, I don't mean that. I mean, well, is it.... Well, of course it is. Mexican, I mean. But is it... well, don't worry. I understand. It has things to eat, which is very good, because I, for one, am famished. Seems the liquor makes me hungry the next day. I think it's the toxins screaming for the antidote, which is good nutrition. How about you? Are you famished?"

"Sí. I have hungry."

"That's so cute. You mean, dear, you *are* hungry. Listen to me, correcting you. I can't speak a word of Spanish. Well, I can. I can say simple things like *gracias* and *mañana. Hola. Uno, dos, tres.* But I could never carry on like you do. I thought about private lessons and actually planned to fit them in. But I swear I don't know where the time goes. Then I get home and hardly have occasion to speak Spanish, except to the... you know. So I forget what I know, which is nothing, but you understand."

Lyria nods with a half smile, understanding very little of what makes Mrs. Mayfair speak so thoroughly around a subject without getting to the point, if in fact a point exists for getting to.

"We'll do lunch," Mrs. Mayfair warbles. "I think I'll like that. I want to get to know you. You might think that strange or at least unusual. But I would. You know."

Lyria's response is again tentative, and she wonders if Mrs. Mayfair understands the true nature of the situation. She demonstrates her understanding by merely daring to cross those boundaries society sets between two women on either side of the same man. "Antonio speaks of you," she says, then shamelessly coos over Antonio's wonnnderful skills as an entertainer.

Lyria's hunger quickly fades. Why is she prattling on like this, and what does she want? Does she think that I will sing *her* praises and tell her that Antonio speaks of her *tambien*? What good is a girlie talk on life, love, money, and murder with this strange woman, who warbles like a canary simply because the sun is out? I would rather the old sow could ape Toucan, keeping it sparse and low.

She imagines Antonio this very minute and hopes he's alone in a cell, however grim, and not under the naked bulb that shines on contusion, laceration, bruises, broken ribs, and spirit and can as well endanger a man's essential legacy. She drifts briefly to Baldo, wondering what he thinks this moment and, moreover, if he thinks anything this moment. Does he understand the fix his brother is in on his behalf? Is he more concerned for buckets of baby turtles? Does he know how a woman feels in the night when a man—and he is a man, this she has seen—curls up like a baby in her lap as if with a baby's needs? Imagine, at his age, taller than his older brother and for all we know more dramatically endowed, but still so young and wanting such contact from a woman.

VIII

Quincy Makes a Call

Baldo does not stay busy from a self-conscious need to look busy like so many who fear that idleness may lend the wrong impression and lead to dismissal. He stays busy to ventilate his drive and to give that which he came to give.

He guards against intruders, marauders, and predators as his title suggests he should. Even now, with the morning feed secure and the late feed yet to begin, his eyes dart in four directions, up and down. The future is at his feet for his safekeeping. He needs no uniform to underscore his calling but he doesn't mind one either, and feels better than he has in his baggy jams and T-shirt. The babies are fed and changed. They flip their little flippers and keep their tiny noses at the surface, sniffing freedom, as anyone will who senses a calling.

They seem driven to the depths, though for now the depths are imaginary. How else can a thing be to those who have never been? Baldo suspects a certain bubble rising from the dark and groaning fantasy in which a billion tons of water seek languorous repose, and in that bubble is a thought, round and perfect as these little turtles daydreaming of the depths. For the depths reside within and without, and we rise and sink according to buoyancy or density of our vision. We fantasize and become that which we dream.

¿Sí? ¿No?

Baldo watches the babies with their flippers flipping through their dream within his dream. How can a being imagine what it has never seen, as surely these small turtles do now?

Well, that's easy to know, and it's easy to feel a smile spread across his young face for the simple truth, which is that the ages connect from then to now through the imagination. What has not been known is easily imagined because it has always been a part of a turtle's heritage; part and parcel of the way a turtle will approach life and knowing.

A woman in a chaise lounge turns ostensibly to face the sun, but secretly she observes the long lanky fellow who smiles. She smiles back. She moves her molten thighs against each other and opens them to the warmth overhead. She closes her eyes and waits.

Baldo looks left and right and then out to the horizon.

He leans over a tub with a piece of fish clamped in his teeth, teaching his babies to eat. The chaise-lounged woman with more oil on her legs than the spill field around a gusher removes her sunglasses and sits up.

Who is this man? And what is he doing?

In eighty-eight days the hotel will make much ado of what has come to pass, because travelers from *el norte* love a celebration and may factor the high times in contemplation of repeat business. Helping these turtles through their struggle for survival is good management after all.

Management will invite each guest to take a young turtle in hand and escort it to the water's edge. With casual pomp and beachfront ceremony, each guest will gain access to glory and grace. As liberators and saviors and citizens of the redeemable world, they will liberate, save, and redeem.

And have fun, *sí?*

Well, you can't blame the guests for playing out a silly charade while on vacation. It's part of the entertainment package. Nor can you complain. Are these babies not marked for survival?

Baldo doesn't mind and won't complain. The dramatic promenade on the day of release will outshine any walk a boy or man could take on this beach, too often littered with dying puffers and so-called bait-stealers left to suffer, as if one hunger was less viable than another.

He thinks nighttime would be best for delivering freedom to the turtle babies, since a bite of any size is protected by darkness. He might want to escort these babies to the depths himself, since any child leaving home wants its mother's company for the first leg of life's journey. Perhaps he will pick a turtle on the night before the release. Perhaps two turtles, one for each hand, so they might swim together for a while, if they want to. He can easily short the tub-count by one or two, and in the safety of the dying light he can not only deliver his young wards to the sea, he can join them in the depths of the fluid dream.

Now that is a lovely prospect indeed.

Beyond the break and sloped bottom of the most active feeding zone, they can make the beautiful swim. If the big bite comes, so be it. Baldo feels an encroachment that he knows is merely fear, and he smiles, faithful that the food chain defers to spirit, hopeful in his connection to the powers that be, of whom he is one. Confidence derives from neither arrogance nor indifference. He simply knows that a boy or a man can't measure his niche in the natural mystery without walking in the dark or swimming there. He can only have a feeling. Baldo feels the animal angels as well. He has seen them on occasion. His smile grows like a flower effusing in springtime with delicate form and brilliant color.

Meanwhile, for eighty-eight more days he must bear up to the ineffably brown Milo in matching brown swim trunks, who sets up for bingo as if nothing is required but the cards, the beans, the numbered balls, and the spinning cage. Oh, and he'll need a great big tub of lard for a gut hanging over his swim trunks too, which he happens to keep on hand for such occasions. Look, he also brought his pocked, splotchy skin and a nub of a *pinga* pointing straight out.

Baldo can't look directly at Milo because of the awful disturbance the squat man causes in the eyes of the beholder. Never mind. The guests by the pool will fervently embrace their true maestro on his rightful return to power, especially the *gringas*. Of this we can be certain.

"Hokay!" Milo grumbles like a man wakened from death. "It is time for you to have some fun!"

Well, *vamos arando, decía un mosquito al buey.* Let's get plowing, said the mosquito to the ox. Just so, the guests glance sleepily at this fat, gruff man exhorting them. The men smile benignly. The women grimace. It's not the same.

Baldo observes with less tolerance. He will never enjoy the same attention from the women that his big brother enjoys. He doesn't mind. Antonio needs the women, and he, Baldo, does not. Such longings may grow, but that bone can be chewed as necessary.

Yet his smile broadens as he recalls the continuing love between himself and Lyria. He doesn't mind helping her out. He wonders why Antonio refuses her the first smidgen. What could it hurt? She may not razzle dazzle like the shameless ones with their shaved centers and glittering gems, but familiarity and sweetness and certain love make her worthy of a concession. Not that such assistance would be a concession, and you couldn't call it drudgery, because it can be fun, like last night, sleeping in her lap, nuzzling her *chichis* and making them shrink and point while she pretended to sleep, pretending as well to gasp in her dream. Baldo wanted to lift her shirt and suckle, which must run in the family. He wonders if his late father suckled his late mother and hopes it was so. Lyria's shirt wouldn't come up because it was actually a dress, but he thinks she wished it a shirt also just to have her swelling *naranjas* suckled, even if only to moan, *Oh, Antonio...*

Baldo would not have minded that either, because sometimes a brother needs help if he can't see something, and a sister too, which is what she is, although he would not actually want to suckle his sister, even if he had one. But then again, who can know? He's never had one except for Lyria, and he wanted to suckle her, but then that was only for fun. But what other reason could you have, unless you were a little baby yearning to feed the hunger? But that's not exactly how he felt.

Hola, little babies, he thinks, eyeing his plentiful charge.

Baldo also minds the minions now gathering to the south at the scene of the crime. He has constrained himself all morning from going hence to inspect the clues. With a crowd gathering he could look more suspicious holding back. But a man should stay on the job and not leave his post. Still, he goes to see. It's only a few hundred yards down. The skies are clear, the only birds working far south.

He approaches and takes note for future reference that the night will fool you every time when it comes to the true appearance of a car or a woman or a murder scene. Perhaps he has resisted the truth since sunrise, when the birds, all the birds of all the species, continued to feed. Well, he thought, the birds feed, and it's so common for one segment of beach to be the focal point of the feeding. Undertow and side currents can push small fish and detritus to the surface in certain sections of the break. But the birds and fish feed for hours from above and below on the horn of plenty risen and strewn across the sand. Now they rest, the birds, fat as ticks and belching on their rocky ledges in the shade.

Close up, he sees that the carnage is more than a smudge. Big chunks sun dry above the water line, ghastly in sunlight but fading to gray from their ghastlier blues and reds. Bone fragments punctuate the sand. Straggler birds work the beach and dive beyond the break. Among the onlookers Baldo hears the murmured consensus. Quincy was here to fetch the body away.

The body? What body? You couldn't call it a body. It was more like clumps of sand with lumps of dough in them. It was very ugly.

Now he's back, Quincy, with these men in their masks and snorkels, to see why the birds still work this space. To see if something else is just there, beyond the break, attracting the birds.

Baldo drifts from the close end of the crowd to the far end and from the back to the front. He feels calm enough. He tests himself for conviction or remorse and is pleased to come up neutral on all fronts. He doesn't like how the fisherman made him feel any more than he could tolerate the fisherman's behavior. He would kill the fisherman again, given the circumstance, but he wouldn't like that either. Perhaps the kill would be easier next time, just as time eases its strain after meeting the fisherman's wife and seeing his issue. Plenty more of them to go around without wasting the innocent and disappearing fishes. If truth be told, he likes this fisherman being gone for good.

From knee-deep water in front of the crowd, watching the police divers half-heartedly try to learn why the birds frenzy, Baldo knows why. The birds rejoice. It's that simple. The evil man will harm no one else but will end his time on earth as guest of honor at this *fiesta* for the birds and fishes. Baldo smiles at nature's way, which is no mystery to some and renders others speechless, though they too may rejoice. What difference does the loss of a man make anyway, if he can't see or hear what the fish and the birds are trying to tell him?

Baldo is looking up when a voice from above asks, "Did you lose something here?" Or maybe the voice is behind. He doesn't turn around but remembers the fisherman standing in this very spot, poised between life and death where only God should stand. The fisherman too did not turn. Baldo shakes his head.

"Well, then. What are you doing?"

He turns quickly now with the practiced grin of the bona fide idiot, pointing to the divers and diving into his own charade, the one dramatizing his skill as a diver and his certain knowledge of the bottom along this stretch. He doesn't miss a beat or show the least hesitation, for he speaks to Quincy himself. Shaped like Milo's littermate, Quincy is squat and round, with a difference as sharp as a bone shard in the sand separating Quincy from the vast majority of stumpy *gordos*. The keen edge of danger surrounds this one's simple stance and spurious smile. Maybe it's the hemispherical bumps covering his face and neck. Like a cobblestone street, Quincy's visage slows you down.

Unlike most people, Baldo isn't afraid to gaze upon this face and wonder how it got so bumpy. These bumps are not red or blotchy, and they're not pimples or pustules. Or boils.

Baldo reaches out but doesn't touch, so Quincy cocks his head and leans toward the stupefied boy, so the boy can feel one. Baldo laughs and smiles like a boy and retreats, shaking his head. So Quincy eases back as well and feels one himself and says, "Cysts. They're cysts. I could have them removed."

Baldo stares.

Quincy shrugs. "Do you think they're ugly?"

Baldo stares, then looks back up the beach at the plastic tubs.

Quincy nods slowly and asks, "What do you do?"

Only now does Baldo realize that he stands knee-deep in his security guard uniform, never mind, the pants will dry, but not before he is seen, wet and wrinkled, by those who might wish him less than well, like Milo. But never mind Milo; let him come. Baldo points north and pantomimes the surface struggle of a baby turtle with such precision that Quincy laughs. Baldo knows that a laughing man is a man of easy reason, so he volunteers to go get his mask and snorkel and see what is to be seen.

Quincy slowly turns away and slowly nods.

So Baldo runs back up to the hotel and runs through the lobby, which burdens him with the risk of further untoward observance. But what else can be done, except to move with most deliberate speed? He runs out front and catches the bus homeward for his mask and snorkel, and for the pillowcase that the rough-hewn face of Quincy brought to mind. He hopes he won't be gone too long, but after all, he's on assignment from Quincy, himself.

As if the pillowcase full of a fisherman's clothing connects the thoughts of those revolved around it, so too does it materialize in Antonio's third eye. *Ay*, he thinks, too distraught for worry or hope. All is surely lost in a pillowcase. So what's the point of further worry? He continues his pointless worry because a shred of hope survives, that the sharp wits of his beloved or the uncertain wits of his brother will allow for remembering and proper action.

Interrogation wasn't so bad. A few slaps and pokes with a nightstick will not likely leave bruises. More importantly, Antonio can tell when a lesser man holds back for fear of reprisal. How hard could it be to break a rib? Not hard at all, no, the *pollo hombre* held back. And what kind of man beats another whose hands are cuffed behind his chair? The bulb was naked but didn't dangle; it flickered florescence. The questions were easy. Who are you? What do you do? When, where, how much, and why? Filling a gap of twenty minutes in the last fifteen hours was easy as walking for the cake, if you're a maestro and live intimately with the walk. A man with the power of improvisation also knows the value of critical timing on the change of pace, the decompression, the soft touch on the matter-of-fact, and the simple anxiety of an innocent man.

Antonio knows these things as well as any man for a thousand miles, maybe more, including the best in the bistros in Acapulco. He hopes Quincy has nothing to go on but proximity and the personal renown of the golden boy. Not that Antonio is a boy, but such is the figure of speech most employed by admirers.

What else could Quincy have? He has no motive and no weapon, which equals zero. Still, a man who knows the neighborhood might anticipate round one leading directly to rounds two through fifty-six, once the evidence and witnesses line up. Who cares about such a fisherman? It's not like all such men can be or should be so easily cured, but really; a fisherman is not a magistrate. Is he? Was he?

Antonio takes solace in small measure and solitude in the dank, dark cell his betrothed imagines. Lying back, he sees her and wishes her here, so she might see the torment he casually endures. He wonders if Mrs. Mayfair left and feels a small pulse of need down below. He doesn't exactly wish *her* to see him so disposed, nor does he wish her here otherwise, except maybe for a few minutes, for the relaxation available in sweet communion.

Shifting the lumpy pad, Antonio repositions, doubtful that a man can sustain the pulse for long in such a place. He knows the pulse can lose its better sense and fail to distinguish between what it wants and what is available in such a place. Confident the distinction will endure in his own mind, he narrows dark potential to the nagging needs of others. Once prison life begins, really begins, he will spend his days in adherence to the old regimen, push-ups, sit-ups, and crunches, so his return to the world of progress will be carved, flexed, rippling, veined, and popping if not monumental. He will rejoin the living as though he never left. In a season or two this hiatus will blur; a man of certain destiny took time out for family matters. Thank God for youth that allows time for all things.

When the pulse continues Antonio wonders if the place perversely stimulates it, or if thoughts of Mrs. Mayfair carry such power, or if his sheer strength and dynamic spirit pump the blood in spite of the lumps and grit. He chooses Mrs. Mayfair and the short work she can make of any pulse any time of day or night. Deflation is immediate on recalling the first hours of incarceration. Quincy came by to stare and ask, "Why did you do it?"

Antonio stared back for a quarter of a minute. "I did not do it."

Quincy walked away, looking back with his follow-up question, "Then how do you know what it is?"

Antonio had to yell, "Because the guards told me!"

Quincy will be back. Maybe then a few ribs will be broken, depending on what or who turns up, or if suitable glory can be derived from a hapless culprit named Antonio. A man of Quincy's magnitude won't close for the kill until the evidence is gathered, the circumstance proscribed, the potential scrutinized. Quincy will hit the beach. Antonio wishes he knew what Baldo should do, but he can only know that Baldo must avoid error. *Ay.* Maybe it doesn't matter. Maybe wishing on a star or throwing coins in a fountain would serve a man in a cell as much as sending thoughts through the ether. Drifting, Antonio seeks stars and fountains.

Quincy, meanwhile, waits, steadfast and stolid as an immovable object that ferrets truth by simply waiting. The truth will out because it always does. He makes no exception here, backing out of the surf.

The pillowcase is gone. Its absence is obvious. Baldo turns the place inside out to be sure no one stashed it. Ransacking takes five minutes. Reassembly is less thorough but takes another seven. In two more he's back on the bus with his mask and snorkel, wondering if Quincy knows this mad dash is an elaborate choreography. Maybe Quincy is having a good laugh, knowing that any choreography can only entertain the long arm of the law.

Baldo now swims in more treacherous depths than any sea, imagined or otherwise. Once in the water he will lead the way to freedom. The dispirited policemen can't really swim but merely flail like blobs. He will lead them deep and show them a truth that will free all concerned.

With folded arms Quincy watches the water. Baldo doesn't run but picks it up to a trot and laughs at the pasty, pudgy police boys who couldn't get twelve feet on a good day, much less thirty on a Sunday with a four-foot break. Hungover and bloated, they struggle. Who will fear them now, the fish? The current or undertow?

Baldo stops alongside Quincy to share the view; fatsos dunking like donuts in the drink. Quincy turns to eye the lanky figure beside him. Baldo shrugs, holding up his mask and snorkel. What can I do, Your Honor? I am nearly a man, one who understands authority, right and wrong, and building within a community today so that we all may share a brighter tomorrow, so I am willing to try. I will see, if I can, what is driving these birds to frenzy. If it's a big chunk of poor, unfortunate fisherman somehow anchored just there beyond the break, I will see that too. I may as well see whatever Your Highness needs to be seen, if such a view finds pleasure with Your Magnitude.

Baldo feels loose and good and therefore successful in his portrayal of civic intention and social conscience. It is not for nothing that he is his brother's brother, and a bit of the maestro flows through his tender veins as well. But Quincy is not your average poolside guest, and Baldo constricts like an animal in a snare on seeing Quincy's grin. Quincy is known from town to hotel row for his cagey skill. Crime is at issue here, and this sad situation may relate to other unsolved homicides or domestic violence. A car theft or robbery may be tied to this scene. We don't know the full extent of corruption here on the golden coast, with the heat, the liquor, and sudden infusion of cash. Do we?

Quincy views the big picture with no holds barred. He is *comandante*, charged with keeping the greater order, as it were. At the hub of this mystery may be passion or money. Are you familiar with either one? No longer known as Armando Sanchez, he is known now as Quincy, who may be a rerun somewhere but still pulls excellent ratings here.

Some say he is better than Quincy as seen on TV.

Others say he would not seem so smart without his cousin at the newspaper to run his photograph with a glowing profile for every Volkswagen recovered.

Some say Quincy's skill is real. How can such a thing be faked? He *is* better than his namesake on TV and better even than Columbo, they say. Some say Quincy *knows*, because you are lying, and he *knows*. The argument persists but consensus settles like concrete: Quincy can tie you hand and foot with logic for a rope to bind the momentarily unsuspecting suspect. "He was my brother," Quincy grumbles, which of course *en Español* is still a grumble but sounds like *El es mi hermano.*

Caught off guard, Baldo flinches. But youth allows for alacrity and resilience, so the flinch is covered by a rare sound such as a mute might make when his mask strap grabs a hank of hair and pulls it. He looks up again with a sheepish smile and an unspoken, *Qué?* He flicks his fingertips from his lips outward then aims them at Quincy, who now asks,

"How is your brother?"

Quincy knows. Of course he knows. He is Quincy.

Baldo illuminates from this sudden flash and hangs his head to hide, knowing Quincy is behind this point and shoot and will see what is shown or not shown. So he shrugs and looks up again, this time miming constraint within the vertical bars in front of him. He glares at Quincy, who eases into a half smile and says,

"Go. See what you can see."

Baldo goes, shaking his head at the fat boys bobbing, sputtering, and muttering that nothing is below, *nada*, sustaining ineptitude with vigorous agreement. Slipping easily under a breaking wave, Baldo disappears into a spot in the water. Let them watch and wait.

The police splash toward the spot to intercept his emergence and take credit for what he'll find. This will be easy, since such a one will not yell for himself.

Those on the beach watch with more measured anticipation, knowing this is the brother of he who waits in jail, whose skill on stage may well be matched here in the water. Is not skill in the one conducive to skill in the other, even if the stage is up yonder, and here is merely deep and dark? In both we have youth, fitness, lithe muscles, and agility. This one has a mask and snorkel and so must be familiar with the roiling murk, unless he stole them. Never mind, the greater potential here is that the primary suspect's brother may soon reveal himself as the primary suspect. So he can't speak. So what?

Baldo is good for three minutes on a dive after a decent night's sleep. Last night wasn't so bad, but with its distractions and those of this morning, two minutes is maximum and plenty for a casual diver riding the undertow sixty feet out easily enough. Visibility wanes but improves on the upward angle, backlit by daylight. Baldo lets the bottom fall, leveling at thirty feet or forty. He cruises farther and rises slightly for the shallow ledge that parallels the beach and accounts for the steep shore break. Familiar with these thermoclines, he is not surprised by the sudden chill at each ten feet of depth, but something here warms as startling as any thermocline. Feeling for the bottom, he grasps something big with rough skin, perhaps a big, sleeping shark. He feels further, gently to avoid a stir, and straining to see. He can't say it is not a life, nor can he say it is, until its outline delineates, rounding and running far forward and back. This is no shark. It's too firm. It emits a tiny pulse but is too still.

He looks slightly up when the light fades and sees the shark overhead, a tiger big enough to swallow a man, even a chubby man in baggy shorts. Well, big enough for two bites. Baldo knows sharks; this one is a stray, too shallow for a tiger's special needs, drawn here, perhaps, for a taste of fisherman fillet.

Truth rises at last in an upwelling just ahead, a rising spring in shimmering light. Spewing from the canvasback beneath him is a stream of chunks and shreds, not fleshy but what Antonio calls shit *del mar* or chunky *paella*; the solid, rough-skinned form is a sewage line that runs a quarter mile out, which should be far enough to keep things happy.

But here its rupture renders it pissing distance from the beach. Perhaps the fisherman knew this and fished here because endless chum would attract the top of the food chain, and one catch could feed an entire family two days before rotting.

Baldo watches the cruising silhouette fade deeper. He cannot return the way he came, against the undertow that carried him out. So he rises to fifteen feet and swims easily in beneath the surface until he's shallow enough to stand and march slowly out. Catching his breath by Quincy, he holds up a hand until he breathes more easily, he folds three fingers and the thumb until only one finger remains—the forefinger—indicating that he will now explain.

He squats and blows a big raspberry. Quincy is not amused, so Baldo flicks his fingertips from his butthole toward the sand, then wraps his arms around a big, invisible pipe and points to the sand beneath them. In a slow rise he follows its path out. Holding up one finger again for further enlightenment, he interrupts the flow there, just there. His hands erupt for a fissure and little raspberries rising from the break. They drift up and down the beach, exciting the birds and most likely improving the fishing, if it's big fish at the top of the chain you want.

This last he conveys by miming a fish on the feed and then a fisherman with a hand line. His beach drama then conveys the oversize dorsal fin and row upon row of triangular teeth sharpened by nature for peak efficiency in cutting and tearing. Baldo does not fear sharks, so he smiles, dragging a toe across the sand in approximate outline of the shark just seen, then pointing to where he saw it. The shark may soon make the streets safer for those with no uniforms or guns. He removes Antonio from suspicion as well, the shark, who ate the fisherman. The fisherman was so foul that the shark got sick and puked him back up on the beach. Such could be the way of the natural mystery, could it not?

Quincy grins his biggest grin like his hero beyond the break, yet warms no further; not so fast and not so easy my skinny fish, he seems to say. He elaborates no further. Silence is the way of Quincy, who will spell things out only once at the end, just before the credits. Besides, he is walking into the surf, perhaps in afterthought but waving his arms madly and shouting at the tubby boys to come in.

Ponderously as men of law enforcement in transition from donuts to burgers, they confer and agree that this investigation is complete; nothing is here. Quincy yells, "*¡Sark! ¡El grandé! ¡Sark!*" And they churn the water to wash cycle.

Baldo laughs, can't help it. He must return to his duties, for the baby turtles have been over an hour with no one to monitor their safety or hunger or to see if their water needs changing. Or to guard against direct sunlight and attend to his ailing bird. These concerns are deftly mimed until Quincy waves him off one-handed and says,

"We'll be in touch."

Baldo nods and walks away, wondering, Hey, you got a hamster in your pocket, *Señor*? Why will you touch me? Why do you speak of *we*? Perhaps you saw Quincy on TV speak that way.

So the game plays out, each player betting and bluffing according to the cards dealt, according to skill and the influence from above. Baldo feels confident, feeling the influence from all sides and below the surface as well.

In an hour the heat rises to its apex and a man on a grimy mat over rusty bedsprings feels the sweat roll in a steady trickle. Sleep left him dazed and dizzy. So what, if he has only to lie on his back? Doors grind open and clang shut, and the voice of authority asks a question of failing objectivity.

"Has he confessed?"

Antonio can practically hear the dolt with the keys in an audible headshake. Maybe his teeth are rattling. Further interrogation is next, perhaps with a sharper edge now that Quincy has more facts. Antonio wipes his eyes and breathes deeply. He waits. Soon he smiles, for such a delay may mean that Baldo has done the right thing, which is nothing at all or something good. Perhaps the delay is so that conclusive evidence can be processed for proper presentation, so confession can be taken directly.

But that is probably not the case, and in any event, *¡Soy inocente!*

IX

Let's Do Lunch

A mile over and ten blocks down, two women are seated at a delightful table just off the promenade with a fabulous view of the "old fishing village." This last phrase is Mrs. Mayfair's. She bandies it about like her middle name, affixing it to the Mexican adventure that is her life today.

Lyria remembers not so long ago when it was simply a village where tourists paid the boat operators to ride out and try to catch fish, but the waterfront wasn't so cluttered with expensive restaurants and baubles for sale.

"Oh, this does look good. Doesn't it?" Mrs. Mayfair gently touches her fingertips to Lyria's arm, which seems to be a habit of hers, an expression of friendship, though Lyria can't help but think of what else Mrs. Mayfair reaches gently to touch, and with what besides her fingertips. Mrs. M sees her young friend look down at the point of contact and blithely continues. "Anything you want, dear. This lunch is on me."

Passing pedestrians can easily take these two as acquaintances out for lunch to catch up on old times. Few would suspect the principle industry of the day as liberating their common man from the local jail, where he festers helplessly on a murder charge. Well, there's nothing to do now but to kill the allotted time and then call Rudolph to see what can be done.

"He is the very best," Mrs. Mayfair assures. "I mean Rudolph. The lawyer. He'll know what to do."

Lyria nods, certain that the reindeer man knew what to do with the chattering *gringa*.

"You know, I have a taste for Mexican. I mean, not that any of these places aren't, but I mean *real* Mexican. You know?"

Lyria thinks Mrs. Mayfair's appetite is for Mexicans, *real* Mexicans, but of course they're not on the menu. She nods in appeasement of the mouth that won't stop.

Mrs. Mayfair studies the menu, simpering gratuitously and finally ordering *nopole* salad, shrimp cocktail, and a whole snapper, grilled. Lyria is not surprised by the excess but thinks the *gringa* has never tasted real *nopole* and won't like it because it's too slimy. She thinks Mrs. Mayfair orders it to fit in, but then maybe she has tried it and loves it because it's slimy. You know? But then the wasteful *gringa* ordered shrimp cocktail and grilled snapper too, which may be more than Baldo and Antonio would eat in a day. Lyria orders a *burrito*.

"That's all! Child, you must eat. We have a long day ahead of us. Please, bring her... do you have a special? Bring her the special. Please."

Lyria looks down, resentful of superior behavior. Mrs. Mayfair touches her again as prelude to apology. Lyria surprises them both by asking, "Why do you call me child? Why do you touch me?" She waits for an answer.

"It's only a figure of speech," Mrs. Mayfair says, withdrawing. "I am older than you. Not that much older, I don't think. I don't mean to offend you."

"Do you call Antonio child? You are older than him as well. Do you call him child when you make him do those things? Is that why you want *nopole* salad? Because he's in jail?"

"What? Oh, dear. Lyria, please." Mrs. Mayfair flashes color like a love struck squid in springtime. Beside herself with embarrassment, she blushes so immensely that her guilt is proven as surely as if she and Lyria watched an X-rated movie starring herself and young Antonio, who knows less of discretion than he does of caressing. Mrs. Mayfair wonders unabashedly what this girl can possibly mean. I want the *nopole* salad because Antonio is in jail? What on earth can she mean by those things I make him do? I don't know what *nopole* salad is. I thought this would be a good time to try it; I've seen it on menus. I like salad. As far as Antonio's behavior, well, she wants to make a lucky guess. That's all. He could *not* share the details of our intimacy with his prospective mate? Surely not, unless he did.

Mrs. Mayfair's view of Lyria as a young woman mildly jealous over misplaced hearts and flowers is dashed, gone to squiggly snow where a clear picture once was. She seems so sweet, this shy girl practically betrothed to Antonio, and he made no secret about her because it wasn't necessary. But tact is another thing, especially with a fragile heart in the balance.

A teenager in such an egregiously Catholic country could hardly be expected to ventilate a young man like Mrs. Mayfair can. Not that Mrs. Mayfair is simply available, but Antonio is not just any young man. Straining for resolution against the disbelief jamming her signals is the picture of Antonio describing the most private, least inhibited acts of love between a man and a woman, which seems neither practical nor fair nor necessary. Then again, we can't be certain of what he said or did not disclose.

"Let me explain something to you." Mrs. Mayfair touches Lyria with the fingers of both hands and breathes deeply, wondering how best to approach this delicate subject. First thinking euphemism best for the nerve now exposed, she shakes her head and clearly sees that beating around the bush will only widen the gap between them. No, she must come clean and state the case. But which case would best be stated, that she is a woman in her prime who is simply weak for a man in his?

Or that she simply loves him?

Or that she now understands the discomfort and difficulty such a liaison can cause?

Or that she was only trying to help by relieving the pressure on all fronts?

Or that she is willing to give it up, all of it, even the thing he does with his mouth? Moreover, that she will forswear his luscious lips enfolding exquisitely onto her own with perfection unmatched in the physical realm.

Or telling Lyria that she doesn't exaggerate, but promises the utmost of the summit of the grandest mountain known to women, if you happen to be one who likes to climb; that Antonio is simply the maestro, with a jut jut jut and a feather light lick that is so delicate, so simple and undeniable that no other man on the face of the earth has yet to figure it out. Well, we can't be certain that *no* other man has figured it out. Someone else may have. But none of the many men I know about have figured it out, except for this one and only. I mean, call him Latin rough and tumble and rest assured he is, but put that Billy goat gruff behind the first inch of wiggling tongue and you might as well call him Fred Astaire, because Lord, he can dance!

Obviously none of these cases can be presented to anyone's advantage, except perhaps the one about perfection in dancing, if it can be packaged as something wonderful to anticipate. But maybe not, and Lyria must anticipate that scenario and the rest anyway. Left with nothing to explain because the big, blatant picture looms between them, Mrs. Mayfair merely withdraws her subtle touch once again and asks, "What are we going to do?"

They look askew at opposing angles for an awkward moment, until Lyria glances back to see a tear rolling down the aging cheek. "I do love him, you know. It's not what you would call a romantic love, but more of a familiar, playful love. He is a sweet boy, and you're a sweet girl. I could tell you I didn't know, but I did. It's typical of me to think you would share. But I'm not here so often. And I do take care of him, you know, in a way you might not...."

Lyria reddens sufficiently to shut Mrs. Mayfair up, though the elder remains certain she has neither cleared the air nor eased the pain. Lyria wonders how a woman can spend such effort on makeup and then leave the tracks of her tears showing with no attempt to refinish. Lyria considers her own tears and how they may define the difference between two women.

Lyria last shed tears when her father died only a year after Antonio and Baldo's father died, which is already many years ago. Maybe a child who doesn't cry in so many years is abnormal, or maybe the sadness of life is subjugated to her strength, on which her survival has depended. Besides, crying is for children, and she's a woman with a woman's wisdom and a woman's experience. She understands Antonio's weakness but knows of no man more able to endure the rigors now upon him. For his resilience she should cry? No, Antonio did the right thing, because Baldo could neither comprehend nor process such difficulty. Even now the idea of a boy like Baldo, with such a handicap, in jail, isolated from love and understanding, confined in darkness; well, that could make her cry.

The salad arrives.

Mrs. Mayfair insists on sharing and divides the cold green strips into two portions. They eat, Lyria obliquely observing the rich *gringa*, who woofs the slimy shreds as easily as a woman at home in the world. But she seems too circumspect on the squiggles to really be at home. She seems at ease now simply because she's familiar with eating slime, isn't she?

Mrs. Mayfair dabs the corners of her mouth with her napkin and says, "This is so good. You must have it often." Lyria smiles weakly. "It must be full of minerals."

Lyria doesn't look up from forking a small load of the green and slimy into the hopper. "*Todos tiempos,*" she says, leaning over for a look at Mrs. Mayfair's watch. Hardly an hour to go, surrounded by gold and diamonds.

Mrs. Mayfair considers taking the watch off and presenting it as a gift to be worn proudly or sold at a fair price. But she lets that notion go the way of sexual explanation. A fair price can hardly be expected around here, and giving such jewelry is no better than sending cash to undeveloped countries. No, the downtrodden need conceptual guidance and hands-on instruction. An aging beauty queen can still yearn for penance and prove her commitment. She doesn't need Lyria's friendship, but anyone past a certain age knows that friendship is best. This isn't a matter of guilt, because no woman here is guiltier than Antonio, or that other one, Baldo, for that matter. This is only an awkward moment in an otherwise delightful lunch. The waiter brings a whole grouper, a six-pounder as warranted by such a gem-studded watch, splayed and grilled.

"Oh, my!" Mrs. Mayfair says.

El Planchar del Capitán Mexicali comes next, eliciting another whimper. Mrs. Mayfair calls for extra plates, and they share. The enchiladas and burritos are only average tourist fare, but the fish is superb, enough so, Mrs. Mayfair feels, to ease tensions with the best remedy, something good-tasting and warm inside them. "Isn't this yummy?" she asks.

"Compared to what?" Lyria asks back.

"Compared to the cold beans and tortillas some people are having for lunch," Mrs. Mayfair says. "Listen, dear. We don't have to be friends. We don't have to be friendly. I only thought it would make things easier. We have some important work ahead of us, and I, for one, prefer a friendly atmosphere to a hostile one."

Lyria looks down. "I'm sorry." Then she looks up. "But how can I know that you won't... When he gets out, that you won't..."

"That I won't what? Love him to death? Listen, dear. He's your betrothed. Not mine. I'm leaving in a few days. I'm sure you wouldn't begrudge a lonely woman her fond farewell in exchange for saving your fiancé from prison."

Lyria can't argue against such reason, nor can she appreciate the logical result.

"Like I say," Mrs. Mayfair says, pulling a long, curved bone from between her lips, setting it on the edge, and licking her fingers. "I would think you would be relieved. Of the pressure, I mean."

Lyria stops eating. "It is because of you that I have no pressure. The dam bursts into your head! It should be mine. Mine!

"Oh, my. I thought... I mean, Antonio said, well, he didn't exactly say it, but he gave me the impression you were...waiting!"

"No, *Señora*. I wait only for you to leave."

"But I'm not here, dear. Twice a year I visit, but the rest of the time he's all yours, and from what he tells me and, I don't mind saying, dear, what he shows me, you're waiting!"

Lyria fumes. "Waiting should be my say-so. Not his. As long as you give him what he needs, he won't need me. So of course I wait. Alone!"

"You want him unfulfilled?"

"I will fill him! I want him to need me, to beg me, to demand satisfaction from me, not from you! I will fill him!"

"Well, if you don't mind my saying, dear—"

"My name is Lyria. Lyria! Not dear."

"Yes. If you don't mind my saying, Lyria, I've had some experience with this sort of thing."

"Oh, yes, I know."

"How can you know?"

Caught in the matrix of her own hostility, Lyria realizes she can't know but can only surmise that a woman whose ears are grasped while her head is pumped full of *pinga* has tried this trick with many men. "I can know just as I know the sky will be blue tomorrow!"

Mrs. Mayfair dabs her mouth with her napkin. "Unless it's hazy. Or overcast. In fact, Lyria, you can't know and you don't know. It's obvious you don't know, because a woman with experience knows she doesn't need a year or six months to make a man crazy with need. A man like Antonio is good for *The Grand Prix of Oaxtapec*. He's good again in forty-five minutes. Or twenty. You want him to sit in traffic? Come on, sweetheart. Wake up and smell the coffee."

"What is grand prix? Is it a big *pinga*?"

"No. It is not a big *pinga*. It's a race. All out, very fast with no holds barred. Do you get the picture?"

Lyria gets the picture all right and wants to order a big fat *chorizo* so Mrs. Mayfair can suck on The Grand Prix. Yet she wants to know more of what this woman of experience might tell her. Because she, Lyria, does not know. And experience can fool you. Her own experience closer to the earth is deeper and more dynamic than that of a pampered, rich *gringa* twice her age. Still, this decadent *gringa* is not stupid and must have learned a few things from the many men standing behind the many *pingas* she has known over the years. Lyria fumes, dabbling with her fork, picking at her *frijoles* and an *enchilada*.

Mrs. Mayfair passes the *salsa* and says, "I don't know very much about cooking, but I think everything here is very good. Don't you?"

Lyria picks and eats. "Okay," she says at last. "What do I do?"

"What do you do? About what?"

"About Antonio. He treats me like a novitiate. He won't look at me like a man should look at a woman. I wait for his face to redden and his hands to shake, but he is like stone. I think it is because you come here twice each year to relieve his pressure."

"Honey, that boy has pressure for twice a morning, twice an evening and then some."

"So what is wrong with me? I think he...loves me. I think he wants one day to...to marry me. Is he afraid? Maybe he is afraid I will look like my mother. He wants to see a picture of her when she was young. I think he is afraid that if she looked like me, then I will look like her."

"You might," Mrs. Mayfair says, finishing half a fillet and lifting the bone clear. "That's why God invented plastic surgeons."

"What has my *madre* to do with toy fish?"

Mrs. Mayfair stops eating and stares, then blushes for the innocence facing her. "No, dear. I mean, Lyria. Not a plastic sturgeon; a plastic surgeon." She pulls her cheeks back and smoothes the skin on her neck. "They keep you young looking. That's all a man wants. These are my own, by the way." She hefts her breasts with the backs of her hands. "I wouldn't have wished for them, but they have their advantages."

Lyria looks at them and down at her own. "I have small ones."

"You have lovely ones."

"How do you know?"

"I can tell. The boys are wild for you."

"One boy is not. His brother gives me more of what a woman needs than he does. His brother is only sixteen. Almost sixteen."

"His brother? You mean Baldo."

"Yes, Baldo. He is a boy but very tall. Nice-looking but a boy. He wants to rub them at night. He thinks I'm sleeping."

"They're all boys, and he knows you're not sleeping."

"How do you know?"

"Please, let's dispense with that. Why do you pretend you're sleeping?"

Lyria thinks and then shrugs. "Wouldn't you?"

Mrs. Mayfair laughs, "I think I'd rise and shine. Oh, my. Sixteen."

"You think sixteen is good?"

"Lyria, dear. Sixteen can be a woman's dream if it's handled properly."

"You mean asking him to grab my ears?"

"What?"

"You know, grab my ears for the *pinga en la cabeza*."

"What? Is that what Antonio told you?"

Lyria nods.

Mrs. Mayfair fairly gasps, to think that Antonio could say such things to his *girlfriend*! She wants to tell Lyria that it's not true, but Lyria believes it so, leaving Mrs. Mayfair no leeway around a flat denial. "It isn't so. I mean it just isn't so."

Lyria seeks the elder's eyes, to tell if she's lying.

"I mean, Lyria, we did what a man and woman do, but it wasn't nearly as rowdy as I hope it will be for you with him one day."

"What day? I think you would like to be there with us."

Mrs. Mayfair rocks her head from side to side. "You know, there was a time when I would have refused that on the spot, but I'd consider it now that I see what happens in fifty years. I don't know what I wouldn't consider, as long as it was fun and nobody got hurt. And I was fond of the people involved."

"So, you are fifty?"

"No, I'm not. Not yet. But I think I will be before you're forty."

"Can I get you anything else?" The waiter waits.

Mrs. Mayfair hesitates on wrapping up the leftovers, it seems like such a schlep, but then wasting seems rude, and suggesting that Lyria take home the leftovers might be misconstrued. She asks Lyria with her eyes if the lunch is worth wrapping.

Lyria nods, "*Si claro. ¿Porque no?*"

Mrs. Mayfair orders grapefruit juice in a large glass with ice and *reposado* and encourages Lyria to try it as well. Lyria nods again, willing to learn what this woman knows. Soon it's only twenty minutes until time to call, with a fair repast under their belts, a few fences mended, and the warmth of a smooth tequila easing them into the afternoon. Mrs. Mayfair makes the call.

Making a connection on the second try, she is told by Rudolph Balsom that contact has been made through proper channels, that a certain lawyer in town is available and on the case right now. He's an old acquaintance of Mister Mayfair. Dialogue is underway but must proceed methodically, through proper channels. The young man in question is suspected of three additional heinous homicides and represents a windfall solution for several key parties involved. Solving these unresolved crimes further represents significant value to said parties, so solutions close to home will be quite dear. Processing will continue through tomorrow with efforts to establish a negotiated settlement, to see if justice can prevail.

Mrs. Mayfair offers listless gratitude and tells Rudolph Balsom to hold the line. She conveys the situation to Lyria, in the end bemoaning the inevitable night ahead, in jail. "Lyria, dear, I will spare no expense, but we can go no faster."

Lyria begs to differ. "Mrs. Mayfair. They will kill him. He cannot stay the night. We must help him escape."

"They won't kill him. They'll have no settlement if they do."

"They will harm him terribly. You don't know. They need him to be guilty."

"Rudolph, the young man's young lady is quite upset. She feels that a night... Yes. You do? You will?" Mrs. Mayfair responds to the lawyer's assurance that he knows what will happen tonight.

He asserts further understanding, which Mrs. Mayfair will not repeat. "I won't ask the nature of your involvement, Lena. But I suspect he's Mexican, which makes things no less harsh in a Mexican jail. I should think him a bit of a man and likely tempered to it. Beyond that, we must remember the gravity of the charge, suspicion of murder. Getting him back on the street tomorrow morning will be pretty darn good if we manage it."

"I'm sorry, Rudy. I just..."

"Yes. I know. You're a tender heart."

"Will I need to be there?"

"You must deposit a retainer with the lawyer, *Señor* Simón Salvador. He'll review his fee schedule and the other expenses with you. He's in contact with your husband, so some of these things may already be taken care of."

"Thank you, Rudolph.... I don't know.... We'll see.... Yes. Goodbye.... I don't know. Perhaps...."

Lyria gets the gist of Rudolph's proposed meeting.

Mrs. Mayfair blushes and calls him a rascal but a dear one. She hangs up with grim resignation, on the verge of great sadness.

Lyria watches until she regains composure and assures that "everything will be okay," which it may not be. With nothing more to do or say, it's time to go. They walk a block in silence, catch a cab, and ride two more silent blocks until Lyria shrieks that the plastic bag containing the pillowcase is still under the table.

¡Ay!

So they ride back for it and continue as they had, in silence. Mrs. Mayfair worries that Lyria will be fired. She says nothing, in order to avoid unnecessary stress.

Lyria wonders how strange it would be to have Mrs. Mayfair at her wedding. But if Mrs. Mayfair doesn't care, then she doesn't mind either, because, for now, at any rate, she likes this aging woman and feels she has learned something. She can't quite put her finger on it; so maybe the wisdom of experience has, as they say, rubbed off. Besides, if a young man is driven to ease the pressure as they all are driven, then better a *puta* of experience and taste than your average streetwalker.

When Mrs. Mayfair asks if today's absence will mean trouble, Lyria shakes her head and smiles, wheezing and coughing, feeling her glands, slumping her shoulders and eyes. "I am sick," she says. "I must not make the guests sick. I have stayed away for them."

Then it's time for Lyria to get out. Mrs. Mayfair touches her arm and says, "I had a lovely time with you today, Lyria. I'll be heading down to the you-know-where in the morning, first thing, say ninish. You're welcome to join me."

Lyria doesn't mean to stare but can't help it, seeing something new in the nemesis of her love. In a gesture of trust she shakes her head. "No. I work. You get him out."

So they bid farewell, not yet ready for the embrace but conjoined in peace for now. After all, the man between them is in jail.

Twilight finds Mrs. Mayfair fixing her evening face above her evening self, pulling her tummy in on a half twist for full advantage in the mirror. The lovely reward is not what it was, but then again it's more. She frowns. She smiles. She smiles wholeheartedly; there it is, the puss that won the west, or a fair corner of it, anyway. Not that Wendell Frederick will score the prize. He wants it so bad he can taste it, and he's a nice enough man with an unimposing disposition, which would put him in the running if the world were a better place. But score he will not, because he'll snore long before the witching hour instead of ordering more drinks and hungering for one more dance and then begging like no tomorrow, please, just this once, you and I. But no, dearest Wendell has neither the skill nor the stamina for romance.

Faithfulness seems a further·stretch to a hussy intimate with middle age and a hot tamale who's in jail. Still, an old gal winks in the mirror at the feeling between Antonio and herself. She calls it the love of her life as a joke and knows she isn't so old if the sap rises so readily in such a vital young man. Cocking her head in flamboyant resignation, she reaches slowly for the stars, closing her eyes and letting her beautiful hands light on her still-lovely loins, from when they slide, gently, for the silky feeling.

Milo sends Baldo home. Only a maniac would want to guard the little turtles night and day. Baldo nods vociferously, because he is and does, but Milo sends him on.

Baldo resists, miming last night's attack from the *tijerillas*.

Milo insists that another attack will not occur with Luís and Tomás on sentry through the night.

Baldo leaves with his injured bird, who rides beneath the wing of the protector. But they circle back to clarify hazards with Luís and Tomás, both of whom pledge diligence against a sneak attack until sunrise, when *El Capitán* will return.

So Baldo heads home at last, weary as a boy can feel, anticipating the comfort of cleaning himself and sleeping at home. He arrives cautiously, anticipating Quincy's secret troops. The place feels forlorn as a ruin of ancient times, empty of the life once lived there, deserted and cold.

Everything is as he left it except for the telltale pillowcase. He secures his bird beneath the table with an oyster shell of water and a piece of fish on the side. He plops onto his hammock for a short rest before personal hygiene, after which he will prepare for tomorrow and then go for something to eat. He falls asleep quickly and wakens to Lyria, arriving with dinner for a king.

Half a grouper surrounded by *Planchar* deluxe and nearly half a *nopole* salad sit him up and remind him how hungry he is. Lyria smiles and ruffles his hair and runs her cool fingers up and down his ribs like slender mallets on a xylophone. They practically stick out through his T-shirt—the ribs—and he writhes and squeals at her touch. He eats like a boy, but she gets him a beer because he looks tired as a man.

Entering her own house for a beer, just one, Rosa the mother waddles from the bedroom with a quixotic smile and a small item in her hand. Rosa breathes short, blushing and nearly tearful. "Here, Lyria. What you wanted."

In Rosa's hand is a photograph of herself taken a year before Lyria's birth. They stare at it together, until Rosa holds it next to Lyria's face for the spit and image that are one. Rosa cries, but whether she weeps for the joy of parenthood and the blessings bestowed upon her, or for the cruel fat awaiting her fair daughter is a matter of speculation.

Lyria hugs her huge mother in response to both potentials, because a mother like Rosa elicits love easily as a blue sky draws clouds. And such a hug hides her own tears.

"Come. Look," Rosa says, leading Lyria to the stack of pictures she has found.

By the time Lyria returns, Baldo is finished. The room smells of soap and he softly swings on the hammock, shirtless in fresh jams with his eyes closed. She sets the beer down within reach and watches him, until he opens his eyes and sits up with his pillow in his hands. He wants to know where is the telltale pillowcase.

She explains it is okay; that the woman with the *pelotas grandes* has disposed of it or will dispose of it. Baldo looks unconvinced but takes the beer and drains half of it and lies back. He scoots over to make room for her, for the solace siblings have to offer each other, she tells herself.

She removes her sweater to ease the constraint of too much clothing in a hammock and lies next to him. Soon she is focused on the ceiling, wondering what it is actually made of, breathing short and fantasizing that a growing boy given a beer will soon complain of needs unmet, that he will need milk.

This is because Baldo has lifted her T-shirt as casually as a pup burrowing through the fur to snuggle in for a nice suckle. She can't help the high-pitched sounds emanating from deep within herself and knows that this is one of those things that only a woman of experience can understand, and now she does. She smiles from within at the sound of cooing that only her love can release from the skinny brother who wields the vengeance. She wishes the lights were off, but then what would people think?

Next door, Rosa has a beer of her own and then another. Remembering those days and honestly feeling no different from then to now, she has another and counts what is lost and gained.

A few miles down the road in a cell with limited ventilation but not too many horrible noises, the darkness turns darker. Then it turns black. Complete lack of light opens Antonio's eyes to utter stillness. He anticipated the horrible sounds of men confined too long and driven to horrible acts. These horrors feel conspicuously absent in the tingly perfect blackness surrounding him. He senses something, but it's only fatigue creeping in, and his eyes gently close. They squeeze shut when a blinding light blasts him from sleep and a deep voice says, "This will take as long as necessary. We have some questions."

You have to wonder: when does Quincy sleep? Here it is six o'clock or ten or maybe it's two a.m., and he's still here, trapped like a prisoner instead of enjoying life out on the town with drinking and dining and perhaps some dancing, and maybe later some hoochie coochie fun.

Quincy settles like the troll under the bridge, first to his haunches, then to his pork-fed butt when a lackey brings a chair. He sinks affably to a full slump in the gut and shoulders, breathes laboriously, but seems happy to be here. With mordant satisfaction, he assesses what he's earned that nobody can take away, least of all the pitiful prisoner now in the unfortunate intersection of the cross hairs of his focus.

Antonio seeks facial adjustment to best reflect his own fortitude, somewhere between confidence and innocence with a dash of irritability.

Quincy says, "You know..." And a smile takes shape, because he *is* happy. His many teeth reveal the extent of his happiness. Antonio does not know, nor does he ask what he should know. Or who is meant by *we* in we have a few questions.

Who? You and *el pequeño* in your pocket? No, Quincy has nothing in his pocket but holes. Nor can he derive satisfaction like a normal man from the answers to a few questions.

Both men wait for the time it takes to measure the other.

Antonio measures the fear simmering inside as well, wondering how this casual approach to a few questions can indicate anything but the most horrible potential of all.

X

Sunny Blue Skies and a Brand New Day

It's all a ruse, a game, a formidable but futile attempt to intimidate by veiled threat. Antonio knows this in the first hour or two but will not succumb to arrogance, nor will he submit to what is not true. Well, he might submit; what else can you do? But he won't confess, because he's innocent. Quincy has nothing but stumbling utterance of his brother or someone else's brother, or you know, or he knows.

Get some clues, hombre!

Antonio wants to yell it or convey it with a smirk. But among the lessons assimilated early on by a young man on the fast track is the practical value of the low profile. Punch lines might be golden with a straight man wry as Quincy making the set-up. But such a rickety stage can make for hazardous delivery to a policeman, and Antonio knows it is sometimes better to concede the spotlight to the pudgy straight man with the bumpy face. Let him shine and have his say. See what follows, laughter or applause or the numbing stillness of an empty cell. Any way it goes, where can the fat man go from here?

Quincy may be fat and have a bumpy face but he's far from pudgy in the brain. He's lean and mean between the eyes. With his first twenty plays scripted on his clipboard he paces the sideline, at a distance, watching, seeking greater control.

Antonio answers carefully, weaving elliptical obtusion and dialectic lexicon like a seasoned apologist of the smoke and mirrors school. The exchange is tape-recorded. So why say anything that can and will be used against you? It's not easy to feign a most sincere yet obscure regret while staying on your feet and giving the illusion of progress.

You know what happened on the night of the twenty-second on the beach near the Hotel Oaxtapec, when Esteban Silvestre was murdered.

What? That's it? Is this a question? Or one of those veiled accusations designed to draw reaction, a confession, as it were? A twitch, a blink, a furrow or uncertain, nervous flex can give you up for guilty, but nobody speaks body language more fluently than Antonio; with chin up, back straight, eyes proud and everything relaxed, Antonio budges not one milimicron as he sighs, "No, sir. I am sorry to say that I do not."

"Your brother did it."

Who would respond to such nonsense? Not Antonio, who can stare into next week. He will offer no denial or equivocation. The statement has no more meaning than, say, the sky is green Jell-O.

So they sit and stare.

Antonio won't blink but finally states for the record, "*Señor*, my brother is a boy of fifteen years and a mute."

"Do you fish?"

"No, *Señor*. I'm sorry to say that I don't."

"Did you ever fish?"

"Yes. A long time ago, with my father."

"Your father is dead. Is he not?"

"Yes, *Señor*. He is."

"Did he...make you fish?"

"No, *Señor*. He did not."

"Then you liked to fish?"

"I liked being with my father. I can no longer be with him, except spiritually."

"Did you know Esteban Silvestre?"

"I don't think I know him."

"You know he is dead?"

"No, *Señor*. I don't know that."

And so on round the bend, slow and rickety as a cart dropping junk off the top now and then when Quincy mumbles aside something like, "Your brother carries a machete."

Antonio treads carefully behind the wagon, neither retrieving the trash nor stumbling over the big pieces, like this one that merits a nod and a clarification. "He uses a machete in his work."

"What is his work?"

"He opens coconuts for guests at the hotel."

"Hm. He doesn't take care of the turtles?"

"Yes. As of yesterday he takes care of the turtles."

"Where is his machete?"

"I don't know." Here Antonio slips with a half-smile tweaking past as he notes the need for a disposition on the machete. But the need is Quincy's; the machete has yet to be found.

Furthermore, Quincy misses the slipped half-smile because he reviews his play list too closely, proving the superior benefits of improvisation. How can you go to question nineteen just because it comes after question eighteen, if nineteen is a digressive query on turtle care after eighteen exposed a flank on a missing machete? You will surely miss your chance, and Quincy does.

Antonio hides his irrepressible relief with another sigh and a slump, which is not a loss of posture but a ruse, a distraction, in which he stares at Quincy's hair, calculating the mix between natural oil and bottled oil that lubricates the sheen. So the telltale smirk is not avoided but not detected either.

The game goes on. Into the night they volley from opposing baselines with neither man rushing the net. A tennis overlay gives a maestro a system in which to work that is better than free form. Let Quincy mumble innuendo and insult. Antonio hangs back and lets the ball come to him. No need to hurry the point.

In a few hours the harsh florescence loses its edge as first light fills the windows. Quincy rises too, saying that should do it.

Antonio doesn't ask what it is, but sits still as a trained, professional witness.

Far from insensitive to such acute skill, Quincy doubletakes on his initial hunch that such a performance may actually prove his premonition. He hesitates, and Antonio trumps him by taking a bumbling initiative that a trained professional would never take.

"You work very hard, *Señor* Quincy."

"Please. My name is not Quincy," Quincy says, but he doesn't say what his name really is.

"I think sitting in a jail cell all night asking questions must not be your first choice."

Quincy allows for another smile, the first since his last smile, and he sits back down. "No it is not. Tell me something. What is *your* first choice?"

Antonio smiles big; it's a fake, but Quincy takes the bait. "My first choice, *Señor*, would be for something good to eat and then maybe a beer, and then I would like to go back to the hotel, you know, if something is on TV, or else I will read from a book. I like to read books on business and the American stock market."

"Is that what you did last night? Go back to watch TV?"

"No. We only went back to bring something to eat to my brother. He is guarding the turtles now and he's very diligent. We had too much to drink. You know, Saturday night. We fell asleep."

"But you have a room at the hotel?"

"No, *Señor*. I watch the TV in the lobby bar."

Quincy takes notes for the first time, then stands and nods and again says that should do it. He moves ponderously on, taking leave, but turns abruptly to ask how Antonio, making better money than most in the area, could risk everything on a simple hatred.

Antonio squints for meaning, confident that he hates nothing.

Quincy spells it out. "Hector Diàz. You bludgeoned him for no reason on his way home from his office. Or maybe you have a reason. Lorenzo Lorca. You killed him with a knife in a similar way." Quincy waits.

Antonio looks up and says, "No sir. I did none of these things. I do not know these men. I'm sorry you cannot solve these crimes."

Quincy leaves, leaving Antonio to wonder if this last exchange will in fact *do it*. Perhaps the bumbling human touch helped assuage suspicion. A maestro must often depend on the corollaries rather than on assessment, and this is one of those times.

The corollary in this application is: *Who knows? Nobody can know until later. So why worry? It can only mess you up.* He reclines to the soft comfort of the corollary and closes his eyes to sleep.

In a short time he is comfortably certain that his final flourish was effective in diluting suspicion. He also realizes that he can't sleep with the sun rising, and here he is, on a tortuous side road off his proven path to development. Then again, no man is absolved from detours like this one, with its harsh conditions and disrespect and critical doubt on personal progress and, with the onset of fatigue, doubts on life itself.

Antonio has lived blessedly free of doubt, first as a child and then as a man who clearly perceived the changing world and its intolerance of caste. All the noise over *Mestizo, Castizo, Espomolo, Mulatto, Zambiago, Cambujo* and the rest of that ancient, hand-me-down constraint has no place in the modern world now geared to performance. Just look around.

Take a place like Jimi Changa's, where the dance floor goes wild with people meeting the common need, swinging, flailing, writhing, and grinding, enjoying life to the maximum, because that is all we have.

Do the wild dancers ask who your parents or grandparents were? I don't think so. Do they consider the lowly shrub that represents Jaime Ruíz's family tree? It doesn't matter, because Jaime Ruíz is now Jimi Changa. And what's that? A cross between the rock icon Jimi Hendrix and the deep-fried gut bomb called *chimichanga* is what. It works, because people see and laugh, which is all they want to do, because it's all they have time for. Even Quincy knows this is true, though Quincy appears far less tuned to modern times and most certainly doesn't laugh.

Antonio remembers his late father recalling the ancestors of two and three generations ago, with tales of caste distinction and of proper rising through the ranks of structured society. *Borquino, Cambujo, Mestizo, Coyote, Mulatto, Alvarazado* and the rest. Who can know which was best or worst? Who can say that one person is of higher birth than another? Look at Antonio Hector Molina Garza, with a touch of the yellow, a dash of the red, hued dark as madrona and lit above all by the rare spark of the maestro. What does Quincy know? Perhaps he too is aware of the ancestors and their superstitions that imbued the people with fear and constraint for too long. Surely Quincy can see in today's world who exactly is whom and where they are going.

Yet a short while after these comparative analyses between the rigid past and the overwhelming present in which each man will adapt or fail, interrupting the marginal numbness of the half-sleep, two men enter the cell. Perhaps now it is time to go home.

But then, why two men?

But of course Antonio Hector Molina Garza knows why two men have come to visit, just as he knows of the rigid past. He sits up as they sit him up, and he thinks again of the laughter that is a potential with every audience and, moreover, that every audience requires the laughter, no matter how bad the weather or their mood or state of digestion.

Except of course for this audience, who have come to work themselves, to extract that which fills a different need, to warm him up, as it were, in spite of his stormy night and foul outlook. They have brought another chair, a metal one just for him, and several lengths of rope. They bind him to it, hands behind and feet below. He wonders why not the cuffs again, but then he knows why not. The cuffs are also metal, which tends to scorch the wrists, which looks unsightly and reflects poorly on the investigative team.

One of the men goes back out for a small table, on which he sets a dirty jar of chili powder and a tall plastic cup of soda pop with three straws, no ice. The label on the jar is smudged with dirty red fingerprints, but Antonio can read it with little effort: *Tehuacàn*. It is the brand most famous for its complexity relative to hot surges, and for its efficacy in *tehuacanazo*.

One man reaches for Antonio's *cojones* as the other steps out again, this time for the twelve-volt battery and the jumper cables. The negative cable is clamped to Antonio's balls. The positive is set on the leg of his chair. The second man dumps three spoonfuls of chili powder into the soda, and as it fizzes, he sticks all three straws into the foam. Two straws go up Antonio's nose, which he can easily resist, until the positive cable is touched to the appropriate battery post, and resistance becomes Pyrrhic.

With two straws up Antonio's nose, the cap is secured to the rim of the plastic cup, and the second man blows into the third straw, driving the spicy foam up and into Antonio's head.

He has heard of such a thing but never in his wildest dreams anticipated its practice so close to home, or at least not on such a one as himself. In less time than the best schtick in the world can make the gamest audience giddy with laughter, Antonio Hector Molina Garza understands that a few things can never go away.

At least it seems like never, once your brain comes to a boil on chili pepper and your nuts soak another twelve volts concurrently.

When Quincy re-enters, Antonio's eyes are bigger than ever, and the bumpy-faced man smiles his sweetest smile, perhaps at this rare moment of professional efficiency.

"Now, *Señor*. We will try again."

Suffice to say that Antonio Hector Molina Garza proceeds posthaste on the path to maturity, instantly learning what makes a man. It's the pain that tells him he is a man beyond the doubts of boyhood and into the full power of manhood. The single transforming influence is pain. Some men take years to feel enough pain and make the change. An unfortunate few cross over in a mere minutes.

Antonio Garza will admit to murdering your mother or your son.

He will confess to illicit sexual relations with a turtle or his fiancée's mother.

Mass murder or any of the unsolved murders that Quincy wants to solve? *No problema.*

He will scream on cue.

He will blow huge red wads of snot from his nose and hock similar gobs from his throat. He will believe that blood is mixed in, and he will laugh, though his laughter is silent and within.

He will brace for the crack to his shins and his ribs. He will believe them broken and proceed to further confession; whatever is required.

Quincy says he doesn't like this, but then asks what else he can do. He can repeat the therapy, but then at a certain point, the questions twist so only a clear mind can follow them. And what good will a confession do for anyone if the suspect is screaming, "*¡Siiiiii! ¡Siiiiii!* I killed them all!"

Quincy remains calm, even in witness of such apparent pain. "How can you say you murdered the fisherman as well as the nun and the bartender, when you were working on both the thirteenth and the seventeenth?" Twelve volts and some spicy foam complete the question.

Antonio can only screech his confirmation, "*¡Siiiiii!*"

A very long time later, Quincy and cohorts fade away, leaving a twitch and a scorch in their wake. And maybe a whimper or two.

Antonio awakens far down the road, beaten to a daze, sweating into the heat of the day. He jolts with alarm, sensing human presence, and he feebly fends off the hands reaching toward him.

But it is only Simón Salvador, a man maybe fifteen years older than himself and impeccably dressed in a suit of apparently Italian cut and shoes that look as soft and pliable as Mrs. Mayfair.

And there, beyond the initial haze of disbelief, are Mrs. Mayfair's *tetas*. They press into the sartorial arm. Not to worry; she slides them on around and heaves them forward to their place of greatest comfort, nestling under Antonio's haggard face. She touches him gingerly as heirloom china that might chip or break. The well-dressed man steps back with austere indifference and authority. He winces in disgust and calls for the guard.

This man waits for no woman or sundown or payday. He is official but not governmental. His dress and demeanor make his independence as well as his position eminently clear to anyone entertaining the slightest doubt that here stands the other side of power. The man smiles as coldly as Quincy did, but unlike Quincy he offers his hand for a shake, which gesture conveys magnanimous dimension, because this man should touch nothing here, including a trembling client and especially if said client survives a recent and most personal inquisition. Which may be why the impeccably dressed man of power shakes only with the tips of his fingers.

But who can blame him in such a sty?

He doesn't look at Antonio but rather through Antonio. He pauses for calibration, and in a voice smooth as silk, soft as cashmere, and as notably scented by curiously strong mints, he says, "Come with us. You're going home."

Mrs. Mayfair is beside herself with constraint. This is not the time or place to demonstrate joy or relief or even the slightest affection. Besides these considerations of tact, who wants snot all over her taffeta? She steps back like a representative of society's divisiveness, as it were, approaching her love on the one hand yet avoiding him on the other.

Like a man rising from the ashes, Antonio rises. Testing his mangled senses with a blink, a nod, a bow, and a feeble grasp, he follows the lawyer out, leaving Mrs. Mayfair to bring up the rear.

Let Quincy see this entourage and wonder who's who and where we're going.

Outside in mere minutes, Antonio Hector Molina Garza experiences that phenomenon so common among professional athletes, politicians, and convicts of *el Norte*, which is that of the rebirth. Keening less on the instrumental injunction of *Jesu Cristo* than on the wealth and influence of Mrs. Mayfair, he steps simply into the outside world as if for the first time. His arms open in cruciform deference to suffering, and he breathes. Muscles ease their grip on bones, and the harsh imprint that no man wants on his curriculum vitae falls behind, already part of the past.

That's the kind of man he is, a man who knows his potential, who will redeem and follow his potential as long as the heart of Mexico pounds in his broken chest.

He knows now as well what some men know about freedom by way of its denial. Breathing deep for the clean, fresh feel of it, even though the air is hot and muggy and tainted with an oily mist, he savors the difference between here and just inside.

Señor Salvador recognizes the symptoms of severe inconvenience. But, he suggests, now is the best time to retire to his office to build a solid foundation, upon which can be erected the bulwarks, framing, and final polish of the sturdiest defense.

Antonio is speechless. The all-night interrogation proved his durability, but he has nothing more to say. So he shrugs and falls in line again, because nothing is left in him with which to resist. He wonders briefly what else is gone for the short term or the long one. Never mind, every battery needs a chance to rest. With faith in the magic that comes from nature, he will recharge just like the twelve-volt battery in the jail and soon be restored to proper energy. He turns to Mrs. Mayfair and nods in affirmation of everything she might suspect, including the horror of last night and the fantasy of the night ahead. Surely she understands. He senses only a dull, singed pain where once his *pinga* would have wagged playfully as the tail of a happy dog, a purebred with proper training who lives on a hacienda.

Well, it's hardly been an hour. The surge will return.

For now he is supremely relieved to be among friends and the other power. Happiness abounds, and he can't keep his arms from wrapping around his soft and scented savior, the female of the liberation. Slowly they embrace, which is quite a moment for both—clothed and far from playfulness or the physical conjunction binding their past.

They tremble as one, perhaps feeling a bit of the hard-earned manhood acquired last night.

He shudders with a wave of relief.

In their first such embrace the spirits join in the meaning of *abrazo*. Yet he falters, ever sensitive to unseemly appearance; this looks like a gamy mismatch. He is so dirty. She is so clean. "Never you mind," she whispers. "We'll get you fixed up right after. Good as new."

Grossly frayed around the edges, Antonio wants to know the cost of such a splendid defender, as if practicality must be measured against the extreme violence he would surely suffer again if the money weren't there. The question is hazardous and tasteless. For one thing, it could establish a debt that could set him back years on the rapid rise. For another, an act of love has no monetary measure.

So he doesn't ask again but simply sits and retells the evening of the twenty-second from beginning to end three times for *Señor*

Salvador. He further enumerates the names of those apparently dead people who are still in need of an identifiable murderer.

The kinks untangle at the soft, skilled hand of the splendid lawyer, who obviously doesn't care what's fudge or embroidery; each has its place in times of need. He laughs at the people named, some of whom he says are only half-dead and in need of facilitation but not yet in need of Antonio as a fall guy.

With focus on cohesive timing and placement, they buff the smooth transitions for a snug fit of the fifteen-minute intervals that comprise the night in question, intervals now on the table like body parts awaiting reassembly after a crude dissection.

A few documents are signed here and here and here.

Mrs. Mayfair signs a few too, scanning them quickly with assurance by the impeccably elegant Simón Salvador, who encapsulates those terms and conditions already discussed with her spouse, the esteemed Mister Mayfair. In short order it's down to farewell and heartfelt wishes for safe passage.

Antonio takes note of this *Señor* Salvador, who has nothing on anyone's historical or cultural legacy and who obviously mastered the lessons of rapid rising at an early age. The man is perfectly free of friction, so smoothly does the world turn in his presence. Antonio hopes his own foundation will lead to *élan* and *savoir-faire* of equal dimension.

Señor Salvador brings his heels smartly together with a quarter millimeter to spare between them. Silence underscores his departing drama, as he bows to kiss Mrs. Mayfair's hand with his gaze aimed directly at the floor rather than the dazzling abyss between her breasts. Ignoring this splendid buffet as only a giant among men can do, *Señor* Simón Salvador hopes they will meet again soon. He steps forward for a timorous fingershake with Antonio and says, "All of us will meet again." His perfectly manicured hand settling onto Antonio's back makes for self-consciousness in the once and future up and comer. But residual grit and grime from a night in jail become incidentals equal to *cero* as *Señor* Salvador presses knots in the rippling muscle mass. Working them deftly with a soothing touch, he counsels no worries; Quincy has *nada*. "¡*Nada!* Footprints in the sand are what he has. Ha! He better hurry. Do you hear me?"

Antonio doesn't say that survival the last thirty-two hours was hinged on this same presumption but rather says thank you.

Mrs. Mayfair slips into moderate flirtation, which includes the subtle but suggestive pucker that dazzles with a fresh application of lip gloss. Gratitude is capped with an easy cleavage squeeze and a sultry "Thank you so much."

Then it's down the stairs, out the door, and into a cab, alone together at last, on their way in the wondrous glow of another lazy afternoon. Silence is golden and more. They hold hands, Antonio and his heroine in humble ardor.

In a few minutes he is compelled to ask aloud if he's best served by going to the hotel just now. Moreover, should he not go home to relieve the tension for his brother and Lyria, and to clean himself?

Mrs. Mayfair says he could call them if they had a phone, which they don't. So going home is indeed necessary, except that it will pre-empt what will best serve her, which is to care for his wounds and clean him up. And, perhaps, to clean him out by opening and clearing the passageways of his manhood, which is not to suggest a claim on him or his time, except for the next two hours. Because she has, after all, sustained terrific expense and, worse yet, suffered profound anxiety herself, which isn't like what he suffered, but still. She asks only a chance to participate in the warmest homecoming a man or woman could ever want, which will enable him to pursue a proper homecoming at home. Because he can't very well check in with his fiancée and then check out for a little while for some of the hot and sweaty with his savior.

Well, she has a point. And a man on the far side of a hard lesson in the value of freedom does want to let it ring, wants to tell the world with a cock a doodle do that it might be sundown but it's the dawn of life anew. Besides, she will send word by way of a note that she can compose right now and have this very taxi deliver. Besides that, he can tuck his shirt in properly and stand tall and use the side entrance and take the service elevator. Then who's to know? And what if they do?

Finally, besides all that, she'll have him home by eight, eleven at the latest.

Oh, and besides that, they must review the legal documents and plan strategy and budget the defense. She slips the b-word in there slyly with a wry eyebrow so he won't feel tacitly indebted, but give a gal a break.

Antonio knows the score and in fact appreciates the leverage. Freeing him from free will, it also allows for the most efficient means available of calming everyone down, alleviating tension, and settling back to life as normal, which is what life should be.

Besides, she says with a tormenting look of sadness and joy, she is leaving tomorrow because she must, or maybe the day after. This will not only be a reunion but a farewell.

She has a point here too, and Antonio feels a tinge of regret for his failure as a noble man, who catches himself counting the four hundred fifty pesos surely accruing to such an evening. For shame, after all she's done. Do you think the spit-shined Simón Salvador would even answer the telephone for four-fifty, much less make a personal trip to the jail on behalf of a scorched and beaten client?

No, he would not, nor would he likely be so crass as to count mere tips where real loyalty is displayed. "But, my beautiful woman, I must ask you to be patient."

"Patient?" The wry eye waits for sophistry.

"I have suffered. Quincy has possibly hurt me. I must go very slowly. I don't know if I can…. You see…"

But Mrs. Mayfair saw hours ago that the fundamental process of caring and cleaning up would require the softest touch with a purr and a coo to see what is ready and what needs a day of rest. Her needs and ministrations come from spiritual love, only love.

Well, perhaps a half-hour of rest will do for starters. Who can know at this juncture? But still, care must be taken to ease the delicate parts back to the job they do best.

Compelled to atone for the sins of greed and ingratitude and for the other sins that never stop lurking in the shadows, he concedes her point of view. In mere moments he is laughing courageously at the sight of himself, the once and future maestro reduced to filth and grime, ascending if not truly rising in the service elevator.

Gladly yet slowly, peeling off his shredded clothing as if shucking his torment, he promises to be brief in the shower. By the fifth minute, however, the steaming hot luxury is so far from the muggy dungeon, he can hardly break away. The mistress enters with exotic gels and lotions and the soft touch that will soon tell them both the condition of the patient.

Redemption appears to be conditional and marginal, then breaks free to fulsome recovery for a thorough thank-you. Expressions of gratitude work out conveniently in the shower, so dinner can be savored without the nagging pressure. The savior and the saved dress partially and settle in to dinner by candlelight, which arrives shortly after initial hellos.

Following a light white wine with a smooth cognac, desert, and a reasonable step up in pace to a rightfully romping homecoming, the hours roll easily past eight and eleven, but not much past midnight, when consensus holds for departure.

The documents are signed, the man groomed, decompressed, and presentable.

"I may stay another day," Mrs. Mayfair sleepily says, reaching for a hug and advising, "Take a cab. The bus doesn't run this late."

How does she know the bus schedule? But what she knows is incidental to what she does with a roll of bills, which is stick it into his pocket. She tells him he is the very best of the loveliest men she's known, and she would be a fool to leave him in jail.

"And you too," he says in the way of freebooting men. Feeling spry and pleasantly numbed and certainly free of pressure, not to mention rigor, he ambles out the main elevator to the lobby and asks José for a taxi. Who cares who is looking? It's after midnight, and in this pocket are—hold on, wait. .

He tells the taxi driver, "*Noches. Calle de Madera, por favor.*"

And he counts: one, two, three, four(!), five hundred pesos! *¡Caramba! ¡*What a lady!

He rides as if weightless on a magic carpet, keenly aware of the difference one person can make and where he would be this minute without her. Strolling into the little *casa*, he is quiet so as not to waken Baldo. He lights a candle, and there they are, Lyria and Baldo, sleeping in each other's arms like children, as he and

Lyria once did. He feels another wave of gratitude for love so bountiful it drives his fiancée and his brother together in his absence, as if their love helped bring him home. He thinks it did but feels something more, which is hard to place but has to do with innocence and the changes life holds in store.

Look at Lyria. She is pure as the day he first remembers them in the same bath. She retains that innocence, always has, though his innocence feels long gone, traded, as it were, for the benefits of development. Such is the toll life takes. Good life, hard life; it doesn't matter. At least the rise of Antonio will continue to bring the whole family up. Let no man or woman doubt the loyalty and devotion here.

Yet a tinge of remorse accompanies his gratitude for this day of liberation. Torture leaves a permanent stain. The days of innocence are gone. Then again, a certain type of man is grateful even for the opportunity to make sacrifice, lest so many lives be lived without a chance for improvement.

Never mind the regrets; his pain shall be everyone's gain.

He undresses and slips into his own hammock, grateful as well that Baldo is man enough to fill his shoes in his absence. Who better to comfort such an innocent than his perfectly innocent brother? Well, maybe not perfectly innocent. That will take some sorting out. But he is innocently motivated, at any rate. And he never said an unkind word about anyone or anything.

Antonio resists the urge to wake them and celebrate, to tell them all that happened, and to learn about the pillowcase and the machete. He knows what they've been through, working as if today was simply another working day, tormented by not knowing. But he slides in quietly and joins the peace, sighing deeply as a man whose homecoming is now complete, surrounded by those who love him. Hardly as insensitive inside as he often appears on the surface, Antonio closes his eyes to better halt the welling tears.

He regrets the whole turn of events but feels worse about the pressure imposed on his own family. We cannot know if Esteban Silvestre was a bad man, but we can get a fairly good sense of it. We saw him in ruthless murder, as if no life counted but his own.

A man given to killing so freely should sense the eternal presence of the Greater Judge. In this case God moved through the hands of the bailiff, an innocent who merely carried out the sentence of the court.

Antonio looks aside at the raft moving slowly downstream to join his loved ones in sleep. He is on board, yawning hugely where the delta meets the sea, drifting further on placid waters until the sorting process settles flat to every horizon.

Is a solid foundation as a maestro a good place from which to begin a career of elegance and good taste in the legal profession?

And soon all slumber.

XI

Life Goes On

The unfathomable dimension of some women, Antonio thinks, no matter how much their minds are open to learning, is the one where they keep their moods. They most often fail to fit the moment, these moods. Like now, with the sun about to rise and relief overflowing, she seems tentative and uncertain. Perhaps the truth is too much to accept all at once. Surely she can't be pouting over the few short hours of delay in the homecoming. They were required for gratitude. Still, she seems nearly nervous.

Not Baldo though; like a pup left home alone, he's all romp and ready to go, a certain beast of simple pleasures but noble in his simplicity and motivation. Lyria gathers her things about her loosely and hugs her betrothed, telling him they will talk in a little while, but for now she must hurry home to prepare for work. Today is Monday, when everyone must look sharp. And be sharp.

Baldo stretches like a rubber man, bringing a smile to his big brother, who must look up today to meet Baldo's eyes. Antonio laughs, "Two days I'm gone, and you're grown higher than the top of the door."

Baldo stands tall under the door to see if the top of his head will touch the frame.

"Mm," Antonio says. "Monday already. What a lovely weekend."

Baldo nods, moving to the table to stoop and care for his bird, who gurgles and squawks when he pushes a piece of fish down its maw. At the sink he squeezes too much toothpaste onto his brush.

Antonio watches him brush with pneumatic vengeance, but the elder brother only smiles. "Baldo. Where is your machete?"

Baldo mimes the hurl over the breakers, flinging toothpaste in his ardor.

"And the pillowcase?"

Baldo indicates Lyria and the other, grasping imaginary *melones* for the other. He shrugs.

Antonio nods. It seems too slapdash for comfort, but at this point a reasonable man can only feel good, having Simón Salvador on his side rather than having an underpaid civil servant, even if the civil servant was as resourceful as Quincy and Quincy had nothing.

In a few minutes the young threesome stands together close enough to hug, because it's Monday, and the bus is full.

Antonio feels the giddy current among them.

Baldo makes elbowroom when his bird complains.

Lyria looks annoyed, as only she can be over such simple things.

And Antonio grins for no other reason than life goes on in the sweet air of freedom to bring his life to its rightful fulfillment. The future feels intact. Which is no small feeling and certainly nothing to sneeze at. Whether more hurdles await is another story that must be examined sooner or later. But not today. Today is meant for joy.

Baldo feels it too, laying his head first on Antonio's shoulder, then on Lyria's.

Lyria adjusts to a reality too good to be true, looking at one and then the other and then at neither, as if sorting a reality that only yesterday seemed out of reach.

Antonio shivers in mere anticipation of the rich, hot *cafe con leche* that will soon flow through him as prelude to the renewed flow of life's simple pleasures. In a few minutes more he tastes the warmth and richness, sipping in overview like a lord of the manor.

To the west, just inside the laundry room, stocking her cart, Lyria is industrious, stolid, a strong-willed woman with a pleasing if not dramatic figure, with good hips and handsome *titas* that already point and swell in preparation for Antonio's own two hands. One day soon she will be his. She will bear his sons and, in keeping with the modern world of right values, his daughters. Soon seems sooner still with advances into the future like last night's, filling the jar with another five big ones. At this rate, the rim will be met by the end of the year, and they will wed. That will be something, both the wedding and the wedding night with such a rare tomato, so pure and ripe she nearly splits with too much juice. Antonio will ease her in as only a man of experience can do, with gentle compassion for the inexperienced.

Does marriage portend the end of Mrs. Mayfair?

He needn't make any drastic decisions just yet. For one thing, twice a year can hardly be called unreasonable. For another thing, little Tono boy will want the very best in clothing and education, and such a standard can hardly sneeze at five hundred a night. For yet another thing, Mrs. Mayfair must be disengaged easily, both as a sensitive, generous woman and a proven and trusted friend.

For one more thing, there she sits, making the most of her last day, lying back with her eyes closed, watching the replay that makes Antonio smile as well. She seems happy, all greased up for a last hurrah of Mexican sun, her grasping hands bikini lifting and spreading as if revealing her heart for sacrifice to the gods of poolside joy.

And there is Baldo, archangel of mercy and justice delivered. Antonio observes his brother's oblivion and focus, as if recent events are merely part of life's spicy mix, as if killing and caring are equal to a time for every purpose under heaven, as if he, Baldo, is the meadowlark on the fencepost singing this sentiment sweetly.

The bird is swaddled in a clean bandage and feeds again.

Each baby turtle is lifted and inspected and in silence encouraged to grow and be strong, as the silent boy has done. Anyone whose heartstrings ever plucked a chord for nature knows the tune flowing into the little turtle ears. The babies listen in perfect stillness until he's done, then they flop their flippers in thin air as if the depths are felt by what he imparts to them.

Antonio feels the richness rising with the rising Sun, who seems equally pleased with his lovely planets in orbit. Soon Antonio is ready for the new guests who have come to let their hair down and have fun! With his cards neatly stacked, his dry-bean jar full of new, clean beans, his numbered balls loaded in his spinning basket, his public address system tested and working with hardly any warp or static, the first morning bingo can begin. "Er! Er-er! Er-errrr! Wake up! Wake up, everybody. No more *siesta*!"

Oh, how they moan and groan but move lovingly in compliance, rising for their cards and beans. This looks like a very good group indeed.

"Okay! Not even lunchtime, so we play for one Bloody Mary! You need it, so only one line, up or down or diagonal. Okay! Wake up! No more *siesta*! Er! Er-er! Er-errrr!"

With only a brief respite after lunch so that Antonio can relax on the eighteenth floor to revive and refresh himself and further repay the generosity shown him, life returns to normal.

Mrs. Mayfair merely touches his cheek with her fingertips to thoroughly convey her sentiment. She will miss him. Gone by one, airborne by two, she is winging overhead by two oh five, looking out the window as he looks up. *You are my saint*, he thinks.

Oy, the pillowcase, she replies. But looking down on the adobe and asphalt miasma called civilization, she reckons that a taxi was likely the best place to lose Exhibit A. Lingering in the few thousand feet between them is her promise to see him soon and his fervent desire to make it sooner.

So the days and nights settle as they once were before Mrs. Mayfair's last visit.

Antonio saves his money.

Lyria works hard and then works some more, and though her beloved wonders what happiness she finds in life, he doesn't press.

He rather goes along with her unspoken premise that these shall be the days of struggle so that those ahead may fill with ease and security. He marvels at her resilience and womanly resolve at such a tender age.

Baldo will not come home until way after dark, until the night sentries arrive, most often near ten o'clock.

So Lyria takes him his dinner, which he eats on the beach by the turtles, or else he takes it with Lyria to the laundry room, where a good maid can sort her needs for an orderly tomorrow. She looks healthier now, though her diet has not changed and she gets no more exercise. She fills out like a woman does, her breasts rising and heaving like competitors sprinting in the stretch. Not as big as Mrs. Mayfair's, they grow rounder with a youthful exuberance defying gravity and the aging process.

Antonio keenly observes this change with pride and pleasure, not to mention anticipation. Yet he is fearful as well. For one thing, a bosom so resplendent will draw strays no less than stink will draw flies.

For another thing, hefty *chichis* are one thing, a good thing. But they often precede hefty thighs that chafe and blot all light in the gap beneath the sacred place, and that's a thing of a different nature; call it bad. He fears the way of Rosa, and his heart and eyes grow heavy with apprehension of a *gorda* wife.

Just so, she reflects his worry. What will he do when she grows fat, go fishing?

He presents her with a pair of shorts, rayon and form fitting to show off the mystically succulent orbs, *donde las espaldas pierden su nombre*. But reference to where the back loses its name is only polite language; her luscious buttocks ride high and inviting with such luxuriant spread that any man popping an eyeful will need no words, polite or otherwise, to convey his love. Ogling as well her rich, tawny thighs, Antonio realizes that his mad lust can only derive from love. And from waiting, as purity and virtue dictate.

You can't really avoid the stray dogs sniffing the bush on a package like this one. Antonio wants to see her figure on display, because soon she will be his, fore and aft, to have and to hold for all time, and seeing her exquisite componentry now will provide a baseline from which to compare the fat, if it comes. He won't press her to wear the shorts for fear of another emotional failure like the one following his innocent request for a picture of Rosa in youth. She will wear them in time, maybe not until the night of nights, but she will. No woman can find peace forever in a maid's baggy dress.

Meanwhile, life brings a change for the worse to Rosa, who takes to drink and melancholy. No one can say why or when, except that the evening of finding the old photographs and drinking through her nostalgia seems to mark the beginning of her downturn.

Baldo and Antonio awaken most mornings to retching sounds from the *casa* next door. They try to ignore the awful discharge, until Antonio winces and shakes his head. Sometimes he mutters about an old, fat woman who can't control her drinking in spite of the awful dues she is made to pay.

Baldo shrugs and shuffles to the table where he stoops to feed his bird and then shuffles to the sink to brush his teeth.

So life fills another day with bingo, pool volleyball, beach volleyball, swimming pool aerobics, and shapely *gringas* shamelessly exposing themselves. Now and then they make shameless proposals that a practical man pursues only when the return is handsome.

Stocking the cart and cleaning rooms, feeding the turtle babies, and changing the water in each tub, counting and encouraging and staying late; all these things roll together next but not as tedium. No, they form a rhythm. Life is good with repetition and method.

Antonio feels himself change as well. His compliance with the rich *gringas* is now casual compared to his former exuberance.

Hello, how goes it for you? Thank you for your business.

He accepts these women as they accept him, as a convenience and a bounty, just as every sunrise needs a sunset in order to come again. Between the two are the goodly pursuits of every day. Antonio cashes in on his rippling abdominal rack, pectorals that look cut by a sculptor and veins popping on his biceps. He knows that these things too shall pass. In the meantime, a hundred sit-ups and a hundred push-ups are insurance. Money in the bank, *mas o menos*, as long as a demand needs a supply.

Crunches?

Mañana.

Baldo too finds a new complacence, no longer holding each dead baby as if grief can bring it back. Learning that life brings grief no matter what, he inures to difficulty, plucking the dead and walking them down the beach to the water's edge, gurgling incantation in his muted, hoarse way until hurling it with God speed over the surf. From the hundred twenty-three babies, a hundred four survive with only six weeks until release.

And on a day like all the rest with no fanfare or indication, it's time to give back that which nature gives.

Baldo unwraps his convalescent bird for the last time. It huddles uncertainly, perched on his arm, so he sets it on the arm of a chaise lounge and opens its wings, working them gently, stretching them to flight position. He holds a piece of fish up to the bird, who reaches for it. But this time Baldo pulls the fish away. He shows it to the bird once more and flings it toward the water.

By now the guests on the other chaise lounges sit up and watch, and those poolside gather for the show, which isn't a show, really, unless your contact with nature is limited and most often expressed with sunscreen.

Baldo ignores his audience with aplomb equal to his brother's fervent courting of the same audience. He lifts the bird to his arm again and walks it to the water's edge, all the while whispering something confidential in its ear. Perhaps he reminds it of the beauty of flight and freedom. Perhaps he asks it to refrain from eating *las tortugas chicas* and warns it as well to stay clear of the nursery. Perhaps he assures this exquisitely winged creature of the rich days and nights ahead that only such a bird will experience.

The guests can only speculate, which they warmly do, some enthused to the point of emotion.

With a gentle uplifting of his forearm, he delivers the gift of flight, delivering the bird to its proper life again. He watches for a minute in a fanciful flight of his own. Turning away, he wipes a tear from his eye and sees on his walk back up the beach, as if for the first time, that many guests observe him.

They cheer with a standing ovation. He is the man of the hour.

Nobody from management praises Baldo, because Milo squelches all praise not for himself. Even so, any fool and Milo can see the lavish good cheer of the guests. They view *las chicas* frequently now and talk of the amazing man who guards them.

Baldo doesn't mind the turtle babies being held for photos, but only after inspection of the hands for sun grease and other hazards.

They love his diligence, the guests, and he brings home tips no one could have foreseen, especially Milo. Not as big as Antonio's tips but formidable; these tips rising from the heart, not the pocket.

Whoever heard of tipping the turtle guard?

Nobody is who. But on another eventful Saturday a quiet man from Chicago and his quiet wife, both decrepit and very near the end of their journey, give Baldo a hundred dollars.

They smile and say nothing in deference to his special dialect.

He stares back for what appears to be a lengthy exchange, until they too shed tears and hug him. He gives the money to Antonio, who puts it in the jar with a fervent Er! Er-er! Er! Errrr!

Milo sees. Milo knows. Who cares?

Nine hundred twenty pesos are more than a tip; they are tribute. They make history and set the bar so high that no man or woman will clear it anytime soon.

Baldo is known, and then he is renown. He is secure in security, and top management takes only an hour to grant his requisition of six more plastic tubs to accommodate the babies, now twice as big as six weeks ago. A second requisition comes from his big brother, always with an eye on the future, who foresees the day after the day of turtle liberation, when *El Capitán de las Tortugas* stands alone with nothing to guard.

Antonio makes a memo to management, through Milo, in which he anticipates continuing need among those guests experiencing thirst and hopes that a position to serve such thirst can be reinstated on the staff ledger. Job description: coconut cleaver and server.

Anyone who can't see through this transparent nepotism is enlightened by Milo, who protests that his own annual efficiency rating is based on service relative to payroll, and that another person poolside is unaccountable, as well as irresponsible and frivolous and, for all we know, dangerous. No, Milo insists, we cannot justify an addition to the staff. Brother Baldo will certainly be considered next year for another stint as *El Capitán*. We'll be in touch. Thank you.

In the meantime, what? You think we would allow him near our guests with a potential murder weapon?

Checkmate. No other persons are now required.

Antonio coyly concurs, but in the cordial aftermath he suggests that we're not talking increased overhead here. We're talking standards in service.

My assistant can cut and serve the coconuts. He has experience. With his young charges already beating the reaper by a hundred percent growth with only twenty percent mortality, and with care and feeding down to a routine that *El Capitán de las Tortugas* can do in his sleep, slicing a few coconuts amounts to *nada*. What's more, Baldo is now a man of esteem, willing to serve it up with expertly presented coconuts.

They love him, the guests.

This proposal requires a day and a half gestation, but it too achieves new life from on high. Halfway into week seven as *El Capitán*, Baldo approaches Antonio himself in tips, because now he, Baldo, has two sources, which anyone even remotely aware of personal advancement can tell you is better than one source.

Antonio anticipates approval and buys a new machete, since a requisition for that item could draw attention to unsavory and as yet unresolved circumstance. Not that circumstance remains unchanging. In week two and again in week five, *Señor* Simón Salvador himself makes personal visits poolside in irrefutable proof of Antonio's innocence. At least such a visit proves Antonio's inevitable exoneration, or at the very least it proves that Antonio's benefactress is deeply solvent and will go the distance on this one.

Antonio rises to these occasions of svelte, suave dialogue with a man in a tailored suit and shoes of appropriate pliability. In his heart of hearts, Antonio wishes *Señor* S would wear a different fine suit from one visit to the next, from the many fine suits obviously hanging in his closet. Never mind; the staff won't notice that it's the same suit as last time, what with three weeks between visits, and the guests can't know, because they only arrived last weekend.

Señor Salvador assures his client, though he describes a reality based in motions, filings, response times, defaults, summary judgments, and possible proceedings. This is all very good indeed, *Señor* Salvador reiterates, assuring Antonio that Mrs. Mayfair is staying in touch, just as he too will stay in touch. So don't worry.

Well, to tell the truth, Antonio wasn't worried, not like he is now, for Mrs. Altmont Caruthers of the Dallas Carutherses steps serenely into the personal space between Antonio and the lawyer. She glistens in full sheen between the two, plucking a pesky gnat from its death wallow in the grease pooling just below her sternum. The portentous tributary running down the center of her chest is not as spectacular as that of Mrs. Mayfair with her grasping hands, but Mrs. Caruthers knows how to work a crowd, even if only a crowd of two, as long as they're men. "You are so good at that water exercise. Are we going to, you know, do it again today?" Not waiting for the affirmative but turning quickly to *Señor* Simón Salvador, she offers her hand. "Hello. I'm Elizabeth Caruthers. Call me Liz."

"*Con mucho gusto.*" *Señor* S responds on cue with his instant non-click of the heels and a gracious bow that puts his lips a hairsbreadth from her greasy hand, his nose a whiff's distance from the dazzling cleavage. Antonio smiles, proud as a facilitator on ascent among the long-standing denizens of the social stratosphere. He feels perfect, knowing when to stay as mum as a mute brother so nature can take its course, which it most often wants to do.

Mrs. Caruthers understands that *Señor* Salvador is of professional status in the legal field and wonders if he might be available for, you know, legal advice on the purchase of real estate here on the, you know, beach.

"*Si claro.* But please, Liz, I am not well versed in such matters. I have a friend who will call on you, if he may."

"Well, yes, I suppose. I just thought it might be nice to..."

"Yes. It will be very nice. We will be in touch. Tomorrow. Or the next day."

Mrs. Caruthers is unaccustomed to such power that can avoid a well-preserved woman, more easily than a mighty river can avoid a rock.

Here may lie a lesson for a young man on the rise. Would not a romp with Mrs. Caruthers be a good and possibly lucrative experience for a rapidly developing portfolio? Of course it would. Yet this man long ago risen tells her that it may be a good thing, and maybe not.

¡Ay! This is power.

So a time is set for nature to play out, which may be tomorrow or the next day. Or never! Such is the whim of power.

At this juncture Antonio worries less and accepts more the idea that the steep fees piling up are well spent. This is not only defense but also continuing education toward the advanced degree. Besides, the expense of a thing is of no concern to a man so thoroughly covered.

Two weeks later, just after Baldo's promotion to the double tier, *Señor* Salvador returns. He waits in the shade watching Antonio until a break in the action presents itself. Antonio is schmoozing with a guest, delivering happiness and the exotic charm that memories are made of, if you're a certain kind of guest. He pours it on so *Señor* Simón Salvador can see the substance of his performance.

Señor S nods warmly, indicating his appreciation of a job well done and says that it's time. The hearing is set for next week, in which the future may be told, whether they will proceed to further legality, or if the matter will be resolved with prejudice. The lawyer is optimistic toward the latter, anticipating best-case scenarios and potentialities of varying parameters. Antonio need not attend. Strategy calls for a straightforward motion for summary judgment in favor of the defendant. The appropriate, shall we say, powers are, shall we say, in place. Mrs. Mayfair will be here.

"With prejudice?"

Señor Salvador broadens his smile in effusive tolerance of the legally uninitiated. Grasping the muscles across Antonio's shoulders again precisely on the sore spot, he tweaks it with uncanny effect. "Don't you worry, my friend. It is good." He scans the face of his client as the little massage finds deep tissue.

Antonio bows his head for the relief of the thing if not in abeyance, and he moans. Yet he wonders how a best-case scenario can be good with so many variable parameters.

Señor S says, "I know you're a busy man, and really, I must go."

Antonio is left standing alone rubbing his own shoulder and assessing legal prospects. He smiles over prospects for a romp with Mrs. M, only a week away.

True, he releases the pressure from time to time among the poolside women, but such frolic has limitation and risk. A man in the spotlight with such a fantastic body must never initiate sexual contact with a guest, no matter if she is *gringa* or Mexican, for that is grist for the harassment mill, and many would as soon share this spotlight as soothe the swollen *pinga*. Besides, after a day of nonstop entertainment and optimism, a nonstop night can leave a man sorely pressed to shine tomorrow. And what if the level of tipping is less than decent? Sure, it is mostly enjoyable with these women, once initiative is established as hers and the charming chitchat is done and the piston properly slides in the cylinder at adequate rpm so the little engine purrs. But with the lights out it all feels the same. Maybe not exactly the same but close enough. Falling fast asleep at two a.m. with a rise and shine only four hours away, the days seem terribly long. They start again with too little rest in between.

At least with Mrs. Mayfair initiative is foregone and it's money in the bank. The cock crows an hour before sundown and an hour after with gymnastics uniquely hers. Then it's all comfy cozy with three pillows each, lying in bed with thirty-two channels and the remote in hand. He wonders briefly if Mrs. Mayfair will have enough money to see him through. But of course she will.

He wonders how a natural beauty like Lyria could approach her prime in life and turn suddenly morose. Like now, with one foot in the laundry room and one foot out, sorting and folding and watching the clouds in sad resignation. He suspects she is hitting the bottle with Rosa and hopes this is the case. The bottle would explain her depression and sudden weight gain. He has seen a special report on heredity and alcoholism. Could it be the gin that turned Rosa *gorda*? Her gut, Rosa's, is not the low-slung tub of fat hanging like a water bag from most *gordas* but is round and firm like Joaquin the bartender's.

Can it be that Rosa has guzzled gin all these years when he thought her so nice and so caring and so much the mother in place of his own? Of course it can be, and such a state of affairs would require re-examination of those events, in which Rosa was actually dead drunk on gin. She must have been. Drunkenness wouldn't make her less loving.

If it's the whiskey gut growing spherical on Lyria too, then she can be spared. With help and guidance and Antonio's encouragement, Lyria can break any habit.

And yet: *Caras vemos, corazones no sabemos*; faces we see, hearts we don't know. Could it be that a thing exists of which he had no clue whatsoever? If so, what else could be misperceived, misconstrued, and unknown?

At least he doesn't need to wait ten years or ten months to see if his betrothed will turn fat, nor must he press his beloved to quit the gin to spare the *gorda*. In a month or two we will see if a thing is true, a thing so strange a man can hardly imagine. He will speculate no further, because worry is a futile endeavor, and numbers cannot lie.

The women in their last days of voluptuous glory need what Antonio can give. They pose and look their best for sultry seduction with many cocktails and low lights. They love the power of a Latin hot-blood with tantalizing charm, high spirit, and rippling body. They swoon to conquer, then whimper in submission. Yet they know nothing of humble origins or manifest destiny. Except for one who does, who offers respite from his current uncertainties.

Soon Mrs. Mayfair will arrive. Perhaps she will help sort things out.

XII

Rapid Development in its
Varying Phases

Antonio Garza has long felt his prime approaching. He anticipates seasoning with bulk and definition to age thirty-five or even forty, because even an old man has more power if he's developed. Due diligence on a hundred fifty times three each morning will lead to dominance on all levels. One hundred forty-six. One hundred forty-seven.

Besides the practical return, a grunt and a sweat can also remove a man from thoughts of greater difficulty. How can you worry about romance and what simply cannot be true but is, if you're straining to complete your reps?

One. Two. Three. Four.

Yet a pain seeps into his heart even in triumph over physical limits. Blood vessels bulge on bulging muscles while breathing is controlled. Focus seems secure but warps with the burden of life and its wily ways.

Is he not kind and compassionate, willing to give back love for love? He thinks he is, and that his heartfelt anticipation of Mrs. Mayfair's arrival is not a sign of weakness but rather a symptom of what Mrs. M herself would call maturity. The women of the world raise a common voice against the men who want nothing but to feel the *chichis* and pump the bushes. Then they're gone, the men, with a frivolous *adios amiga* that gives nothing to the women who give their all.

Antonio Garza is not like that, or least that part of him fades as he moves ineluctably toward his prime.

Mrs. Mayfair is the bearer of many wonderful openings that welcome his surge, and she loves him for it. But she is more now a true friend and confidant, not to mention savior. Is he then wrong to count down the days from one hour to the next until her arrival, until she relieves the pressure with a vengeance and tells him life will be good again, just you wait and see? No, he is not wrong.

But the arrival of Mister Mayfair along with Mrs. Mayfair jolts Antonio in this tender phase no less than a blind speedbump on the *autopista* at night in the rain with the wind blowing. What is *he* doing here? What will he think of his wife's lavish expenditure on a man with abdominal muscles like his?

That she merely enjoys his company?

Well, of course she merely does, but surely her own husband knows of his wife's weakness for horizontal recreation. Unless he is old or infirm or no longer inclined to the wild dance. Antonio can't know until they meet. But meeting the husband won't assuage the terrible pressure of these lonely weeks of not knowing and not ventilating, unless of course the Mister is willing to have a few dozen drinks in the lobby bar while Mrs. M and Antonio merely enjoy each other's company.

Ha and again ha.

Ninety-one. Ninety-two. Ninety-three.

Baldo is waking up with his guttural complaint, processing his own difficulty, which is no more than a reach for consciousness. What a simpleton he really is.

Antonio winces at these harsh thoughts toward his younger brother, but some things are unavoidable. To think, their father insisted that Baldo possessed a mystical knowing just because the younger could say nothing to prove his stupidity. Truth be told, Baldo gives poignancy to the adage, *es burro que no rebuzna porque olvidó la tonada.*

He is a burro who will not bray because he forgot the song.

He behaves as if nothing is changed, nothing is wrong. It may be natural for a woman to take something to eat each night to a man she loves like a brother. But this is not such a love. For days

Lyria has not shared a word with Antonio, which wouldn't be cause for alarm, since she can hardly share more than paltry dialogue with Baldo. But she swells in the womb, and this is no *gorda* blossoming.

No, she retches and cries, and Rosa wails.

Baldo merely drags himself up, drags his legs over, and stands like a man in a dream. He yawns and stretches and slumps again, asleep as a man can be.

Look at him, also swelling in the gut like a man twice his age with nothing to cause it but an excellent repast each evening that begins with *tamales* and ends with a nice serving of *sopapillas* as only Antonio's beloved can muster.

A hundred forty-eight. A hundred forty-nine.

Perhaps the standard should be raised to a hundred seventy-five. Well, maybe tomorrow. You give in to whimsical modulation any old time; next thing you know, the rapid rise to anywhere is derailed. No, a man of diligence and reason will encounter those times when the left foot must go forward and then the right. Change nothing for now. Don't worry about the pain. You cannot know now what you will know in due time.

Rising and wiping the sweat from his face and chest, Antonio counts the due time. If he calculates correctly, due time will be in August, when the sweat rolls most. He throws the towel aside and prepares for another day that may well be the day of days.

Who can know?

Hardly spitting distance away comes the awful sound of reverse squishing, then the retch and lament. Baldo turns to hear better, then he turns away, on his way to brush his teeth.

Antonio lights the stove and puts the water on and watches and watches and watches and realizes he is no closer to the sterling coffee service with real cream available this minute to both Mrs. and Mister Mayfair than he was two years ago or twenty. He is no closer than the man in the moon. No closer than he will ever be. Today is merely a day like the rest, and maybe this insight is part and parcel to the developmental process, however rapidly or slowly it transpires.

I am a clown who leads a bingo game by the swimming pool, and sometimes I make money on the side as a gigolo. And there, just there, drooling like an infant is my half-wit brother, who is also a murderer who makes ficky fick with my beloved every night after dinner.

She cooks.

In a few months they will be three, and then what? Do they move in here and send me over for a happily ever after with Rosa?

"Then what?" he calls softly. "Then what will you do?"

Baldo looks up and over at Antonio, who waits for an answer. Baldo smiles, leaving the toothbrush in his mouth and grabbing the sink by its sides. He humps the sink in eerie playfulness as a high-pitched squeal rises from him. Antonio nods; how nice it must be to live blissfully as a half-wit, now or then or ever; it's all the same.

He wants in the perverse way of men to know how it happened thus far. Did she come to him? Did she initiate? Or was it his idea? Did she resist? Did he force himself upon her? Did she resist? Of course she doesn't resist anymore. How could she? His beloved?

Growing larger than the nagging questions of a man betrayed in love is the question of a man betrayed by life. How can a man work so hard and care so thoroughly for his brother and his betrothed, and then receive such harsh treatment? Maybe he is more sensitive to the short shrift in view of Mister Mayfair's arrival, which may leave a stunted clown of a man alone outside, leashed to the steps like a dog because he no longer fits indoors.

What is he supposed to do, go down to the pool for the cock-a-doodle-do and a rousing round of bingo for a beer, and then join his wealthy friends from *el norte*, the Mayfairs, for brunch?

Well, in fact that is what he's supposed to do, but truth be told, he would rather crawl back in the sack under the covers and sleep. Is this a symptom of maturation? Maybe it is, and maybe today it would be best *darle un beso a la botella*, to give the bottle a kiss. Such a quench seems suitable to the thirst now burning. Today feels like bits and pieces before we even begin.

Waiting for neither his brother nor his formerly beloved, he selects a new T-shirt saved for a special occasion. Not the *ciento-*

peso number showing Toucan in splendid surroundings but the one Mrs. M bought last time. This T is plain white and properly reflects the stark reality he feels inside, the one no cartoon can adequately convey. He slips into it and checks his posture briefly before striding out the door on his way up to the bus stop.

People on the bus smile as if they know, but they don't ask about his brother or Lyria. Nor does he invite their questions. He stares out the window, and thinks the bumpy, smelly ride a perfect backdrop to his thoughts.

He walks through the lobby without a single hello or nod or wave, and out at the table by the pool he turns the microphone on, knocks it twice, and somberly says, "Testing. *Uno. Dos. Tres.* Okay. Bingo. You want to play, come get your card and your beans. You want to sleep, Okay by me. You be dead a long time, maybe then you will wish you could play bingo, but, never mind, okay by me. Bingo. Take it. Leave it. Okay? Five minutes. *Cinco minutos. ¿Sí? ¿No?* Okay."

A woman poolside in a lumpy one-piece stares incredulously, then laughs pitifully. This is not the kind of delight Antonio wants to generate, so he returns her stare with a smile and asks, "You want to play? Three beers, one line, up, down, diagonal. Three beers. I think they will make you happy. *¿Sí?*"

The woman declines, more in disdain than direct response.

So he mumbles, "*Gringa puta*," just close enough to the mike to raise eyebrows among the staff around the pool. Fortunately, the woman doesn't look back but walks up to freshen her coffee. Who cares about her, every day with her poo poo eyes for bingo and volleyball, joining in the pool aerobics but never once getting excited or saying thank you for a very nice time?

Who cares? Lumpy one-piece. Who?

And who cares if only one woman wants to play bingo? She seems nice, skinny and pale, most likely a schoolteacher from Chicago, who looks in need of three beers. But "You can't have a three-beer game with only one player. You can't even have a game with only one player. So, here. Here is a chit for one beer. You win just as if you played. Now go back to sleep. You win."

She is nice, lolling her head, smiling shyly, glancing quickly at the maestro's abdominal section and perhaps as well at his *pinga* before returning to her chaise lounge and the rest of her nap.

She's having fun, which everyone can clearly see, but the maestro underscores the moment with the microphone. "Okay. Back to sleep. In forty-five minutes we play volleyball! Okay. Too early for you to play bingo, all of you except for one. She wins. Have your coffee and have some more. Er errr! Go back to sleep, then wake up. Forty-five minutes. No more!"

Antonio Garza has never experienced such a morning, in which all the parts are properly placed but none will fit the puzzle. He can't find the old momentum. Is it his fault if the system fails with so much failure around him? Does he not waken every day to the combined and compound failure of his brother and his beloved? What next?

I'll tell you what next; I will move into my own *casa*. I will not begrudge them money in times of dire need, because I would not do such a thing. But basic need? They're on their own. When the daughter is twelve and the worries begin over the proper morality or lack thereof that got her mother into this fix, Lyria will change.

So fast it will seem like overnight, she will gain the weight a *gorda* needs to gain so she can become caring and loving. At least she won't tilt *my* bed. But truth be told, she won't tilt Baldo's either. He'll be long gone by then. Won't he? I think he will. He's worse than half-witted. He's impulsive to the extreme. First murder and then ficky fick with his own brother's beloved. He knows not right from wrong. So what should I do, justify this behavior too in terms of natural innocence? Maybe he is the archangel of justice for me too. And maybe for Lyria. Time will tell. But I justify nothing. Baldo will seek a life of instant solution to his private problems. The instant of truth is all he can grasp.

This is the knowing that grows and gnaws in Antonio's head and in his gut on such a worrisome day. Though it's only forty-five minutes to volleyball, he looks up again at the clock and it's only twenty. Has he been standing here twenty-five minutes thinking darkly of what has come to pass? Was his brow wrinkled? This is not the pose of confidence.

He will have Mrs. Mayfair and in the meantime, plenty of Mexican women come here too, single women from families who have taught them the proper morality.

He awakens yet again from the loss of ten more minutes, this time by the waving hand attached to the delicately jeweled wrist of the evenly tanned arm leading up to the pouting lips and down to the fulsome breasts and supple thighs of Mrs. Mayfair. She is sitting between *Señor* Simón Salvador and another man of equal spit and polish.

In spite of a physique that was years in the making and widens the eyes of hungry women, Antonio pulls in here, pushes out there. This is not in compensation for anything lacking, except of course it is. And lo, what is this, the result of tainted sausage from the buffet line that now causes this squeeze in his gut?

Stage fright? The maestro?

¡Nunca! It is merely a chill in the air that accounts for the queasy tremble in the kneecap region as well. Or maybe this weakness is from so much preoccupation and so little of the old verve. It may be the latter, because such symptoms were long ago purged from the man of proven resilience in ascension.

Tainted sausage? Cool breezes? Never mind.

A man must suck it up and move, mindful that each step approaches independence from the distraction undermining his strength. Even so, the earth quakes beneath his humble left, right, left as he approaches that to which he aspires. Well, it's not the earth that's quaking but the atmosphere surrounding it, not that an atmosphere can actually quake. It's made of air, but still. He's no drunk and this is no hangover, yet beneath him is the timorous gait of a man with marginal confidence.

She is all heart, and he wants to nestle under her wing, to take succor until the shakes go away so he can rise again and drive her down their private byway of madly careening love. Of course such is not the next step up. The obstacle before him calls for clarity, for strength but softness.

It requires dominance but sophistication. He must display wealth in the classic mode, which has nothing to do with money.

He calls on the power of few words and rises to the occasion, aided for starters by a more level playing field. That is, Simón Salvador now wears baggy jams and *huaraches* below. Above is an elegantly tailored shirt in the *campo* cut worn open to reveal a hairless chest on which reposes a silver fist on a silver chain. The single earring is a simple stud and wasn't there before but now matches the earring worn by Mister Mayfair, who is dressed in casual tailoring of equal elegance. The two men touch shoulders and sit slightly apart from Mrs. Mayfair. With body language as efficient as any verbalization Baldo ever made, they tell a story of a thousand words with a simple picture.

Antonio fixes the warmth onto his face and reminds himself of what is said, *cada perico a su estaca, cada changa a su mecate,* which allows each parakeet to pick his perch, each monkey to choose his vine.

The threesome gazes at the approach of Mrs. M's young ward as if waiting fulfillment of an exquisite anticipation, which is his splendid presence at last.

Antonio turns his stage warmth up a notch to match what he sees, sensing plenty of room at the top for those who qualify. Though *Señor* Simón Salvador has already met *Señor* Antonio Garza on several occasions, this is an occasion for equal footing with everyone here.

This could be a day that may endure among the days. Isn't this the way it goes? You feel so bound for destiny, for your chance to face your best crowd yet. And once finally in place to give your all, you feel reduced to hardly more than your half. Never mind! Stand tall, take control but only subtly, emote and be happy, or at least display happiness.

"Antonio!" Simón Salvador exclaims, standing to meet this up-and-comer.

"*Hola,* Simón." Antonio feels the surge sputter as the old verve turns over. First names are a presumption on both sides, a good one.

"*Hola,* Antonio. I'm Thornton Mayfair." Mister Mayfair offers as much warmth; well, not as much as Mrs. Mayfair, but still. He offers his hand for a hardy pump but still sits, presenting a dilemma early in the lift-off phase. First-name presumption here could be bad. He offered it but does not stand, maybe because he's older or comfortable or had too much breakfast or feels his superiority might be called into question.

Antonio adapts instantly with a move borrowed from his close friend, Simón Salvador. He brings his heels quickly together, which is perfect because they don't click, because he is barefoot, which some people might view as appropriate to his station in life but he knows is appropriate to the responsibility of assuring the comfort, ease of mind, and sheer happiness for hundreds of guests. So he nods, bringing his eyes into focus on the ground, which is the focus they bulge onto as Mister says, "Mrs. Mayfair has told me everything..."

¡Qué!

"...about you."

Ah.

But he calls her Mrs. Mayfair, indicating the preservation of distinction between classes, or maybe that's just ages. He is what? Sixty? Not so fat, decent color, hardly bald. So what?

Antonio smiles with magnitude now, careful not to slip into the grin but reaching deep for substantive camaraderie. He pumps Mister Mayfair's hand with feeling and allows the playful truth to romp in his head: *I'll tell you what; you cannot do for her what I do. That's what.*

But wait—Antonio glances over at the Mrs. to see her reaction at this meeting of her men.

Nothing changes. What a woman. She is like a warm spring in her tireless, endless flow. Surely she has told her husband about Antonio, but not about you-know-what. He's her *hus*band, so it isn't at all the same as telling such things to Lyria, even if you call Lyria his betrothed. Because Lyria has been like a sister all along, a sister he would not touch in that way ever. Well, maybe not ever, but by then she will be more than a sister. In the meantime, she is surely grateful to know that another is easing the pressure, which isn't the same thing at all as telling a husband.

No, that cannot be. Can it?

The contemplation of that question is set aside, because another glance in the next fractional moment reveals warmth of an equal nature exuding from Simón Salvador.

"Sit down, Antonio. Do you have time?" The invitation to sit is from the lawyer.

"A few minutes. Yes."

"You know, we're very pleased with progress on the case. I have to be perfectly honest with you. *Falta lo mero bueno.*" Simón Salvador allows a dramatic pause so the news can adequately twist Antonio's face. He explains for the Mayfairs, "We are not out of the woods yet. But..." He turns back to Antonio. "We feel that your prospects for complete exoneration are excellent." The salvation trinity beams its approval, for which Antonio wants to mirror effusive gratitude and tries heartily to do so. "You know, this man they call Quincy; he has nothing. Really. Nothing." Another beaming consensus is strung up the flagpole for a salute.

Mrs. M takes initiative and orders a round of drinks.

What can be better? What can feel better? Liberation and independence appear to be ongoing. The sun is shining. Antonio has risen from despair to this, his destined echelon, the rare atmosphere in which happiness is an abundant resource requiring management.

Mister Mayfair leans in and says with authority, "We want to move on to new business."

And so they do, beaming, nodding, sipping, and trading trinkets of dialogue relative to nothing but an extension of life as we know it, which could be viewed as the same old same old on a dark day of somber reassessment. But a different feeling is available to those who will grasp it. That is, the summit of development is no different today than it ever was, except of course for one difference.

The difference is that today Antonio is here.

Lyria observes these things from under the shade tree she once leaned upon languorously to elicit the admiration of her former suitor. Oh, Antonio will nearly burst from pride and will feel like the man of destiny he wants to be, once he repeats in hearing range the job he has been offered. So what? What does he want from me? Regret? Misery? Shame and poverty? Will that make him happy or crown his glory?

Lyria sees clearly as if it were written on the page before her that Mister Mayfair likes to have his ears grabbed as well, especially by *Señor Rico Suave* the lawyer, who perhaps is willing to lower his fees in trade. How convenient a ruthless beheading on the beach at night is turning out to be. Maybe these two gentle men will make further arrangements for further convenience along with separate rooms for Mister and Mrs. If they throw in a nice job for Antonio it's a regular happily-ever-after, which is the least the men of power can do in appreciation of their young ward getting the old lady out of the way.

Lyria has only now come from cleaning Mister Mayfair's room on the twelfth floor. She found both beds mussed with *Señor* Simón Salvador's personal brief case on the dresser and one foil packet on the floor.

Only one in the twelve hours since their arrival? These men of power could take a lesson from the old lady and the maestro. Then again, maybe they were tired from travel.

Then again, Lyria doubts that the number of foil packets can measure the dirty habits of anyone in the whole ear-grabbing family.

Prospects for hygienic safety are greatly enhanced on her own. And on her own is where she will stay. How can it be otherwise?

XIII

The Things a Young Woman Must Consider

Baldo is a boy and worse. You can't very well call him a simpleton in all things, because in some ways he exceeds the insight and skill of most men. Experience is limited in a young woman like Lyria, but she suspects few people anywhere can commune with little turtles as well as Baldo can. She suspects him gifted as well with his sexual skills.

Granted, he is of the tireless age, but he is more, so slow and deliberate and sensitive to a young woman's needs. He makes eerie sounds and sometimes wants to commandeer awkward positions, but that's only an effort to ape his hero. Lyria wants to keep this phase of experiential data collection simple, straightforward, and concise, and she maintains authority quite easily, given her superior age and wisdom.

Okay, so she allowed an ear-grab once to see what there was to see but will not try it again. For one thing, it doesn't work so well. With his *pinga* pointing skyward and him squeezing her ears, nothing fits properly. No, lying down is the only way. Besides, what's to see? A scenic coastal drive this is not. Please, leave my ears alone. For yet another thing, she will not do that again. It is disgusting and made her gag, and riding the tapioca flood, Baldo shrieked like a monkey, wild with flailing and flopping.

Well, a girl can learn certain things only by experience. Now she knows. She might try these things again, but only with the man who takes her for a wife. Short of marriage, she might consider these contortions with he who is willing to keep her in a *casa chica*. In either case, repetition will not be with Baldo; he is so far removed from the practical world.

This interlude is merely an experimental phase for all parties concerned, because experience is the best teacher. But who is she kidding? Who would take a woman for a wife when everyone knows she is soiled? Antonio will not. On this we can depend.

She briefly considers enticing Antonio shamelessly to the ficky fick, but he's too smart. Even if she succeeded, he has only to count the months. But maybe if he becomes very drunk. Well, maybe, we shall see. We can only be certain at this point that the little fling with Baldo will not survive the experimental phase. He is crazy. *Le patina el coco.* He could hold his head in one hand and a coconut in the other and not know the difference. Worse yet, he is a boy who needs constant supervision.

Already the line is drawn ending his nightly indulgence, except for last night, because he really is very good, and once a young woman knows certain things, she can't very easily forget, as if she doesn't know. She knows; yet knowledge comes at no less expense than originally paid by Eve with her apple and Adam with his serpent.

The lesson was there all along; no sooner is knowledge acquired than it reveals vast ignorance. The simple question rising from the ashes of recent experience asks what a woman can do now. A gawky fellow with huge hands and many teeth on TV assures her that she can do anything she imagines with a properly directed mind. He will direct for her if she attends his seminar for only nine thousand pesos, which seems out of the question, even though Lyria knows where to find the down payment. It's in the jar under the dirty clothes Antonio keeps in the corner. Well, she could borrow it and then pay it back, once she gets direction and some money coming in.

But what good is guidance for a woman big with a child? No good at all is the answer, because the condition is a direction all its own that will not detour to whim or fancy. Of course there is the other, but abortion would haunt her the rest of her life. Then again, a child would haunt equally with far more needs, unless of course she was married to a proper husband to support her and the baby.

But she is not.

And an abortion would be known by herself and the church and by Rosa too, which seems altogether too much to bear for now.

Well, a raven-haired beauty with big, dark eyes and a figure as svelte as the disco dancers on TV should need no seminar to test her fortune. The world demands maximum efficiency in resource utilization. This is the fallow field waiting only for sowing. The village may not be optimal for testing potential, but then what is a girl to do, ride the bus to Mexico City, where beautiful women abound on every corner? No, she can test things at home, where failure is easier to absorb.

So she shortens the hem of a rayon dress and tries it on with no brassiere, which might have worked on a bold day before the swelling, but not now. Except of course it works very well to heighten the drama of the presentation and erase all doubt on potential, once the mind is properly directed to the objective at hand. She's not yet lactating and does want to measure the market that is the real world.

So why not?

She has no reason not to proceed, and besides, she will not be a prostitute, never that. She only wants to test the water, so to speak, for a relationship acceptable on practical terms. Prospects for a young man of wealth and gentility would be greater in Mexico City, but there is time enough for that if this works. In the meantime several more months as a maid will help with a down payment on the trip. The focus for now is faith that a big fish will take the bait. Besides, testing skills in the city would require new equipment, like brassiere and shoes. Staying home represents savings for now.

She shaves her high thighs, shins, and armpits smooth as peach skins. She hurries, because a girl with a few more months knows that the swelling is relentless, one week to the next. Still, she takes time in applying her resources, conveying warmth to a world in need of warmth, to assure perfect strangers of her weakness for sweets and liquor, and of course comfort and security. Who can know what luck will bring before time runs out, and life will be foregone?

So she eases seams here and there and squeezes in. Make no mistake; heads will turn to see such a woman with no brassiere. Natural beauty will lure them in. Just look: slowly twisting before the mirror as Mrs. Mayfair did, hips forward, she draws the skimpy dress tight across the *chichis*.

She reaches up as if to hail a cab, bends over to pick up two hundred pesos and saunters casually down a street.

The mirror gives back with each practiced pose the riches so critical to a young woman in a bind.

Oh, she will be seen; visibility is a given. The problem will be the billy goats and geezers. How can a girl know who is which? Not that a billy goat or geezer can't have the money to keep such a prize, but a younger man with nice looks would be so much better. That's another thing; how much money will it take? The hotel pays a hundred a day to clean rooms.

But what difference does that make? Can that compare to cleaning a man's tubes? Is a thousand a day too little or too much? Certainly a handsome man with a nice body could keep a prize for less. But where does a girl start the bidding?

And how does she hook the right fish, since she really doesn't know the difference between trolling with a lure and dragging a net? She does want a young one, but he should be old enough to have the money worked out, and it should show, the money, the manners, and the gentle touch, like Antonio.

She smiles sadly and struggles against the tears, realizing he would not qualify because he has no money for a *casa chica* and his manners are those of an exhibitionist. But he can be gentle, and something feels terribly lost.

Does her pain rise from the love between them that will never be? Does the child they would have made but is now displaced by the taller, lankier seed sadden her? How can such harm come from one moment of weakness? If her back itches, and she can reach it, should she not scratch? That's all it was.

Except of course it was more, allowing the brother of her beloved to put his *pinga* between her legs. But what could she do?

Twenty-two years old already and practically serving her luscious self on a platter to a fool who remains spent on a gamy old *gringa*.

Well, looking back in sadness is for those who don't mind turning into salt, which is not the case for Lyria Elena Alvarez, who learned at a tender age that tenderness is for those with the basics provided. The rest must look ahead, only ahead. Now she is providing for two, maybe three, or will it be four?

No, she will never let that happen.

Baldo will not be her ward but will remain his brother's charge. Maybe some weakness in this time of drawing the line didn't hurt anything more than it's already hurt, but now the experience will stop. Well, maybe it won't stop, but it will go in a new direction. Maybe it was only natural between a ripe young woman and a quite naturally beautiful young man, but it changed everything, and he also happens to be demented or criminally insane or something other than normal.

So yes, it must stop. And I mean stop, not tomorrow or next week but right now, without even fifteen minutes' notice, which is really all it takes if you don't count the time he needs to worry like a woman over his little turtles when such a hot dish could well be cooling. No, it will stop now, because it's been enough. Well, maybe not enough, but enough of him and enough for now.

A young woman has enough of stumbling over sevens and eights every step of the way without an imbecile and his buckets of turtles to worry about. She doesn't even have the right shoes. What can she wear? Maid shoes that look like nurse shoes with their wedge heels and chalk white color? Or *huaraches*? New shoes will cost a hundred pesos, two hundred if they're to last.

These and other concerns accompany Lyria two blocks to the shoe store, where life and love take a breather for new shoes at a hundred eighty. The heels are only six centimeters, but that's enough to show off her shapely long, smooth calves. Besides, the tall ones are four hundred and make her look too beautiful for any one man, which really is all she wants for now. So she settles on the moderate heels and wears them, putting her sandals in the plastic bag.

To tell the truth she'd rather have new shoes than a new brassiere any day, and it's high time, and a girl needs to feel good about something if she hopes to look good enough to make someone else feel good about her. Not that a man needs much more than the fleshy basics to feel good about a woman. Not at first anyway. Romance will come, if you take your time and use what you know and are careful in your selection.

Ask Mrs. Mayfair for advice?

¡Nunca!

Well, not before trying things out alone. Let the old woman see what her endless needs have caused. What does Mrs. Mayfair know, other than that a man with a rippling stomach leaves the yellow stain in her panties? Antonio was a good choice for Mrs. M, which a girl can know in her mind even with the bitterness in her heart.

The bitterness seems to be going around. How does Antonio feel about things? To tell the truth, he seems hurt but not bitter, as if his brother cannot be held accountable. How does he hold me? If not accountable, then what does he think, that a woman will fail sooner or later, given the chance?

Isn't that like him?

What can I do, sympathize? He thinks I'm made of rubber, and his tales of happy ear grabbing will bounce off easy as that.

Do I have no heart?

Maybe it's too early in the afternoon. A woman can look good in mild perspiration, but this is sweat, rolling like a river.

And look, there is my only admirer, a dirty old man. Perhaps the air will be cooler in the shade by the water.

So Lyria forgets her destination with a laugh, since she had no destination in the first place and isn't quite sure how to define one to reconcile her need and disposition. She heads west to the waterfront, where iced tea costs more than a beer anywhere else and a beer cost the same as a meal. Such is the price of what the tourists want most, which is what they call a view. Lyria wonders what they view at home as she strolls casually toward the touristic waterfront. At least the short benches in the shade cost nothing.

Perhaps a tourist would be best for starters, to sample the experience and measure the money available.

Sitting in the shade, she sustains productivity by trying different poses, crossing her legs, uncrossing and turning her knees aside, because a working girl keeps working just as a fisherman keeps his bait in the water if he hopes to come home with dinner.

A boy stacking crates between buildings across the promenade tries to look up her dress when she shifts her legs. Then he drops a crate. If she times her changes properly, he can't stack and peek without dropping crates, exposing him as well to unsavory consequence. They scrimmage like a point forward and a goalie. She can't help the moment of exposure between positions, and then she doesn't care.

He's just like the rest, willing to waste his time and accept an ache in the back to stay at ground level for a little peak at her you-know-what. She won't give in but knows he craves what he knows nothing about.

Who cares?

Lyria stares off at nothing as if seeking resignation from the world of woe, striking a pose of indifference. With acceptance comes the slump and a new pose, beauty in utter dejection.

It is this beauty in its sad splendor that Viorica Vicente Valenzuela first sees. She approaches clandestinely and observes from behind as Lyria turns to a pose of weary resolve. With a wary voice the new woman softly announces, "*Hola*. I am Viorica Valenzuela." She pronounces it Vi·OH·rica and gives her last name as a matter of habit, allowing a new friend to consider her formally. "I am visiting from Venezuela," she says in a moment, allowing time to separate Valenzuela from Venuzuela so a new friend might be spared unnecessary confusion, or perhaps to displace one confusion with another.

The two women meet in the eyes and share a half-smile like old familiars meeting again. One is light-spirited with a practiced caution. The other seems innocently uncertain of social expectations in the real world.

Viorica Valenzuela is beautiful and glamorously finished as Lyria Alvarez can only hope to be. And look: heels rising to every inch of fifteen centimeters make her no less pure than a statue of the Blessed Virgin or Liberty or someone like that.

Viorica offers a splendidly finished hand that has suffered no ammonia or cleanser, much less touched the insidious stray hairs on a toilet rim.

Lyria takes it softly to explore its texture and smoothness. Not hands to wipe or scrub or make beds and grasp the vacuum cleaner for a thrust under the bed to suck up who knows what kinds of filth, these hands have absorbed the finest lotions. Lyria looks up at the face above the hands.

It smiles warmly down now and asks, "What is your name?"

"Lyria. I am Lyria Alvarez. I'm sorry." Lyria straightens her knees and slides over to make room. "Won't you sit down?"

Well, yes, Viorica Valenzuela believes that she will, if you don't mind. And here they are, comfy cozy in the shade with a view, time and tide converging serendipitously at last, bringing randomly drifting women together for a visit as only soul sisters can understand. In no time the two are giving and receiving. Each counsels the other as needs prevail and as only women can do. Minutes ago total strangers, they form the bonds of like-minded souls with vastly similar experience, lost and alone but found in the most pleasant company.

The world whirls about them with men, money, shoes, dresses, and cruel indifference to a woman of nubility who only wants to get along and maybe a little bit ahead. So much is understood between them as they fast forward to now from their common past that they rise to tacit agreement in a very short time. A ravaging hunger for trust and confidence is slaked by simple friendship. Like found money, each is observed by the other with the feeling that now my luck is changing.

Well, perhaps their past is not so common, considering the one's familiarity with cleaning agents and thrusts under the bed, and the other's explicit ignorance of manual labor and familiarity with thrusts of a more delicate nature. But two women sensing lasting friendship will attest to the giddy euphoria accompanying prospects for a girlfriend and fun.

Lyria advises no, this section of town is not the best for dining, unless you are a tourist, which you are, but still. The best and most romantic places are there, six blocks over, four blocks down.

Viorica asks if Lyria is here for the dining. No, Lyria is only here for the shade and slight relief from the heat, available near the water. Forgive me; these places are suitable for dining, if you're hungry and feel too hot to walk so far.

A man's voice erupts from the bar by the alley where the boy finagles his crates for a view up the dresses of *dos putas* now seated for spectacular potential. The man exhorts another man, who listens listlessly, that he does not like the tourists; they're so drunk, with such cows for women. Not even as good as our waitresses are these tourist women. So stupid; they will order anything if you tell them it's special and charge too much. Like the special of the house, which *is Consomme con Pollo Rojo*, which is a cup of chicken broth with a boiled chicken leg cut roughly into chunks with a machete, bones and all, and served in a bowl mixed loosely with ketchup and tomato paste. "They love it!" The man bellows. "Because I tell them it is so good!"

Lyria blushes but doesn't know what to say, so Viorica touches her arm and says, "Many men are like that man. Others are only persistent, like the boy. But some men have better manners. That's the best we can do. That and some money."

"How can you know these things?" Lyria asks, blushing again. "I mean, I know how you can tell what kind of man he is, because he is so gruff and loud. But how can you tell with a man you don't know?"

"You must know. You can know. Have you never had a boyfriend?"

Lyria feels like a *labriego estúpido* just come to town from out of the dirt. A thousand times she has passed this way, but now this way is different, like another place and time. She wants mightily to speak decisively with worldly knowing but can only smile. Out of the blue sky has come a fairy godsister with no requirements or expectations, an angel who seems willing to share.

Well, it's a hazy sky and not an angel but a very nice woman she can trust. She knows these things and feels confident like she did only a few months ago. Certitude restored eases her burden, allowing cruel knowledge to be shared.

Lyria knows a few things, all right, but cannot account for the deep and dire cost of knowing. This may sound similar to the very first burden of the very first woman in the very first garden, which was vaguely similar to current surroundings, but what else can a woman come to with only men from whom to gain the knowing? Because the way of the world is very little changed in all these years since the beginning of time. If you think it otherwise, then you must be something other than a woman.

The lesson of the ages is the same as all men have always tried to teach all women, if the women are gullible enough to accept it. Yet gullibility is too simple in this case because of the love involved between Lyria and her boyfriend and his brother. Well, he's hardly her boyfriend anymore, but he was and lingers like he is, and maybe in a way he still is. But of course he's not.

Viorica listens attentively, as only a patient and trusted friend will do, until asking incredulously, "Are you saying the boyfriend is not the brother?"

"Yes. I mean no. I mean they are brothers. One is…or was my boyfriend. The other is his brother. But I have loved them both as brothers. I have loved one as a boyfriend, and the brother, I have…" Lyria falters here, perhaps realizing on simple verbalization the magnitude of her behavior.

Viorica reads the rest of the sentence on Lyria's face. "You have been romantic with the brother but not the boyfriend?"

Lyria reddens deeper still and hangs her head. "Yes." And so it hangs, ready for the lop of Damocles, who surely swings his sword from the ether of all knowing.

Viorica laughs and touches Lyria serenely, gently as Mrs. M had done. But this feels different, and the difficulty hovering overhead like a sharp presence these past weeks and months suddenly vaporizes. With a touch the ominous ether turns to sprightly mist—or sprightly humidity, anyway. A bit of sprightly laughter blows it away.

The trouble and the dark presence are no more than bird squat, so easy to avoid stepping in. So why step in it? Why not step around it and step ahead? Because what we have here is a long and happy road in front of us, in which youth, vigor, and beauty pave a way where few can tread. All this flows over the little bench with a happy laugh. Viorica makes lightheartedness official when she says, "You are quite a woman. You will have to tell me more. Come. I want to buy an iced tea for you. Or would you rather have lemonade? Do they have lemonade? Surely they do."

In mere minutes a day of difficulty becomes a momentous change in time, in which the huge, crusty doors of relief swing open at last. Moreover, the laughter is shared. This is the most potent of all tonics, curing Lyria in stature and spirit. In fact, this is more fun than she can remember, much more even than the knowing she so longed for with a man. This is knowing of a different nature, at least as fulfilling, and though she feels far removed from the electricity that arced her loins and released strange, unearthly sounds from within, this knowing wants to go on and on. It will leave no mess and no doubt. This, a girl can feel. She smiles in response to the soft current from just as deep inside as that other current.

Leaning her elbows on the table and sipping lemonade through a straw, she revels in Viorica's touch when the older, wiser woman gently plucks a lemon squidgy from above her lip. She nearly trembles in the silence, savoring the camaraderie that can allow such comfort with no words. She's never done this, simple as this pastime may seem to a worldly woman on tour from another country. Such a thing should seem simple to anyone. Now it seems simple to Lyria as well. She cannot say why she has yet in her life to enjoy a lemonade in the shade with a girlfriend.

Does life not pass quickly as an afternoon? Should it not hold some relaxation and shade and lemonade for a girl who takes care of her mother and works hard and endures a living hell for one little slip? Well, the slip is probably up to ten or twelve by now but is categorically still one.

Here she is twenty-two, or good as, and never yet wasted an afternoon talking, laughing, and savoring the unknown. She knows full well that a tourist is headed home, and with guarded anxiety she asks, "How long are you here, Viorica?"

Viorica smiles with a big, inverted smile and exaggerated shrug that seems to say, *as long as it takes*.

Lyria wonders how long it could be, and what it is.

So Viorica touches her gently again and says she's been visiting from Venezuela for two years now, but you haven't seen me because I spend so much time in the city.

So Lyria asks the next question that seems natural enough, though she will learn in due time that such a question is hardly *de rigueur*. "What do you do?"

"I am looking," Viorica says, looking at Lyria to see if such an answer will do.

But Lyria is not stupid; she is merely uninformed, waiting for this situation to change.

"I am looking for, shall we say, investments."

Lyria looks aside, perhaps wondering if a girl of her background is not meant to know certain things. She knows the word investment indicates money, the kind of money that is not counted in pesos by the hour but is much more, say, enough to keep a beautiful woman in a *casa chica*. Well, a person would actually need more money than that, for a man wouldn't keep such a woman with the main portion of his wealth but only with money he doesn't need elsewhere.

Besides that, Viorica doesn't mean she's looking for investments; she's looking for investors. Isn't she?

"Don't you mean you're looking for investors?"

The new girlfriends join anew in a blush for the ages, as if such redness is ordained to make them one with the very first blush. They agree, sharing each other's eyes that they'll have no more of difficulty, or at least avoid it where they can. Lyria blushes for her unbridled presumption in getting so personal so fast. Viorica blushes for the truth, which may sting a bit at first, but such a sting is not of her making.

But though Viorica Valenzuela is an easy match for wrongful knowing, she rights the world around her with a most extraordinary beauty. She turns a blush to radiance easy as that, displaying as well her skill at quick recovery. With simple technique she effectively allows them to back up from their dead end to begin again. "And you?" She asks, hardly ruffled. "What do you do?"

Never in her life has Lyria Alvarez doubted what she does or why she does it. She simply does what needs to be done. But something sticks in her throat now no less than a bone in a bird's craw. Clearing the blockage, she glances both ways as if seeking an easy crossing of this difficult thoroughfare. With eyes cast downward, she smiles sheepishly and nearly mumbles, "In a hotel. I work in a hotel. I am a maid. I clean rooms in a hotel."

Viorica looks quite stern now, jutting her chin and shaking her head. "This is a waste. You know this, don't you?"

Well, it's another moment of knowing. Realization is harsh and sudden, arriving from the blind side and whacking a young woman square in the emotional jaw. After all, it's been quite a day of change and reassessment. Yet in an instant Lyria must agree that much has been wasted. Her face skews to match the inverted smile recently learned, but Lyria's is different from the charming, practiced exaggeration of Viorica's.

Lyria's sad smile is that of a baby, twenty-one years after the fact. Like a baby who is cold and hungry but can't yet verbalize her need for warmth and succor, her face contorts in failure. Finding no words to express her frustration, she fails again, reeling from the impact of the horrible truth upon her. Breathing becomes difficult, just like acceptance of what is surely true.

She wants to contain herself, to preserve an element of dignity here in the face of a new friend. Limited success holds the big tears in the corners of her eyes. Another silence enfolds, this one far from comforting, filled with the tension and strain of growth. The picture now is not one of beauty but only sadness.

What is ever gained in life without losing something else?

Two lemonades warm between two beautiful women, one of whom feels her face twist like a rag until droplets rise. The other watches grimly, reflecting her new friend's anguish.

Viorica reaches across the table and takes Lyria's hand in both of her own. "I want you to know something," Viorica says. But the touch of another who has come so close so quickly to share the burden that was carried so far all alone is like a touch to a droplet hanging by sheer tenacity. Itself failing, the droplet falls with no concern for the end of its life as a droplet contained. Every droplet falls to the earth or dries up, and it doesn't matter, because all rise like spirits do, up to the heavens where new droplets convene.

Sometimes they gather with ebullient energy in lightning and thunder. The valley brightens and booms in monsoon. This deluge feels biblical in its torrential proportion but is just as unavoidable in curing the world around us. On a personal level its embarrassing nature may be the crucible of understanding between new friends.

Afterward all is calm, with little droplets clinging again where they may. "I want to tell you something," Viorica begins again. But again she must wait for another torrent to flood the valley.

Lyria cries her eyes out.

Who cares what Viorica is looking for in this shell of a town gone to tourism or what she does with investments or investors or what she has to say? Lyria squeezes her new friend's hand and only wants to know how much longer they can be friends. She hopes it can be forever, because she can't bear these burdens all alone with nobody to talk to but the lint and stray hairs and the high whine of a vacuum cleaner to answer her questions and pose its own.

The sun stops in its slow, greasy slide. The breeze huffs like the idle buffoon in the bar over there. Neither breeze nor man can quite make the point.

The two women sit, holding hands, waiting for the flat spot of the afternoon to sink in. When Lyria' tears slow to a drip, and her breathing only trembles at the top, Viorica says, "I want to tell you. I have men following me, calling me, and begging me to be with them. Rich, powerful men."

"Why?"

"Why? Because they want to be with me. Some have been with me and want to be with me again. Some only hope to be with me and never will, unless, well, maybe. But it's what they want. It's all they want. It's how they are."

"No. I mean, why do you want to tell me this?"

Viorica smiles sweetly and leans closer. "So you will know."

Lyria tries to smile back and nods. "I know."

So they sit and wait, sighing and sipping, until Lyria asks, "What happens?"

"Nothing is what happens." She waits for Lyria's puzzled look, and there it is. "Nothing until I say it is okay for this to happen. And here is what you will pay. My dear, sweet Lyria. They must be made to pay. They know this in their hearts every bit as much as they know their mothers and wives are beyond payment. They must pay as much as they are able to pay, because they have nothing better to do with the money."

Again the more seasoned woman waits for absorption, but even a young woman with limited experience needs little time to know the meaning of these words. "You are a prostitute. The men are the investors you seek."

"Please. Lyria. Prostitute is such a judgmental word. What were you looking for today? You wear these cheap shoes that are no good to anyone and hurt your feet. These shoes tell me that you want something different but are afraid to commit to the right shoes that might cost more but will make you comfortable and more beautiful. What is your mother looking for today? What will the three of us have in common in a hundred years? Lyria, I'm not looking for investors. Like I told you, I'm looking for investments."

They sit a while longer, waiting to know more, pondering long time and short time. Lyria has heard this word *judgmental* in passing reference on morning TV, where the women seem to agree that it is wrong. She wonders how these TV women always know what in the world is good and what is bad. She wants to know more of such wisdom beyond her limited world.

Viorica is serene again, relaxing in the shade, a paradigm of quick recovery to rhythm and stride. What else can a woman do in a world of hurdles?

Lyria thinks and nods, displacing bitter tears with tart, sweet lemonade down to the sump sounds at the bottom, where Viorica brightens with an easy question. "Where do you live?"

Lyria tells her, seven blocks over and four blocks down.

"Well, then," Viorica asks, "Do you want to come for a visit to the hotel? We can freshen up and visit some more and have a drink."

Lyria would like that very much but must be home soon or her mother will worry.

Viorica smiles, reaching across the table for another touch, and says, "So sweet."

Lyria again matches her new friend's smile and feels the elixir flowing between them. This too is sweet, and out of the clear blue sky comes another vision, more of a recollection, actually, of Antonio with his faults, which are the faults of all men, except for the single damning fault of all men but him.

He only wanted to love her more than she deserved.

Viorica will explain the nature of love and deserving. She will know why fault has no meaning in assessing either one. She will offer insight to happiness and its transitory nature, and when she meets Rosa she will see the mold that cast the clay.

Rosa will see as well and nod in understanding or resignation.

But explanation will come later tonight after more drinks and a sunset walk to the quaint hotel in town where Viorica is staying. For now the day steams at the apex of its heat. Flesh slumps on bones and most people lie back to pass this lazy time in *siesta*.

Lyria feels weary enough to sleep but can only stare at the thin air and wish Antonio could learn to love her again as only a few weeks ago he did. And she cries again in a torrent over all she's lost.

XIV

A Season of Growth

Baldo is more sensitive to the changing ways of loved ones than either his brother or the one who is like a big sister can imagine.

Well, she was close as a sister, sometimes close as a mother.

Do they think him numb to their cold indifference? Too much cold can lead from numbness to death, but that can't be what they really want.

Can it?

Are they not the foundation of his days? Yet the one who makes him feel like a man and begs him not to stop until she finishes gasping like a fish out of water treats him like a stranger or worse. She is more beautiful now than ever with her new appearance and her body that is no longer too skinny, but the distance grows between them where once it was only he, Baldo, growing between them.

Who cares if he ever grows again? Who cares if he has no place to put his love? Love is the one thing he's learned. She taught him. He was a boy, but now he is a man.

He loves it so much. He gets it no more. And no one seems to care.

The other one who doubles as father and doubles again as paragon in the world of business and doubles yet again as hero in the world of life, yes, his own brother, joins her in what feels like a conspiracy of detachment. Of course it cannot be a conspiracy.

That would require discussion and planning, and they no longer speak to each other or to him. What did he do that was so wrong? Did he not help those he loves by assisting each with their needs?

These and other mysteries burden the boy who now fears the manhood upon him. If maturity puts him deeper in the wilderness, who needs to grow up?

This question first posed by Peter Pan echoes from the dog-eared book with the fanciful pictures, the book Lyria read to him years ago. Peter Pan can fly, because he never feels this heavy. It seems a lifetime ago that he, Baldo, cuddled in her arms as she read and pointed to the pictures and explained the nature of fancy and then turned the page, sprinkling pixie dust on his otherwise barren childhood. Where now is the magic dust, under the rug with the happy thoughts?

It seems nearly as long ago that she spoke civilly to him. Now she only beckons with frustration and need. Who can know when or why? Who can anticipate? And what about something to eat?

Antonio is a joker. This we know. The lesson brought home time and again is that the world wants to laugh. Yet Baldo wakes to Antonio staring. Baldo gets up, and Antonio stares. Baldo drools toothpaste over the sink. Antonio stares. Baldo humps the sink for a laugh, but Antonio only stares. He won't laugh.

So what? What? What can he do?

Well, the answer is simple for he who guards the most important guests in the history of the *Hotel Oaxtapec*. He knows that a few babies will die. This is nature's way. He feels relief for those with the white fungus over their eyes whose struggles finally cease. With guttural lament he plucks them from the tubs and carries them to the surf in his open palms so their lingering spirits might slip into the immensity that will be denied their physical selves. He won't throw them in any more for fear of establishing an appetite beyond the break. He rather carries them back up the beach and sets them in a smaller plastic container with no water. He covers them with sand and later takes them home, where they lie in repose while he cleans himself. Sometimes he sleeps.

By and by he carries them to the waterfront in town, where he commits them to eternity. Appetites in a boat harbor have no rhythm but attune themselves to the tidal flush that removes the shit and putrescence, more or less, which is also nature's way, modified.

In the morning he returns to the task that defines all that is left to him. It's a substantial love remaining if you count a hundred two babies who look up in need and dependence as he once looked up with love and trust.

Thirty days remain.

Already they are grown too big for most beaks or bills, and they're too heavy for most birds to carry. In thirty days they will stand the best chance. He watches them, feeding some by hand if they need help from their mother, he who speaks like a turtle.

He doesn't mind when they grow presumptuous as adolescents and strain to swim away in the thin air. Independence is necessary, and motivation in this early phase bodes well. He sets a particularly feisty turtle in the sand one morning, and it races headlong for the sea; it *knows* the direction in which life begins. It knows, just as Baldo believed it would, because such things are known as they've always been known. He intercepts the escape attempt and consoles, *Not yet, my compadre. Soon, but not yet.*

Fed and changed, the young turtles are safe by themselves for a while. They're too big for the phantoms of infancy, so Baldo walks up the beach to see what might align from a distance.

He observes the morning fishermen who remain oblivious to the lanky boy behind them and the suffering nearby. Baldo can't tell if the stranded puffers have been hooked and then flung high and dry to die slowly, or if the surf put them there. They look dead, until he picks them up. Some wiggle vigorously and need only a helping hand back to the water. Others wiggle weakly and need a supporting hand under the surface, until the water flowing past their gills revives them sufficiently so they can swim through the surf to escape the roiling that would tumble them to death.

Some don't move. These he lays into the water and watches them spin and roll to eternity. One has a hook and length of monofilament streaming from its mouth, but alas, no one fishes just here.

He presses one gently, looking for life, and he looks up at the sound of girls his age giggling as they pass. He presses gently again, but to no avail. Holding the dead fish, he looks up and down hotel row as if lost, checking his bearings, seeing where his is and what comes next. Perhaps it isn't here, even with Antonio paving the way.

Perhaps the priesthood or something equally soft and compassionate would best suit his love of the other animals and his deficiency in dealing with his own species. But maybe not, the priests seem so rigidly bent on suffering in the here and now. Baldo wants none of that for himself or his friends. Besides, he knows now what communion he loves most, which isn't the same at all as what the priests appear to long for.

He stares back at *Hotel Oaxtapec* where Lyria prepares to clean rooms on the twelfth floor and Antonio prepares for poolside games, unless Antonio is drinking liquor with his new friends and chewing on the glory just ahead.

Like a beacon of simple wonder, he stands and stares.

Antonio sits up, stretching his neck for a better view to the south, where his lanky brother sways like a lone weed in the breeze. But there is no breeze this early in the morning, nor is there a reason for Baldo to be that far down the beach.

Antonio's new friends, Sally and Thorny, watch their young protégé and crane as well to see what the eagle-eyed maestro has spotted. They ease back, seeing it's only the little brother, and they laugh warmly over Antonio's fatherly concern.

Ha, ha, Antonio agrees, squinting to see if Baldo's left arm is twenty-four inches too long and too sharp for anyone's good. But it's not. The wayward boy has only drifted off his moorings to play with the dead fish. He'll drift back in due time. With no machete in hand, he'll not likely encumber the otherwise peaceful morning with violence and death. Antonio eases down in his chair, nodding warmly now to match the lingering warmth on the table and in the excellent coffee and *Kahlua*.

Ah, and here come the *huevos rancheros* basted to a turn with a few nice links on the side and some toast, which makes more sense than *tortillas* if you think about it. Mm, so good. This feels much better than chasing a crazed youth down the beach and sweating out of breath and otherwise suffering the loss of composure for an orderly evening or morning to cover for his brother's psychopathic crime spree. This is better than jail too, with its lumpy mattress and certain torture. Mm. The taste is different. But of course it would be.

The men eat and agree with low moans that this is very good. Soon the Mrs. will join them, just coffee and juice for her, please. Then talk will proceed to new business and further development, real progress at last, with bricks and mortar and elevators and alabaster tiles and a gift shop with T-shirts like the toucan T Antonio now wears.

In fact the new T-shirts for the new gift shop will be better because they will be new. Just as the hotel will be new. Well, maybe not *new* new, but newly remodeled, which is just as good and much, much quicker, even if the existing building is so old and small. Never mind, it will be new and, more importantly, newly open for business in less than eight months.

"It's like our baby," Thornton says, causing a brief but startled reaction from Antonio, who still needs a moment to sort phraseology *en inglés*, where the words come so fast and so shameless tease an ardent listener with glistening promise.

The new hotel will be called *La Mexica, the Resort*. The first part of the name is, of course, after the huge lake to the east that was filled in five hundred years ago so the conquerors could build Mexico City. *La Mexica* will capture an Indian essence that is no longer anathema to the spirit of the country but is rather pivotal to its mystique.

By showing the tourists as much difference from themselves and their world as possible, you will see peripheral sales go through the roof. T-shirts are only the beginning once you let them feel something, which is anything other than what they come from.

"We're talking carved wooden toucans, toucan candleholders, glass toucans, toucan candles, for Christ's sake. You want panthers, tree frogs, rutabagas or whatever they're called, those little weasel guys that live in the sticks over there; we'll have them. Look, we're not saying we don't understand the need or the niche for a few strip malls, and it doesn't even matter if we don't, because, let's face it, they're sitting across the street, and they're *not* going away." This overview is from Thornton, who is called Thorny by Sally.

But Antonio can't quite get comfortable past Thornton and Simón.

Thorny holds a bite of *rancheros* within striking distance and adds, "At least they're not going away for forty years till the paper gets paid off. Did they write forty-year paper over there?"

"Mm," Sally grunts, stanching a drool. "Thirty."

"Okay, thirty years," Thorny smiles. "They're not going away for thirty years." He grins. "We'll be dead or good as. The point is: we're coming on with the real item. Authenticity. That's our niche." He savors the steaming bite as his eyes roll back so far they seem to push the wrinkles up on his forehead. "Mm," he agrees. "I don't know what it is. You just can't get *rancheros* like this at home." The three eat, Thornton continuing with, "*The Resort*, on the other hand, will let them know they're in their own backyard, the one they aspire to anyway, with the pool and amenities and much, much more."

Antonio wants to participate in this seminal dialogue and to perhaps bring his particular influence to bear on the direction of *La Mexica* in its thematic phase. But he does not want to step in *caga*. So he treads lightly, hovering, as it were, in the weightlessness of pure theory. "Tell me something, so I will know," he begins, gaining the attention of his mentors who eagerly anticipate this first opinion of their young protégé. "If I walk into the lobby here at *Hotel Oaxtapec*, I have a certain feeling. Tell me; when I enter the lobby of *La Mexica, the Resort*, what will that feeling be? Will it be different? How will it be different?"

Thornton Mayfair and Simón Salvador share a quick eyeful of most definite approval and possible relief that the protégé can indeed grasp merchandising at the conceptual level, beginning in the stratosphere of theory, which is a feeling, an instinct, and intuition, and he has it. The question is good, the *caga* avoided. "It will be different," Thornton says. "The resort will feel the same as this hotel in some ways, but different in others."

"It will be new," Sally says with a nod that Antonio instantly matches, as if comprehending the difference between the *Oaxtapec*, and something new.

"More plants," Thornton says. "Many, many more plants. Sure, you have plants here. But tell me something; do you know the indoor plant budget here?"

"No, I do not," Antonio concedes, squelching the urge to explain that he's a maestro, not a gardener. Surely the mentors know the difference. Yet he blushes, which can hardly be avoided in light of the opportunity missed by not knowing the plant budget here at *Oaxtapec*.

"Suffice to say," Thornton says, picking up steam on his cooling eggs, "ours will be much, much higher. We plan on roughly five times the foliage. Five times!"

His fork is upside down now, grasped firmly to work better with his knife. "We're talking huge palms, those gigantic ones that grow up to what? The tenth or fourteenth floor? *And* we'll have the full array of ornamentals down lower. Everything in the lobby! The feeling you will have on entering *La Mexica*... Let's just say your entrance will stop. I mean you will stop in your tracks for the breathtaking moment you'll need to take it all in. You won't only be entering a modern resort hotel; you'll be stepping back in time too, into the teeming, tropical jungle that rightly belongs on this very beach and in fact is still here!"

He thrusts again and chews, then points his fork at Antonio. "Authenticity," he nods, first to Antonio and then to Sally. "That was a good question, Antonio. A very good question. I think you understand what we want to do here."

Still treading cautiously, as if in first light through the tall grass where stray dogs passed in the night, Antonio ventures further. From modern concepts for modern times he meanders cautiously to the abstract periphery, which may be his realm of expertise, where he senses enhanced margins of dizzying magnitude, not to mention greatness. On a slow nod he comes into focus. "Okay. I walk through the lobby, stopping my tracks and taking my breath. I marvel at the jungle that belongs here. That is here. I walk through the restaurant, which I want to know about, and you will tell me, and I want to eat there too, and I walk out to the terrace. I approach the pool. What will I feel at the pool? Will we have a cabana with a high bar on one side with perhaps a spectacular arching roof system of giant bamboo? Will we have a water bar in the pool where a casual swimmer can drink a *piña colada* after pool aerobics?"

Both men nod quickly again at this excellent follow-up question.

Sally shrugs. "You will feel no different from one phase of *La Mexica* to another, meaning from the restaurant to the terrace to any one of three or four bars around the pool. The overwhelming difference between our resort and the rest will remain consistent from the lobby to the cabana. Authenticity. It will merely change flavors along the way."

"Hmm," Antonio ponders authentically changing flavors. The other two wait nearly playfully to see if an excellent follow-up can be followed by still more excellence. "More trees," Antonio says at last, taking the safe but logical path.

"Bingo!" Thornton says. "Where are my three beers?" And the threesome enjoy a hearty laugh at the witty humor of Thorny Mayfair, who is, after all, the money maestro of the modern resort for modern times.

Antonio shrugs and nearly says that he loves trees, which would be a witless thing to say, so he's glad the enthusiasm of the moment hangs him lisping on the cusp and carries forward sufficiently to preempt this blunder, leaving him dabbing little flecks with his napkin.

"I mean bingo as only one man can lead it," Thornton says.

The others laugh again and nod at this continuing display of wit, until Thornton pushes his plate aside with apparent finality if not disgust. Wiping his chin with direct dispatch, he leans close for a serious note in confidence. "Do you have any idea what you mean to this place? I mean here, this *Oaxtapec* place? We're surrounded by concrete and water. Period. The end. It's Sleepy Hollow with horrible insects and sunburn, without you. You might think yourself casual and playful, my friend, with your little Er er-

er er-errr. But you and only you can wake them up. You draw them out. What we have in mind is to steal you."

Antonio's eyebrows rise reflexively at the recognition missing for so long, now arriving in confidence, like a secret, as it were. He further perks at the mention of a theft, a bold move that will lead to massive development with himself as the valued commodity in question.

Sally smiles at the outrage of it all.

Thornton tosses his napkin onto the table. "If you're not a free agent, then I'm a *paisano*. You think they've been good to you here? I won't burst your bubble, but I'll ask you one little question: where's the money? I think I have a fair idea of your income. You don't need to tell me, but I think it's somewhere around, say, a hundred to three hundred pesos a day, say ten to thirty-five dollars. Am I right?"

Well, of course Mister Thornton Mayfair isn't lobbing a Hail Mary this early in the game, nor should Antonio's income here at *Hotel Oaxtapec* bear on the future as it has on the past. Give Mister M credit in gentility for his obstreperous good taste in ignoring Antonio's moonlighting and income generated by the evenings, when he can make a few pesos more. This display of *savoir-faire* sets a proper tone in which concepts converge and objectives can be met. It further reflects Thornton Mayfair's sense of fair play, or at least reflects his rectitude for business without clouding the issue with distraction.

Why quibble over a few pesos when we're talking magnitude? The man understands free agency, which may be a high, inside curve to Antonio Garza who has yet to see the sense of most free agents, declining millions in hopes of more, then moving from free agent to holdout, losing prime time and all hope for the playoffs.

Why would an up-and-comer turn down thirteen million to pump the jam in free agency for two million more? You can't even get a line on *Jesu's* odds for next season's cut what with waivers and injuries and salary caps. But so many today hold out—out in the cold, as it were, for a chance to scrounge a little bit more lunch and bus fare. No, this idle bandy of tricky terms is best avoided for the untimely trap it may well be. What is a maestro in free agency to do, hold out for more with an ultimatum?

No, he is not, because more is one thing, and happiness delivered as a way of life daily and often nightly is quite another. This is what separates those of us with authenticity in our hearts from our compatriots in *el norte*, who think *siesta* is only a nap. We don't grind straight through for more, more, more. We go home to where we live and come back refreshed, offering our products and services into evening where we continue to live with spoken discourse among ourselves rather than giving in to the TV. If a life is rich with give and take, who needs to be a millionaire?

The offer lingers, but Antonio instinctively spins from the number of pesos per day. "I have my family to consider as well," he says. Even mundane reference to the brother renews the ache, but this is no time for conservative play; these moves will shape the game.

Sally stares at Thorny, who waits with grim resolve. "Yes," he says. "We know. We want to consider your... what should I call her, your fiancée?"

"She is my friend."

"Yes, yes, of course. Your friend. We want to consider her for the program as soon as we have an opening. Your brother is..." Sally and Thorny tick their heads in toothy display designed to convey stalemate; difficulty and desire cannot resolve, so the grin struggles against the grimace and loses. "...shall we say, ticklish?" Sally looks down and then up to deliver the news. "Listen, Antonio. You're a noble man, a man we can trust and depend on. We want to discuss your brother, but we want you to consider a few things as we must see them."

For the first time in these rich, rewarding minutes, a pall ensues. Here is an obstacle, front and center, seemingly insurmountable. This is far worse than stepping in *caga*, which can be wiped off. What can Antonio do?

Should he bear a grudge against those who have shared his life forever for transgressions against him a few weeks ago?

Does anything short of death warrant the dismissal of kith and kin? No, because a man who can shimmy and fake to compromise his family's interests could not be Antonio Garza. How could he be, with Gustavo and Tiny Jesu looking on?

No problema aqui, because assessment defaults to instinct, and a path is suddenly revealed.

For one thing, Baldo will always be a brother, as in flesh and blood, the same as their poor, dead father. For another, if this is free agency, emotion defers to money. What difference does it make if Baldo is on the staff of *La Mexica, the Resort* or not, if enough money is on the table for me? I can hire him myself. Let them pay me, and *I'll* pay Baldo. Every maestro needs a grip.

What? What was that I heard just there, rustling like a leaf? Signing bonus? Did you say, signing bonus?

"What kind of things must we consider?"

Thornton Mayfair softens his grimace just like Quincy, with neither mirth nor humor. "This dialogue won't help anybody. So we won't have it now. We'll have it later, when we're better prepared, once we've all had time to thoroughly consider the practicalities." Thornton hangs his head. "I don't mean to leave you out on a limb, Antonio. I realize that without you here, your brother will likely lose his job."

"Likely?" Antonio lopes for the score, challenging the defense with pride if not arrogance to show its stuff. Let's see what you got now, my fair-weather friend.

Thornton nods. "I know. Let's table the subject for a while and see what we can work out. I assure you we'll have resources that may very well enable your brother to get what he needs."

Antonio doesn't ask what his brother needs beyond a job, but he suspects psychiatric help is what Thornton M has in mind. Such therapy will further the interests of none but the psychiatrist. Oh, yes, the shrink will agree that a simple, innocent boy needs therapy much more than two grown men behaving like drain snakes in the same hotel room. Well, Baldo isn't so simple or innocent, but then of course he is, on the one hand or the other.

"*Señor* Thorny, I am grateful to both of you. I promise to consider the practicalities, since nothing can be of greater importance. I only ask that in your consideration you remember the brightest spot for these guests at the pool. It is there, in those little plastic tubs with those little baby *tortugas*."

Thornton Mayfair puts his forearms on the table now and leans his closest. "Those turtles are very popular," he concedes. "But the turtle program is only ninety days, leaving two hundred seventy days of uncertain disposition for your uncertain brother. I don't know how else to say it, except that..."

"He is *loco*, your brother. *Más loco que una cabra.* Surely you know this." Sally speaks.

Antonio shakes his head at this unwarranted accusation comparing Baldo's temperament to that of a goat. Well, maybe it's warranted from time to time, but this is hardly the time.

"*Señor.* We are all *loco*, are we not? Many people would look at each of us and shake their heads and say, '*loco*, that one. Just look what he does.'"

Antonio waits the perfect moment for the blood to fill the faces of his breakfast companions. "'Just look what he does, talking of such a decrepit sorry place as *Los Burros Beach Hotel* as a modern resort.' You know that this would be true if they knew what plans are on this table. Many would call us *loco*, no?"

The blood recedes with tedious slowness.

Antonio facilitates composure with a deft change of pace. "It is not only the turtles these guests want to see. Do you think the jungle that is rightfully here is sterile as a hotel lobby? A jungle is alive. It is the birds as well they want to see, and the flowers that grow only here, but only with a caring hand to nurture them. Do you think any person can give you the jaguar orchid or the six sacred bromeliads?"

Antonio stares with lofty reverence at the horizon, allowing him to scan his mentors peripherally. Can they see the garden path with its fantastic, exotic, breathtaking specimens, or do they stumble in the dark?

Jaguar orchids? Sacred bromeliads? Hey, why not? The question here is not one of authenticity, because who makes up names for things anyway? Humans do. Does a ravishingly beautiful flower know what it's called in a book? Or does it care?

No, it does not. The question goes to merchandising. What? I am showing this to them?

Will the guests buy these things? Will the guests love these things? Antonio nods steadily even as his mentors squint at the idea of sacred jaguars. Because the guests will love and buy.

"*Señor* Thorny, the question here is not one of authenticity, because who makes up names for things anyway? Humans do." Well, maybe this thought played better internally than it does to the stone-faced mentors. So he fast-forwards, touching strategically on merchandising, buying, and loving.

The mentors don't exactly nod, but they no longer squint either, which means they're at least paused momentarily in the realm of pro and con.

Antonio returns to *terra firma*, with its needs and practicalities. "I will consider things as you suggest, for the foundation of everything should be consideration. But let us not forget our flamboyance. How can you put a number on color and movement? You can't. What could be more authentic than a mute boy who speaks the seventeen languages of the animals? I see Baldo as curator and caretaker, as a dynamic component of *La Mexica, the Resort*. I hope you might see the practical benefit of such a thing as well."

Score the next silence as his advantage, Antonio feels, because they're thinking. Confirmation comes from Thornton Mayfair who, in a half-slump and simple head turn, asks, "Can your brother provide us with these specimens? I don't mean the flowers. We can get the flowers. I mean the animals. The birds and maybe a few, what do they call them? Those half-raccoon, half-cat things you used to see on the road all the time."

Antonio senses danger, considering the response of his half-crazed brother to a request for the collection of exotic animals. What do you think makes him crazy? And why talk halfsies? No, such a proposition should be made from a distance with no machetes allowed. Laughing short at the ludicrous result of such a request, Antonio attempts a maneuver he has observed but has yet to try, the obfuscatory back-pedal. Well, he has yet to try it in such a big game.

"My friends, my brother Baldo loves nothing more than the animals. He raised Toucan from a tiny pup. He rescues the little fish." Antonio pauses for the blood to surge and recede and then moves quickly on. "Now he raises the little turtles, which everyone knows would perish in terrible numbers without his care and protection."

The mentors wait for specific response on collectibles.

"You know Toucan? He lives across the street at Jimi Changa's, the discotheque." Antonio nearly grins and grinds his hips, scrunching his shoulders and stirring his fists over his congealing *rancheros*. Who can resist such a rhythm?

He is done making his case.

A Thorny stare at the dissipating rhythm with a slight tick tells Antonio that the question remains on the table unanswered. The pointed eyes slide to Sally, who speaks on cue.

"Tono, can your brother find us these birds and furry animals? Can he bring us young ones from the jungle?"

"Well, you know the jungle is not what it used to be. I mean, with the roads now and the animals moving... And then, of course, my friends, we have the question of intent. My brother is, shall we say, sensitive. You understand. He will only help those animals in need. I don't think he will..."

"Antonio."

Antonio nods deeply, sensing arrival at a consensus on a fair airing of the issues. Discountable only moments ago as a *loco* boy, Baldo is now conceptual and complex with a lingering note of dynamic potential in the face of liability. In a word, he is still *loco*, but perhaps he is justifiable as a collector of animals.

This is the fine line on which astronomical deals sometimes balance, though in this application the balance remains to be found. Balance as a concept is understood here, like that between scorn and flamboyance, which is the balance these two understand best. A load should tip precariously to neither side.

So it is in the balance between authenticity and liability. You want Baldo collecting animals from the wild to live in a hotel lobby? Well then, perhaps we can view the exotic specimens in terms of, say, a wildlife rescue program. Or a, what do they call it?

A genetic assurance program to guarantee forever the guests' rights to see what was here long after we achieve our greatest level of development. We can capture a few for making babies for their own good and for ours and everyone's. Moreover, the question of money has been effectively deferred to contemplation of exponential magnitude, as it were, factoring family and friends in the best possible light, which is that of real value.

"My friends," Antonio intones in the somber voice reserved for complete control of the situation. "We can only ask. My brother is sensitive to the perceptions of nature held by those around him. He is unique among men. He is nothing if not honest. He will tell us."

The mentors look at each other as numbers and concepts briefly muddle, until Mrs. M herself preempts contemplation of value and flamboyance. High heels clicking on the marble floor like a metronome time the eternal elegance that will not fade for many years to come. Her beach robe in translucent saffron highlights the womanly embers within. Billowing no less than flames fanned, it opens on the glowing thighs that don't chafe and hardly jiggle.

But who's looking at the thighs anyway with such boom ba ba boom up top? Red silk crisscrosses the mountaintops like bandoleers. It runs around the back and up as well to hang from the neck. Thornton Mayfair smiles tolerantly.

Simón Salvador seeks the attention of a waiter, because it's time for sweets and more caffeine.

"*Buenos Días,*" she says.

"Good morning, dear. You look ravishing, as usual."

"Mm," she purrs. "I feel more ravished than usual." She doesn't touch Antonio or look at him, but the touch and look are hardly necessary to reference the marathon intimacy of last night's homecoming. Going to midnight might not seem so late, unless you begin immediately after cocktails, as a man engulfed by loneliness and disappointment is wont to do. But why these people seem so driven to wallow in their own indelicacy is beyond the reason of any man. Now it's Antonio's turn to feel the blood rise and shade his tawny good looks to undeniable magenta.

Thornton Mayfair stares with amusement. How can this be? Well, of course they have a modern arrangement, but still, some things are very hard to understand.

"Taking the morning off?" She asks Antonio, who jumps from contemplation of ficky fick and an enriched future back to the moment with its practical need. He looks at his watch, the new one with the combination silver- and gold-linked band and the gold-rimmed face.

¡Ay! Nine o'clock already.

Stretching again, he sees that the pool is lined with guests. Some are sleeping. Some sip coffee. Some stare into space. All verge perilously on boredom or worse, a review of their lives at home, down to the commute, the years remaining on their mortgages and lives, their paltry joys, and the hours of the days.

"*¡Chihuahua!*" he lowly moans. "My guests are thinking."

"See what I mean?" Thornton Mayfair says with conviction.

"No," Mrs. M perks. "Tell me what you mean."

XV

Where Love Lay Hidden All Along

Lyria Alvarez lies awake in the bed of her own making, which is not to say her own bed but is rather that of Viorica Valenzuela. She's far from home, where she lay only this morning, wondering how she came to feel lost and alone.

How did she arrive here, only four blocks down and two blocks over, to feel anything but alone? "Love is like life," Viorica whispers. "We cannot arrange it neatly on a shelf. We can't do anything about it. But we can play and have fun. So why not?"

Surrounded by soft light, linens, and the soft caress of Viorica, Lyria feels the knowing sinking in. Smiling in the dark, she opens the little door in her heart for the one patiently knocking since a brief and random meeting only this afternoon. A poor, confused hotel maid who barred the door grants entry and now steps back, unafraid.

Viorica breathes gently beside her. Viorica fills her with a touch. Viorica fills the room with the presence of a goddess. How can this be so? Do not women lying together face holy repercussion? But if sin is to be feared in the eyes of God, then why is this presence so easily revered? How can it feel so good and provide such relief?

Like a prisoner loosened from her bindings at last, Lyria stretches lazily and feels her soul yawn with awakening.

Viorica wakens beside her and feels the soft, smooth flank as a sculptress might feel a finished marble.

Lyria turns to Viorica and wonders who could see such a beautiful face and guess the unlikely place it most wanted to be? She smiles at the thought of it, which is funny in its way. She trembles with the warmth welling inside her, her smile stretching to laughter, which puts her at the top, however briefly, of the difficult mountain called life. If Viorica wants to do those things in her gentle way, things that Antonio revels in so boisterously, what's the harm? Lyria feels herself between the legs and trembles again at the thought of it.

"This is easy," Viorica says, picking up the thread of Lyria's thought from where it dangles. "You're pregnant with Baldo's child. You must make a choice now, because you can't make a choice later. If you wait until later, the choice you didn't make may well haunt you and your child, who may wish she were never born. Believe me. I have had such a wish."

"You have wished to miss your own birth?" Lyria asks incredulously.

Viorica's diffident half-smile is a sad, stern confirmation.

"But you're happy," Lyria says. "How can you wish you were never born? If you were never born, you could never be happy."

"You've been going to church," Viorica says. "That's where you learn to think without logic. If you were never born, my dear, you could never be unhappy. Believe me, happiness is very capable of getting along without us. I'm happy now, because you're here. I learned a long time ago to take happiness where I can. It doesn't last. It's no deeper than the time it takes it to go away. I want to experience Lyria Alvarez. I admit that I want this passionately. I think perhaps that passion is the depth of happiness. Already I have her body, and I think her mind will be as sweet. How long can we stay married?"

"Married?"

They roll apart and lay side by side, staring up.

"Exactly. The two of us in bed having our fill. Like we were married. I think I like this more than you do. It doesn't matter. How long until we seek something different, something new? You make me happy. In a little while or a long while, happiness will go away. You think I help you see things in a different light. Soon you will see for yourself. Maybe you will help me see something. Maybe not. I'm not saying this is bad, or that I don't want to be alive right now. I'm only saying that life is up and down. I used to wish that I'd never been born. Now I think I wouldn't mind if I'd never been born. This is an improvement. No?"

"This is very sad."

"It's only sad when you make me explain. Happiness is when you feel no need to explain anything. It doesn't come along very often, unless you're alone. I like being alone. But I like being with you better, for now."

They lay silently in flickering candlelight watching the playful shadows, until Viorica turns and says, "You make me lose my thought. You must choose now, which is every woman's right, no matter what the men say. You must choose to have your baby and raise it and care for it and work to make the money with no help from the father. This you know. Or you must choose to spare it the suffering with an abortion."

Lyria does not move but scrutinizes the shadow play on the walls and ceiling. She turns to Viorica's gentle countenance, fairly certain of the preference therein, which leans toward independence and freedom from responsibility.

How blessed the comfort of a sturdy, soft bed to diffuse the burden of choice. How heavily the burden presses, yet it eases. Waiting for an answer to arrive on its own seems the best thing for a young woman to do, until Viorica reads these thoughts too and admonishes those who wait. The answer will not come by itself, without your help. It must be chosen.

"I think you can help me with either choice I make," Lyria says, feeling suddenly mobile in the world of knowing.

"Yes. I can," Viorica says, leaning in for a kiss on Lyria's neck, a kiss she, Lyria, would call disgusting if it passed between Antonio and the old *puta*. But this is different; not that Antonio or anyone will have the chance to call it anything. "You don't need to choose right now. But soon. You must also make another choice."

Lyria waits fearfully for the balance of her destiny to be told.

"You must choose to remain a hotel maid, or to become a woman of financial independence."

Lyria smiles and frowns. She casts her eyes down and then up. "You mean that I must be a maid or a prostitute?"

Viorica laughs quietly. "No. I think a prostitute has sexual relations for money. She will for the most part have sexual relations with anyone who can pay the price, with as many men as possible, if they can pay. Wives have sexual relations with these same men, perhaps not so often, but then the money is also less and must be begged. A woman of independent means chooses her client and is very well paid for her affection. If she chooses carefully, the affection is not so difficult and in time may become natural."

"You make it sound natural. But you also sound like these arrangements of affection are only temporary."

Viorica shrugs. "Like I have told you, this is the nature of happiness. It's the same as love or flowers or anything that's nice. It goes away. If it didn't, it wouldn't seem so nice while it was here. Maybe you'll find the man to grow old with. Maybe you'll win the lottery. Anything is possible."

They wait for things to settle, and soon Viorica sleeps again.

Lyria thinks until she's too sleepy, but the middle of the night is time for sleep, unless your head caroms with this and that, demanding resolution. The little flame flickers but will not die.

Lyria loves the way her choices were presented, not as ultimatum, with either one dependent on goodness or badness or assuring damnation from one school or another. These are separate choices, either of which can be correct. She can have a baby or not and be a *puta* or not.

Yes, I know; it's not a *puta* because of blah, blah, blah. So why, Miss Smarty pants, does all of society consider such women to be *putas*?

Viorica slips deeper and soon verges on a dainty snore.

Lyria knows the answer. It is because society knows what is best for those at the top of the heap. Society is valued and defined by those in comfort, those who have seen Lyria Alvarez wiping the rim and sucking the lint and foil wrappers from under the bed, those who would see her into the future as a hotel maid.

Or a *puta*.

The thing of it is, Lyria as a maid is easy to see, and the other is nobody's business but my own. But then who will pay for the affection of a beautiful woman, which is exactly what I am, with a baby? Or a child, or a teenager, or a young adult? Because a baby will surely go through life in phases as I have done, which seems tortuous on reflection and a very good reason for independence and freedom from responsibility. And what would a child think of a *puta* for a mother? The answers require no mystical analysis. Every car has its buyer. Some have more or fewer buyers, depending on make, model, and options. And of course the mileage, unless the maintenance has been good.

Anything is possible. As far as the baby's growth and changing phases, she can only hope for happiness.

Isn't that what the church says? This is very difficult. What if a woman wants someone to grow old with, and he wants his own son?

The answer here too seems known, because the likelihood of a man wanting his own son is no greater than that of a man willing to accept the son that comes to him. After all, standing naked in low light as Viorica bid her do so the last vestige of the lower life could be shorn away, Lyria could see the beauty for herself.

Viorica traced the curvature of her body with fingertips and lips. Viorica called her beautiful, and assured her that beauty is often taken for granted; it seems such a simple contour but in fact outlines the greatest longing of men. It is the most valuable resource granted by God. Affection does not come from the loins but from the heart. It is something else, perhaps not entirely removed from this lovely curvature with its curious bumps and crevasses, and it can be learned in time, with patience. In the meantime, we can practice patiently on each other.

But doesn't that mean that a well mannered, properly schooled woman like Lyria Alvarez will be expected to behave like Mrs. Mayfair in her later years?

This too is simple. She, Lyria, will have no need for such wanton flamboyance, so it will not be necessary.

Happiness depends on faith, which is exactly what the church has been trying to teach. Faith must be its own reward, in case the happiness doesn't follow. These and other thoughts clarify their meaning in the dancing light, even as Viorica gently snores.

Lyria slips down into the soft warmth, causing Viorica to shift in deference to her dream. Their bodies snuggle precisely and meld with matched breathing until all knowing is as easy as falling off a log.

The little flame expires: hsst. Lyria's muscles loosen on the cinnamon-scented smoke. She moans and nestles in. Viorica squeezes gently from her dream, and they sleep.

They surface when darkness ebbs.

One wakens and slides under for that which the other has only heard about before yesterday. Hearing of such a thing falls short of the actual event, with its many surprises and sensations, its dynamic range of pace and vigor and, if you're lucky, it's tireless pursuit, until the little birds flutter out of nowhere and take riotous flight to everywhere.

So wakens the other, yielding to the torrent nature provides.

The one rises to the pillow next door with a soft, "Good morning."

The other feels indebted, as properly schooled girls in the region will feel. The love at hand is creamy rich. They wallow in it, until each feels indebted, neither will resist, and the happiness may be shared. Cautiously yielding to guiding hands for proper alignment of smiles, they yield to pace and vigor. Control is not so cut and dried once initiative becomes mutual, and happiness is soon secure for both.

Moaning and gasping feels overwhelming and further removed from an ear grab than *Oaxtapec* from Uranus. This nuance and subtlety and numbing wave of lovely comfort go hand in glove with tireless persistence and, if you will, with a certain character found only in women. On this last critical point, the one insists: not in men, but only women.

The other will understand, even as she wonders what was subtle.

Full claim and comprehension will come with *cafe con leche* and *jugo de naranja* and *tamales con mole*. Breakfast comes after the flock screeches and sings to the horizon and the steaming shower and the shampoo massaged thoroughly to displace prior thought. Then the cream rinse and leisurely dry and some lovely new things and another walk, this one light and clear as the brand new day. It's only the café two blocks down and six over, but it fits with what Lyria has learned, that happiness is hers for the taking, if only she will.

The catch is that it must be taken, or it will not be.

She cannot love Viorica Valenzuela as Viorica might love her, yet she loves this feeling of relief and…and everything. She would tell these things to Viorica but feels certain Viorica knows.

Viorica affirms the feeling with a shrug, meaning that every now and then we find it. She takes Lyria's hand, because now they have found it together.

Lyria nods and can't keep from grinning, which Viorica can't help but mirror, as if the joke is theirs to have on all else. "What? Tell me, *chica*. What?"

"I don't want… I don't…"

"What?"

"I will have my baby."

Viorica rolls her eyes. "If that's what you want, then good. You have thought and made a choice. So few do, you know."

Lyria blushes. "I only want it…" She hesitates, fearing a blunder and the appearance of stupidity. She proceeds to test the mettle of her new friendship. "I only want it to be Antonio's."

Viorica's eyebrows arch. "You want what would have been easy. Now it could be difficult. Let me think…"

Viorica thinks. Lyria waits.

Viorica speaks, sharing the process of solution. "I have too many times considered a thing impossible. Some things are impossible, but most are not. Most things are only as we see them. I will think on this, because what we have…"

She stops when Lyria is suddenly startled. "What?"

"I have missed my work."

Viorica shrugs. "So? You have made your second choice. Besides, I'm thinking."

But Lyria's head shakes vigorously now, because Viorica obviously doesn't understand that work is not like life; it is much more necessary and much less forgiving. While the end of one is blessedly beyond pain or desire, the end of the other is unemployment with the rent due and the cupboard bare. "You don't understand."

"Yes, I do. You need money on Friday. Am I right?"

"Yes. I must work to live." Her eyes lower so she can speak with pride, preempting what she senses. "I cannot take money from you."

"I want you to work for me."

"I know that. But I am with child. How can I work with you? I mean for you."

"It is not a problem. You will need some time off, but not for a while. By then, you will make more money than any hotel maid ever dreamed of."

Suddenly the tamales look cold. They shrivel under the congealed *mole* with a skin on top. It looks like glop and smells mephitic. Perhaps those words, *by then*, bring home the reality of this newfound comfort and mobility and leisurely breakfast in a café, not to mention the warmth and understanding, which will continue until *then* only by allowing the *pingas* of many men to slide freely between her legs.

These thoughts twist her face with resistance. She wants to spit, thinking as well of such traffic between the legs of her friend, who once again sees and knows.

"*¿Hola? ¿Chica?* This is ground control to Major Tom. *¿Hola? Por favor.* You are very sweet to fear for your life, but your life is already gone. Only today will you begin to live. Trust me. You do what I say. I will pay the money the hotel would pay you. You don't have to do anything. Except maybe meet a man. Just meet him. Say hello and whatever you like. Nothing else. Then we talk, so you can tell me if you like him or no."

"But what of...my *chica*?"

Viorica shrugs. "We won't introduce her. It's too early. Don't you think so?"

Lyria smiles grimly, unconvinced.

Viorica says, "Did you ever hear of the child who was born with the gift of speech?"

"No, I have not. It was a miracle?"

"Yes, of course it was a miracle. The little baby came out, and the doctor held it up and slapped it on the bottom until it could breathe, and it looked up and asked, 'Are you my papa?' The doctor told the little baby no, I am not your papa, then handed it to its mother. The mother held it gently, and it looked up and asked, 'Are you my papa?' The mother said 'No, I'm not your papa. But here comes someone you can ask,' and she handed the little baby to its papa, who also held it gently, and the little baby asked, 'Are you my papa?' The papa said, 'Yes, little baby, I am your papa.' So the little baby reached up and put its arm around the papa's neck and said, 'Let me ask you something. How does this feel?'"

Viorica reaches gently around Lyria's neck and pulls her head near. Then with the stiff fingers of her other hand she pokes Lyria's forehead repeatedly. "'You like this, huh? Does this feel good?'" And she laughs, because it's a joke.

Lyria does not laugh.

"Lyria, this is a joke. A joke." She won't ask if Lyria gets it for fear of having to explain.

"I thought you said it was a miracle."

"It would be a miracle, but it didn't really happen. I was telling you a joke."

"You think it's funny, when a little baby is poked in the head with a *pinga*?"

Viorica smiles. "Yes, I do, especially when the little baby comes out complaining about it and then pokes the man back."

Lyria nods, pondering the humor of the situation, wondering if the *chica* inside her also hears but doesn't laugh and instead fears what must come next. "When?"

"When what?"

"When must I meet him?"

"Soon. We are in no rush. Would you like to go shopping today?"

"You mean shopping for this man?"

"No, my pet. You suddenly have no faith. Please, leave the men to me. I mean the man. There will be no men. Not all at once."

"Do you know him?"

"I have an idea of him."

"Just one idea?"

"No, I have several ideas. We hardly ever find a perfect match. Not in life or in love or in the practical world. We'll find the best of the lot for you. Don't worry."

"Don't worry? This is easy for you to say and maybe easy for you to do. Maybe you are rich. Maybe you have many men who want to be with you and some of them are rich and so you have money. But I don't. I only have worries over money. Now I have worries that you are...with too many men whose health you may not know."

"Yes, it's easy for me to say. It's easy for you to say too, if only you will. You spent all that time in school and in church, and for what? Yes, I have money, more money than I can ever spend. My father is an oil producer. Do you know what that means? As for health, we will try our best to find you a married man. These are the healthiest. They must also be careful, and that is all you can ever have, the benefit of some thoughtful caution. Believe me, Lyria. You will be pleased. That you will be pleased is my guarantee. If you are not pleased, then nothing will happen. Now, would you like to go shopping?"

"Shopping for what?"

"You need a brassiere. And shoes."

XVI

Liberation

With only three days remaining until the young turtles will be officially free to find their way in the watery world, excitement is stirring at *Hotel Oaxtapec*. New arrivals are thrilled with the timing of their vacations, especially on learning that they too may participate in the ceremonies leading to and including the dramatic finale of the grand liberation. Each guest will be given a turtle to escort to the water's edge, to instruct and assist in a little prayer, presumably to God, who is sure to be listening.

Guests scheduled for departure prior to the ceremony can only wish they'd known, and many promise to time their vacations properly next year. Some bid farewell and luck to the young turtles, most often with a wave and a cheerful "Goodbye, little turtles!"

Down on the beach in personal isolation, swaying again like a solitary weed as his habit has become, Baldo stands between the world of his alienation and the one that beckons.

These days are most troubling to Antonio, who feels the sting of loss of tips rightfully accruing to Baldo, who has brought the turtles along, but now they're going down the drain, the tips, or worse, into Milo's pocket.

Milo also sees but won't complain with tips coming in. He urges more, assuring well-wishers that donations will go directly into the turtle fund.

The turtle fund? Antonio will see about that.

Baldo gazes longingly seaward, but a man can't go live in the sea. Baldo knows this with each breath he takes, as he knows he must continue to breathe, unlike the fish, who can live indefinitely underwater. Then again, it's not like they don't breathe. They do. This we know. They breathe between the water, which a boy of unique insight to certain things knows and has, in fact, experienced. Even if it was only a dream, it was real.

Baldo could breathe between the water in his dream. He could surface easily as a turtle, but still, he is too soft and has no shell to tuck into. Then again, neither do the turtles have a solid defense against those who would take a bite or even a nibble. Some survive for many years for no other reason than they are chosen to survive. Perhaps the animal angels protect them, or maybe a spirit residing in the infinite depths chooses who will live and who will die, as surely we must live until we die, each in his way.

In keeping with the Law of Life and Death, the depths beckon with their clarity and soothing sibilance. Do not the depths offer a greater freedom in life, no matter how long that life will be? Who can say if a being is chosen or protected, or that a life will be a short one or a long one?

The poster proclaims the little turtles will soon be Officially Free. Isn't that just like the world of alienation, to burden freedom with organization, administration, pomp and ceremony?

The turtles know better. Baldo senses this as well.

They may live for more years or fewer, but wisdom comes easier to a turtle than to a human. Just look in their eyes and sense their longing for the deep blue sea. Watch their reverie in only a few feet of water, and you will see a grace and compassion the humans can only attempt to organize and administer and still fail miserably at learning. What human was ever so sanguine at ninety days? Who needs to count the days anyway?

Baldo knows who was ready ten days ago and who needs a few days more. Still they will go together for the benefit of the guests, as if the guests too will throw off a yoke of their own making and for a while be free of the tubs of their own making, where they are destined to struggle for air eternally between feedings.

This morning a new uniform waited on a hanger in a plastic bag. Baldo wears it now, but its color and decoration lose their zest. Epaulets and colorful badges on the chest and sleeves give the shirt a festive look, because the march from the plastic tubs to the beach will have the trappings of a parade. It will be as if *Hotel Oaxtapec* won the cup and will now roll slowly down the main street for the hometown crowd to cheer.

Baldo will wave the big baton. He's not in the Navy, nor does he exactly understand what *El Secretario Pesco* does, but he has the patches. Oh, well, it would have been fun and a great sendoff for the babies who have waited for so long.

Some are now five inches across. Some only four. Some weigh half a kilo, *mas o menos*. Baldo observes them for symmetry and stroke, haunch and focus.

Do they look this way and that, or do they gaze straight ahead in their paddle through thin air? Do they eat their fill? Do they peck back when pecked? And what about posture and stance?

Baldo will pick two young turtles for early release, perhaps these two who now swim in mid-air with considerable excitement, which is understandable here, for the first time so near the sea of their dreams. They can see that it's real, has been real all along, that they were right and never lost faith, even in the confines of a world called Rubbermaid® where no one would listen or believe.

Just look. There it is.

They can see and smell it and know that dreams come true. The big one thrusts his head high in the air and would arch his back and neigh while standing on his hind legs if he could.

The small one is more circumspect and perhaps uncertain, but she's certainly unafraid. She only finds her way more slowly, which is no slower than fast, given the infinite nature and timeless schedule of the deep blue sea. What's the rush? She may need companionship is all, until she grows a bit bigger. Mario will lead. Baldo and Chiquita will follow.

Of course these are merely the idle thoughts of a troubled boy. What can a silly daydream amount to but foolishness and perhaps a little time harmlessly wasted? Still, he has chosen to wear the colorful new uniform three days ahead of schedule, because he thinks he will wear it now or never. He's never had a uniform like this, reflecting elevation and importance in the world of men, and it is fun. Or, if not fun, at least it lets him sample the feeling of a life in uniform. Perhaps, given a chance of a different nature, he would be on the rise to become *El Secretario* himself one day.

Even as the bright and frilly uniform feels more and more like every day, people pass by and stare and talk privately to each other. So it must be impressive. Let Quincy see this and wonder who's in control. Baldo contemplates a life of garish color, in which he will take his place on the reef and guard his home from intruders. Officially.

He sets the young turtles in hand onto the sand and holds them gently but firmly in place so they will know to wait there. Don't move.

He pulls his machete from its makeshift sheath that hangs from his belt and raises it in the air, because the leader of a marching band must show those behind him where he's going, so they can see and follow. Baldo knows no one is behind him but himself in long-lost youth. Still, he looks back. He could have told you what was there; it's nothing but sandy beach up to the pool deck where Antonio sits with the two soft men who eye the baby turtles frequently and now and then eye their keeper. Baldo suspects an appetite for turtle soup to go with a little brown round steak.

The softies listen intently to Antonio, who seems to speak mechanically while staring across the beach, which is nearly empty today under gray skies. A few tourists walk it, but Antonio is watching his former brother, the unlikely bandleader who waves his machete in the air but has yet to march, maybe because of the difficulty presented in high-stepping with flippers on his feet.

Hot today and breezeless, the stillness resonates with Antonio's voice in the distance.

Antonio strives to make a point that he saw concisely illustrated in a movie not too long ago. That is, a moral message can outweigh the appearance of violence and maximize the gate if the set is sufficiently lavish and the effects are up to snuff, which seems obvious, of course. But this particular movie really illustrated the point like no other, though he can't remember the name of it. So he sits back and calls the waiter for more coffee. Nor can he be entirely certain what it was about, which illustrates another point, *mas o menos*, that content doesn't really matter, as long as you entertain from frame to frame, which is actually what Thorny and Sally have been saying all along.

The soft men adjust to new positions, and the darker-skinned one asks who was in this movie.

Antonio pauses on the verge of speaking. He prompts himself and snaps his fingers to indicate that it was, uh, uh, you know, uh. "I will remember in a minute."

The lighter-skinned one asks what kind of movie it was.

The breeze whispers nothing as Antonio thinks, until he looks up with a nod and decisive smile and says, "It was made in California."

The soft men nod and shrug, so Antonio proceeds with elaboration on further theory of this, that and the other that will no doubt enhance margins and bid formidably for market share.

The soft men shrug and nod some more.

Baldo tries these gestures on himself to see how they feel. He wants to know if the feeling will somehow tell him what is next felt, just as his new uniform lets him know how something feels. He nods and shrugs and nods some more. He prompts himself with a forward rolling hand and snaps his fingers on the verge of speaking. He listens for what the still, muggy air will tell him.

He stops listening and looks down. Scanning quickly left and right and then dead ahead just in time, he sees Mario and Chiquita poised on their tiptoes ten paces ahead. They brace at the top of a wave wash that tickles their chins, for the first time in direct contact with Mother Ocean, who bathes her baby turtles with seawater untouched by human hands.

Baldo sheathes his blade and slides the sheath around to the back as he steps forward slowly. He moves with the awkwardness befalling those species who find grace most easily in the water, yet must walk on dry land from time to time.

The wave wash recedes and now tickles his youthful *compadres* from the hind side. They give into it and crawl with difficulty to knee-deep and then shoulder-deep, which depth is, of course, much easier for them, adding buoyancy.

It's only ankle deep for Baldo, who slowly follows, watching over and above them, casting an eye as well beyond and beneath them. In a few paces more they swim and seem happier than they ever could have imagined, or maybe it's the action of the shallow waves tossing them about that makes their effort look like a romp.

Dos tijerillas fly overhead and circle back until Baldo pulls his blade and spreads his wings to convey the message. With sincere conviction, he lets them read it and further informs all parties that he will deliver the message if either bird swoops to swinging radius, even as he peers to see if one is perhaps his own *Tijerilla*. Such is the way and the hand of God, who surely listens and knows and moves through this, the hand of His agent.

He thinks neither of these birds is his, but even if one is, we have come now to the law of nature, which cannot be broken no matter who thinks it can be.

The birds read the message clearly and fly away.

Meanwhile, Mario merely treads while Chiquita has no doubt. It's only a phase he's going through, in which he needs a minute to adjust, or he senses something, or maybe she's the one who senses. Never mind; it's time to go knee deep and watch his young companions give in to seduction and find their stride.

Baldo slides his mask from his shoulder where the strap of it squeezed an epaulet. Trussed up in a fancy shirt but looking very peculiar indeed with flippers on his feet and no trousers, well, at least now, with a mask over his eyes, he can see. Looking away from one dimension and into another, he sees that dreams are real—just look at Mario and Chiquita!

This shirt would best fit a clown, but if it is left here to catch the next wave just as a mute boy once waited to catch the next bus, so too is trouble left behind. And confusion.

Beyond the break, nothing breaks. It undulates receptively, and a lanky boy finding his rhythm moves into it with faith.

The clouds cleave. The sun shines. Beneath is a clarity Baldo has seen nowhere but here. There are his friends, Wrasse and

Tang, Butterfly and Angel. And there are his great good friends Trumpet fish and Puffer.

¡Hola, mis amigos¡ Hey, Mario, Chiquita, wait for me.

And so on a gentle transition from vertical to horizontal, Baldo Garza eases into a soft, gentle stroke similar to that of a young turtle. He urges Mario along, because it's time to go and there is nothing more to sense here in the shallows than the deep blue sea before us, which is plenty to sense, especially at first blush, with so much infinity and eternity drawing us in.

Mario must learn that stopping for every feeling of immensity that comes along will open him to attack no less than a sitting duck. Of course he, Mario, is neither sitting nor a duck. But treading water isn't much different than sitting still, and you're still smaller than a duck and just as defenseless.

So you move through the fear to the feeling that will be known as home, until the feeling too disappears, and all that is known rises in a bubble through these, the waters of our forgetting.

With luck we'll have time until then, perhaps a long time.

Mario finally catches up with Chiquita, with Baldo's help, and the two small ones rest, treading lightly but mostly resting. Shadows play across the bottom at fifty feet, and a swimmer can easily tell where clouds block the slanting shafts of glimmering light. He can tell which shadows are cast by denizens of the reef, and which ones move in tandem with three young siblings of two different sizes.

Baldo hovers and feels his skin tighten with knowing. He cannot be certain what he knows, but he knows it with certainty. The chill upon him is removed from official scheduling, and he thinks it will pass, given a minute to warm up. Then Chiquita dives for the feel of it, and he follows. She only goes ten feet or fifteen, and the chill surges with circulation.

Mario follows for cavorting at far greater depths than a tub could allow. Then they return to the surface and make their way.

Baldo knows the way. It draws him in, as a homecoming will welcome a weary traveler.

Such is the departure forevermore of Baldo Garza, who will be known in the short term as a *loco* boy who killed himself because he was depressed. Some will further speculate on whom else he may have killed or if he impregnated his brother's fiancée.

In the long term he will become the legendary turtle boy who swam so far out with his young charges that he joined them in spirit and may still be swimming. Perhaps he will age gracefully and live for many decades with barnacles on his shell. Or maybe he turned right and swam back to shore farther south to begin a new life as a cabaret mime in Acapulco. He was really very good, you know.

In the moment he only swims, watched by the brother who has witnessed his progression from the edge of their father's grave to appointment as *El Capitán de las Tortugas*. Antonio ponders the net effect of brotherly guidance and briefly considers mortal sin as a lingering shadow on a family. One brother is shamed and the other sways like a weed, staring idly through once-idyllic mornings.

What difference does a brother make? What is the difference between watching Baldo over gruel and *tortillas* and watching him over power brunch? *Nada* is the answer. Nothing makes a difference. Nothing will help. Nothing is what Baldo will come to, and so too what he touches.

Yet Antonio watches to keep his own peace of mind. He doesn't worry, because Baldo can't harm anything by standing on a beach or going for a swim. Tourists pass by, but he only gazes back dolefully, harmlessly, unless they, you know, break the Law of Baldo's Land.

Which they will, surely as that gang of monkeys will type the National Anthem of Mexico, given a decent chance. Inevitability plagues Antonio's days no less than the mosquitoes plague his sleep. Here he loses his train of thought at a critical juncture, a point worked toward and longed for, only to find himself forgetting the names of fabulous movies and their stars. He agrees distractedly to Thorny and Sally's continuing perambulations on margin enhancement, and he watches.

Baldo's new uniform looks different with a machete on his belt and a mask and snorkel on his shoulder, but not for long. He's putting the mask on now and taking off the shirt and leaving it in the surf. And, *Madre de Cristo*, what is that tiny splashing in front of him? Well, he won't hurt the little turtles. But why release them now? Where is he taking them? Antonio watches his brother's awkward walk to the sea, his casual disrobing and easy stroke, herding two little swimmers in front. What difference can it make if two little turtles go now? Baldo can swim to the rock and back without flippers if he wants to, even if it's twelve miles round trip and might take till noon.

But what is he thinking? How can he leave his brilliant new uniform tumbling in the break? Let's face it; he's *más loco que una cabra*. Only Baldo and a goat would shun success. And Antonio might as well eat tin cans as apply reason to one so troubled.

XVII

A Dream Come True

Antonio dreams that he and his brother swim side by side in the dream they now share.

Baldo says he is happy, not in so many words but rather with his inimitable conveyance of what should be known. Baldo says he is home at last with the animal angels, who are no different than the animals that inhabit the depths. This is because the depths are every bit as lovely as they are alluring. He says his migration is ongoing and good, and don't worry because his recent departure was inevitable, not a learned behavior but hard-wired from the beginning. It was only a matter of time.

Baldo flexes gracefully as a ray and dips below the surface. The machete doesn't slap his thighs if he's under water but waves like a barb at the base of his spine to warn those who may not yet recognize him.

Antonio wakens at two or six in a sweat, each time dripping wet as if freshly emerged from the briny deep. Waking suddenly from such a dream of his brother in the act of finality leaves him with a pounding heart and the disturbing sensation of water all around. He breathes deeply and reaches to feel the air and perhaps to feel Baldo still swimming alongside.

But this is no nightmare. No horror fills the room or constricts the dreamer's breathing, for the dream is merely what Antonio believes. Or maybe he only thinks he might believe it, or should believe it. At any rate it is the stuff of Antonio's evolving faith.

Faith in what, he cannot say. But he thinks, perhaps, Baldo's long, easy stroke is tireless if not eternal, that a boy so touched by spirits may in fact find his way back to the land of the living. Or at least he may avoid death, or may have, or maybe not.

Baldo swims ahead into the darkness and fades, as he must.

The morning of the release of all the little turtles is great cause for celebration with ceremony and speeches of self-congratulation. Turtles have been slaughtered but now may be restored and revered; so shall we pause to reflect on what sets us apart from our kind, which is our heroism in the face of massive development.

The two *can* peacefully coexist. This we have proven here.

Along with the pitter-patter of tiny feet, the hotel guests approach to watch, some in awe and wonder, some in sleepy awareness of this turtle thing they're making all the hoopla over down on the beach. Some hug each other. Some hug themselves. Some cry for the little turtles, so alone in such a great big sea. Or maybe they cry for all the turtles lost or something else that's lost. Some carry their tiny wards very slowly, whispering secrets to the young turtles who don't listen but flip madly for the freedom to begin. Some want to know if the big coffee percolator will be wheeled down to the beach so they can wake up reasonably. God *damn*, that was a humdinger last night.

Wasn't it?

Some ask why not wheel the percolator down here where it is needed. It has wheels! Wouldn't it be perfect if they wheeled a buffet table down here too? They have wheels too, you know, the tables. So why not?

A few guests swim out with the young turtles, but not too far because of potential danger beyond the break, where *El Capitán de las Tortugas* may have been lost. But maybe he wasn't lost, or if he was, maybe it happened much farther out. Or maybe he swam back in and has yet to call home. Or come home, since he can't very well call. Maybe he's only stepped out for a few decades and will be home later.

With no Grand Marshall to lead the parade, ceremonial duties fall to Antonio, who understandably begs off in deference to the anxiety and grief he now suffers for his brother. *No problema* with

Milo on hand, who mumbles and laughs over what you've been waiting for, and so now here it is.

Clouds drift in and a breeze stiffens but *las chicas* have only one thought, and they stroke through ninety days of waiting in the next few minutes, making double time for the depths.

What's the rush? Predators abound. Just look.

A few of the liberated wander north or south in their excitement, but the herd in general heads directly out to sea as if something urgent awaits them there. Stragglers and misfits are redirected to their proper course, and soon all shrink in the distance, gone in the troughs, splashing bravely on the crests.

The last guest waits until the last turtle is out of sight, and then it's over.

The night after the morning of the release is the occasion of another dream, this one equally fluid and as well removed from the fear or ghastly presence of a nightmare. But this one is different for the toll it takes on a weakened heart. You could call it a bad dream for its wanton taunt of a man's grief, but then growth often requires pain and more pain, until the carapace of a former self cleaves asunder and the new man swells to his rightful place in the world.

In this dream Lyria comes to Antonio's bed in the deepest part of the night, where even a light sleeper remains groggy and may think he's waking up but then knows he only dreams of thinking he's awake. Just so, Antonio thinks he's awake even as he realizes the deceptive nature of the dream.

"Sh," Lyria says dreamily.

He moans and rolls to face the image in the dream and settles again to the depths. He feels a foreign warmth, not fuzzy but smooth, like her body. It feels as he imagined it would feel in texture, firmness, shape and contour. He feels her breath on his neck. Then he feels nothing, until a soft landing on the peninsula of his essential self rouses the troops to attention.

Well, it rouses the rowdiest troop who assures the others that waking is not necessary. Leave this to him; he'll stand up and look around to see what's going on.

He, Antonio, opens his eyes in his dream and moves his hands up her body in a slow, soft way he's never done before but has often imagined.

The nature of a dream allows gentle exploration; a thorough probity unavailable through mere image and waking fantasy. In this embrace the body parts awaken and mesh. Antonio realizes he is having a wet dream and will soon soil the sheet on his hammock. But this dream is too good to will himself awake, so good that it allows tangible difficulties to fade away. This dream is pliable and flexible, allowing ficky fick in a hammock, flowing freely in the dark, in sleep, where no words are required. Yet she whispers, "You are my love," as he emits into the night. Love sentiments are conjured from his subconscious mind, another facility of a memorable and endless dream that then ends. The broken heart is salved with love, yet the ache is compounded with loss. He sleeps.

In the morning he awakens and grasps at the dream, rising not to a day of days but rather to a solitude stanched by his brother's absence. He can neither exercise nor count his money.

He needs time to heal, but he fears the process cannot begin. Never and ever can it begin with such a void in his life.

Discounting everything gained and what more was wanted, he thinks only of what he has to do today. It's another day like the rest. He cleans himself and brushes his hair with perfunctory dispatch, no posing and no adventures in styling. He pushes himself through these tasks, because they define the difference between a man who is alive and one who is not. He dresses simply in a button shirt and Bermuda shorts as conceptual breakfast with his mentors dictates.

Today they will review options relative to the size and shape of the pool and the possible addition of a cabana, which is Antonio's idea, even though guests want more sun than is good for them. A cabana will open the pool area for commerce in rainy weather. He has the attention of the mentors. He moves like a man in a dream, wondering what to do with it, the attention of his mentors.

Lyria does not salt the wounds between them with her presence but is careful to avoid him. For several days now she has taken an earlier bus in and a later bus out. But today she waits by her front door. She wears a new dress of flimsy but flattering material that clings to her and shows more of her chest than she has shown in the past. The neckline swoops daringly to reveal a lacy brassiere that must be new as well and makes her *chichis* look bigger.

He smiles briefly and looks away.

She waits, as if the bus will pull up right here and not up the hill, across the road. She gazes softly at his idle movements, movements aimed at nothing and accomplishing only the minimal act of defining a man with a pulse. He feels her gaze but ignores it as he rearranges things out front so she may have an opportunity to leave alone and spare them what they both want to avoid.

She must have slept late. But she waits until everything out front is rearranged and finally calls so softly that she could easily be unheard if he chose not to hear her.

"*Buenos dias.*"

He looks around to see if perhaps a hotel guest has wandered far afield. Or maybe she's practicing for a promotion to the restaurant. He looks again to see, and yes, that's what's different; the new dress reveals more leg and has no sleeves, and all the fuzzy parts are shaved clean. He would ask to see her armpits, but he knows they're also shaved, and besides, he can't ask.

She waits until he has nowhere else to turn but to her, and she whispers again, "You are my love."

A heart so burdened with ache that suddenly hears the words of reprieve can very well burst under the anguish of dying and living. Such pressure from inside and out is too much, even for a man in peak physical condition. He can only stare back, still and silent except for his face, which now reflects all that has come and gone between them, which is mostly a love nurtured since youth and in a very short time gone away, unless you count what lingers.

She walks the few paces between them and stands before him. She touches his face, which responds with a twist and downward squeeze he's never felt before, much less shared with another.

And there between them evolves another element of his faith. It takes the form of a secret they will share for years, which is this: the heart of a woman with its womanly weakness pounds inside this man, who breaks down and cries, who covers his face with his hands and weeps for what has come to him.

His loss is overwhelming. He can't go on.

She embraces him softly, briefly, and leads him back into his *casa* and to the edge of his hammock where she whispers yet again, "You are my love," in case he forgot. In case he forgot his recent dream, she doffs the new dress in a single slinky shimmy. Then come the lacy brassiere, and finally the panties to match.

Her obtrusive nudity gives rise to a morning of incongruity, the first being the unlikely time for romance at this time of mourning.

Second is the unabashed shamelessness of the woman saved for so long. Of course she blushes and can't meet him eye to eye but stoops to the task at hand, which is a fervent rousing of his cockadoodle do, which is also brooding and mourning but will set anything aside for a sensitivity session.

The gentle touch of romance is soon displaced by urgent needs, her own as well as his, and she works as if to get a job done, oblivious to recent events or the morning's agenda or anything in the world. With knowing efficiency she replaces mourning, death, and pain with what any man is weak to resist, which is brief and intense eradication.

Suffice to say that in a short while Antonio Garza stares at the ceiling again. Again he is dripping as if freshly emergent from the briny depths. But this time it is different, lying beside the former woman of his dreams, Lyria Alvarez. Equally dazed by the rigors of the romp, she too stares at something far away, perhaps something long gone, which is the childhood shared with the man beside her.

Here they are, thrust, as it were, into the future. Just so, the past vanishes as quickly as a wake dissipates to that level which water can't help but find, which is its own.

She searches the ruins for a keepsake, scans the future for what might be built on this shaky foundation.

Words won't come to either one of them, and constraint draws tight between them so they cannot express themselves verbally as they did only minutes ago physically.

He looks about the room, in his mind rearranging the clutter. Rolling his way, she stares sweetly. She blinks like a fawn at sunrise to assure him yet again of his place in her heart. He stares at the ceiling, sorting, moving, thinking. She wants to tell him that such mental gyration is circular by nature, that we can only round the bend to round the bend again, that love and life and what each deserves and each gets can only be assessed in the present, not the past. But these thoughts are as new to her as her new dress that fits well and feels good but will take some time getting used to, for all that is revealed. She wants to live by these new thoughts, but she's not yet ready to share.

So they wait.

In a while he rolls to meet her eyes. He feels her skin and then her breasts with amazement that such fondling is so accessible. Putting his tongue where his eyes have never been, he flicks the tips of her *chichis*, unseen since sharing the bath so many years ago, assuring her of mutual affection.

She whimpers.

He nibbles, sliding his hand down the lovely curvature to her belly of another curvature, which is not unlovely and may in fact be shaped only as nature intended. Because six-pack abs are for men, and wombs with room for babies are for women.

She reaches for his *pinga* with her own evolving faith in Mrs. M and is affirmed by thumping resolution, ready again. So she pushes him over, crawls on top and hovers so his eyes can feast and send the message to his brain for forwarding due south. Every man needs a woman to look up to, but she needn't explain such things to a man who can see for himself.

They look down at the junction as if for proof of their convergence, bumping heads in the space between them. Together for the first time in this, their new life together, they laugh. They hardly notice the bump or the pain because of the vaster pain displaced.

She slides down the fire pole with five-alarm urgency. Their eyes meet in sweet agony as they wonder if this is love. As if doubting his comprehension, or maybe fearing his blindness to her capacity and range of love, to her commitment and earnest intent, she tells him again, "You are my love."

Soon he rides the bus alone, after she tells him that she will no longer be a maid in a hotel, because he is her love. Drifting further from his moorings, he spares himself the need for specific bearings.

We can dispense with navigation and logic this close to home. For years the one and only prize bull of *Oaxtapec* anticipated a grunt and a snort of fearsome dimension that would roll up the hill and down through the valley (or at least the lobby) once consummating his destiny with the essence of purity known as Lyria.

Instead, the future and the world and everything anticipated has come to this: he feels nothing, which can be better than something if the prevailing sensation these days is one of failure. This is the best he's felt in weeks. He knows she loves him as she always has. She said as much, and said it often.

The mentors have eaten and relax over coffee, assessing tangible benefits to a modern resort like the one next door that will have its own beach peddlers on staff. Pricing will be fixed, so the best peddlers can finagle as expected and make the most money. Meanwhile, *La Mexica, the Resort* can maximize margins and assure top quality through volume buys, like Costco or Wal-Mart but with authenticity, with the trees and the beach and everything, *hecho en Mexico*, as it were.

Antonio should eat quickly and hurry to his post. Some guests are napping by the pool already. Worse yet, some are staring and thinking. Worse yet, the fog enshrouding the once-vibrant maestro has settled, unmoving, with visibility close to zero.

He eats casually as the mentors tease him on the difficult schedule of a young man on the rise.

Mrs. M is in her place, already in full array. She's back to grasping hands and lies in strategic overview on a chaise lounge angled to present herself to the sun for maximum *sauté* with an optimal view of her husband and his friends. She seems basted with more cosmetic than usual, but that could be the direct morning sunlight that reveals the depth of her foundation and perhaps is melting it as well.

Antonio clearly sees through his fog that she is a classic beauty under the putty, and no man could tire of what the plastic hands tirelessly grasp. Mrs. M is in fact amazingly reminiscent of the sex-goddess/film legend Tina Torino, whose defiant beauty at fifty-two also denies the aging process, whose very face tells us this sculpture is stone, not clay. This beauty is for the ages and will not sag.

Tina Torino was on TV and said she would never grow old. She's coming here. She said so. Antonio eats, trying to remember the name of the daytime series that took the country by storm and gave her a household word for a name.

Clouds drift to the horizon.

He catches himself staring and sends the M an assuring nod. He will be willing and able to meet her briefly for years to come. If Tina Torino wants to relax by the pool, she too will be made to feel welcome as any beautiful guest. What else can he do but what he does, no matter what numbing clouds distract him?

Mrs. M calls softly, "Are you okay?"

Antonio laughs. He has heard this question often in the movies made in California, and he knows the answer. "Yes," he calls back. "I am okay."

Out front a taxi pulls up to deliver a beautiful movie star to the luxury of *Hotel Oaxtapec*. Perhaps her fame is yesterday's newspaper, but it was, and so it is. She is no longer prime for a poster shot highlighting her taut nipples for ogling by millions of teenage boys across the lower quadrant of the continent. But *Part of our Lives* is the indelible imprint she will carry to eternity. Her beauty is classic, her stardom an easy memory.

The door staff and lobby staff gather round for recognition and welcome, if not homage.

The taxi driver stares at the two *pesos* this notable woman has left for a tip. With her jewelry and plastic surgery, her scent of dying flowers and haughty airs, she is ignorant of the needs of a poor driver with children and a wife to feed. Does she know the value of two *pesos*? Two hundred pesos won't even pay for this welded chain steering wheel only twenty centimeters across. The chromium *paint* was fifty!

He wears the red-and-yellow plaid shirt he found in his taxi along with the houndstooth trousers common to the kitchen trade. The *huaraches* are a little snug but will loosen easily with slight cutting here and there. Perhaps this clothing is slightly the worse for wear, but it's clean and freshly stitched across the chest and thighs.

These repairs were a good deal of work but seemed warranted, the trousers and shirt fit so well and weren't all that threadbare, so what should he do, throw them out?

XVIII

The Pinnacle of Developmental Success

Lyria Alvarez and Antonio Garza will soon marry. They don't yet have a date but hope it will be prior to the birth of their child. Yet commitment to a date is made problematic by the vagaries of the construction schedule for *La Mexica, the Resort.*

Antonio wants his wedding poolside for spiritual reasons, for it is by the pool that success continues in all things. It only makes sense when you consider the dynamic symbiosis between himself and a perfectly dazzling pool surrounded by guests.

On a practical level a poolside wedding will prime the pump, as it were, on the idea of poolside weddings, which commerce will engage the entire hotel staff and generate much tipping and will carry a handsome premium on catering and rental rates.

Antonio can't officially conduct weddings, but he can keep the receptions lively with singing and dancing for a pretty peso, which shall be billed *a la carte* by *Maestro de Ceremonia LTD.*, a private concessionaire.

Are you kidding? Weddings? Who is dry-eyed or sober at a good wedding? Moreover, everyone is so—what is the word?— *verklempt*, that higher prices for everything just slide on by with hardly a notice. So why not reap what we have sown?

The new hotel will be everything the investors and Antonio had hoped for. The pool will be bigger, some say much bigger, with a cabana for continuing festivities in inclement weather. With twenty floors instead of merely eighteen and a higher rack rate, *La*

Mexica should attract a better crowd, meaning a crowd with a higher demographic, meaning greater discretionary income and increased upside potential. The stats have yet to lie. More money means more affluence if not influence, which can only lead to more of the same, and of course much, much more.

Cyclical prosperity is expected and factored into the equation for less traffic in the off-season or downward trending seasons. Traffic can only be sustained through the long, sultry summer with a lower demographic, meaning less revenue on greater volume. What can you do? Only peons and cheapos come to a sweat camp like this in August.

Unless of course they were not so cheap and are already dead, bringing us to the next level of dynamic enterprise, the rest lawn, which has a much nicer feel even in the saying than does the cemetery. *The 19th Fairway* will be down the road three miles and on the other side, closer to the trees than to the beach, because, well, let's be practical. Though three miles down, *The 19th Fairway* will be nonetheless adjunctive to *La Mexica, the Resort* in all manners pertaining to administrative function, flawless service, aesthetic excellence and, of course, spirituality.

What difference can a few miles make if you're, you know, and besides, *The 19th Fairway will have an excellent view* (as if anyone needs a view with golf on the wind) of the eighteenth green, which is where every golfer wants to finish.

More importantly is that this kind of diversification will bolster cyclical softness while shoring the bottom line with plenty of bench strength. Let's face it, the cheapos aren't going away, and we really don't want them to. Who else will fill the steamy months?

With the airlines putting more seats in the air at ever-lowering prices and then offering special-combo packages, as if every seat and room isn't already taken, is it any wonder that we work for less in the most difficult time?

Still, things are looking plentiful, with more on the way. Happy guests who ponder life and the thereafter may soon ponder frequent flyer miles earned at *La Mexica* through flight partnerships. Those miles may apply toward the eternal flight at

The 19th Fairway. Why shouldn't they travel first class and earn the peace of mind that comes with arrival at your final destination in luxurious tropical surroundings?

Antonio asks this last question and waits, not with the cocky presumption of a young man on the rapid rise, but rather with the seasoned confidence of a man who knows his rhetoric is solid gold, a man himself arrived. The answer to the question of first class and tropical luxury through frequent flyer miles is so obvious it need not be uttered. This could be the eternal essence of frequent-flyer partnership.

Well, of course it is, and its simple beauty nearly screams at you, once you've been made to see it, as Antonio so deftly makes the vision accessible to his colleagues. Moreover, as a seasoned man of proven instinct, his ascendance is assured. Antonio Garza is the maestro and more; he will also be the poolside manager of *La Mexica, the Resort.*

Antonio has no need to service the hungry women anymore, except of course if an occasional young one persists. As it is said, *el campo fértil no descansado, tórnase estéril.* All work and no play make Antonio a dull boy. Or practicality calls when an elderly one now and then needs a service for a thousand-*peso* minimum, which is a very fair rate once you factor devaluation. A thousand *p* is not what it was, and besides, it's all play money to them. Like Tina Torino, looking hardly forty in the prime of her preservation. Her flourish and flamboyance are grist for a maestro's mill. So seasoned herself, so capable of appreciating what is made to look so easy, she understands show business. Her compassionate observation fans the flame in a man of uncanny skill. They have seasoned equally, he and she, concurrently on different sets but with the same timing, nuance, and ellipsis. Instinct hones to a fine edge in both of them.

These things come to Antonio with the bittersweet tang that any person surviving the seasoning will taste. Life goes on.

The numbness nature provides to deaden the pain soon inures the man to his past. Like waking from a deep sleep with still-sleeping limbs, he feels them tingle. Circulation returns slowly, and so does Antonio.

It's true that he stares seaward with notable frequency. Still, he again counts push-ups, sit-ups and crunches, though now with conviction that only a young man needs to press the limits. A man of continuing maturation requires moderation, such as that reflected by sets of one hundred, three days a week, schedule permitting.

His stomach still ripples like a washboard if he's standing up. It fairly ripples when he's lying back on two pillows with the remote control in one hand and a *resposado* in the other as the tight-skinned Tina Torino takes her fill of what she calls her favorite protein smoothie, who is, of course, Antonio Garza himself.

A thousand pesos? How about five thousand? Or ten? And fun?

This is a woman for all seasons, or at least for this season for a man of seasoning. He is a man of service, after all, humble and proud as Grandfather Garza, who worked livery at *Hacienda Torino* and likely polished the boots of *Señor* Grandfather Torino. We can't very well be certain it was the same Torinos. We may ask by and by. In the meantime, the traditions continue in their way. If this development does not factor the past and the future with dynamic overlap, then what?

Comfort settles in his bones as his eyes close to conjure the scene of one old man blacking the boots of another. The old men look down, one at the boots, the other at the servant beneath him. Antonio opens his eyes and looks down, as his forebears did in the same spirit of giving. Yet he is sensitive to the needs of a once-megastar and will not laugh at the TV comedians while she is eating him.

Of course from time to time a joke or a line that is very funny will make such constraint impossible. Still, he has learned: better to hit the mute for the sake of keeping the peace, because Tina Torino is easy to discourage and much easier to admire; she is so...bold.

Home life flows with equal abundance from the cornucopia of life at last. Lyria busies herself with preparation, also rising to growing fulfillment of what the early years promised. Happy as a shorebird feathering her nest, she preps the nursery and talks to the infant as yet unborn.

Antonio suspects the little one might even appreciate her words of comfort, solace and patience, though in many ways they only postpone what the child must inevitably learn. But what harm can they be? She will make a good mother, though he worries over time spent with the one from Venezuela, the pale, frigid one who speaks *castellano* and can't be trusted and seems significantly removed from nature's intention. Yet not one peep will be uttered by the father-to-be.

Why not? Just because.

"You think we're disgusting, don't you?" Viorica asks.

"You have never heard me use that word," Antonio responds. "I would not call you or what you do disgusting even if I thought such a thing. I only said that lying with another woman is not the normal behavior of a satisfied woman." Unmoving as a stone that dares to be pushed, he waits for her response. But Viorica Valenzuela will not respond, because she too has learned the value of keeping the peace.

Still it wouldn't hurt to hear confirmation from his beloved relative to satisfaction. What would it cost her to give the support he so often feels lacking? But Lyria only avoids the eyes of her intimate relations, perhaps embarrassed in mixed company, or maybe she still maneuvers internally through the sordid twists encountered on the road to love. So he shrugs and shakes his head, indicating with adequate certainty that his beloved is in fact among the most satisfied of women. How could she be otherwise with such frequency and attention to detail?

Viorica shakes her head too and says there are some things she will never understand. But one thing she sees clearly is the very good deal Mister Antonio is getting here, so don't complain or the rates will go up.

Rates? What rates? Forget it. She speaks gibberish. Why torture a thing for meaning when the words flop around randomly as jumping beans? Why take the notion of a woman to task when it can only lead you in circles? Besides, the day is only begun, and a man of many missions has a few stops yet to make. So it's *hasta la hora* to the beloved and the shrew, over and out. Up the hill and down to the office, which is not an office per se but is nonetheless the axis on which his world turns.

Mrs. M will soon return here forever, she says, as soon as her penthouse suite at *La Mexica, the Resort* is complete. In the meantime, she will soon leave for a while. So timing is tricky, which is nothing new for a master of ceremonies who moves among moving parts like a river moves through flotsam, easily with the flow. Who among men needs the complications of a snag? No one is the answer. They are simply unnecessary and avoidable, the snags, if movement is sustained.

The M, as all the guests at *Hotel Oaxtapec*, is tediously aware of Tina Torino's grandiose presence, but we can't be certain she, the M, knows what's up. She must suspect the worst, but surely she views her one and only in beneficent light. We can only speculate on who knows what or how much, but then how much can these sordid details matter to an older woman coming to terms with fading glory?

The M is a beacon of womanly wisdom who comprehends that physical beauty must one day end for all women. So? What does she want to do? Or be? President of the *Women's League of Oaxtapec*? Antonio can help arrange this; not that she will be president overnight, for all women begin in the League as mere members. Is it flowers she wants? Queen of *The Orchid Society* might also be an appropriate elevation from which to view the golden years.

Except that it's also not for nothing she's the M and knows how to season the stew. So hold your physical, queenly horses.

Hardly a devious woman, Mrs. Mayfair nonetheless approaches on cat's feet bright and early this morning immediately after brunch, silently arriving behind Antonio, where she stands still as a tree.

Prepping his cards and balls, he watches the former megastar Tina T saunter across the deck to her place of exquisite repose.

Speaking so soft and low that the hearer doesn't even flinch, Mrs. M whispers, "There but for the grace of God."

What grace? What God? Antonio freezes in her headlights that don't exactly blind him but press him to stillness from the rear.

Remembering the primordial rule of seasoned men, he thaws to a smile under the morning kliegs, matching her bright and shining eyes on a slow turn to display his pleasure on seeing her. He blinks innocently and asks, "What?"

"I only hope I don't get that way."

He considers philosophical ramifications, because her wish hinges on a faith as old as the missions and as thoroughly unyielding. She hopes, as many women do, that what is seen and known is not true, that she will beat the rule because of who she is and what she's seen in the eyes of her admirers. Still, a woman must come to terms with reality as much as any person.

Surely she knows the ultimate development is dust; a woman's years are what they are, no matter what she says or tries to show. Life and death in the end allow no compromise.

He thinks she does know. Why else would she grow content to have him merely park in her private space without the old contortion or *salsa* squirting every which way? He knows the reason; it's what every woman and man wants, which is company in the shadows, a companion with whom to face the last shadow, the one with the hood and scythe. What else could account for her changing needs, for wanting more talk and more hugging? She can rightfully fear the hooded one but should not think that he will forget her. Will the sun forget to rise? If the League and orchid women won't do, Antonio will make her Empress of the Stars. She will shine among the greatest beauties, and nighttime will be best as well for its low light.

Mrs. Mayfair sucks her stomach in and thrusts her chest out, moving in a slow, perfect writhe resulting from diligent years. She knows the effect and is affirmed by the growth in his jams. Yet she slumps when he asks, "How can you not, you know, change?"

Of course she can't not, but that's hardly the issue here. The issue is love and support and their meaning as applied to daily life, like today. Her hurtful look lets him know how unloving and worse, how mean he can be. She hits home, causing Antonio to cringe with regret. She caught him playing with matches and forces his hand.

What can he say, Oh, her? No, I don't want some of that? Or, No, I've had none of that? Or, Hey, it's only a practical thing, you know? Or, What?

Well, at this point he need say nothing because the damage is done, the consequence of carelessness. Putting the fire out may be achieved by letting the river flow over it. He puts his arm around Mrs. M and pulls her near.

Resisting coyly in demonstration of her better judgment she finally relents and nestles in for a most lovely snuggle by the pool under the sun among the seductively rustling trees for all to see, especially those nosy has-beens seething with envy. It feels perfect, until he pats her on the head and tells her there are plenty more miles left in the old gray mare before anyone should even think about the pasture.

"What? What did you say?" She removes his hand and arm and tells him he really should consider a private tutor in English or a personal trainer in etiquette, and she glides to her own place of elegant repose.

"What? What did I say?"

Too late. The exotic plumage is ruffled but can't hide the love she's in, and she knows it and knows he knows it too, which makes matters worse for her, though he feels progress in the making. He stoops to conquer as he did so many years ago on serving her first *piña colada* poolside with an offer to protect her from the sun. So he now stoops to offer a brief solace upstairs.

Matters will trend downward for a while anyway, and Mrs. M comprehends more than Antonio imagines. She knows, for example, that life and love allow no winners except for those dying very young. She plans to be around a few more decades herself and knows full well what the romp will come to. For now an easy score seems propitious. So she rises in her majesty and leads the tawny, muscular one by the hand for the service a has-been movie vamp can only remember from a script.

The long walk down the length of the pool jostles the former movie queen, who in fact also adapts to a pesky new phase in life, which is that of competition. She ignores Mrs. Mayfair's obsequious gaze at the goddess of victory for now. Soon enough she will draw a line in the sand, demanding that Antonio say where she stands.

A maestro smiles at all in passing, moving with the rhythm. A man must make do, and in a few short hours when the sun goes down, he must make do again, which calls for pacing, timing, nuance, and of course the seasoning so visibly underway.

Baldo is not mentioned in Antonio's presence. Nor do friends and acquaintances commonly discuss the younger brother's effect on him. The common belief is that Antonio was a basically happy man given to gregarious contact with life on a daily basis and soon will be his old self again. Such happiness is the source of his innate skill and must return.

Everyone agrees that such a man must naturally take a fall in the course of life, and *de la subida más alta es la caída más lastimosa*. Antonio is a very important man even at his tender age. Perhaps a fall as hard as this one should have been foreseen, given the steep grade he chose to scale. Disagreement prevails on the net result of Baldo's absence. Some say losing a younger brother is a terrible thing, but this younger brother was not exactly cherished. This one was rather a liability and may have caused severe trouble, rendering his demise a blessing and a relief.

So why do you think he, Antonio, keeps staring at the sea? Does he expect his brother to come walking out of it?

Everyone sees. Some have remained quiet but come forth now to insist that Baldo was cherished more than your average brother. Baldo and Baldo alone proved that a young man so driven for money and power could also be a man with a caring heart. Now he, Baldo, the proof, is gone. Who else could teach Antonio the lesson of selfless giving if not Baldo?

The answer to some is obvious: Lyria would have done so just as she does now and will into the future with their sons. Others say no, she knew nothing of magnanimity until it swelled inside her and forced her to give. And this, too, derived from the younger, perhaps deranged, brother.

But assessment is brief and for the most part idle, limited to sparse opinion over beer with a few nods at Antonio, who continues to keep them moving, bodies and minds. He keeps them happy and entertained, albeit with occasional glances you-know-where.

XIX

Y Colorín, Colorado, este Cuento se ha Acabado

And they Lived Happily Ever After (*mas o menos*)

With authenticity in mind along with residual consolation to Antonio, the mentors present a concept deferring to the spirit of the jungle that rightfully belongs here on the one hand, and on the other hand is the spirit of a late and most authentic naturalist.

Simón Salvador does the talking, one countryman to another, as Mister Mayfair observes. The idea is that a foyer alcove be set aside in the lobby *of La Mexica, the Resort*, designated, as it were, to specific purpose. In it, among the creepers and flowering vines, the bromeliads and ferns, including the dazzling staghorns and radiantly aromatic cereus, will stand a bronze likeness bigger than life but proportionate to the myth of Baldo in baggy jams and an open camp shirt revealing his lithe and sinewy self.

Sally pauses to let the drama and beauty of the thing sink in and perhaps to let the meaning of life itself absorb into the pores of the threesome gathered for their regular review of the general situation.

The pool next door at *Hotel Oaxtapec* seems distantly past and just as empty.

Here at *La Mexica, the Resort*, we see and feel what greater minds hath wrought. The fronds here simmer more seductively in a profusion never dreamt next door. Seething greenery balances the greater abundance of chaise lounges around the greater pool that will soon serve the greater number of guests. Seventy-eight percent occupancy isn't bad, especially when you factor a nine-week waiting list until the next available Sunday for renting *The Little Wedding Chapel by the Pool.*

Antonio Garza made the market and began a family of his own in one fell swoop. It was the swoop that culminated his efforts these many days and years and now places him in enviable overview of his realm. He sits back with the apparent languor of a man of power, a landed man with a beautiful wife and a healthy baby named Teodoro after his great-grandfather who worked livery on a hacienda so that he may thrive today.

And of course the doting Venezuelan nanny who is not a nanny per se visits often, though this peculiar nanny will not soil her hands with Teodoro's mess, nor will she rise in the small hours to feed and comfort the *chica.* Who cares what people say of the nanny's demands and the baby's inordinate length and small diameter and continuing silence?

Sally presents Antonio with the consensus among the directors: both long-term and short-term margin enhancement can be achieved through the fabrication and installation of the bronze likeness of said brother, to be followed directly and pointedly by promotion and mythical embroidery at the expense of *La Mexica, the Resort.*

They, the directors, want Antonio's assessment of the idea and will not proceed without his approval. His contentment is just that critical to the operation, they say. They wait in surreptitious repose, their eyes underscoring their pregnant anticipation.

Antonio lets his own eyes wander in a casual drift with impressive indifference, the kind of indifference that best profiles a position of strength in a seasoned man at a bargaining table. In a moment his chin juts as if to make room for the assessment that approaches completion, but will not yet flow from the mouth.

He turns seaward momentarily and turns back, but not to the mentors. He stares obliquely at something or other, perhaps at a phantom still eluding form.

Simón Salvador is more than a colleague. He is a friend and is hardly insensitive to the difficulties at hand. With a quick glance at Thornton Mayfair he is granted a nod at the same, quick pace, and he proceeds.

Antonio is a vital cog in the freshly spinning machinery, he says, which vitality has been factored into this concept. That is, a bronze statue will bear significant cost, at this phase more appropriately considered as additional capitalization. Not to worry, because many new hotels around the world have proven the efficacy of terribly expensive sculpture so guests can feel artistic, or in the presence of art or something of that nature. These things are factored as being worthwhile. What remains to be determined is the capital budget for such a monument in the lobby.

Antonio returns to the living with a laugh. "Budget? What budget?" Perhaps here he surpasses benign indifference with a dip back to the old, cocky presumption. The mentors share another brief eye lock in possible concurrence that such a dip may be an integral spice to the general seasoning. They laugh along with him, until he asks, "How much can it be?"

Sally digresses here to delineate this opportunity to clear the air and claim the history that will in time, we feel, be fundamental to merchandising.

People want history as a destination in their travels now, because they experience so little of it at home. Here we have all the movement and color a history could ever want. Baldo was not merely *El Capitán* or the coconut boy, Sally contends.

He was the turtle boy. He was the *tijerilla* boy. He was *Toucan, Comadreja, Pantera y todos los pescados.*

He was the archangel, human as an animal can be, animalistic as a human can be.

Thorny nods, though his chin can't dip too far for hitting the fists that support it.

"You know, Antonio. We feared him, but we loved him," Sally says. He further embellishes on the abiding spirit that should not be forgotten but should in fact be the stuff of legend and lore.

Baldo should stand here where the jungle rightfully belongs. Here in our lobby is where he should live forever in bronze.

The mentors relax in a moment of silent devotion to the spirit on the table that may well be embodied, and *pronto*, in this monument to Baldo. Antonio relaxes with them, perhaps savoring nothing but the silence.

"All that we want," Sally resumes from the blue, "is to offset our capital requirements by considering a merger. We want to join the forces of *La Mexica Inc.* with *Maestro de Ceremonia LTD.* Antonio, let's face it, you make more money on a wedding reception than the hotel makes all day at seventy-eight percent occupancy, which is where we are, my friend. Of course our occupancy will increase. *p+17Xincrease. In you have once again shown us where impressive margins may derive from the thin air. We run seventy-eight percent all week, and you are at a hundred percent on Sundays for months in advance. You must also be aware that we can require all hotel functions to pass directly through food and beverage at any time. We don't want to do that, because, after all, you are…our friend."

"I am the maestro," Antonio corrects. "That I am your friend does not enter into our discussion here. You are free to offer your own services through food and beverage. You may enlist the services of Milo. I think he's a free agent these days."

Antonio rises in his seat and cranes to the north.

"There he is. He will look striking once you dress him like a *vaquero* and teach him to dance. Don't you think so?"

Sally and Thorny's next shared glance arcs with the short circuitry of certain disadvantage.

Antonio eases down and leans in for the easy score, which is this: "I will gladly merge my company with your own, because we have grown to be friends who love and trust each other. You may have all of my company and with it comes all of my services at no extra charge. Weddings, funerals, bar mitzvahs, whatever you like, *no problema.*"

He pauses for absorption of magnitude, but the mentors are way beyond the delusion that any lunch is free.

"For myself, I ask only three percent of this company, which now shall include one hundred percent of my own. We shall sit together on a single board of directors in the capacity of senior management. That's three percent. One for me. One for my new wife and one for my baby, who is doing quite well, thank you, and may one day stand on the edge of this very pool to call the numbers and keep them happy. You know, my friends, genius cannot be taught. So, we can only hope it will be inherited."

The mentors feign abusive scorn at the ravages of their new, official colleague who just raked them over the coals for *three percent!* This percentage will derive from the net, not the gross, of course, which derivation shall occur after management salaries and shall only derive for purposes of payout when the aforementioned net is greater than zero. What? He should merger into liability? Or loss? *¡Por favor!*

Said percentage shall accrue as soon as money stops passing through this place like scratch through a goose and starts to stick where it should, which shouldn't be too much longer with any luck. How long can it take to turn the tide with a new format featuring special event services with a maestro included in the package—*in addition* to the airfare, the car, the room, and not one *piña colada* daily by the pool but *two*?

Antonio openly shares Sally and Thorny's secret smirk. Who doesn't know twenty-four carat potential when they feel it? Who can't see that these two *dar la suave* with their anguish? Do they think I have never polished a wormy apple? Besides, what do I have to lose? Will they foreclose on my employee housing? Three percent! Take it or leave it! The league is big and very hungry for a free agent.

You wait and see what happens to occupancy here at *La Mexica, the Resort*. Format? I'll give you format.

So the likeness of the late brother is first drawn and then modified as necessary according to the recollection and guidance of the elder brother. Baldo is granted the stoic resolve of their poor, dead father. Likewise, Antonio suggests a manlier chiseling of the face, but of course not beyond the soft compassion predominantly characterizing both his late father and brother.

But whom do I kid with soft compassion? Call it soft in the poor, dead father and potentially murderous in the missing brother. Still, it is common to both, the compassion. *De tal jarro, tal tepalcate*, as the saying goes. Let them see for themselves that from such a pot, such a potsherd.

Following artistic modification to enhance the essence of his inner self, Baldo is cast and poured, not actually in bronze, but there *is* some bronze dust in the mix, and you can't tell the difference, really. Besides, this mix does alleviate some capitalization pressure.

The statue is then burnished and set in place.

Unveiling is a quiet event highlighted by lifting the peak of the bed sheet and revealing the statue. "Here is to my brother, Baldo," Antonio says with little ceremony, as he insists Baldo would want.

The molded face is alert and benign. The left hand hangs down. The right hand is offered in friendship or peace or giving or something. Vines are planted at the feet along with a few shrubs, and mounted at the base is a small plaque that says, *Baldo Garza, Turtle Boy and Abiding Spirit.*

Guests come and go and in time swerve on their course to review the unusual shrine with its little hedge and bronze statue of this fellow who saved the turtles from something, something they heard about, and now here it is. They can see it.

In only a week the vile children left to run untended through the lobby at night tape a machete to the left hand so it hangs like it did, as an extension of the arm.

Antonio sees this modification the very next morning on his stroll through the lobby. He stops in his tracks for the first time since first stopping there to gasp for the benefit of the mentors. He can't say why, but the addition of the machete seems an improvement, bringing the statue in greater alignment with Baldo's actual presence. Baldo carried a machete more often than not. Who needs to know the foul deed such a blade committed? This machete is good.

Yet only two days later a coconut sits on the open right hand with two lime slices for eyes and a pineapple wedge for a nose and a little paper parasol for a hat. And a piece of dead fern for a long, droopy mustache and thick, congealing salsa for blood that streams down the coconut face.

Antonio removes the vile object and carries it back out to the front and tosses it into the hedge out by the street, which he crosses to the gate of Jimi Changa's, which is locked now, since all the revelers are passed out cold, all the disco dancers fast asleep.

Climbing a wrought iron fence may seem normal for a boy or even a young man, but it seems unseemly for a man of seasoned distinction, not to mention distinctive seasoning. Never mind; hurdles are made for clearing.

With only his hoarse gutturals interrupting the easy sounds of morning, Toucan whispers from somewhere under the blanket covering his cage. Perhaps he complains of a life sacrificed to perverse timing, in which nights are for staying up and a blanket covers the mornings. Unveiled by a tug at the peak of the bedsheet, he gazes into the light, a little bit bleary-eyed from such a late night, perhaps recognizing the brother of his former mentor.

Antonio opens the cage and takes a chance on love by presenting his perfectly hued and muscular forearm to the weary bird, who takes a single step forward and then another to catch up with himself and then a few more to ascend toward the shoulder, as some birds want to do.

Back across the street Toucan takes another step, onto the metal likeness of his former mentor's forearm. He looks up and looks around.

Antonio thinks the bromeliads and ferns in masonry pots nearby may be very heavy but will never come near the amazing burden a simple mop bucket can come to. Besides that, a man should not be so muscular for nothing but show. Then again, these aren't clay. They're concrete.

Again, never mind, it is not for nothing that a man or an animal knows the difference between adaptation and slow death. Well, nobody needs to die over a little transplanting.

So he goes to the buffet for a serving spoon and a bowl of berries while he's at it, and in a shake he's back at the alcove off the foyer near the entry of the lobby, digging in.

It's a mechanical, thoughtless little project first thing in the morning that lends itself to sprightly contemplation of life in simple terms, like roots and dirt and water and abiding spirits and the amazing difference between two brothers.

Toucan eats his berries from Baldo's bronze hand.

Antonio hears the berries squish and wonders if this is all that Baldo knew or cared for. Of course Baldo understood more than the imbecilic happiness derived from a measly feeding of a bird. Yet his happiness seemed singular with focus on the moment and greater in proportion to the moment's proximity to life in its most basic element. Is this what their poor dead father believed was so unique as to verge on magical, when it's really nothing if you think about it? It's nothing but the sound of the dark dirt displacing briefly to accept a new plant.

Nothing is what he hears but the tinkling of water pouring forth from this pitcher with life for these plants.

Nothing else is heard but the tender squish of berries in a bird's beak.

Antonio looks up with a sudden chill. Goose bumps rise in a breaking wave, head to toe, on sensing immensity in these simple sounds of comfort and growth. How can a life reconcile so much love and loss, much less the strange and awful knowing, on such simple terms?

Hey, wait. What is that? What is that rasping sound striving to gain an octave on its guttural rumbling toward melody?